THE
DEVIL
in
OXFORD

ALSO BY JESS ARMSTRONG

THE RUBY VAUGHN MYSTERIES

The Secret of the Three Fates
The Curse of Penryth Hall

THE DEVIL in OXFORD

A RUBY VAUGHN MYSTERY

JESS ARMSTRONG

MINOTAUR BOOKS
NEW YORK

This is a work of fiction. All of the characters, organizations, and events portrayed in this novel are either products of the author's imagination or are used fictitiously.

First published in the United States by Minotaur Books, an imprint of St. Martin's Publishing Group

EU Representative: Macmillan Publishers Ireland Ltd, 1st Floor, The Liffey Trust Centre, 117–126 Sheriff Street Upper, Dublin 1, DO1 YC43

THE DEVIL IN OXFORD. Copyright © 2025 by Jess Armstrong. All rights reserved. Printed in the United States of America. For information, address St. Martin's Publishing Group, 120 Broadway, New York, NY 10271.

www.minotaurbooks.com

The Library of Congress Cataloging-in-Publication Data is available upon request.

ISBN 978-1-250-37465-3 (hardcover)
ISBN 978-1-250-37466-0 (ebook)

The publisher of this book does not authorize the use or reproduction of any part of this book in any manner for the purpose of training artificial intelligence technologies or systems. The publisher of this book expressly reserves this book from the Text and Data Mining exception in accordance with Article 4(3) of the European Union Digital Single Market Directive 2019/790.

Our books may be purchased in bulk for specialty retail/wholesale, literacy, corporate/premium, educational, and subscription box use. Please contact MacmillanSpecialMarkets@macmillan.com.

First Edition: 2025

10 9 8 7 6 5 4 3 2 1

For J and the boys.
You are an endless source of inspiration and joy.
P.S. I'm sorry I have yet to include a pet chicken into the plot as requested. One day.

The Devil *in* Oxford

Chapter One

En Garde

Oxford, England
December 1922

IN my thirty years of existence, I had come to know myself fairly well. Oh, I harbored no delusions of being redeemable, as I had more than my share of flaws: headstrong—though Mr. Owen, my employer, would say mulish—a *mite* impetuous, and most certainly unsteady in affairs of the heart. Yet, as I lay there flat on my back upon the brightly polished wooden floor of the Artemis Club with a blunt-tipped saber pressed to the two-month-old scar on my chest, I realized one other essential truth about myself.

I, Ruby Vaughn, had never, *ever* before lost upon the fencing strip.

Not even when said piste was little more than a makeshift rectangle hastily hashed out in the dirt behind a military hospital in France. But I supposed in time everything must change—even me.

"Best of three, eh, Vaughn?"

I glared through my mesh mask at Leona Abernathy, whose saber remained pressed gently against my breast. My muscles screamed in protest as moisture soaked through my thick white fencing jacket. Gasping, I stared up at the ornately carved white scrollwork adorning the ceiling. Around us, the sound of metal upon metal rang out as other pairs practiced with their blades.

Leona laughed, tugging off her own mask, and offered me a gloved hand. A shaft of light came in through the window, catching in the dark browns and umbers of her hair. She hadn't aged a bit since we'd been stationed together at that hospital in Amiens. I watched my old friend's brown eyes dance as she wiped the sweat from her brow with the back of her sleeve.

She'd gotten far better since our wartime duels. During the bloodiest months of the cataclysm, teaching her to fence had served as a distraction from the slow, beating drum of death raging outside the hospital walls, and the growing specter of my slipping grasp on sanity. The war had tested me in ways that I did not wish to think on. Certainly not *here*. In *Oxford*. During the week before Christmas. The past—*that particular past*—had no business in my present.

"Best of *three*?" I gasped indignantly, rolling over onto my hands and knees. "Are you trying to kill me?"

"Where'd be the fun of that?" Leona tugged her long dark braid over her shoulder and ran her hand along it loosely. I sprang to my feet with a grunt. I seldom had the opportunity to fence nowadays, spending most of my time in the stuffy old bookshop I ran alongside my octogenarian housemate and employer, Mr. Owen, back home in Exeter. Life as an antiquarian-turned-lady-sleuth-detective had clearly taken its toll on my body.

Though by all appearances, time spent in scholarly pursuits hadn't taken a toll on Leona at all. She looked much the same as she had during the war, with large brown eyes set into a heart-shaped face and the sort of effortless beauty that would have launched a thousand ships in another lifetime. She was lithe and strong, possibly stronger than she'd been back then. Who knew that sorting through antiquities and translating ancient scrolls would do such wonders for a girl's health?

She nudged me again with the saber, drawing my attention back to her. "Besides, you're here for two more weeks. I'll wait at least until the new year to finish you off."

"Wonderful . . . I shall eagerly await my demise." I adjusted my grip on my own blade, lightly bouncing the hilt in my palm, gaze drifting to the gray world outside the windows. Bundled-up shoppers passed the faintly fogged window as the first fat snowflakes began to fall from the afternoon sky.

My afternoons with Leona at the Artemis Club had become a respite from my worries of the last few months—the increasingly peculiar situations in which Mr. Owen had gotten me ensnared, my multiple brushes with death, the fact that I'd fallen in *love* with a witch who possessed an uncanny ability to hear my thoughts. Dreadful thing, love. Of course, my indecision put a quick end to that short-lived romance. So, when Mr. Owen informed me that we would be spending Christmas in Oxford to attend the annual gathering of his antiquarian society, I leapt at the chance to escape the doldrums of my life and nurse my aching heart. Unfortunately, the trip had the opposite effect—for Mr. Owen's antiquarian friends had been taking up more and more of my time with each passing day thanks to Howard Carter's recent discovery of a new tomb in the Valley of the Kings. Egyptology and, consequently, my ability to read both hieratic and demotic scripts had kept us quite busy since arriving in town.

Leona nudged me again. "Where'd you go?"

"What do you mean, *where did I go*? I'm right *here*."

She frowned, pursing her lips, and gestured vaguely at my chest. "Your body is standing there, but your head has been elsewhere all day." She tapped the side of my mask with her forefingers. "It's no wonder you lost the match. You're distracted and it's left you flat on your back twice now."

"I'm fine," I huffed, swatting away her fingers. My breath uncharacteristically ragged as I tugged off my own mesh mask, gulping in the warm damp air. "And much as I would love to let you beat me again—I'm late as it is. Another dinner with the antiquarians. Mr. Owen will be terribly cross with me if I don't show myself."

Leona laughed merrily, taking a challenging step closer. "The Ruby Vaughn I knew never lost, nor did she worry about being late for a fusty supper full of conversation with men old enough to be her grandfather. Come on, once more for old times' sake? I'll buy you a drink after?"

It was tempting, to be certain, but I loved Mr. Owen—far more than I ought, considering the messes he'd gotten me into. "I'd love to—truly. But I can't. I've been busy with the antiquarians from the moment I arrived here in Oxford. You would not *believe* the things they've pulled out of their moldering attics for me to examine. I do not know how you stomach it day in and out at the museum." I laughed, placing my saber beneath my arm as I fiddled with the fastenings on my jacket. It was unbearably *hot* in here, as if someone hadn't bothered to turn down the radiators. I fanned my neck with my glove as another irritating bead of sweat found its way between my breasts.

She grinned. "Welcome to my life. I swear, for the last two months I have been mostly living at the museum. Poor Annabelle must feel like she's a queen, living by herself in our little flat, with no roommate to bother with. It's enough to make me wish Howard Carter had never gone to Egypt at all. Let that poor soul rest in peace and not be subjected to all this—" Her hand flung out to the side.

"But you're happy working at the museum? Truly? You never speak of your work in your letters."

There was an odd flicker in Leona's smile. "Of course. And to finally be respected. Treated as an equal to the male scholars there . . . it's a heady thing, Ruby. I truly recommend it."

I smiled back at her, brushing the sweaty curls from my face. It was rapidly growing dark as the sun sank low in the December sky, casting long dramatic shadows across the herringbone floor. Mr. Owen had likely already arrived at our host's home and begun holding court around the fire with a bottle of Scotch if I knew him.

A ripple of nervous silence spread across the room like waves surging upon the shore. I turned to see the source of the disturbance. My blood stilled as any thought for Mr. Owen evaporated into the ether.

It was a man.

In the Artemis Club.

Men were never allowed past the front reception. And it was not just any man who'd breached the gates of our veritable feminine sanctuary—it was my very own solicitor. "Christ on a cracker, it's Hari!" Mercifully he'd not spotted me yet, caught up in conversation with a woman at the front entrance. I heard her—whoever she was—laugh, a sign that the stubborn man had employed his considerable charm to reach this inner sanctum rather than employing the law for his aims.

Without a thought, I took Leona by the hand, dragging her across the floor and into the far corridor leading to the changing rooms.

"Hari Anand?" she squeaked. "You've taken up with *Hari Anand*? Please tell me *he's* the reason your fencing has become abysmal!"

"He is *not*," I grumbled, rushing the pair of us down the corridor. "And *I* have not."

"Oh, Ruby, I've always adored Hari, ever since he first came to the hospital! I haven't seen him in years."

I let out an exasperated sigh, pausing alongside a fragrant glass jar holding branches of wintersweet, its papery yellow flowers catching in the fading sun. "Keep your voice down! I've not taken up with Hari—he's my solicitor, for goodness' sake!" And truthfully, the man was more of a brother to me than anything else. He'd been badly wounded when I first met him in Amiens, but the two of us struck up an easy friendship that endured long after the war.

Hand in hand with Leona, I stormed down the darkened hallway before shoving her bodily into our private dressing room and slamming the door, locking it behind us.

The walls inside the dressing room were covered in a pale pink patterned fabric that muted the sound of our voices. Likewise, all the furniture was soft and plush and various shades of the hue, giving me the amusing image of being wrapped in bunting. We weren't, of course, but there was something delightfully absurd about the room—at once utterly darling and not at all suited to me, for I was anything but darling.

"If he's not your distraction then why, may I ask, are you hiding from the man like he's unexpectedly seen you in your knickers?" She laughed, slumping into a sumptuous porcine-colored velvet armchair, and began tugging at her shoes, one by one.

"It isn't Hari the man that I am avoiding. It's Hari the solicitor." I finished with the fastenings of my jacket and tossed it over an ornamental screen before stepping behind it and slipping out of my pants. "Hari the man is perfectly agreeable."

"You're not in trouble, are you?" She nervously folded her long fingers into her lap. "If you were—I know I don't have much money, or much else for that matter—I'd help you if I could."

My high-necked indigo evening gown hung on a hook behind me. I slipped it off the wooden hanger and stepped into the dress, tugging it up over the fresh scar on my breast before peeking my head back out from around the floral screen. "It's nothing like that. It's a legal matter, that's all. I don't want to deal with it before Christmas."

"So *that's* why you came to the Ashmolean today."

"Partly . . . ," I admitted, struggling with the tiny pearl-studded buttons up the back. "My housekeeper, Mrs. Penrose, told me that Hari intended to call upon me this afternoon—I needed some air . . . I needed . . ." My pulse thundered in my ears as I debated whether to speak aloud the true ghost that had been haunting my days. The reason I'd lost sleep, the reason for my increasing nightmares and for dodging poor Hari like a bridegroom at the altar. "You see, there's another imposter."

Leona sucked in a sharp breath, the words hanging between us for several seconds.

An imposter. A fraud. Yet another charlatan pretending to be my dead mother. I swallowed hard as the awkward silence stretched on.

"Oh, Ruby, that's terrible. *Another?* I thought they'd finally stopped coming after the war."

As had I. It had been years since another crept from the shadows to plague me. "It's *fine*. Truly. I'd hoped to put off the conversation until January. I'm not overly sentimental about Christmas, but there's something about this time of year that makes me rather melancholy. Perhaps it's the greenery. The fig pudding. Who even *likes* fig pudding?"

"Or the fact that everyone is with their families and yours is dead?"

"There is that . . ." I wrinkled my nose. "But I have a cat, as well as a meddling octogenarian who has taken up the mantle of paternal duties with aplomb."

She reached out, taking me by the arms, lips pressed into a firm line. "Darling, of course you're bound to be sad. *Anyone* with a heart would be sad. I miss my family terribly in winter and they're simply in Egypt. The nights are dreadfully long. It's dark. Cold. It isn't the holidays that are causing it, it's the weather that makes a body lonely!" Leona enveloped me in a warm hug, the scent of her jasmine perfume filling my nose.

Loneliness? I chewed on the word for several seconds. Perhaps that was all it was. A logical, reasonable little thing. She stepped back, holding me at arm's length, appraising me from head to toe. "Enough of that, you have a horde of antiquarians to entertain."

I let out a wet laugh, wiping at the moisture that had strangely gathered beneath my eyes. Perhaps I did have a functioning heart after all.

"That color suits you. One might even confuse you for a lady."

I laughed, grateful for her change in subject, as she stepped back. I flopped onto an absurdly puffed-up rose-colored ottoman and began rolling my stockings up my leg, affixing them with an old velvet garter. "One might be mistaken on that score." I glanced to the closed door. "Do you think you could occupy Hari until I can make my escape?"

Leona raised a brow, looking from me to the ground-floor window behind me. "You do realize that's a five-foot drop to the street."

I wet my lips and nodded. "Perhaps I'd better wait to put my shoes on once I land then, hmm?"

Leona laughed. "Very well, I can buy you a few moments, I suppose. For old times' sake. But first . . ." She stood and came closer, tucking an errant curl behind my ear. "There. You look beautiful. Even if you are still rather damp from fencing."

I grinned, pressing a gentle kiss to her cheek. "You are a darling. Same time tomorrow morning as usual?"

Again, a strange expression crossed her face. Precisely as it had when I last mentioned the museum. She gave her head a slight shake. "I don't think tomorrow would be a good idea."

I gathered up my beaded handbag, fastening it. "Whyever not? We meet here every morning. I know they've been keeping you busy, but surely you don't have to be at the museum at *dawn*."

She stared at the snowflakes falling outside the large leaded glass window, her fingers running absently on the wooden sash. "It's nothing. It's only Reaver has this project that's consuming him, and he insisted I be at his side all day tomorrow."

I stared at her unblinking. "Frederick Reaver. . . . You work for *the* Frederick Reaver?" The words came out as a squeak. How on earth had she omitted that tiny fact? The man was a legend among Mr. Owen's set. Universally adored by the papers as one of the great minds of our age. "Why didn't you mention that before? Leona, that's a *boon*! No wonder you're happy at the museum."

"I'm s-sorry. It must have slipped my mind," she murmured, picking at the cuticle of her left thumb.

This sudden reticence worried me. I took a step closer, laying a hand on her shoulder. "Is everything all right?"

She rubbed her left eye and shook her head. "I'm fine, Ruby. Truly. It's only a headache. It's come on all of a sudden." Her voice cracked and she flashed me a small smile. "Off with you. I'll keep Hari occupied. Maybe even have him buy me supper somewhere expensive. He can certainly afford it if he's having to keep you out of trouble."

Leona was behaving strangely, but I hadn't time to parse out what it meant. Perhaps it was only a headache as she said, or perhaps she simply wasn't as happy at the museum as she'd implied. After all, I knew how hard she'd fought to be taken seriously by the academy. And for her to have a permanent position at the Ashmolean—one of the most respected, if not *the* preeminent museum in Britain—and under Frederick Reaver? It was everything she'd ever dreamed of.

The heavy wooden sash groaned as I lifted it. A gust of wind sent a maelstrom of wet snow inside, striking the side of my face. My fancy shoes in my left hand, I threw my legs over the side, balancing there—half in, half out. "With your headache, shouldn't you fix yourself some tea and go to bed? I'm sure Hari won't mind." I'd meant the words kindly, and yet Leona stiffened as if struck.

But whatever it was would have to wait until the morning, I was already late for supper with the antiquarians, and that would never do.

Chapter Two

The Prodigal Protégé

THE snowstorm raged outside the thick walls of Emmanuel Laurent's stately townhome. I'd been here for over an hour now and yet my stockings had scarcely dried from where I landed on the snowy street outside the club. I stretched my toes in my shoes. Every so often, the very walls of the home would groan as a stiff gale whipped down the winding narrow street between the tall yellowstone buildings. Oxford was a lovely town, with the University the beating heart of it. Ever since arriving here, I could not go two steps without running into someone who was connected to the place. Even our kindly host Emmanuel Laurent, who was currently angling to be the next Member of Parliament for Oxford itself, was a former professor—having taught anthropology for decades before turning his attention to politics. The University connection was how Mr. Owen first became acquainted with the fellow, and how I ended up nursing a glass of champagne alone on a settee feeling utterly sorry for myself—at half past eight o'clock on a Tuesday. Or was it Wednesday? I tilted my glass to one side—the days had turned into a blur. An endless morass punctuated by random pangs of guilt for how I'd left things with Ruan.

I nearly groaned. *Ruan Kivell* and my confounding feelings for the man were a constant plague upon my thoughts. I took another drink, staring at the fine rug beneath my shoes in a desperate attempt to think of something other than the intriguing folk healer I'd met in Cornwall last August. It must be Oxford itself that kept him so close to mind, as he'd been a student here before the war. Granted, almost *everything* made me think of Ruan as of late. The man managed to capture my bitter heart in a way I'd not expected. Running from my feelings for the dreadful man was half the reason I so readily agreed to join Mr. Owen in Oxford. I thought being away from home would give me time to forget my wretched inaction in Scotland. The man laid his feelings for me bare, and I'd . . . I'd said nothing. I let him walk away—entirely unaware of how deeply I cared for him. I swallowed that unwelcome memory along with the dregs of my champagne, setting the glass on the ornately carved cherry occasional table beside me.

Where was Mr. Owen? I scanned the room, before spotting him holding court alongside the great carved-stone mantelpiece at the far end of the room, decorated with a cheerful garland of braided ivy. I recognized some of his compatriots as men I'd seen at the bookshop, but there were other people here too, ones I was less familiar with—those who'd known him when he was the Viscount of Hawick, a fact I had only recently learned myself. Mr. Owen still *was* the viscount of course, but he'd gone so long by his nom de guerre that he tended to prefer it to the title he'd been born to.

"Do you suppose we will be snowed in here?"

I jerked my head around to the voice, lost in my own festive display of self-pity, to find our host standing beside me with two coupe glasses of champagne in his hands. Emmanuel Laurent was a remarkably handsome gentleman, a decade or two younger than Mr. Owen, with dark gray eyes that put me in mind of the slate quarries I'd seen back in the mountains of New York when I was a young girl, long before scandal sent me away to Britain.

My hesitation to answer must have worried him as he quickly

changed the subject. "Are you enjoying yourself this evening, Miss Vaughn?"

If one considered reciting one's greatest failures *enjoyment*, I supposed I was. The edge of my mouth curved up into a ghost of a smile. "A bit."

"I should hope more than a bit, my dear. It's nearly Christmas after all." He held a glass out to me, the pale effervescence from the liquid catching in the electric lights.

I reached up accepting it, murmuring my thanks. Mr. Laurent sank down into the chair opposite me, thoughtfully twisting his own glass.

"More than a bit," I conceded. "You have a lovely home." The statement was not at all polite conversation. Emmanuel Laurent had an exceptionally elegant drawing room. Each of the pieces carefully curated and positioned to use the room to its maximum efficiency. There were no awkwardly placed settees, nor any stacks of wayward tomes with forgotten teacups balanced precariously on top here. The man had impeccable taste and style, that extended past his drawing room to the person himself. Mr. Laurent was clean-shaven, with a warm, kindly affect. He wore his hair short and slicked back as was the fashion, the ebony strands warring with the silver at his temples giving him a learned air, which was to be expected since he'd spent most of his life lecturing on anthropology here at the University.

I glanced past him to the heavily frosted windowpane. "You might be right about the snow." Almost at command, the glass rattled again in its wooden casing. "I haven't seen a storm like this since I left New York."

He gave me a sympathetic frown, sipping his champagne at the mention of my past life—it was no secret that I'd been sent to Britain under a cloud of scandal at the ripe age of sixteen. No one spoke much of it anymore, but mention of my life in America was oft met with similarly polite nods. *That poor Vaughn girl.*

"You must be terribly bored tonight, all anyone wants to discuss is either bookbinding or Julius Harker's mysterious disappearance. I confess, I cannot decide which is more loathsome."

I laughed at the serious expression upon his face. "You mean the fellow running the curiosity museum in town?" The city and the antiquarians both had been abuzz for the last two days regarding the elusive Julius Harker. I'd not paid much attention to it, for I knew all about those sorts of *curiosity* museums and the type of people who ran them—the ones who would wire a cat skeleton to a salmon and call it a mermaid all for a few coins.

Laurent made a low sound in his chest as he finished his champagne. "The same. The fellow was invited by none other than Frederick Reaver to present a lecture at the Ashmolean some three days ago. Though why a man like Reaver would lower himself to entertain a scoundrel like Julius Harker, I certainly don't know. Regardless, in typical form Harker did not appear, and no one has seen hide nor hair of him since. Rumors are swirling whether he'll even appear for this grand unveiling of his Napoleonic cache tomorrow night."

I worried my lower lip as the fire popped merrily in the hearth. "How very strange."

Laurent let out an exasperated sigh, his eyes warm upon my own. "The two men have been at odds for years. It would not surprise me if Professor Reaver had invited him to speak with the intention of embarrassing the fellow, and Harker simply one-upped him by not attending."

"That's a great deal of effort for a simple rivalry."

"You've not met many true academics then. You cannot challenge the ego of a genius without facing repercussions of some sort. The pair of them are like tomcats circling one another. Always have been."

Laurent must have misread my expression, for he quickly continued. "Oh no, my dear. That's not to say that Frederick Reaver is all bad, we have been trying for years to have him join our antiquarian society, but the museum takes up all his time. It's even worse now that Carter found that new tomb. Fielding newspaper interviews, and requests for lectures. I'd be surprised if he doesn't pack his bags and disappear back to Egypt before long." He gave me a sympathetic smile, his palm resting lightly on the table beside me.

I glanced behind me to Mr. Owen, who still boisterously held court near the fireplace with a half dozen of his comrades, all of whom were deep in their cups and flushed. "I am sorry I'm not a better conversationalist tonight. You've likely escaped a riveting debate about dust mites. And now here you are discussing long-dead pharaohs and academic grievances."

His dark gray eyes sparkled in the dim electric lights as he leaned closer to me. The spicy scent of his cologne tickled my nose. "I never regret abandoning the mites for a new acquaintance, my dear girl. Tell me, do you care for archaeology as much as Owen does?" He inclined his head in Mr. Owen's direction. "You seemed terribly interested when I mentioned Professor Reaver."

I was grateful for the discreet change of subject. "Far too much if you ask Mr. Owen."

"Does he not care for scientific discovery?" The older fellow's brows rose comically.

"Oh, Mr. Owen cares a great deal just as long as said discovery does not discommode him. It's why I wasn't allowed to join Howard Carter's expedition to the Valley of the Kings earlier this year. He needed me at the bookshop, not off gallivanting with archaeologists—or so he claimed."

"Not allowed?" Laurent wore an endearing look of affront on his face that Mr. Owen would *disallow* his employee to do anything.

"He had a half dozen jobs for me to do instead, and as frustrating as he can be, I am fond of the old man. So I told my dear friend Mr. Carter that I could not go."

Laurent let out a low sound of appreciation and rose from his chair, holding out his arm indicating I should join him. "Though I must say, to have been part of Carter's most recent discovery would have been a feather in your cap. While I don't have the glories of the Nile here in Oxford, I might have something else you will enjoy all the same. Perhaps it will cheer you this evening. Though I suspect the weather does not help."

"No, it does not. I am getting cold even thinking of the long walk home. I may see if we can catch a car back this evening, even though it isn't terribly far." I laughed, standing and scooping up my glass. I rather liked Emmanuel Laurent, even if he was a politician. He had an affability about him, a way of listening that made you feel truly heard. *Understood.* It was a dizzying thing, or perhaps it was the three glasses of champagne I'd had on an empty stomach.

I laid my palm on his wool-jacketed arm and allowed him to lead me away from the rest of the group, down a quiet corridor and to a great door at the end of the hall with a lovely silver knob in the shape of a lion's head.

"It certainly isn't as thrilling as Mr. Carter's discovery, but I hope it will lift your spirits for one evening." He paused for emphasis before placing his hand in the mouth of the silver lion, and turned, pushing the door in.

I peered into the well-lit library and could scarcely believe what I saw. For such a small townhome, Professor Laurent had created a veritable museum of early British archaeology inside his library. The room itself had been combined with another to double its size, and it was lined with floor-to-ceiling cases. Over the years he'd lovingly affixed old, mismatched, glass curio cases to the walls, until the room was essentially one giant collection. Some of the boxes were open to the air displaying large fossils, while others were sealed shut to protect more delicate contents from the elements.

There was a cobbled-together grace to the whole thing—a studied disarray, unlike the rest of the home—that made it all the more welcoming and warm. I pored over the shelves, uncertain where to begin.

"You can start wherever you wish. There is no beginning and no end. I tried to go thematically rather than chronologically. Likely not the best interpretive choice, but as it's my personal library, I make the rules." He smiled broadly but I was already hooked.

This room bore none of the holiday decorations from the more public areas of the house. It smelled clean and crisp, of old wood and leather soap. I took a step farther into the room and paused at the first case, taking in a small collection of four intricately twisted golden torcs.

"That set was a particularly lucky acquisition," he said with pride.

"It's extraordinary . . ." I whispered, moving on to the next case, which housed intriguing, old, beaded jewelry. I flitted from case to case, stretching up on the tips of my toes, greedily absorbing it all. Everything from broken bits of pottery to Bronze Age tools and even a recovered bit of Roman mosaic that he had carefully preserved and affixed to a section of wall.

"That tilework was one of my earliest pieces. It was found at a site not far from here sixty years ago." He gestured to the mosaic. "It had been mostly consumed by the woods. That section is all that remains. Sometimes I like to sit here and think of the hands that made the tile, the ones who laid the pieces—all of it nearly two thousand years ago. It's awe-inspiring, is it not?"

"It truly is." I wet my lips, strangely moved by the humanness of the notion. The unending need of man to leave a mark upon the world behind him. "Do you ever pause to think of all the myriad lives that have been lived in its presence? I wonder sometimes if the pieces can recall what came before, and all the people that have appreciated them over the years."

"You are like him . . ." He smiled fondly at me before checking his watch. "It's uncanny."

"Like whom?"

A cloud covered his expression, like a storm across a summer field. Sudden and sharp. "My dear son . . . Ernst. I lost him during the war, but he would say those very things from the time he could form sentences. Come crawl onto my lap in this room. *Papa, do you ever wonder . . . ?*" He gave his head a shake. "It's been years. Do not mind me, it's an old man's reverie. I suppose it's the season making me miss him all the more. He did love the holidays. The sweets, the colors."

My own heart ached. "I am sorry."

"It is nothing. A memory, that's all, and memories can't harm us." Laurent cleared his throat, turning back to his collection. "I thought this room might buoy your spirits. You looked quite sad earlier in the drawing room."

I gave him a faint smile, stunned that I'd been so easy to read.

He patted me on the shoulder. "It seems I have found a kindred spirit here amongst the antiquarians. I shall leave you for a moment to explore. Take all the time you wish. Dinner will be delayed a bit longer as I am awaiting our final guest—an old pupil of mine whom I haven't seen in an age. One of the most extraordinary lads I'd ever had the privilege of teaching. I've not seen him since before the war, but he had been a dear friend to my darling Ernst."

The deep pain of regret echoed in his words. A sentiment I keenly knew.

"Don't worry about me. I am perfectly content here. Please return to your guests. I think I might enjoy some peace with the artifacts after all."

"I thought you might." He gave me a conspiratorial wink, the shadow of melancholy lingering at the edges of his eyes. "If you'd like, I can ask that your supper be brought here. It is no bother."

The large leather sofa in the center of the room *was* appealing. Just a few moments alone wouldn't be too terribly selfish. "I shouldn't. Mr. Owen would be very cross with me."

"You need some quiet, my dear girl. It is written all over your face. Sit. I'll make your excuses. Owen will have to answer to me if he objects."

I ran my fingers over the edge of the sofa, weighing the options. "You know, I think a little quiet might be nice."

Laurent flashed me an answering smile before dipping out the door and into the darkened corridor beyond. He was right, of course. A little quiet would do me a world of good.

Chapter Three

Amiable Lord Amberley

I woke the next morning fully determined to spend most of the day as horizontal as possible with the serial novel I'd picked up at the bookshop on Broad Street three days before. Preferably curled up with a plate of Mrs. Penrose's saffron buns and my substantial black cat, Fiachna, purring at my side. Leona's peculiarities at the mention of her employer, Frederick Reaver, weighed upon me. How was it that she worked for the most important man in the field of Egyptology, save for Howard Carter himself, and she failed to mention it to me? That was not the sort of thing one ignored. It was almost as if she didn't want me to know. I didn't know why the thought bothered me as much as it did. Perhaps it was simply that Reaver was at the forefront of my mind, thanks to my conversation last night with Laurent. After supper when I had rejoined the antiquarians, the conflict between Reaver and Julius Harker, the enigma who had been cast out of Oxford under a shadow of scandal, was all anyone could speak of. The men were two sides of a coin. One utterly respected, the other similarly despised. Purportedly, the disreputable Julius Harker had even once taught alongside Reaver and Laurent at the University before being unceremoniously thrown out on his ear.

No one spoke of what Julius Harker had done, but whatever it was had been bad enough that he could not return to polite society. People visited his curiosity museum, but few publicly associated with him. Which again raised more questions than answers, but I was done with my lady-sleuthing days. No more investigations. No more crimes. No more murder.

However, my dreams of saffron buns and literary assignations were short-lived, as just ten minutes after waking, Mr. Owen had come upstairs with another request, and I'd been foisted once more unto the breach of inspecting ancient tomes.

Today's quarry was Lord Amberley's copy of Copernicus's *De revolutionibus orbium coelestium*. An exceptionally fine piece, with no surprises and few imperfections. I had a sneaking suspicion that Mr. Owen wanted the book for his private collection and had no intention of putting it in the shop at all. Amberley was yet another of Mr. Owen's antiquarian friends that I'd become acquainted with since arriving in Oxford.

Once we said our goodbyes and with book in hand, the two of us stepped out onto the curb and began the long walk home. The snow clouds from the night before had given way to a brilliant golden sun that made the already gold-hued town appear even more gilded. Piles of snow that had been cleared from the street this morning lay melting along the curbstones. "I do hope it doesn't snow again tonight," Mr. Owen grumbled to himself, tugging his long woolen coat tighter.

"Why should it matter if it does?" I tucked the carefully wrapped tome more securely against my body, cautious not to catch any errant melting ice from the eaves. "I, for one, fully intend to return to my own book now that this business is over. It's my Christmas present to myself. And you *did* promise me a holiday, yet for the last week I've been so busy that I have not been able to read one single sentence for my own amusement. I deserve a plate of ginger biscuits, a bottle of wine, and my book, Mr. Owen. I daresay I *need* it after the year we've had."

Mr. Owen let out a harrumph. "About that, my love . . ."

I paused, turning to him as a motorcar rumbled past on the cobbles, the heft of the book solid against my belly. "About *what* exactly, Mr. Owen?"

"It's only I have a pair of tickets for tonight . . ." His dear wizened face was downcast, hiding his expression behind the wide brim of his gray homburg hat. "I thought you'd be pleased . . ."

I racked my brain for what Mr. Owen might have procured tickets *for*. We often went to the opera, an occasional play from time to time, though usually those were at my insistence, not his. He had a penchant for motion pictures, but we had just been to the theater three weeks ago. Brow raised, I shifted the book in my arms. "What have you committed me to now?"

"Nothing terrible, lass." Mr. Owen let out a dry laugh. "Last night while you were rusticating off only the gods know where in Laurent's townhome, I promised a few of the fellows we'd go with them to the exhibition."

"I would like to point out one cannot rusticate *inside* a townhouse. I was simply enjoying a moment of peace admiring Laurent's collection." The familiar pinch of a headache formed between my brows. One caused by a meddling octogenarian bookseller. "And please tell me this exhibition doesn't have to do with that Julius Harker fellow." My heart sank. The exhibition *was* supposed to be tonight, and this Harker person was all any of the antiquarians could speak of. "It *is* the exhibition . . . isn't it?"

Mr. Owen coughed, starting off down the street with a speed that only confirmed my worst suspicions.

I hurried off after his sturdy form. "Mr. Owen . . ."

"Aye, lass?"

"I take it we *are* going to Harker's exhibition." I met him step for step, shifting the weight of the book in my arms.

He made a grunt in the affirmative.

I blew my hair from my eyes. "Do you even *know* this Harker fellow?"

Mr. Owen dodged around a paperboy and continued at his breakneck speed. For a man well over eighty, he hadn't started to slow down one bit—that is, unless his gout flared up. He glanced back over his shoulder to be sure I was still following. "No, my lamb. But I mean to. After all, he's quite possibly the most interesting man in Oxford and that makes him someone I'd dearly like to meet. Besides, it's going to be quite the spectacle. He's unveiling a cache of Egyptian antiquities stolen by Napoleon himself. Can you imagine?"

I let out a very Mr. Owen–sounding harrumph. I could indeed imagine the scene, and despite my desperation to join Howard Carter on his excavation of the Valley of the Kings, there was a darker side to archaeology. One that led to the wholesale looting of graves performed by many purported *scientists*, and it was *that* sort of thing that made me ill at ease.

Standing there in the wide entrance of Harker's Curiosity Museum that evening I immediately knew I'd made a terrible mistake. Dread clawed up my throat as the room before me opened into a sea of people. The warmth from their bodies combined with the radiant heat gave the wide-open main exhibition room a claustrophobic feel. I stretched up on my toes searching for Mr. Owen's fluffy white hair, but he was nowhere to be found. I had sent him along to the exhibition ahead of me, as I was running late—as usual—but he ought to have been here by now.

Palms sweating, I moved quickly through the main room toward a quiet corner as a sudden peculiar sensation fluttered in my chest.

My palm found its way to the spot, resting over the hidden scar on my breast. I drew in a shaky breath, then a second, before swallowing hard and moving deeper into the museum, only to be besieged by cloying perfume and a cacophony of voices springing up around me. The hard walls and exhibit cases created a world of discordant echoes, making it difficult to focus on anything at all beyond the voices rising up around me.

"Do you think he'll show?"

"Where is he?"

"You know he's likely drunk, or worse."

"Could be in a gutter, knowing him."

It was no wonder Mr. Owen had insisted on attending. He'd never been one to pass up a scene and, judging from the people already here, tonight would be quite the show.

Moonlight filtered in through the open metal and glass of the domed ceiling, helpless to compete with the old-fashioned gaslight flames burning nakedly overhead. Something about the scene—the excitement, the scent of the gaslight, the nearness of other bodies—reminded me of the traveling curiosity exhibits of my childhood. My father thought them silly but Mother adored them. Utterly captivated by the possibility of what could be, and she insisted on taking me along with her. I tended to walk a line between my parents, never fully taken in by the spectacle and never fully skeptical. I was a pragmatic, sensible girl—if terribly trusting and naïve. But despite all that, I still found an almost childlike wonder in the unknown. The inexplicable that drew me in against all good judgment.

Which was likely how I ended up working with Mr. Owen dealing in rare, arcane, and *occasionally* illegal books. My curiosity about the unknown was likely also the reason I remained stubbornly captivated by Ruan. Not that *that* mattered anymore. He was unfortunately consigned to my past.

The main exhibition room broke off into smaller wings, each devoted to a different era. PRE-HISTORY, THE NATURAL WORLD, THE

UNNATURAL WORLD—whatever that might be—ANTIQUITY, and lastly THE INDUSTRIAL WORLD. The museum grew hotter by the moment, the bodice of my gown dampening with sweat.

Desperate for a breeze, and perhaps an inch or two of space amidst the crowd, I sidled past the great stage already set for tonight's spectacle. The dais was shrouded by a deep jade velvet curtain rigged up like some sort of macabre holiday package. On each of the four corners were large flaming torches. Edging around the flames, lest I knock one over and send us all to perdition, I hurried back outside and down the twelve steps onto the sidewalk. Lazy snowflakes drifted down from the wispy clouds overhead and landed on my dark hair. More snow. Poor Mr. Owen. He always did detest the stuff.

I leaned against the wall of the museum, tilting my face up to the moonlight. The icy wind pricked my exposed skin. Yesterday's snow had only begun to melt, and now it was refreezing, leaving the ground around me slick with ice. Perhaps we'd hire a car home. Better than walking at any rate.

I rummaged in my pocket for my silver cigarette case, opened it, and pulled one out before putting it to my lips and lighting it. I drew the smoke into my lungs and blew it out again into the night air.

"Good evening."

I flicked the ashes into the gutter before looking up. A strikingly handsome gentleman stood before me. He wasn't much taller than me, with ashen strands laced through his sandy hair. He wore a clever houndstooth suit that fit his athletic form a bit too snugly for current fashion. There was a carelessness to his dress, presumably intended to be alluring, but the effect struck me as a bit too studied. I took another drag from the cigarette rather than answering. I was used to fellows like that.

"Professor Frederick Reaver." He tried again with a game smile.

My pulse stilled. Or perhaps not fellows like *that*.

The man had uttered the only three words in the English language to catch my attention this evening. *Professor Frederick Reaver*—the Keeper of the Egyptology collection at the Ashmolean Museum. In the flesh, the man was nothing at all like I'd expected. Instead of a pinched and thin academic in a tired jumper, this man could have stepped straight from the pages of a men's fashion advertisement. Not to mention the way his jacket stretched at his shoulders—he was muscle upon muscle. How very curious.

I toyed with the paper of the cigarette with my thumbnail.

"And you . . . if I do not miss my guess, are Ruby Vaughn."

"You do not miss." I barely concealed my surprise. "Though I must confess I'm curious how you knew."

"You have an unusual face." His smile melted away as he mirrored my frank inspection before checking his watch and glancing over his shoulder at the rapidly emptying streets of Oxford. Nearly half the city had crammed itself inside the museum wondering if Julius Harker would truly arrive, and doubly curious how this Reaver fellow would react to the exhibition.

"I've read all about your adventures this year. You're becoming a bit of a celebrity on these shores with your knack for finding trouble."

His jab about my previous exploits was nothing I did not already know. I did not relish the fame that had been following me these past few months thanks to an irritating journalist . . . *V. E. Devereaux*. The man had made a point of sensationalizing my every move. If I ever met him . . . I would certainly give him a piece of my mind. For the whole reason I'd settled in Exeter in the first place was to avoid the notoriety that came along with being that *scandalous Vaughn girl*. Little good that did me. My life with Mr. Owen proved to be a greater scandal than the one that sent me fleeing America.

Reaver's expression faltered, revealing a deep dimple in one cheek. "I apologize. I am often told my manner is too brusque for polite company and that I belong up to my knees in dirt in the field—not in these hallowed halls with my coarse manners." He tilted his head down the street in the direction of the Ashmolean. The museum itself was not visible at night, but I could make out the shadowy gothic spire of the Martyrs' Memorial from here, even in the darkness. "It is only that Miss Abernathy told me you were in town and that you spend your mornings together before she comes in, and I've learned that a friend of hers is well worth knowing."

She might have told *him* about me, but she'd scarcely mentioned him at all. In truth, when he came up yesterday afternoon, she skirted the subject. "Is she here tonight?"

Something shuttered in his expression. "I doubt it. Miss Abernathy was occupied with her research when I left her at the museum." Professor Reaver watched a group of young men coming down the street before training his attention upon me. "Care to join me to watch the spectacle, Miss Vaughn? I daresay it will be quite the show."

He was acting the perfect gentleman, but something about him gave me pause. I hesitated before laying my palm on the fine wool of his jacket. He tilted his head in acknowledgment to the young men now flanking him and one of them hurried ahead to open the door for us. The roar of sound from inside Harker's Curiosity Museum flooded out into the street as I returned to the maw of the beast, wholly unprepared for the spectacle soon to unfold.

Chapter Four

Harker's Final Show

IN the handful of minutes I'd been outside the museum with Frederick Reaver, dozens more people had joined the throng of onlookers, making it difficult to navigate between the bodies. All the discordant sounds from their hundreds of conversations made my pulse thunder in my veins. Raw, unbridled panic began to surge through me.

I hated crowds.

Had loathed them ever since my misadventures in Lothlel Green this past summer. I could scarcely be in a room with twenty people or more without becoming rabbity, but this—this new sensation was nigh on unbearable. My head began to ache as I thought of my days in that godforsaken hamlet. Was this what Ruan had meant when he'd refer to his uncomfortable ability to hear people's thoughts? He'd told me once that it was *akin to a train station . . . a sense of something coming*. If so, it was no wonder the man remained in his remote Cornish village most of the time. I'd shun society as well if I could hear their every waking thought.

Good God, why could I not get him out of my head? He was a plague and a pestilence. If only I could forget what had come between us. What had *almost* happened. Of course, my attempts to forget were stymied by the fact I'd invited him to join us in Oxford in a gin-fueled missive, apologizing for the way I'd left things. But he'd not deigned to come, instead he'd sent a response that was all of two words.

I SEE. R

Five damnable letters. One period and no indication whether he forgave me or not.

That was my answer, I supposed. Our would-be romance was over before it had even begun. My fingers itched for the flask that was once my dearest companion, but I'd left it at home. Hiding in the bottom of a bottle of gin was yet another habit I needed to break—regardless of the status of my wounded heart.

Across the room by the shrouded dais, Lord Amberley—whom I'd seen earlier today—was speaking with his son, gesturing at the flaming torches by the curtains. At least I presumed the fellow with him was his son, as the two might have been twins, albeit ones separated by a good forty years. Amberley waved me over with a broad smile. He was a man of about Mr. Owen's years, with a balding pate and a gentle face.

"I'd been waiting for you, dear girl. Owen was here a moment ago asking for you." Amberley strained, craning his neck looking around for Mr. Owen before giving up with an affectionate sigh. "I must confess I do not even know why I've come tonight. I've always found this sort of display vulgar."

Amberley's son was tense, glancing around the room. A faint sheen of perspiration glistened on his brow. I couldn't fault him for his discomfort, the crowd was unbearable. He blotted at his brow with a handkerchief.

"As do I." I laughed, struggling to focus on Amberley's face amidst the irrational unease that grew in my chest from the closing-in crowd. "It must be our mutual affection for Mr. Owen that makes us do these things. They do so bring him joy."

"That and a dash of morbid curiosity—most certainly." Amberley's rheumy eyes sparkled. "Don't let anyone persuade you otherwise. Half of Oxford has been wagering whether that cur Harker will even bother to appear tonight after shunning the Ashmolean as he did . . . Did you know he's not been seen in days? It's a bit of a surprise as much as the man adores being the center of attention." A trace of acidity laced his tone as he spotted the distinctive figure of Professor Reaver on the far side of the room surrounded by a half dozen young bucks vying for his ear. "Dear me, even Reaver is here with his army of acolytes. The business with Harker at the Ashmolean must have truly set him off." He clapped his hands in delight. "This *will* be a show. Reaver's a cold one, more likely to ice a fellow out than to show up and challenge him directly."

Reaver's fair head was bowed as he listened to one of them. There were five of them surrounding him, each of the young men even wearing their hair in the same style as Reaver's, having modeled themselves upon the fellow down to his sartorial choices.

Amberley leaned closer. "He is constantly trailed by that passel of pups from the University. All of them jockeying to claim the title of his prized pupil. Every year since he returned from the war, he selects one lad to be his pet for the year. It's all nonsense if you ask me, but what fellow of that age has any sense?"

"Was he teaching here before the war?"

"For a time, but he'd been away from the University for several years before the Germans marched on Belgium. By that time, he was already in Egypt, making a name for himself in the field. Then the war came, of course. Terrible business, that." Amberley gestured to the shrouded dais before us. "If Harker had an ounce of good sense, he'd have accepted Reaver's offer to speak at the museum the other night, played by the rules, and smoothed over the scandal once and for all. But oh no, far be it from Julius Harker to choose the safe course and mend fences."

I started to ask him about the scandal at the University, as no one else had been able to tell me why Harker had been abruptly cast out, but any concern I had for Julius Harker disappeared when I spotted Leona—not ten feet away from Professor Reaver. Her long dark hair was braided much as it had been the previous afternoon and hung loose over her shoulder. Her expression drawn with panic as she scoured the faces of the room. She was searching for someone. A frisson of worry climbed up my spine.

She wore a crisp white blouse, and a half-unbuttoned waistcoat. Her shirtsleeves were rolled up and even from this distance I could see the careless stains of ink upon her forearms. A few tendrils of hair had come loose from her braid, giving the impression she'd run the quarter mile here. Reaver said he'd left her at the museum—doubted she would come, and yet here she was. Leona's disarray stood out in stark contrast to the other attendees who were dressed for an evening out on the town.

"If you'd excuse me . . ." I murmured to Lord Amberley, slipping away from the fellow. There would be time enough to puzzle out what he knew of Julius Harker's scandal later. Something was terribly wrong if Leona was here. She detested these sorts of affairs. I squeezed between bodies, murmuring out apologies as I headed in her direction. My own fears warring with logic.

This was an exhibition in her field of study, after all. And she *was* Egyptian, having been raised in Cairo by her grandfather and aunt after her mother died. Her father had been a British officer, if I recalled correctly, but Leona seldom spoke of him. I wondered, sometimes, why she settled this far from her family, but never asked. It wasn't my business, and she scarcely spoke of the *why*.

It *shouldn't* have been unusual for Leona to be here at Harker's exhibition—and yet I knew it was. It was in her dress. The look on her face. Leona was always so meticulous about her own appearance and how she was perceived by others. She knew, unjust as it was, that to be taken seriously in a man's world she had to be twice as clever. Twice as perfect. Utterly flawless. And it was that small detail that had every warning bell in my body ringing. If Leona had come here out of scholarly interest, she would be dressed like the rest of the audience who had paid good money to attend. Whatever brought her here was more important to her than her scholarly reputation—and that concerned me a great deal.

I lost sight of her for a moment, before spotting her again, this time on the far side of the dais. Within seconds I was at her side and touched her elbow. "Darling, are you all right?"

She jumped at the contact. Confusion and fear flickered across her face. "R-Ruby, what are you doing here?"

I cocked my head to the side. "I presume what the better half of Oxford is doing: waiting for the exhibition. I didn't know you were coming tonight, or I'd have come with you. I scarcely know a soul here."

"I didn't . . . I mean I wasn't . . . I came to find someone . . . it's important. I need to—" Leona's expression grew stricken as she strained up on the tips of her toes. She was a good three inches shorter than me, making it difficult for her to see over the tops of the heads of others.

"Are you looking for Professor Reaver? I ran into him earlier. I can show you—"

Her eyes widened and she swore. "He's here? Where? He cannot see me here . . . He cannot know I've come."

I leaned closer, taking her by the hand. "What has he done, Leona?"

She squeezed my fingers, leading me deeper into the crowd. "It's not that . . . He would be cross. I promised him that I wouldn't set foot in this building today. I'm fine. I promise you."

"You are not *fine,* you look as if you're running from a ghost." And I should know, considering my previous forays into the occult.

She struggled to school her face. "I'm fine, Ruby. It's only that I need to find someone. You startled me when you came upon me like you did." She laid a hand on my forearm. "All is well."

Liar. I squeezed her hand, and rather than pull away, she wrapped her fingers tighter around my own.

"Who are you looking for? I can help you without drawing attention," I insisted, as a man smelling of whisky and cigars bumped into me, pushing me against her.

She worried her lower lip and began to deny it but then dropped her voice to a whisper. "Julius Harker is not here." She checked an ancient silver pocket watch, snapped it back tight, and slipped it into her waistcoat. "He should have been here by now."

My skin pricked at her words. "Good God, no wonder you don't want Reaver to see you—you can't mean to say that you're acquainted with *him*? Leona, Julius Harker's reputation is beyond repair. Your position at the Ashmolean . . . you'd be . . ." *Ruined.*

She waved the thought away. "Don't pay mind to that. It's not important. What matters is Julius is missing."

She called him by his first name. I didn't like the sound of that—not one little bit.

My stomach knotted as Leona fiddled with the silver chain on her watch, running it between her fingers. "He should be here. I need to go—" Her expression fell at once and I turned to find Frederick Reaver standing behind us, his jaw strained and tight, revealing his singular dimple.

"*There* you are, Miss Abernathy!"

Leona's fingers squeezed mine even tighter as she froze in place.

Reaver looked her over much as he'd inspected me in the street. "I thought I'd left you in the reading room?"

Leona stiffened, slipping her hand from mine and folding her arms across her lithe chest. "I came to find you. I . . . I was having trouble with a text."

Professor Reaver's jaw relaxed, visibly relieved by her lies. His brows drew up in confusion. "But were you not working on the *Saqqara* scrolls when I left you earlier? You should not need me for those." The emphasis he placed on *Saqqara* struck me as odd, but I didn't have time to think on it, as the crowd's roar died to a hush.

A short, round man came out onto the stage, saving Leona from fabricating yet another excuse for her presence. He dabbed at the perspiration on his brow with a freshly pressed white handkerchief. A second, younger man joined him, and the two drew back the deep green curtains, revealing a sheer inner veil obscuring the cache. The four torches flickered as the overhead gaslights were dimmed. Only the shadowy outlines of a sarcophagus, or perhaps a funerary box, along with some jars were visible through the gauzy inner curtain.

"Is that fellow Julius Harker?" I whispered.

Leona's lips were pressed into a thin line. "No. That's Mr. Mueller, his business partner. Mueller handles the books. This isn't like Julius at all." She craned her neck again, scouring the crowd. "Where can he *be*?"

"Evidently hell bent on destroying what's left of his reputation," Reaver muttered.

Leona's body tensed.

Mr. Mueller blotted his brow with the handkerchief and began to address the increasingly restless crowd. Leona's concerns were echoed by the disorderly audience.

"Where is he?"

"Harker's done it again!"

"Perhaps he's late."

"Harker's never late."

All the confused voices crashed into an angry sea of confusion and anticipation.

Reaver leaned close to Leona, whispering something into her ear. His voice low enough I couldn't hear, though her spine straightened and a faint bit of color rose to her cheeks. His hand rested possessively on her other elbow, fingers curled around the exposed flesh there. She did not pull away—not at all fazed by his familiar gesture.

Leona eyed Mr. Mueller's anxious form on the stage for a second too long before turning to me. "I have to go." She turned and made her way deeper into the crowd with Reaver at her side. I was right to mistrust the fellow when we first met. I didn't know what was happening between Leona and him, but I didn't like it. Not one bit.

I watched after the pair, perplexed by their interplay. She had appeared almost afraid of him at first, but now? She went along with nary a word. She didn't flinch at his touch, did not even move away from him. She simply obeyed. In the time we'd been reunited here in Oxford, she'd scarcely mentioned this man—or Julius Harker for that matter—yet it was clear as day that she was very familiar with them both.

Chalk that up to another thing we'd be discussing at the Artemis Club when we met in the morning. I blew out an irritated breath, wishing that Mr. Owen had left me to my book and biscuits for the evening.

"If I could have your attention!" Mr. Mueller cried out over the noisy crowd. He and his young assistant tugged the filmy shroud back, revealing the cache at long last. A great canopic box sat in the center. The goddess Nephthys with her kite wings spread high was carved on the side nearest to me. Her sister, Isis, was presumably depicted in a similar position on the far side. Dozens of canopic jars and small statues surrounded the box, all lit by small glass luminaries giving the subtle illusion of movement among the artifacts. A neat trick, but this was a rather disappointing cache all told.

Only a handful of artifacts, and nothing particularly rare. Certainly not rare enough to warrant such fanfare.

And where *was* Mr. Owen? I turned from Mr. Mueller and his accomplice, looking for a familiar tuft of white hair amongst the crowd. The low, barely lit gaslights flickered overhead as I spied two of his antiquarian friends from last night. They'd cornered some poor soul in the shadows behind a curio case full of enormous ammonites, excitedly nattering away at the fellow. Better him than me.

"Blood! There's blood!"

A woman let out a loud shriek from my left.

I whipped my attention back to Mr. Mueller's sturdy young assistant, now retching out the contents of his stomach onto the wooden floor below. The shouts and flickering lights slowed my thoughts. Mind unable to keep up with what I was seeing.

Blood? Blood from where?

I stepped around the tide of people scrambling to get away from the dais and edged closer. Mr. Mueller was frozen in place with the top of the funerary box clutched in his blood-stained hands. He stared in horror at whatever lay within the box.

A sickening sensation settled in my gut as I hiked my skirt to my knee, and took the big step up onto the raised platform. I gingerly maneuvered between the canopic jars and glanced down into the great stone box.

I found Julius Harker.

He hadn't been late after all.

He'd simply been dead.

Chapter Five

A Penchant for Peril

THE body of Julius Harker had been awkwardly crammed into the great stone funerary box. His mouth gaped open, dark blood pooling around his head like a garish halo. Something about the sight put me in mind of that German film that Mr. Owen had been going on about before we set off for Oxford. Something to do with vampires. I'd not paid much attention at the time, thinking it another silly picture I didn't care to watch, but perhaps I ought to have, considering my recent experiences with the inexplicable and arcane. I certainly couldn't discount the notion of such things as easily now as I once had, as Mr. Owen's *otherworld* was far more a part of *our* world than I'd ever imagined.

Harker's legs were unnaturally contorted, as the box was not long enough for him to fully extend inside this temporary grave. His hands were scraped and cut; nails broken below the quick with dried blood on them indicating he'd been wounded, then entombed alive, left to bleed out or suffocate—whichever came first.

Wrinkling my nose, I leaned down with half a mind to adjust his jaw to see if he still possessed a tongue. It *appeared* to my untrained eye that the thing had been excised entirely. I grimaced at the thought. Who would take a man's tongue . . . and why?

But before I could get any closer to the body to prove my hypothesis, a rough pair of hands grabbed me hard about the waist, pulling me down from the dais and into the crowd.

I yelped, elbowing my assailant in the ribs, fully prepared to shove my hip into his groin, when my mind registered what my body somehow already knew. I'd been struck with a familiar green scent. Calendula, feverfew, rosemary. Angelica.

Either I'd gone utterly mad—not an impossible situation—or Ruan Kivell had *actually* come to Oxford.

My pulse raced as I spun around and found myself looking up into his green eyes. Pale in color, except for the dark gray cloud in one that stretched across to the iris. I wasn't mad. Not at all.

I swallowed hard, as he let go of my waist and glowered down at me before taking me by the shoulders and turning me away from him. "Why is it that dead bodies follow you around like kittens?" Ruan began marching me through the crowd away from the funerary box and into one of the darkened alcoves near the towering mahogany curiosity cases.

How was he *here*? I glanced over my shoulder, greedily drinking in his familiar features in the darkened museum. He'd lost that dreadful beard he'd had in Scotland and his dark hair was longer now. Though the deep divot of worry remained etched between his brows. My fingers longed to smooth it, but his worries weren't mine to ease. Not after the way I left things.

I sniffed indignantly, folding my arms tight. "I don't find that imagery amusing. Not one bit. What are you doing here anyway?"

"What am *I* doing here? What are *you* doing running toward the first dead man you see?"

I opened my mouth, then snapped it back shut. "I did not run. I walked. And I ask again, what are you doing here?"

"*You* are the one who invited me to join you in Oxford. Though had I realized that the very evening I arrived there would be yet another corpse at your feet, I might have reconsidered boarding the bloody train to begin with."

I huffed, peering past him out into the exhibit room. It was easier to be annoyed with Ruan if I didn't have to look at him. The man was a weakness I did not need. Not with my own frayed emotions. I couldn't be this near him or else I'd cut myself on the jagged edges I'd left behind.

He grunted, before again taking me roughly by the shoulders and pushing us deeper into the shadows of the museum, behind that same ammonite case I'd noticed earlier. Suddenly I knew precisely who Mr. Owen's friends had been talking to with such animation. Ruan had been here the whole time.

"What do you want?"

"To speak with you."

Liar. If he meant that, he'd have come to me straightaway. "You've come to torment me, that's what you've done. Flaunt your—" I gestured at the substantial width of his shoulders and made another very Mr. Owen–sounding sound in the back of my throat.

"I called on you earlier, but you were out. Mrs. Penrose said I could find you here."

Fabulous, my own housekeeper betrayed me, *and* he was eavesdropping on my private thoughts again. I'd not quite gotten used to the fact he could do that—a part of me felt violated by his ability to *hear* my thoughts, though it wasn't as if he could control it. Our peculiar connection made certain of that. "You still didn't answer my letter."

He stepped closer, reaching out to touch my hand but then caught himself, shoving his gloved fist into his pocket instead. "I did write you."

"Two words, Ruan Kivell. You wrote two words. Besides, this isn't the time for this conversation. In case you've forgotten, there is a *dead man* in a box on the other side of this cabinet." I tapped the glass with two fingers.

Ruan peered through the edge of the panel to where he could get a better view of the crowd still huddled around the box. "I'd say it's the perfect time to settle this between us. The police are on their way, and you know as well as I do that neither of us will be leaving the museum until they've talked to each and every one of us."

He was correct on that score. I'd first met Ruan in Cornwall, where we'd investigated the death of Tamsyn's dreadful husband, Sir Edward. Then again, we came together in Scotland to investigate the death of a medium. "Fine." Best to get it over with. "Why could you not at least answer me? I laid myself bare in that letter and you—"

He let out a strangled sound, hand resting oddly over his jacket pocket as he watched me. "I would like to remind you that you are not the only person in the world capable of feelings, Ruby Vaughn. What was I to say to that absurd *thing* you penned me? I still am not certain what it *meant*, let alone how to respond." He pulled a well-worn piece of paper from his pocket and held it up in the light before beginning to read. "'Ruan, I will not apologize for how we left things in Scotland. Nor will I apologize for not knowing how to respond to your *unseemly*'"—his emphasis, not mine—"'show of emotion. As you ought to know, I live my life with no regrets and few entanglements. Unfortunately, you have dug your way beneath my skin, and I do not know what to make of the situation. You certainly should have known better than to encourage my affections.'"

I glanced over my shoulder to see the police had finally arrived. "You truly do not have to read it to me. I recall what I said. I wrote the damn thing." I *didn't* actually, as I'd had the better part of a bottle of gin when I'd finally worked up the nerve to write it. But he didn't need to know that. I stretched up on my toes, scanning the crowd for Mr. Owen. Where *was* the old man? Surely he was around here somewhere. "I think that's quite clear how I feel on the matter."

"Of course you do." He let out a hoarse laugh. "I, for one, couldn't quite tell if you were throwing me over or asking me to tea. I am your friend—I will always be your friend, Ruby, you must know that by now. But you are going to have to decide what you want because I will not throw myself at your feet again."

"Ruan . . ." My stomach twisted at the bitterness in his words.

"Despite what the people in Lothlel Green believe . . . despite what *you* might believe, I am not made of stone."

"But you came anyway . . . why?"

Ruan rubbed a hand over his jaw. "The gods must know, because I bloody well don't. Anytime we are within the same county, someone ends up dead and I end up with a half dozen more scars for the effort."

"That's not our fault." I glanced back toward the funerary box. By now, there were a half dozen uniformed police working their way through the crowd. Lord Amberley was speaking with one near the front door alongside Mr. Owen, who was now gesturing widely—I could only imagine what it was he was telling the officer. I let out a sigh of relief at finally spotting the old man in the crowd. I scanned the room, suddenly realizing that neither Leona nor Professor Reaver were here.

Had they managed to leave before the body was revealed? It had only been a handful of seconds at most from the moment they took their leave of me to when the box was opened—less than a minute. Surely, they couldn't have escaped the museum that quickly. My pulse quickened.

"Do you suspect her?" Ruan asked, changing the subject from the uncomfortable topic of our thwarted romance back to safer terrain—murder.

"Leona?" I placed my hands on my hips, watching the detectives surround the dais. "No. She hasn't a violent bone in her body. But I do wish you'd at least *try* to not eavesdrop on my thoughts."

"Would that I could. But this Leona person is numbered amongst your friends. I have to question that point."

He had me there.

The edge of his mouth twitched as he fought a smile despite the anger he must have felt toward me. But if he *was* angry, why would he come? I turned away. "You may not be wrong on that either, but I don't think she's involved in *this*. Leona was . . ." I weighed how much to tell him about her, but this was Ruan. He'd find out anyway—even if we were at odds. "Concerned for Harker . . . She must have known he was in danger. I don't think she could have feigned that worry. She must have known something was going to happen here. Known or feared."

Ruan cocked an eyebrow in challenge.

"I do hate how you do that—it's terribly unfair. But I am done." I held up my palms, wiping them in the air to underscore my point. "Done with murderers, done with mysteries. And as soon as these lovely gentleman"—I gestured to the nearby detective questioning a middle-aged matron—"have finished here, I will go home, take a bath, crawl into bed with my cat and my book, and forget this evening ever happened."

"Will you?"

"Of course." Though both of us knew that was not to be.

Several hours later, I sat in the kitchen of our cozy townhome alone with Mrs. Penrose. Mr. Owen had been deep in conversation with Lord Amberley at the museum, so Ruan promised to stay behind and see the old man into a car and safely home. I tucked my legs up beneath me on the bench, bare feet off the cold floor as my housekeeper poured a kettle of boiling water into a blue china teapot. "Bad business, murder." She frowned. Mrs. Penrose wore a serviceable woolen dressing gown pulled tight over her own nightdress as she set the teapot to steep on the table between us.

I nodded absently, running my thumb over an imperfection in the wooden work surface. "It's peculiar. Whoever killed Harker had removed his tongue, then left him in that box to bleed out. Why would a person do something like that?"

"Hungry, my lover?" she asked, the familiar Cornish term of endearment bringing the first smile to my lips in hours. I let out a startled laugh, glancing up from the wooden tabletop. "No. I'm afraid seeing a dead man tonight did in my appetite."

Mrs. Penrose chuckled. "I suspect it would do that, maid. Have a cup with me. It'll help you sleep."

She didn't bother waiting on my response and set about fixing my tea, then placed it in my hands. She groaned as she lowered herself into a chair across the table. "It's been a day. I meant to tell you, young Ruan Kivell came by earlier. You didn't tell me he was coming to stay. I'd never been so surprised in my life to see the lad this far from home." Her long graying hair fell loose over her shoulder, and I could have sworn that she looked younger in the months since she'd been living with Mr. Owen and me in Exeter.

I frowned. "I didn't know he was coming either. I only saw him for the first time at the museum."

"Did he say where he was staying, I was hoping he might—" But before she could continue, the telltale click of the key sounded in the lock. Mr. Owen must have finally escaped Amberley's attentions. I stifled a yawn into my fist, not bothering to look up from my warm cup of oolong.

"Why, hello there, my 'ansom! Back so soon?" Mrs. Penrose shot to her feet. I turned in surprise to see my housekeeper launch herself across the room, wrapping her arms around Ruan's neck. Ruan froze, standing half in and half out with his haversack slung over his shoulder and tattered valise in his hand. He wore a low-slung cap over his brow, and a few snowflakes clung to the dark wool of his coat like stars in the night sky.

Mr. Owen shooed Ruan and Mrs. Penrose into the room then

closed the heavy door, knocking the bits of snow off his boots. "I was telling Kivell here, that with a murderer in Oxford, I thought it best he stay with us. The lad was going to stay at a boardinghouse and I told him that Dorothea wouldn't allow for her countryman to stay with strangers, not when we were staying in the same town. Didn't I, Kivell?"

Incredulous, my eyebrows shot up. "Mr. Owen! We hardly have room for the three of us and the cat. Besides, what will people say?" Though truthfully, I knew good and well no one would bat an eye at the unusual living arrangement. Times had changed after the war, upsetting the social order that had placed restrictions upon my sex. Women had entered the workforce, others had taken lovers, and as long as one remained discreet, most of society did not care one way or the other. Especially when one was past the first blush of youth as I was. Of course, my money also went a good way to protect me from social censure—a thought that rankled. For a wealthy heiress who breaks the rules of society becomes an eccentric, but their gilded doors always remain open, as there's always someone in want of her money.

"Since when have you given a damn what anyone said?" Mr. Owen grumbled. "Besides, you're here with Dorothea and me. Even in *my* youth, that would be chaperonage enough to protect your virtue." Mr. Owen's dark brown eyes glittered with amusement. He knew good and well I did not want Ruan here invading my space, I'd given Mr. Owen the rough outline of the sad affair after we left Scotland. Mr. Owen had urged me to apologize, to fix things before they became irreparable, and I'd stubbornly refused.

Mrs. Penrose held his face in her hands and took a step back with a maternal muttering. "Nonsense, my lover, we have a room in the attic. And I'd take mortal offense if you didn't stay under my roof, Ruan Kivell. Your mother would never forgive me if I even thought for a moment of putting you with strangers. I will not have it."

She squeezed him again, and he shot me a helpless look over her shoulder.

Serves you right for not writing.

Then another thought struck me. That empty room in the attic she'd mentioned . . . it was directly across the hall from my own.

Fabulous. Just fabulous.

Ruan and I would sort out this strangeness between us one way or the other, and Mr. Owen—as usual—would be squarely in the middle of it.

Chapter Six

A Mourning Caller

EARLY the next morning, Mrs. Penrose burst into my darkened attic bedroom, shaking me hard from my sleep. "Up, maid. Up with you!"

I slowly opened my eyes, the last whispers of sleep rattling from my head. It had been my first solid night of the stuff in weeks too. My nightmares had been growing increasingly worse over the last year—to the point I now rarely slept more than a few hours at a time. Sometimes it would be a recurring dream—over and over—warning me of some impending cataclysm. Though lately those had taken a more sinister turn. I no longer *saw* things but felt them instead. An unending, suffocating stillness I could not escape.

My nightmares were half the reason I met Leona at dawn for fencing each morning. First it was the dreams. Then the imposter. Now Julius Harker's dead body. It was no wonder I couldn't sleep. It was still dark, not nearly time for me to go to the club. I grumbled, struggling to focus on my housekeeper's face as I swung my feet to the cold wooden floor. "What time is it?"

"Too early, maid. Too early, but there's someone here for you."

"Here? *Now?*" My eyes darted to the darkened window, sleep vanishing at once. "What's wrong?" I snatched an embroidered black and red silk dressing gown and pulled it over my short white nightdress, tying it at the waist. "It's Hari, isn't it?"

Mrs. Penrose let out a martyred sigh at the mention of my solicitor, the same one she'd helped me evade for the past week. He must have been desperate indeed if he'd showed up here before dawn to catch me. "No. Not him."

I ran a rough hand over my face.

"Though you should see the poor man before he takes a fancy to breaking down the door at this hour too." Her gaze narrowed at me for a half second before her expression shifted back to concern. She brushed a gray strand of hair back into her low braid. "But no, 'tis a maid this time. She said it was urgent, or I'd have sent her away to come back at a more Christian hour. She looks a fright."

Fear prickled at my throat. *Leona.* It had to be her.

"Right frantic she is."

This did not sound good. Not good at all. I left Mrs. Penrose in my room and ran down the narrow townhouse stairs into the kitchen, the silk of the dressing gown rustling in the quiet of the cozy house.

Leona sat on the same bench I'd occupied earlier, alongside the low kitchen worktable. She was dressed as she had been when I last saw her. Her green skirt was covered in dust, with a peculiar dark stain at the hem and a tear near her pocket. Her waistcoat had been similarly ripped, and her ink-stained skin was now smeared with dirt.

"Darling, what's happened? Where have you been? I was searching for you at the museum after Reaver grabbed you."

Pale tear streaks had dried on her cheeks as she held a china cup unsteadily in her shaking hands. Beside her sat the little blue teapot and a tray of sandwiches. Leave it to Mrs. Penrose to make sure a body is fed in a crisis—even at four in the morning.

"They've arrested Mr. Mueller," she whispered, half to herself. "They've *arrested* . . . Mr. Mueller . . . for murder."

I watched her warily, noting the flicker of fear on her face as the words sat in the air between us. "Julius Harker's bookkeeper?" The man nearly died of shock himself after discovering the body of his colleague. Certainly not the reaction of one who was guilty of a crime. "When was this? I watched him leave the museum not long before I did. That was"—I leaned against the cool porcelain face of the sink and reached for my pin watch, which was unfortunately still upstairs on my dresser, and sighed—"hours ago. . . . Why would they arrest him? If anything, he needs a stiff drink and a few days' rest after such a shock."

She flicked the rim of her cup with her broken nail and my eye caught on the bloodied edge. Her damaged thumb traced the smooth china rim, running it back and forth, seeking comfort from the repetitive motion. Outside a dog began to bay in the night, low and deep.

I crossed the kitchen, covering her hand against the rapidly cooling cup before tilting her chin up with the crook of my finger, forcing her to face me. "You have to talk to me. You've come here for a reason, and I cannot help if I don't know what happened tonight and what you need of me."

Leona swallowed hard, staring off into the distance at some imagined spot on the floor.

I crouched before her. My dressing gown pooled around my feet, as the cold from the stone floor seeped through my skin and into my very bones. "The last I saw you, you were leaving the museum with Frederick Reaver. Did something happen at the Ashmolean? Because dressed as you are, you appear as if you've clawed your way out of a . . . *grave*." The final word evaporated on my tongue. I'd not connected the thoughts before, but the state of her fingers very much resembled Julius Harker's hands, except he hadn't escaped his tomb. Dread lodged itself in my throat. "What happened to you?"

She shrugged away from my touch, shooting to her feet and

moving to the far end of the table. "I did this to myself. I've been in the archives all evening seeking . . . *something*." She studied my skeptical expression for several heartbeats before adding, "A book, Ruby. I was looking for a book—all right? It has nothing to do with poor Mr. Mueller."

I raised a brow. Goodness knew I'd spent many an hour digging around in old books and never ended up in that condition. "Where did Professor Reaver go? Was he looking for the *book* too?"

She shook her head, lips pressed into a thin line, oddly defensive of Reaver. "He left me in the archives and returned to his office. They are two separate matters." Leona clenched her wounded fist. "What is important is that Julius has been murdered." She sat the teacup down with a clatter and covered her face with her hands. "I cannot believe he is *dead*."

"You were friends?"

Her dark lashes fanned out over her cheeks. She raked her hands over her face, struggling to put herself to rights. "Freddie—Professor Reaver—" She caught herself. "He told me he'd found something at the museum earlier that day that he needed my assistance with. I had spent all day with him there. But if I'd known that Julius was dead in that box, I would not have left—" Her words were swallowed up by a mournful sob.

"There's nothing you could have done—nothing at all. Gauging from his body, he'd likely been in there for a day or two. It's probably why he didn't show up to the Ashmolean for that lecture earlier this week. The poor fellow."

Leona grew gray at the thought. She clenched her hands to keep them from trembling. "Oh, Julius . . . He did not deserve this. Neither of them does . . ." Her wounded finger began to bleed again and she shoved it into her mouth to stop it.

My eyes drifted over her torn and dirty clothing. "Leona, I want to believe you that you were at the museum—but the state of you—if you could only see yourself as I do. Where were you truly?"

Leona's gaze narrowed. "I am not lying. I was at the museum. Reaver dragged me over there and then left me in one of the subterranean storerooms to assist with a plinth he was having trouble dating. He left me there, I presume to return to Harker's museum—said he had things to see to. I locked myself in because it was late, but the door was stuck—"

"You said moments before you sought a book. Now it's a plinth." I narrowed my gaze at her. "Why are you lying to me?"

"I am not lying. Not about the museum. You must trust me on this, my trip back to the Ashmolean had *nothing* to do with what happened to Julius Harker."

I did not believe her. Not one bit. "Reaver did not come back to Harker's museum after the two of you left. He wasn't there when Mr. Mueller discovered the body. Did he even return with you to the Ashmolean or is that something else you are keeping from me?"

"Why are you behaving like this?" She stared at me dumbfounded. Her mouth opened, then snapped back shut. "Of course he came back to the Ashmolean, but I do not know where he went after. He left me in that storeroom. Had he stayed, I wouldn't have broken my blasted nail trying to get out the jammed door."

I wanted to believe her—I did—but her story didn't make sense. I softened my voice. "Darling, I promise you. He didn't come back to Harker's museum. Do you know where else he might have gone?"

She sank back onto the bench in disbelief, tugging her long dark hair over her shoulder, braiding it loosely in her worried hands. "No. Professor Reaver doesn't always entrust me with his secrets, and yes—I know what you're thinking—he can be terribly brusque, but he'd never harm Julius. He's not a violent man."

Again, that low baleful howl came from farther down the lane. I shivered, wrapping my dressing gown tighter around me. "What about Mueller? What makes you certain he is innocent?"

Frustrated, she slapped her palm on the tabletop. "The man

collects *teakettles*, Ruby! What cause would he have to harm his oldest friend?"

That *was* the question, was it not? I'd already ascertained that Julius Harker was *persona non grata* in most academic circles, and yet Leona cared for him. *Deeply.* Add to that her peculiar relationship with Frederick Reaver. The two men could not have been any more different. One, the favorite child of the academy; the other, its black sheep, and I could not—for the life of me—understand how Leona fit into all of this.

The winter winds raged at the windowpanes, rattling the glass in the sill. I leaned over to the table and took a sandwich from the untouched plate beside her. I gestured at the others, with my little finger. "Eat. Please. Mrs. Penrose will take it as a mortal offense if you don't."

That earned a half-hearted smile from Leona as she tentatively picked up a sandwich, pressing the soft bread between her fingers.

"How well did you know Julius Harker? You'd never mentioned him before . . ." Truthfully, she had omitted a great deal, but Julius Harker was the safest place to start unraveling the truth.

She eyed the darkened doorway behind me leading back into the main house with a sigh. "Everyone knows him." She wet her lips, weighing her words. "Most serious scholars do not associate with him openly. Frederick thought my continued dealings with him would reflect poorly upon the museum and discouraged me from continuing our friendship."

I took a cautious bite of the cheddar and chutney sandwich. I had to go slowly with her for fear she'd stop talking altogether. "What did Harker do to be the subject of such scorn?"

Leona finished off her sandwich before taking a second. "I'm not entirely sure. I know Frederick and he taught together for a time. When the scandal occurred and Julius lost his position at the University, Frederick had already been in Egypt for a year or two. He'd left to work in the field. To make his name."

Leona's casualness with using Professor Reaver's first name struck me as odd. Yes, the two worked together closely, but there was an intimacy in her tone that I wasn't sure I liked. "Do you think there's a connection between the two?" Each new question risked her shutting the door on the conversation entirely.

"I don't know. I don't *believe* so. Whatever it was that Julius had gotten involved in was bad enough that no one spoke publicly about what happened. Rumors spread like wildfire that he'd been involved in *unnatural* things—but by that time Frederick had been gone for years."

My mind flitted to the *unnatural* world exhibit at his museum and a shiver went up my spine. "What sorts of things . . ."

"It's all likely nonsense—but you know the type. Whispers of secret societies. *Magic.* No one truly believes it. The magic part at least . . . I mean honestly, Ruby. It's absurd to even speak of it as everyone knows there's no such thing."

Not six months ago, I shared her sentiment, but now I had seen, no . . . *experienced* . . . things with no rational explanation and was far less sure of my own convictions now than I was then. The sharp scent of electricity filled the room around me, like the air before a summer storm. I did not even need to turn to know Ruan was here. The peculiar connection between us had its uses. In the same way *he* could overhear my thoughts, *I* could somehow sense when he drew upon his abilities. *Upon his power.* It always smelled old and strong, like a powerful storm ripping across the land. I doubted he even realized I could smell it on him. An odd thing to tell a person, and I kept the thought guarded. We must have woken him with our discussion. I hadn't thought to keep my voice down as up until this moment I'd blissfully forgotten he was even *here*.

Ruan wore the stern expression of the strange witch I'd first met in Cornwall, his eyes still bore the faintest echoes of silver. It wasn't our *voices* that woke him then, he'd *heard* her distress. Either her thoughts or her emotions. It was the only explanation. "Is everything all right?" His broad West Country accent was thick with sleep.

"It's fine, Ruan. Just a friend of mine. She came to tell me that Mr. Mueller had been arrested for the murder of Julius Harker."

Ruan's expression grew dark. Evidently, he hadn't *heard* that part yet. "The bookkeeper?"

Leona frowned, glancing between the two of us warily. "I'm sorry to have disturbed you, Mr. . . ."

"Ruan. Ruan Kivell. And do not worry yourself—I often wake early." He shrugged, keeping to the shadows of the kitchen.

My chest tightened at the meaning behind his words. Of the hundreds of villagers constantly calling upon him to heal their injuries or broken hearts or to help their constable catch a thief. They might call him Pellar, their *witch*, but Ruan healed more than their bodies. He eased their hearts.

And I'd broken his.

For a third time the dratted hound bayed in the distance.

"I overheard you talking about this Mr. Mueller fellow as I came downstairs. Why do you think the police would have arrested him?" Ruan asked softly from the shadows.

You heard a bit more than that, I'd wager.

Ruan held my gaze for several seconds, an unreadable expression on his face.

"Last night . . ." Leona hesitated, staring at the reddish tiles of the floor. "On the way home after leaving the Ashmolean, I saw the commotion outside Harker's museum. At first I thought Julius had shown himself and done something truly outlandish." Her voice trembled. "But then the police told me that Mr. Mueller had killed Julius . . . that they were going to arrest him."

I paused at her words. Leona lived on the far side of town closer to the castle. The Ashmolean lay between her home and Harker's museum. There was no path she could have reasonably taken that would bring her back to the scene of the crime on her way home—

unless she was returning there for some reason. I kept my worries to myself and crossed the space between, clasping her wounded hands in my own. "You have to tell us everything that you know about Harker. Mueller. All of it."

Leona tensed.

"Ruby . . ." Ruan's voice carried a warning edge.

"I *have* told you everything I know!" Her lovely brown eyes grew wet. "I begged the police not to arrest him. I told them he was harmless—that he'd have no reason to harm Julius. But they refused to listen to me. Why would Mr. Mueller be foolish enough to expose his own crime publicly? It makes no *sense* and yet they threatened to arrest me if I didn't get out of their way and mind my own business."

"You've had a shock, Leona. You should go home. Get cleaned up and get some sl—"

"Do not speak to me like I am a child, Ruby Vaughn," she snapped, wiping hastily at her tears. Even Ruan was startled by her sudden flash of temper. "I am not some delicate creature to be coddled. A man was brutally murdered and his killer is still out there—"

I opened my mouth then snapped it shut.

"I thought you of all people would help me."

I pointed to my chest before gesturing wildly. "Me? What exactly do you want me to do? I don't know this town. I don't know these people."

"Has that stopped you before?" She jabbed at me with her forefinger. "You've solved at least two separate crimes. All I'm asking is for you to help me prove Mr. Mueller is innocent. Surely that cannot be difficult."

I gave her an incredulous stare. "Leona . . . I had no choice in either matter. In Scotland I was accused of the blasted crime and in Lothlel Green . . ." My gaze drifted absently to Ruan, whose own breath was caught in his chest observing the interplay between us.

"In Lothlel Green you helped because it was Tamsyn?" Leona whispered softly, finishing the sentence with words I refused to utter.

Her words dug their way between my ribs. But she was right. Tamsyn had been my dearest girlhood friend, and somewhere along the way we became a great deal more than that. She'd been my confidante, my best friend, my lover. Then she walked away. I'd fancied myself in love with her, but now I wondered if that was so. If instead it was infatuation, grasping for stability, for purpose, for *meaning*.

I took a step toward Leona and swallowed hard. She was right. "What would you have me do?"

"You could start by being a little less dismissive and by trusting me. I came here to ask my *friend* to help me."

Guilt gnawed at me. "It's only that I've been in your shoes more times than I care to admit and often the best course of action is to not get involved—I have been poisoned, I've been shot. Nearly drowned. Please trust me. You do *not* want to go digging into things if you don't have to."

"But I *must*. Mr. Mueller is innocent, and I cannot let him suffer for my—"

My ears pricked. "Your *what* . . . ?"

She shook her head angrily, slamming the teacup down on the table with a crash, and stormed to the door, flinging it open, before looking back over her shoulder. The cold wind rushed in, pressing her filthy skirt to her legs. "You've changed, Ruby Vaughn. . . . Suspicious and skeptical, and I'm not sure I like who you've become." She turned and hurried out into the night, leaving the door wide open in her wake.

What in the world had happened?

I crept across the kitchen and stepped into the alley after her but Leona had disappeared into the inky night. The icy cobbles stung my bare feet as I glanced down the lane, to where a great beast of a dog stood sentinel. From this distance I could not tell what sort of a dog it was, beyond the fact it had to weigh well over eighty pounds with dark fur. It was illuminated by a gas streetlamp. Was this the dog I'd heard?

There was something altogether menacing about the creature when it turned its head to stare at me. I stepped backward into the lane, then darted into the house, stumbling over the threshold, and closed the door tight behind me, heart hammering in my chest.

"Are you all right?" Ruan asked.

I wasn't sure. I wet my lips, staring at the doorway. "In the folk stories. In your *otherworld* . . . what does a great dark dog mean?"

Ruan sniffed, picking up one of the long-forgotten tea sandwiches, and took a bite. "Death usually. Why do you ask?"

I swallowed hard, pushing the image of the creature illuminated by the gaslight from my mind. "No reason."

He narrowed his gaze but let my lie pass. There had been a time not so long ago when Ruan could scarcely keep from being close to me. The casual brush of his hand. A soothing hug. A touch of my cheek. But now he kept a full room's length between us.

I closed my eyes, regretting every single minute of my conversation with Leona. She had known something. Her concern for Mr. Mueller was beyond friendship.

I cannot let him suffer for my . . .

For my *what*?

I should never have spoken to her like that. She had every right to be worried and to ask my assistance, and here I was suspecting her motives.

I opened my eyes to see Ruan standing before me, waiting on me to speak. "What do you think?"

"That she's hiding something."

As do I.

Drumming my fingers on my hips, I paced around the darkened kitchen. "I don't for one moment believe she was at the Ashmolean as she said—but she seemed shocked that Reaver had not returned to Harker's Curiosity Museum. So if not there, then where were they?"

Ruan raked his hands through his dark curls, resting his palms atop his head. "Harker was put into the box before the exhibition. It doesn't matter where they were at the time of the discovery—what matters is where they were at the time of death."

My mind raced trying to add up the pieces, not at all liking the cursory answer I reached. "Harker hadn't been seen for at least two days before he was discovered. The body"—I winced at the recollection—"might have been dead that long. I didn't get a good chance to examine him, but I am pretty certain he was put in there alive. Someone removed his tongue and sealed him inside."

Ruan made a low growl in his chest, keeping stubbornly to the other side of the room.

"But why not kill him first? Why stick him in there to suffer?"

Ruan shifted, cocking his head to one side. "To send a message."

"It does seem that way—but Leona is right on one thing. Mr. Mueller certainly did not kill him. That box was airtight. If Mr. Mueller *had* done it, he could have left him in a storeroom and Harker's body would have turned to dust before anyone ever thought to open it. No one would have ever wondered upon his disappearance, assuming that he'd simply run off due to debts or some other scandal."

"Unless whoever it was who killed him wanted Mueller out of the way too. It would tie things up neatly and send a message to anyone connected to them to not ask questions."

"From stitching up injured children to pondering motivations for murder. I truly wonder at how your mind works."

"I could say the same." That deep divot of worry formed between Ruan's dark brows. "I hate to say this . . ."

"We have another murder to solve, don't we?"

"Indeed, and I don't for one moment believe that this is a

straightforward matter." He took a step closer. Near enough that I caught the heady green scent of him. The warmth of his skin that I'd once had the privilege of sharing. But no more. He folded his arms across his chest, palms tucked against his body. I struggled to swallow.

If Ruan sensed the discord in my thoughts, his expression did not betray him. "I know you have your doubts about the other world. About *my* world."

I let out a huff of air and turned away before I did something absurd like touch him. "I will grant you that witches exist, and perhaps ghosts—"

"*Perhaps ghosts*," he said with a dry laugh.

My brows rose. "I admit there may be some truth to your and Mr. Owen's otherworld, but I am not a part of that world. I'm not like you, and despite the macabre display of Julius Harker's body, this is not a curse or a haunting. This is murder, plain and simple."

He wet his lips wanting to say something, but held his tongue, not wanting to belabor the point. "Perhaps, but I felt the lure of that world at the museum. It pulsed strong enough that I'd convinced myself it was simply your nearness that made me *feel* things that weren't real. Surely you sensed it too?"

I shivered at his words, my mind returning to how uneasy I'd been inside the museum. How hot my body was, the panic that grew each time I allowed my mind to wander. I'd ascribed it to the crowd, but what if Ruan was right and there was something else at play here? Add that to the uncanny dog at the end of the lane. An omen of *death*. I tugged my dressing gown tighter around my body. Not that the thin material stood a prayer of protecting me from what we were about to do.

"Leona said there were rumors that Harker was involved in the occult."

Ruan grunted in agreement. "There were rumors about him

researching the otherworld when I was in school here. It's my understanding he was interested in my kind. Those of us who live between the borders of the two worlds."

"Witches?" I furrowed my brow, scarcely believing I was having this conversation at all.

"And . . . ah . . . other things." He shifted awkwardly.

Ah. Right. As if this were normal pre-dawn conversation. "Do you think that has to do with why he was removed from his post?"

Ruan shrugged. "Whatever it was he was studying, he'd gotten in some sort of trouble over it and it was covered up. Be it the otherworld or simply a radical intellectual position. He'd crossed someone at the University, that's for certain."

"Did he show an interest in you . . . know what you can do?"

Ruan's expression darkened. "No, Owen made sure no one was told what I was. He was concerned what might happen if someone found out the truth. He worried they'd use me, keep me for their own curiosity. I'm grateful now that he took me away from Cornwall, even if I wasn't at the time. It wasn't long after the first mine collapse when he arrived in Lothlel Green and told my mother what he intended for my future. By that time people had begun whispering about my abilities. Strangers would come bringing their sick and dying to our village expecting me to *do* something about it. It wasn't long after when he sent me away to school, and then on to Oxford to finish my education. I was a boy then, with no idea what I was doing or how to control it. Gods, I scarcely know what to do with it now or even what I *can* do."

My heart ached for him each time he mentioned his childhood. Of how hard it was to be so very different, without anyone to confide in.

"It was for the best I had a chance to grow into a man away from that world—away from people who knew what I was. So, no. Harker could not have known the truth about me, and he certainly never treated me with any interest. I was beneath him."

It was for the best that he escaped notice of such a horrible person. "Do you think whatever Harker was involved in back then has to do with his death?"

"I don't know. But I sense we are going to find out, aren't we?"

"I suppose it's good I've summoned the Pellar then."

The lines at the edges of his eyes creased with a faint smile and I could have sworn he started to move closer to me, but I should have known better. Ruan was a far stronger soul than I. He allowed the moment to end, turned, and went back to bed. And with that, I took another bite of my sandwich, sat down at the table, and plotted out my next course of action.

Chapter Seven

An Unearned Trust

TWO cups of black coffee, a slice of buttered toast, and several hours later I was finally ready to seek out Leona to make amends for the way we'd left things when she stormed out of my kitchen. While she was behaving suspiciously, she was right on one score—I had changed. I'd grown skeptical, seeking connections and conspiracies everywhere I turned. She had reason to be worried about Mr. Mueller, and the fact I'd not immediately jumped to her aid sat in my gut like a stone.

The Ashmolean Museum rested gracefully on Beaumont Street, its smart classical lines presumably modeled after some ancient Greek temple adorned with frieze work and decorative pilasters. Had I not known better, I'd have thought the whole building had been scooped up from Greece and planted here in the center of Oxford, were it not clad in the signature golden-hued limestone of the rest of the city.

The oldest public museum in Britain, and with a sterling reputation, it commanded the respect of the world. Its immense collections were meticulously cared for by the preeminent scholars of the day. Truthfully, it was a coup that Leona had secured a position here at all, and part of me envied her that.

I glanced up at the portico, shielding my eyes against the gray morning sky before running up the stone steps to the front doors. The first drops of rain hit the pavement behind me as I reached the shelter of the entrance. I cursed myself for forgetting my umbrella. After this many years living in England, one *might* be prepared for the changeable weather, but not I.

Muted sunlight filtered in through the windows of the museum creating a cozy glow inside the quiet of the bustling space. The main hall had been adorned with festive ribbons and greenery. Sprigs of mistletoe bound in red velvet ribbon hung from the doorways. Only a few more days to Christmas and to 1923 and all the fuss and bother that comes with a new year—though if the last few months of 1922 were any measure, I dreaded to find out what the new year would bring.

I hurried down the slippery stone stairs to the basement reading room where Leona usually worked. Nudging the door open with my shoe, I stepped inside the cramped room with its low ceiling. The walls on all sides were lined with overburdened shelves holding bits of stonework and books stacked upon books, at least two deep. Leona shared this space with a middle-aged librarian named Mary. Mary, for her part, scarcely ever said more than three words to me—instead politely peering at me above her glasses, before returning to her work.

Leona sat on the far side of a long study table with her forehead resting upon her palm—her long dark hair was braided and wound around her head, pinned up and out of the way. Silver spectacles sat on the tip of her nose. Her crisp white blouse and navy skirt were a far cry from the similar dusty and torn outfit she'd worn in my kitchen this morning—though the dark bruises of exhaustion beneath her eyes told me she'd slept no more than I had.

"Tommy, I told you—" Her expression fell as she saw it was me rather than Tommy who had interrupted her studies. She gave an exasperated snort and returned to her book. "Come to tell me I'm overreacting again?"

Perhaps coming here was a mistake. Leona was nearly as stubborn as I was when in a temper.

She closed her book loudly, then turned to her colleague. "Mary . . . might you give me a moment with my *friend*."

Mary eyed me with protective suspicion, before slipping out the door and shutting it behind her. It echoed in the room, rattling the framed prints on the wall. I startled, biting my tongue in the process.

Leona came around her desk and leaned her hip against the low-slung wooden case housing larger bits of broken stone awaiting translation. I tilted my head to examine them better. They were very old—perhaps . . .

"It's from Saqqara, yes. Sixth Dynasty. Did you come with a purpose, or did you just want to ogle the antiquities?"

I flushed. She was not going to make this easy for me. She never had. I drew in a breath of stagnant air. "I came to apologize for the way I behaved last night. I had no right to talk to you that way."

She frowned, smoothing her skirt, refusing to look me in the eye.

Heart pounding in my chest, I took a step closer, hands outstretched. "I thought of what you said—and of what I saw inside Harker's museum and . . ." I glanced over my shoulder to be certain the heavy wooden door was closed, even though Mary had slammed it hard enough it might never open again. "You're right. It doesn't make any sense for Mr. Mueller to have killed Julius Harker, then immediately expose his own crime to the world. You should have seen his face, Leona. He was horrified at what he found in that box. Anyone who witnessed that could attest to it. Not even the best actors in West End could have feigned that. The only logical answer is that someone wanted both Julius Harker *and* poor Mr. Mueller out of the way—and they certainly picked a tidy way to go about it."

Leona's expression softened in relief as my words sank in. She furrowed her brow, debating whether to trust in my words. "Then you agree with me?"

Unfortunately, I did.

I nodded, lower lip caught between my teeth.

"And you'll help me prove that he didn't do it?" The unbridled hope in her question was too much to bear. Soft voices came from outside the door, followed by a pair of men laughing as they made their way down the hallway. I waited until after they passed by—not that they'd likely overhear us through the thick walls of this place.

Despite my bone-deep hesitation to get involved, Julius Harker's death bothered me. Something peculiar *had* happened, and the disinterest of the police in finding the truth in it—unable to probe beyond the simplest hypothesis—was enough to drive me mad.

I cannot let him suffer for my . . . Leona's cryptic words from last night came back to me in a flash. *For her what?* It was on the edge of my tongue to ask Leona more, and why she felt responsible for Mr. Mueller's fate, but I kept that question to myself. Last night, she'd almost blurted it out but caught herself before lashing out in anger. I could not risk the same thing today—not when we'd come to an uneasy truce. "Have you spoken to the authorities again this morning? Have they changed their minds?"

She drummed her fingers on the top of the cabinet housing the roughly three-thousand-year-old carving. A hollow tum-tum-tum on the surface. "Without proof? I don't even know where I would begin. It's why I came to you."

"I'll go speak with Mr. Mueller. He's the logical place to start. Perhaps he'll be able to point me in the right direction or know who might have wished harm upon his friend."

"And what do you think he'll tell you that he hasn't already told the authorities?"

"I'm not certain. But we must start somewhere, and he is the obvious place to begin."

Before I could realize the ramifications of what I'd promised, Leona threw her arms around me, pulling me into a great hug. Her clean jasmine scent filled my nose as she squeezed. I closed my eyes and allowed myself to hug her back, all the while wondering how long before I regretted my hastily made promise.

COLD RAIN FELL in torrents, making a mess of what remained of the previous two days' worth of snow. I ducked my head, stepping out the front door of the museum determined to make my way to the Blue Boar Street Police Station once this rain eased. I loitered beneath the portico outside the museum watching a young mother pushing a pram down the street, a big black umbrella covering them both. I tugged on the fingers of my gloves, cursing my lack of forethought. *Umbrellas, Ruby. Why do you never carry an umbrella?*

I was of half a mind to go back inside and peruse the galleries until the weather turned. It *always* turned. And there *were* a few intriguing Renaissance bronzes that I'd not yet inspected. At present, the thought of being warm and dry inside the museum was vastly preferable to getting soaked to my skin in search of a killer I wasn't even certain I wanted to find.

What foolishness wouldn't I do for the people I loved? I blew out a breath, resolved to wait for a break in the rain when I spotted a soggy newspaper discarded on the top step. Bending down, I picked it up to dispose of the thing properly when the headline on the front page caught my attention.

MUMMY'S CURSE REBORN?

I swore, scanning the article, which contained no more facts than I already possessed—fewer as it did not mention the damage to Harker's hands nor that his tongue had been removed from his mouth. I was ready to throw the entire nonsense away until I spotted an unpleasant sentence on the very last line.

Perhaps with the intrepid Ruby Vaughn in Oxford, there is more to this murder than meets the eye?

"Oh, for heaven's—"

"Miss Vaughn?"

I crumpled the offending paper, slipping it behind my back in time to see Frederick Reaver approach, his palm resting lazily upon the handle of a large black umbrella. He wore a deep green overcoat from the last century, and an equally unfashionable worn hat with a matching green ribbon. Yet instead of looking absurd, the combination was downright dashing on him. "I see you have noticed the headlines?" He opened the umbrella with practiced gusto.

"Can you believe this nonsense?" I held the offending paper up between us.

He inclined his head in acknowledgment, frowning at the rainy street beyond. "Indeed, I can. I only marvel they haven't come up with more absurdities. Can I walk you wherever it is you're headed? You appear to be in need of shelter."

I snorted back a laugh, discomfited by the paper. "I am, aren't I? I was debating whether to wait out the shower or give in and just get wet." As if on cue, the mocking rain fell harder, splattering off the stone steps onto the hem of my skirt. "I was going to Blue Boar Street, though I think I may wait it out. Surely it won't rain forever."

The lines on his face furrowed for a half second. "That's not far at all. Only a few minutes' walk. I am headed to meet a colleague over at Brasenose College. It's not terribly out of the way. Please let me see you where you're going. I insist."

Another bone-rattling gust of wind swept through the portico, plastering my skirt to my legs and dousing my stockings with icy rainwater. While I wasn't sure what to make of Frederick Reaver, I could see no harm in availing myself of his umbrella for the length of time it took to get to the police station. "That would be lovely. Thank you."

He gave me a rakish smile, revealing that solitary dimple again. I ducked under the shelter of his large umbrella and we started down the steps. Frederick Reaver was an irritatingly attractive man and his physicality only accentuated his enigmatic presence. One couldn't be around him for more than a few moments without feeling the draw. Perhaps that's why I mistrusted him so. I never did care much for beautiful men after having fallen under the spell of one at sixteen years of age, and we saw where that got me—utterly ruined and shipped to another continent for my own safety.

A damp lock of sandy hair curled across Reaver's brow as he lowered his head to speak with me, but the way his eyes glinted in the midmorning light gave me pause. There was an intensity there that took my breath away. Frederick Reaver had the eyes of an eighteenth-century missionary, burning with some unholy fire. This was a man driven by his passion and the sheer conviction of his rightness.

Unaware of my discomfort, Reaver pulled his hideous hat farther down. "Leona tells me you were an ambulance driver during the war and that is how the pair of you met."

I tucked my gloved hands deeper into the pockets of my woolen overcoat as we crossed the busy street. "It was a long time ago. But yes. I was. Leona was the librarian at the hospital. The first time I met her, she was leading a reading circle with the soldiers there. It was quite entertaining to listen to the intense debates amongst the men over whether Austen or Brontë created a more compelling world."

He let out a low chuckle, his stern expression softening at the mere mention of her. "I assume you both had opinions on the matter?"

"I am afraid when forced to choose, I found myself preferring Brontë every time, much to Leona's deep consternation. It felt far more real to me than Austen ever did. There is a darkness in human nature that cannot be forgotten, even in fiction. Leona thought it a dreadfully depressing way to approach literature, but I've never been afraid of the dark. For at least there is honesty in it."

He chuckled fondly. "That sounds like her. It is our good fortune to have her at the museum. Leona is a singularly gifted young woman who never fails to see the good in even the bleakest of souls. I truly do not know what I would do without her."

"Were you also in the war?" I asked, knowing good and well that he had been. I glanced over at him in time to catch a flicker of something in his expression.

"Here and there, but I was grateful to return home after it was done. After several years traveling the world, I found that I'd missed the comforts of Oxford."

We continued, passing by shop windows decorated for Christmas, laden with bright colors and saccharine scenes. "How long have you and Leona worked together?"

He shifted the umbrella, brushing against my arm. "I returned to Oxford two years ago, and that's when I first met Miss Abernathy. She'd been doing translations alongside Mary, down in the archives. But when I was brought on as Keeper of the Egyptology collection, I employed her as my aide. We've been sorting through the old collection for much of the last year. There's been an influx of items coming in since the war and even more in the month since Howard Carter's discovery. I've been tasked with ascertaining the provenance of some of the older pieces as well as sorting out which are authentic, and which are clever forgeries."

"I didn't realize she had such an interest in antiquities."

Reaver laughed, his expression softening. "She is a constant surprise to me as well, but her childhood in Egypt and her skill with language has made her invaluable in this task. She tells me you are also a polyglot." He cast me an assessing glance as we continued along.

My skin pricked. How much had Leona told him of me? I tugged my coat tighter as we passed by a cheerful bakery. The door opened, filling the street with the scent of bread. "You know an awful lot about me."

"It's my business to know a lot about people."

I stiffened, pausing on the sidewalk.

"Does it bother you that I know these things? I told you yesterday, I am a blunt man. I do not have time for pleasantries. Some don't appreciate my manners, but others . . . others grow accustomed to me."

Others, *like Leona*? I brushed the thought away, taking hold of the conversation yet again. "What took you from the museum the night of Harker's death? I don't believe either of you returned . . ."

It was his turn to be discomfited. He sniffed, looking down at me. "I see I'm not the only one to pay attention to details."

"It's only fair."

His cold blue gaze held mine for several seconds. "I needed her assistance in translating something."

"At nine o'clock at night?" I raised a brow.

"She is very useful."

The urge to look away was strong, but I could not. Could not even blink, lest he win whatever battle of wills we were fighting. "Is that all she is to you . . . useful?"

He sniffed and turned away, giving me the strangest sense that neither of us was the victor in this first skirmish. He took off, heading down the sidewalk. "My meeting is soon, we should keep going."

A shiny new automobile passed along the street, splashing water onto the sidewalk as a paperboy shouted out the news of Harker's death and Mueller's arrest.

"A tragedy," Reaver said with a shake of his head as we passed by. "An utter tragedy."

"Harker's death?"

"No." Reaver glanced at traffic before gesturing for me to cross the street alongside him. "It's a tragedy that the police think that Mueller did it. Mueller, who may be the only person in this town who still gave two damns about Julius. I cannot understand why they would focus upon him when there are any number of likely culprits out there."

"Leona said the same." A sharp cold gust of wind pricked my lungs as I hurried along after him. "Harker had enemies, then? I heard that he was kicked out of the University, but no one knows *what* exactly he did."

"You are a curious cat, aren't you?" He hesitated, rubbing at his jaw with the back of his oxblood glove. "Julius always had a keen eye for antiquities and an uncanny knack for spotting a fake from a mile away."

"Wouldn't that be an asset at the museum? Particularly with this project you and Leona have been working on?"

Reaver's mouth curved up into a dry smile as he saw the ornate Town Hall in the distance. "Julius and I did not see eye to eye on many things. He had also made some powerful enemies over the years who never would have allowed him to return to academia without a fight. Certainly not after what he did."

Tugging my jacket closer around me, I brushed a dark curl back from my face. "Leona said there were rumors he'd dabbled in the occult."

Professor Reaver let out a cynical sound. "Utter nonsense. Julius landed in a spot of trouble a dozen years ago that got him kicked out of Oxford. He's lucky it didn't land him in prison. I cannot imagine what he was thinking." Reaver hesitated, weighing his words as a pall came over him. "But I suppose he was not lucky in the end."

"What . . . what did he do?"

Reaver readjusted his scarf, tucking it deeper into his jacket for warmth. "He took something that was not his to take and paid the price for it."

"Do you suppose that what happened then had anything to do with his murder?"

He shook his head, gesturing for us to continue down Cornmarket Street. "No, I suspect it's his recent dealings that caused his demise. Julius had a nasty habit of rubbing people's noses in the fact he was cleverer than they. It was obnoxious at the University, worse yet when he no longer had his position to protect him. Then after what happened three years ago . . ."

I leaned closer. "Three years ago?"

"It had to do with your friend Lord Amberley."

"Amberley? The jolly old antiquarian?" I let out a startled laugh. I could not fathom what Julius Harker could have done to cross swords with the kindly old man.

"The same. Harker went to authenticate a set of seven ancient marble sculptures in Amberley's private collection. They were set to fetch a *fortune* from a foreign buyer. Harker had moderately repaired his reputation by this point—at least enough that the open-minded sort would have him do the odd appraisal or acquisition of this or that. Amberley invited Harker out to his country estate to see the marbles. They had been on display there for decades, set into six alcoves along the perimeter of the room and the seventh and most magnificent—an enormous statue of Athena—situated on a plinth in the very center of the hall. It was impressive, even I had to admit to being moved by their beauty and I pride myself in not being swayed by pretty things."

I'd seen a similar effect on a larger scale at Kedleston Hall on an errand in Derbyshire for Mr. Owen back in February. "Where did the marbles come from?"

"Now that was the question, wasn't it? Amberley claimed they'd been in the family for over a century, but the buyer wanted confirmation that they were real with fair provenance. Thus, they brought in Harker's expert opinion."

I let out another startled laugh. "You mean the buyer wanted reassurance that they weren't stolen like Elgin's marbles?"

Reaver flashed me a rare smile, revealing his sole dimple. "Precisely. Though you must know that's a controversial statement among some."

I wasn't sure how I felt about this newfound knowledge. I *liked* Lord Amberley. But I'd seen where such feelings had gotten me in the past. Sometimes wolves hide amongst the sheep.

"Who was the buyer?"

"No one knows. Someone with deep pockets, and an uncommonly strict moral compass. Though I suspect you know as well as I do that most collectors are more concerned with *what* they can acquire rather than *how* the thing is done."

The waning winter hours grew short, and the sun had already begun its descent, casting dramatic shadows against the buildings. "What happened, then? It must have caused a great scandal."

"It did. For within a day of the inspection, Harker proclaimed loudly to all who would listen that Amberley's marbles were clever forgeries. Oh, he was apologetic—of course—and offered to take them off Amberley's hands for a fair sum."

I furrowed my brow. This made no sense. None at all. "Why would he do that for forgeries?"

Reaver lifted a shoulder and shifted the umbrella to make way for a young delivery boy overburdened with parcels. He stepped down off the curb to allow the fellow to pass. "Why did Julius Harker do anything? Perhaps he felt bad for ruining the sale? Perhaps it was the threat of scandal rearing its ugly head again and he wanted to ease it as best he could. What I *do* know is Harker had money trouble and had for years. How he came up with the funds to purchase the marbles—fake or not—is beyond me."

How does a man with no money buy a collection of marble sculptures? Even forgeries would hold *some* value. "Was Amberley angry?"

"No. Not at all. Lord Amberley is a genial sort, as you've likely noticed. He didn't need the money, it was more a point of pride. Can you imagine what it would feel like to have been flaunting forgeries for the better part of a decade and then be publicly exposed?" He let out a low whistle.

I'd dealt with my share of antiquarians and knew the sort. They took pride in their reputations and to have it tarnished so publicly—now *that* was far worse than any other crimes one could be accused of. "But you don't think Amberley harmed him. If not Amberley, who else would have been angry enough to lock a man in a box and leave him to die?"

Reaver cleared his throat, drumming his fingers along the handle of the umbrella. "Take your pick. Harker dabbled with the wrong sort. Radicals and revolutionaries, the lot of them. If I were you, Miss Vaughn, I would stay as far from this matter as possible. Our *dear* Julius had some very unpleasant bedfellows, and I am quite certain that whatever happened to him, he likely deserved."

I took a half step back closer to the curb, my heel slipping off, and I had to shift quickly to regain my balance. His strong hand shot out to steady me.

"I don't mean to frighten you. It's only that I knew him before his disgrace, and the man who was killed last night is not the same fellow I once called my friend. He had begun making dangerous acquaintances and had grown more and more erratic—refusing to listen to reason. I only fear for poor Mr. Mueller—it would be a tragedy if he swung for a crime he didn't commit."

The distinct shape of the Victorian-era Town Hall was now just across the street, and nestled alongside was the police station.

Reaver frowned, the insouciant dimple disappearing from his cheek. "Please tell me you are not intending to speak with Mr. Mueller . . ."

I straightened my shoulders. "Very well then, I won't."

"Miss Vaughn, let me make it painfully clear to you that you will not like what you discover. I am very aware of your reputation for amateur detective work—but you are in above your head in this matter. I beg you, leave it to the authorities before anyone else is harmed."

That firebrand intensity returned to his expression, fierce enough that I almost questioned my own motives. *Almost.* I blinked in feigned innocence. "Why, Professor Reaver, I have every intention of doing just that."

Chapter Eight

A Soupçon of Subterfuge

I ran my hands over my rain-dampened hair as I entered the dimly lit police station. The wooden floor was scuffed and tired, though recently cleaned—scrubbed with lye soap to within an inch of its life by some poor charwoman. The scent of the soap still sharp on the air. The electric lights overhead cast a jaundiced glow over the dark oak desk. A long low bench made from the same wood sat alongside the opposite wall. The station itself was empty other than a young constable seated at the desk who looked up at me with his brows raised. For a half second I thought of turning on my heels and leaving.

The thought of setting foot inside a police station made my skin crawl—likely due to my own brief stint in Holloway Prison thanks to Mr. Owen's penchant for illegal books. The young constable inspected me from over the tall wooden desk. His fair hair was neatly cut and combed. He had a smattering of freckles across his nose, giving him a boyish appearance. He couldn't have been much over twenty, if that. The same age of those schoolboys following Reaver around the exhibition the previous night, yet their worlds could not be more different. Those boys sat around in their seats of privilege and comfort jockeying for position and prestige—the only jockeying this fellow did was for a promotion.

"Can I help you, miss?" he asked at last, his keen dark eyes watching, uncertain what to make of the strange half-drenched American dripping rainwater on his once-pristine floors.

Right. To the point, Ruby.

I took a step closer and rested my fists on the cool wood of the desk. "I've come to see my uncle."

He laid the paper down, his palm obscuring the headline, but from the edge I could see that it was the same edition I'd recovered from the steps outside the Ashmolean.

"Uncle, Miss . . . ?"

I racked my brain for a half second before spitting out the first thing on my mind and jutting out my hand in greeting. "Evangeline Mueller."

Evangeline? Good God, Ruby, pick something a little more ordinary next time.

His gaze dropped to my outstretched hand as he tapped his fingertips on the newsprint, my pulse echoing the rhythm. "You're Old Mueller's niece?"

I snatched my hand back, folding my arms across my chest as the room tightened around me. The constable was scarcely out of boyhood and yet the way he watched me told me there was far more going on behind his eyes than he was letting on.

The words fell out of my mouth before I could think better of the lie. "I am. I saw in the paper what happened last night at the museum and am terribly worried for him. I wanted to come speak with him, offer my . . . sympathies." I winced inwardly at the insipidness of my words—there was no way this young man would believe my sorry tale. I cursed Frederick Reaver and his conversation. The man had distracted me on our walk here. Granted, I'd learned a great deal about Julius Harker, but I'd entirely forgotten to devise an actual *plan* on what I was going to do once I arrived at the police station. Mr. Owen would be ashamed of my lack of foresight.

The young constable sniffed and then glanced to the wall clock behind him. "I don't see any harm in it." He lifted the hinge on the long dark counter and gestured for me to follow him. "Come along, miss. You'd better hurry before Inspector Beecham gets back. He wouldn't like to find you here. Not one bit."

Stunned by my unexpected good fortune, I stammered out my thanks. "I don't think I got your name."

He flashed me a charming smile as a pang of regret settled in my stomach for tricking him. "John Price, miss. But everyone calls me Jack."

Jack. A perfectly charming name for a very sweet-seeming boy. "You're not from here, are you?"

"Nah, not me," he began, as we started down the narrow dark stairway leading to the cells. The air here was damp and acrid with the scent of sweat, urine, and stale air—a stark contrast to the sterile, clean police station above. I wrinkled my nose, running my gloved hand down the smooth utilitarian banister. "My da is a dairyman up in the Dales."

"That's a lovely part of the world. It's a wonder you left at all." *Keep him talking, Ruby. Keep his focus on himself, not on you, and you might just make it out.* I summoned a light smile that I did not feel.

"Lovely, it is, aside from the fact you're up before dawn milking and feeding and tending. I couldn't get out of there fast enough, miss. That I can tell you. Compared to that, police work is a dream."

I laughed, the sound hollow to my own ears. "I suppose I don't blame you. What brought you to Oxford then? I suspect there are plenty of towns in Yorkshire in need of policemen."

We continued down the narrow, damp stair before reaching the darkened basement. The electric lights struggled down here, and whether real or imagined, the walls around me inched incrementally closer. I couldn't breathe. Couldn't think.

If I was going to succeed in this task, I had to focus on the boy from Yorkshire leading me to the cells and not the vagaries of my own imagination.

"Same story as a lot of lads from the country, I suspect. The war." He let out a small bitter laugh. "The summer I turned sixteen, I signed up."

My voice cracked as I stared at a space between his shoulder blades, desperately grasping onto anything beyond the bubbling panic in my throat. "Weren't you too young?"

He paused, shoving open yet another heavy wooden door with his hip, revealing the corridor to the holding cells. "Mmm, but they didn't know that. I told you I was tired of the cows. Thought I'd get a chance to see the world—but found a lot more than I bargained for." There was a heaviness there in his words as he gave me a rueful smile. "Well. Here we are." He unlocked a small metal cell door and pushed me through, slamming it hard behind me.

"I'll be back in ten minutes, miss. No more than that."

"And who might you be?" Mr. Mueller asked. He sat defeated at the far side of the cell on a hard wooden slab beneath the small iron-barred window. White paint chipped from the bars, adding to the general sense of decay down here. Truthfully, they didn't even need to block the window, as nothing larger than a house cat might slip through the opening. Fiachna himself would struggle to squeeze his heft through the tiny slit in the thick walls—there was no prayer that a full-grown soul might do the same.

Mr. Mueller's back was pressed flat against the damp wall of the cell—no wider than I was tall and scarcely half again that long. Tiny hash marks had been picked on the paint, logging days from a previous occupant. Other walls bore other symbols.

Words.

Thoughts.

Names.

Echoes of innumerable lives altered by circumstance.

I squeezed my eyes shut, trying to will away the peculiar feeling rising in my chest. It wasn't Mr. Mueller who brought about this conflagration within me—the man was clearly harmless—but rather the growing sense of being caged. Trapped like an animal in a snare.

I cleared my throat. "I am Ruby Vaughn." There was no sense lying to him as I had to young Jack, the constable. We hadn't the time for it. A small puddle of something wet and brown sat in the corner. "I am a friend of Leona Abernathy. She asked me to help you."

"Miss Abernathy? What does she think you can do?" He gave me a quizzical look from beneath furrowed brows. "Such a sweet girl, but I fear there's nothing to be done. The police will not listen to reason."

Ten minutes, the constable had said. I had ten minutes and I'd already wasted a good two of them. I glanced over my shoulder to the thick metal door and sighed. "Believe me, I have asked myself that same question all the way here. But I came to see if you had any idea who might have killed your colleague."

Mr. Mueller made a weary sound. He was clad in powder blue cotton pajamas, his feet bare and slightly bloodied. They must have roused him from bed and brought him straight here, not even bothering to let him dress himself. I shuddered at the needless cruelty of it. No wonder Leona was adamant about freeing him.

"I do not know." He rubbed his palm with his thumb. "If I did, I would have told them the first time they questioned me."

"The *first* time? Did they talk to you twice?"

"Indeed. I spoke with them at length at the museum and they thanked me for my time and asked that I share any information I recalled about his enemies should I think of anyone. I was sick over what happened, utterly sick. I went home, poured myself a drink, and went to bed. Then the inspector was at my door before my head hit the pillow."

My brows knit together. "Do you not find that strange that they'd let you go, only to fetch you back immediately? Was there any mention of cause? Evidence?"

"I do not know what *is* ordinary in such things, but I promise you, Miss Vaughn, I did not harm Julius. He was my friend. I do not know what evidence they could find for something I did not do."

I took a step closer to Mr. Mueller, crouching before him to see his face more clearly. There was no doubt that he was speaking the truth. But if not him, then who? I laid a tender hand on his forearm. "And have you any idea who might have wanted to harm him? I've been told he had been making a lot of enemies lately."

Mr. Mueller blinked away the dampness in his eyes. "Oh, turning friends to enemies was Julius's forte to be sure. I have thought upon the matter all night long. And while he had dozens of enemies, I cannot think of a one who would wish him *dead*. He might have crossed people but . . ." He caught himself, shaking his head.

"But what . . . ?"

"But he was *right*." Mr. Mueller weighed his words cautiously as he searched my face for any sign of sympathy. "Julius never truly *harmed* anyone who didn't deserve it, and even then, it was more a matter of nicking their pride."

I raised an eyebrow. People have killed for far less than wounded pride. "Professor Reaver told me that there had been some scandal about forgeries lately. Do you know anything of that?"

He ran his hands over his face roughly. "Of course, but tell me, Miss Vaughn, how much sympathy do you have for the sort of man who would empty another's grave to decorate his dining room? It did not bother me in the least what Julius did to those men. I only wish he'd have left them unaware of the false sarcophagi and forged marbles they'd squandered their fortunes upon." He sighed, wary eyes darting to the closed cell door behind me. "I did notice that he had been secretive as of late. More than usual. He kept going on about how he'd finally figured out how to get us out from under the yoke of oppression."

"*Yoke of oppression?*" I raised my brows. "That sounds rather radical for an archaeologist. Was he the revolutionary sort?" Politics might be a motivation, at least the start of one.

"Heavens, no. Julius stayed clear of politics for the most part, more interested in his scholarship than anything else. I can only think he meant Reaver. The two men had been at each other's throats since their time together at Oxford. I half wonder if it wasn't their disagreements that sent Reaver fleeing for Egypt before the war. But since Reaver's been back . . . he and Julius had been constantly fighting." Mr. Mueller winced, shaking his head. "I told Julius he shouldn't tweak Reaver's nose so, but each month there would be another new public quarrel between the two. There were wagers whether they'd come to fisticuffs at the lecture that Julius missed a few nights ago." His voice cracked at the dawning realization that Julius missed said lecture because he'd been *dead*. "They had been rivals for decades, but after Julius was thrown out of the University, he'd only grown more captious. I think a part of him resented Reaver for his own misfortunes."

Captious. What a delicious word. I filed it away for future use with a frown. Frederick Reaver had gone missing before the body had been revealed. Convenient, as he was not there for questioning. I wet my lips cautiously. "Was Reaver the reason that Julius was thrown from the University? He'd mentioned something about Mr. Harker having stolen something."

Mueller gave a slow shake of his head. "Julius was innocent of the crime of which he'd been accused. Of that I am certain."

We were running out of time. I glanced back to the door behind me. A minute, perhaps two remained? I had to hurry. "Do you think Professor Reaver could have been involved in poor Mr. Harker's death?"

Mr. Mueller inhaled sharply. "Perhaps. Perhaps not. Reaver is not the idealogue that he'd have you believe. He's every bit the radical Harker was, not that anyone in the academy would believe it." Mr. Mueller glanced past me to the closed cell door. "If I had to guess . . . knowing what I do, with how erratic Julius had been as of late, I think he was about to sell something worth a fortune."

"Sell?" My brows shot up. "What would make you think that?"

"Money buys freedom, Miss Vaughn. With enough of the stuff, one can do as they please."

As plausible as any hypothesis and certainly more than I had thus far. "Do you know what he was going to sell, or to whom?"

"If only." He rubbed his thumb over the sores on his wrist from his iron restraints. "He'd spent hours in his office—staying long after we closed, arriving hours before we opened. I think he'd taken to sleeping there rather than at home. He had to be doing something—perhaps he left some answer in his papers or perhaps it is hidden somewhere in the collection."

I wet my lips. "You truly believe Mr. Harker was doing business with his killer."

"I do. It is the only thing that makes any sense."

"Someone he'd offended, or . . . cheated?"

Mueller made a sad low sound in his chest but did not respond. He leaned forward, resting his elbows on his knees. "Everyone was at the museum that night. And probably half of the people in that room had reason to hate him. But why should any of them kill the only truly interesting man in Oxford?"

Mr. Owen had said something similar about Harker. I gnawed on the inside of my cheek. Why indeed?

Angry voices outside the cell door drew closer. Time was running short.

"Do not fear for my future, Miss Vaughn." He gave me a

hopeless smile. "I have lost my dearest friend in this world in the ghastliest way imaginable. I do not care much what happens to me. But tell Miss Abernathy to be careful. Tell her I thank her and appreciate her kindness more than she could ever know. And yours."

Careful of what? was on the tip of my tongue when the door burst open. It sailed into the yellowing wall behind it with a crash. Jack, the young constable, stood in the doorway, his earlier carefree expression marred with worry as an older man grabbed him roughly by the sleeve of his woolen uniform jacket and shoved him into the cell with us. Jack stumbled on the stone floor but caught himself before falling and gave me an apologetic grimace.

My ten minutes had ended earlier than expected.

The older man glowered behind him, clad in a freshly pressed police uniform. Buttons shining in the dim light of the cell. The fellow's face was sour and round, flushed pink with anger. There was no doubt in my mind that this was the inspector that Jack had been worried about. Beecham, I think he'd said. The man was a sturdy enough fellow with a mean expression—taller than me with a chest like a whisky barrel. The sort of man a romantic soul might imagine serving as a boatswain on a ship a century ago—with likely the same amount of humor. He had a bristly mustache covering his thin lips. "Out." He pointed at me with a thick forefinger. "I don't know what you said or did to make this idiot allow you to be alone with a murderer—but out!"

"Accused murderer," I replied hotly, oddly protective of both Mueller and the poor young constable. It wasn't Jack's fault that I'd manipulated him into allowing me down here. "Mr. Mueller didn't kill Julius Harker, he had no motivation to do so!"

The inspector glared at me, a bulging purple vein in his neck pulsing visibly. "Would you like to have a permanent room in the adjoining cell, Miss Vaughn? I could arrange it for you."

I kept my mouth shut and stormed out of the cell, Inspector Beecham at my heels.

"Lock him back up or else it's to the cowshed with you, you bloody idiot," Beecham spat at Jack as the inspector pushed me up the stairs to the main lobby of the police station. "As for *you* . . . I read all about you and your unnatural habits in the paper this morning."

My spine straightened and I paused, spinning around on the narrow stair, making me stand a full head taller than the inspector. "*What* did you say?"

He wasn't at all affected by my biting temper. Inspector Beecham met my stare with one equally as cold. "Dabbling in police affairs, living with an unmarried gentleman—"

This again. It was always a particular narrow-minded sort that grew fixated upon my particular living arrangements. Granted, it wasn't aided by the fact Mr. Owen had a reputation in his youth that rivaled my own. "A gentleman who *happens* to be my employer."

"And who in all of Britain would be naïve enough to believe that *the notorious* Ruby Vaughn needs some old viscount's money?"

Mr. Owen's title still sat uneasily with me. I'd not known that Mr. Owen was the Viscount of Hawick until only recently. Nor had I known that the old man had been a bit of a rake in his youth. Neither of which bothered me in the least.

"He had better take you in hand soon. A woman of your age should have her mind to rearing children. Obeying her husband and tending to her household. Not prancing around the countryside sticking her nose in police business and encouraging wild stories about a mummy's curse!"

My nostrils flared. Of all the insufferable, backward notions. "Only the vilest, weakest, and most cowardly of men seek to control another, and I assure you that Mr. Owen is none of those things. The only person I obey is my own conscience. And if my existing in the same room as a corpse is enough to cause some muckraking reporter to dream up stories about curses—well that sounds as if it is *your* problem, not mine."

He grabbed me hard by the arm, pulling me close to him. His breath stale. "*Miss* Vaughn. I don't know what game you think you're playing at, but this is police business. I have half a mind to lock you up alongside Mueller. And if it weren't for the fact you have such powerful friends . . ."

The little bell rang above the door as an elderly woman entered the station escorted by a young man, interrupting the inspector's threats.

I jerked my elbow from his clammy grasp. "Then it's a very good thing I do have powerful friends."

"I don't want to see your face here again. Do you understand me?" he hissed.

"Perfectly." The word was ice as I brushed past the woman and started out onto the rainy streets of Oxford. I'd simply have to find another way to aid Leona and Mr. Mueller. One that did not involve the authorities—but that would entail a trip back to Harker's museum to see what the police had missed. I checked my watch. The sun would set in a few hours, and then later, under the cover of darkness, when most people were abed, I could return to the museum to see what Harker might have left for me to discover.

Chapter Nine

Caught, at Last

AFTER my poor reception by Inspector Beecham, I did not feel much like going home. Leona was right to be worried about Mueller's hasty arrest—and against all better sense, I was determined to get to the bottom of it. My reluctance certainly had *nothing* to do with the fact Ruan Kivell was likely still there. Nor was it avoidance of the inevitable conversation that would ensue once I laid out my plans for this evening. The man had aided me in past investigations, but I got the distinct sense that burgling remained at the remotest edge of his morality map.

Breath visible in the cold midmorning air, I waited on the curbstone for a passing motorcar before hurrying across the street. A few cold drops of rain splattered my cheeks as I tucked into the Covered Market for shelter. The tall wooden-buttressed ceiling gave the entire structure an airy open affect, aided in no small measure by the high windows allowing in what pitiable light broke through the rain clouds. It was an utterly dreary day, made doubly so by the discoveries of the last twenty-four hours.

Mrs. Penrose had asked me to pick up a few bits and bobs while I was in town—utterly unaware that I would be once again investigating a murder. Besides, she took far less umbrage at my erratic comings and goings when I brought her little gifts. Nothing pleased my housekeeper more than a chance to experiment with an unusual spice, a new vegetable, or a curious cheese. The woman adored a challenge, which was likely the reason she agreed to come work for me in Exeter earlier this year, for we both knew that I was *nothing* if not challenging.

Four pigeons pecked around on the cobbles for forgotten crumbs from a previous patron. A peculiar sound caught my attention, and I turned back to the street as the rain began to pour from the heavens. There in the distance at the corner of Cornmarket stood a slight, fair-haired man. He wore a long military-style overcoat and leaned against the stone front of a building, smoking a pipe in the shelter of the eaves. A thick beard a shade or two darker than his hair disguised his face. At this distance, I could not make out his features, other than to know without a doubt that he was watching me. Something about his shape pricked at my memory, an achingly familiar sensation. I *knew* him somehow, and yet I could not place it.

The man remained there for several seconds watching me, before he dipped his head in polite acknowledgment and turned, walking off into the rain, without even an umbrella to keep him dry. How very strange.

I stared in his direction long after the man disappeared, half wondering if I'd hallucinated the whole thing. It wouldn't be the first time I'd seen people who did not exist, but that had been during the darkest days of the war. And in truth, I think most of us were half-mad during that time, for madness helped make sense of a senseless situation.

Hallucination or no, staring off into the rain wasn't going to get me any closer to clearing Mr. Mueller's name. And as I was trapped by the weather for the foreseeable future, I made the most of things—dipping into a nearby produce stall and setting to work to earn the forbearance of my housekeeper and forget the burgeoning unease in my belly.

An hour and a half later, newly acquired umbrella and sack of produce in hand, I found myself in a nearby tearoom waiting on the rain to finally ease for my walk home. I took a seat at a table near the front window. The glass was terribly fogged, casting the outside world in impressionist shadows. Shapes and hints of color hidden behind the moisture. An occasional droplet of water would slip down the pane, cutting a narrow line to the outside world. A gash as raw as the wound in my heart. An imposter. Another murder. The mess I'd made with Ruan. I was adrift in a sea of turmoil and uncertainty and wanted none of it.

The winter sun had already sunk below the horizon. This time of year, it was scarcely overhead at all, always hanging in that middling space just past dawn and before nightfall. A perpetual twilight that left me craving the long days of summer with their endless hours of sunshine and the scent of the sea on my skin. I missed the water when I was this far inland. It wouldn't be long though. A few more weeks and the days would lengthen again. Perhaps I could convince Mr. Owen to go on a Mediterranean holiday once we returned to Exeter.

I wrapped my fingers around the chipped white cup before closing my eyes and lifting it to my lips, inhaling the earthy scent of tea as a chair scraped the tile floor across from me. I winced, opening my eyes, dreading which of my acquaintances had found me.

"Ruby Vaughn, you certainly are hard to find when you want to be . . ."

I bit my lower lip, struggling to disguise my smile as I saw my solicitor taking a seat in the dainty pastel green chair across from me. "Hari . . ."

He flashed me a dashing smile and folded his neatly manicured hands before him. "Don't even begin devising excuses. I know you've been avoiding me for days and I suspect I know why."

More like weeks . . . but I cocked my head to one side in acknowledgment. "It's nothing personal, dearest. You know I adore you."

"I weep for the soul you truly love." He chuckled, not at all offended by the fact that I had climbed out of a window to avoid having this very conversation. Hari leaned back in his chair, a faint hint of amusement never leaving his lips. He was a formidable man, even dressed as he was in an immaculately tailored royal blue suit with a gray herringbone waistcoat. The dastar he wore was the same jewel-toned hue as his jacket. Everything looked smart on Hari Anand, even the drab khaki of the British Expeditionary Force uniform that he'd been wearing when we first met. It was an understatement to say I adored the fellow. Hari had also been orphaned during the war, and the pair of us struck up an easy friendship that carried us through the darkest of days. It was little wonder that he became my solicitor after the armistice, as he was one of the handful of people I trusted in this world.

"I saw in the papers what happened to Julius Harker." His hazel eyes were fixed upon me as he laid down the offending newsprint on the table between us.

I picked up my teacup and took an indignant sip. "Don't start with the pleasantries, Hari, you did not come here to talk about murder."

"I did not, but as I read your name in the article, I felt compelled to bring it up and be certain you aren't doing anything reckless."

The corner of my mouth curved up. I set my teacup down slightly harder than intended, sending the brown liquid sloshing out onto the saucer to a harrumph of approbation from the matron at the table beside me. "I'm not involved in that—truly." Perhaps that was a tiny lie. I ran my finger over the tines of my fork, testing them against my flesh. "After the last few months, I cannot even walk down the street without someone assuming there's some sort of supernatural nonsense afoot. Don't pay the papers any mind." The weariness must have been evident on my face as Hari's expression softened.

"I had hoped you would say as much." He rubbed his thick beard with the back of his hand. "Ruby . . . you do know why I'm here, don't you?"

"Another imposter, I presume. That's the only thing that would warrant you coming in person and not sending a letter or phoning me."

Hari flattened his palms on his thighs, visibly relieved that I had already guessed his purpose. "Yes, yes there is. And I shall get to the point. This woman is requesting a meeting with you."

Somehow hearing the words from his lips did not burn as much as I'd expected. "Can't you send her away like all the others?"

He raised his eyebrows. "Do you think I have no experience in frightening away these women? Practically since I've known you, I have had one fraud after another showing up at my office door—some with children in tow—claiming to be your mother or Opal."

My eyes burned at my sister's name, but he told me nothing I did not know. Hari tried to shield me from the worst of it. But occasionally an intrepid imposter would require my attention and Hari would come—as he had today—with that same sympathetic glint in his lovely hazel eyes that told me how much it pained him to rehash old wounds.

"I have tried to get her to leave, but this woman . . . Ruby, she is not like the others. I am sorry for it, but I fear you need to speak with her."

My jaw tightened and I swallowed hard. "If anyone should be sorry it is this woman trying to dredge up the past for money."

He hesitated, tapping his finger three times on the table. "You see, that's the thing about this woman. She hasn't asked for money. She's not asked for anything beyond the opportunity to speak to you. I've done everything in my power to frighten her off—but I fear . . ."

"You fear what?"

"I simply wonder if she might not *be* an imposter in the sense the others have been."

My stomach knotted at his words and my skin grew cold. I thrust my hands into my lap, gathering my skirt in my fists to keep them from shaking. "What do you mean *not an imposter*? Hari, my mother died on the *Lusitania*. As did my sister and my father. Unless the woman is a *ghost*, she must be an imposter."

Hari closed his eyes and sighed. The nearby matrons having overheard our conversation quieted as to gather more juicy breadcrumbs. Mention of ghosts and imposters clearly was more interesting than their egg-and-cress sandwiches.

I lowered my voice to a whisper. "What are you trying to say?"

He leaned forward. "You know that your mother and sister's bodies were never found. This woman . . . she knows things. Things that only you've told me. Things that none of the others have known. Things *no one* could know."

"That does not mean she is my mother. Besides, there were plenty of others who were not recovered from the wreckage." I didn't know if the reassurance was for him or myself.

"I know." He worried his lower lip, the familiar freckle there catching my attention. "I don't think she *is* your mother. She's far too young—but I do think you should speak to her and see what her motivation is. You know I have never asked this of you before, and would do anything to spare you this pain, but Ruby—what if there is a chance that your mother is alive somewhere and this woman is key to finding her?"

I bristled at the thought.

"It's a chance I would take if it were me. What if she's out there?"

"Then why would she not come herself?" I slammed my hand on the table, palm stinging. Bitter tears filling my eyes. "She's dead, Hari. My mother is dead. Please don't do this to me. Not you. Not now."

His expression shifted and he stood slowly with a soft sigh. "Very well. I will not push you. I am staying at the Randolph for the next few days." He paused, pulling a slip of paper from his card case and scratching out a room number on the back in pencil before sliding it to me. "If you change your mind, let me know. I fear she will not leave you alone until you speak with her—and it is my experience that it's best to handle such things on your own terms rather than allowing the aggressor command of the field."

My mouth dried and I squeezed my eyes shut. He was right and yet I could not bring myself to agree to do this thing—to rend open that old wound—when it was *precisely* what needed to be done.

"Hari . . ."

"Ruby?" His tone matched mine.

"What if I can't do it?" The words came out as weak and broken as I felt.

"Then I will be here for you, as I have been since the day you saved me back in France."

I furrowed my brow in confusion. "I didn't save you. I simply drove you back from the front. The surgeon saved you when he took your leg."

He gave me a faint smile, his eyes sad. "I beg to differ." And with that, he stood and turned, walking out of the tearoom, leaving me with the most uncomfortable of thoughts. I sat there staring at the paper in my hands, with only one question on my mind—*What if she's not an imposter?*

Chapter Ten

A Curious Museum

"ARE you meaning to tell me that you're actually *investigating* this murder?" Ruan's voice came out scarcely over a whisper. I drew in a breath through my nose, waiting for him to continue with his objections to my plan for the evening.

Mrs. Penrose had long ago retreated to the hall beyond the closed kitchen door with Mr. Owen, carrying on their own conversation in hushed tones—one also focused upon me and my ill-advised plans.

"Was it not this *very* morning, in this *very kitchen*"—I poked a finger at Ruan's stomach—"when you said things were suspicious and that we had another mystery to solve?"

He bit into an apple, chewing slowly, unperturbed by my words. My eyes remained fixed on his lower lip as he sucked a bit of juice from it. "What I say when roused from my bed at four in the morning should not be considered an agreement to commit larceny."

"It's not larceny, I'm simply going to look around—I'm not *stealing* anything." I sniffed, fiddling with the button on my sleeve. "It doesn't matter, because I'm going whether you wish to join me or not."

Ruan glanced out the darkened window then back to me. "Whether I *wish* to come with you is immaterial. There is a murderer loose on the streets of Oxford, and *you* have a habit of getting yourself into trouble. I don't see as I have a choice about going along with you, if only for your own sake."

He wasn't entirely wrong.

"I know I'm not. What in the gods' names even possessed you to walk into the police station today? You are lucky they let you walk out with only a tongue lashing and didn't arrest you for interference."

"Stop eavesdropping!" I snapped. It was hard enough to think around him, let alone guard my thoughts from him as well.

"Stop thinking so loudly and maybe I'll try?"

I rolled my eyes and started up the stairs. "Stay put, would you? I'll be right back."

I could have sworn the ghost of a smile crossed his face as I walked past him. Oh, he could pretend to be exasperated with me all he wanted, but I knew good and well that Ruan Kivell enjoyed these investigations nearly as much as I did. He'd grown weary of his country life in Lothlel Green, and despite any protestations to the contrary, the man would follow me to the ends of the earth if required of him. Not required—he would come at my request—regardless of whether he liked me very much at present. The pair of us were bound together by something stronger than either of us could possibly comprehend. The connection was frustrating, yes—but it was there whether we willed it or not.

After retrieving my roll of lockpicks, I met Ruan in the kitchen and the pair of us slipped out into the darkened streets of Oxford.

No one paid us any mind as we hurried through the narrow streets in the pitch of night. Our path was illuminated by the gaslights dotting the streets, unaided by the meager light reflected from the fingernail moon. The rain from earlier had stopped hours ago, but even still hardly anyone was about.

It was strange how unsettling night in the city could be. In the countryside there was always something awake and with you. A bird. A fox. Insects. Sounds to remind you that you were never alone. There was a comfort in that anonymous companionship—for you could trust the birds to quiet before a predator struck. Their silence a warning to all. But in a city—a space where man had slowly strangled nature into submission—in man's absence grew an unsettling stillness far more frightening than anything nature could dream up.

At least I had Ruan with me tonight. I kept my head down, scarf pulled high around my chin as a bulwark against the winter wind. Dressed as I was, in a pair of trousers and my thick shapeless coat, passersby would assume we were a pair of lads off for a pint after work.

"Do you recall the first time we burgled together?" I asked, my fingernail catching on the smallest of my lockpicks. I nervously flicked the tip. Harker's Curiosity Museum was just ahead. It was smaller than the two university buildings flanking it, like a young child lovingly nestled between two parents. Had Julius Harker intended that when he leased the space? To sit there as a thorn in the side of the place that had thrown him out?

It surely could not be a coincidence. I hurried ahead of Ruan, not waiting on his answer, and opened the narrow iron gate before slipping into the alley in search of the back entrance.

Ruan made a low sound in his throat, his body blocking my view of the street beyond. "I do recall the first time you pulled me along on one of your schemes, yes. And I pray to the gods there's not another dead baronet on the other side of this door like there was that time." He inclined his chin to the small entrance at the bottom of a narrow set of steps. I turned to him, spotting the faintest glimmer of humor in his eyes before it disappeared entirely.

I took three steps down toward the door and sat my rump on the icy middle stone stair, eye level with the lock. The dampness soaked through my trousers and then my drawers, sending the cold straight through me.

Lovely. Just lovely.

The lock was a simple warded affair, nothing difficult. I lifted a pick to the moonlight. *Which to choose, which to choose?*

Ruan glanced down the alley toward the street before he let out a low laugh. "I cannot decide whether or not I should be disturbed at the ease with which you bend the law to suit your whims or to admire you for it."

I furrowed my brow, focused upon the brass keyhole, and jiggled the pick once.

Then a second time. It did not want to give. I sighed, rocking back onto my now cold, damp haunches. "If it's any consolation, I cannot decide either. Besides, I do not consider this *burgling*. I was invited by the museum owner to investigate."

Ruan shifted and I caught a glimpse of the street again and a canine-shaped shadow at the end of the lane. My breath caught. "Do you see that?"

Ruan turned, blocking my view of the street and the dog along with it. "See what? There's nothing there . . . just an empty street."

The hair on the back of my neck rose. "You . . . you didn't see the dog? It was just there." I lifted my hand, pointing to the entrance to the alley.

Ruan's back stiffened as he turned back to face me. "You are telling me that you saw a dog. . . . Does this have to do with what you asked me this morning?"

I caught my lower lip between my teeth. "I know. I know. Omen of death—or so you said. But as we already have a dead man, I think we're all settled on that score."

"I'm not amused. Ruby, if you are seeing *spectral* creatures, I would say that *is* a slight problem."

"It's not a spectral dog. I would certainly know if I'd seen a ghost or a demon or whatever exactly that omen might be." I tried to make light of the concept, but after the things I'd encountered since meeting Ruan, I was not as easily able to discount the *otherworld* as I once was. I cleared my throat. "It's likely a stray, seeking out a spot to bed down for the night. There are hundreds of dogs in Oxford, I'm inclined to believe I've seen one of *those* and not some harbinger of doom."

Ruan grunted in disagreement, but at least he let it drop.

The dog. Then that man outside the Covered Market. I swallowed hard, trying not to think of what *that* meant. Surely I was not seeing things that were not real—not again. I squeezed my eyes shut trying not to think about those days, of how close I'd come to being put into a hospital for shell shock in 1917. They said I'd been too close to the front lines for my delicate feminine constitution. I believed them . . . at least for a time . . . chalking up the inconsistencies of my memories to the trauma of the war. But I was no more mad then than I was now.

I had seen something. Not a ghost. Not my imagination. There'd been a dog. There had to be. But I was wise enough to let it drop, lest I end up in the same situation now as I had been then. No matter how kind Ruan was, seeing things that no one else does never bodes well.

I shook my head and turned my focus back to the brass plate covering the keyhole and continued fumbling with the lock until I felt it give, and the door swung free.

"Now . . . shall we see what Mr. Harker is hiding?"

WE CREPT UP the narrow winding stair until we reached the landing, which opened onto a small gallery before leading out into the main exhibition space. Meager moonlight made its way through the glass dome overhead. We silently made our way through the main hall, neither of us willing to use a flashlight, lest we attract unwanted attention from the sleeping city outside.

"I don't like this place," Ruan murmured, pausing alongside a glass display case from the last century. He laid a gloved hand upon the glass, oddly transfixed by what was inside. "Hurry up and find what you're looking for so we can be gone."

I drew closer to him, peering over his shoulder at the darkened case. "I would like to point out that it is hard to hurry when I don't even know what I'm looking for in the first place."

"Then you'd better get started."

I muttered something rather unkind about *irritating Pellars*, glancing back over my shoulder to the windows leading onto the street. We were far enough from them that I doubted my light would draw much notice. I flicked on my flashlight and cautiously shined it into the case.

The sleeve of my jacket brushed against Ruan's. His breath hitched and he muttered something in Cornish. I couldn't quite decide if it was *me* or the object that caused such a response. Inside the glass case, an old decorative comb lay on a wooden stand with a black satin cushion beneath it. The contrast caused the white of the scrimshaw to glow in the darkness. It was intricately carved with a peculiar symbology I could not place. A language of some sort. I'd stake my life upon it. Though it was none I'd ever seen. Small pieces of pearl and abalone had been meticulously embedded into the edge, catching in the artificial light from my flashlight.

What is it?

Ruan's bottom lip was caught in his teeth as he studied the little comb, his gloved hand on the glass. His conscience warring with him on whether to lift the case and touch it. The spell it cast upon him was unnerving, yet there was something achingly familiar about the piece.

"It's a charming little comb, Ruan. Probably made by some bored sea captain for his wife at home."

Ruan could not tear himself away from the piece. "Do you not hear it? It sings . . ."

My heart thundered in my chest. I was seeing things, Ruan was *hearing* things. Granted, he often heard things, but I doubted he frequently heard *objects*. If this was any indication of what we were dealing with, whatever was going on in Oxford was bad. Very bad. I touched his hand, taking it into my own and gently pulling him away from the glass. It was the first time he allowed me to touch him, but rather than shrink away he simply let me lead him away, his attention riveted to the little comb. "No, Ruan. I don't hear anything. Nothing at all."

One step, then another backward, in a strange hypnotic dance into the shadows of the museum.

"Ruan . . ." My voice cracked as I held his hand in my own.

Whatever trance he'd been in snapped, a nearly audible crack split the space between us as he pulled his hand away and turned from the comb. His face was unreadable save for the deep divot of worry between his brows. He flexed his hand, then folded his arms tight across his chest.

"Ruan . . . what . . . what was that?"

He frowned, slowly moving farther from the comb toward another alcove stacked nearly to the ceiling with natural curiosities. "I'm sure it is nothing to worry about." He cleared his throat, growing grim. "Go on and find your clues, Ruby. I'll be here." I watched his darkened form disappear amongst the towering wall of ammonites and whalebones. The comb and its odd effect upon Ruan had nothing to do with the problem at hand—at least I hoped not. In my experience, murder tended to be a straightforward affair, and the occult rarely had much to do with it. Mr. Owen's *otherworld* tended to mind its business while ours remained hell-bent on tearing itself apart at the seams.

I rubbed my icy gloved hands over my face, trying to summon my conversation with Mr. Mueller from earlier in the day. With all that had come between then and now, I scarcely recalled the details.

Dangerous people. That's what both he and Professor Reaver had implied.

Dangerous people and fraudulent artifacts.

It wasn't much to go on, but it was a place to start. Mr. Mueller had believed that Julius Harker was going to come into money, likely from selling something valuable. But selling artifacts—even those obtained legitimately—was not a quick and easy process. And if the item was stolen, it was even more difficult. This whole endeavor was a herculean task to say the least.

Mr. Mueller and Julius Harker's offices sat side by side within eyeshot of the front entrance to the museum. The badly worn floorboards indicated that, despite his status of *persona non grata* within the academy, Harker's Curiosity Museum remained a wildly popular attraction amongst locals and tourists alike. I tried the first door—the one with Harker's name engraved on a metal placard—but it was locked tight. Mueller's, however, lay wide open. Likely not having been closed at all since the exhibition last night.

Clawing dread made its way up my spine. There was no time for nerves. We had at most an hour here before we ran the risk of discovery. I crept inside and pulled the curtains tight before turning my attention to the desk. Bracing my flashlight between my jaw and my shoulder I began to rummage through the papers, careful not to disturb anything more than necessary. If Mr. Mueller kept the books for the museum, then any financial transactions would be sitting in his records—not Julius Harker's—and hidden in plain sight. Mueller might not have even realized what he had.

Unless there were two sets of books.

A worry for another day. The papers on his abandoned desk were a crisp yellow from long-dried spilled tea. I carefully flipped through them one by one, mindful to neither rip them nor get them out of order lest someone realize I'd been here. Bills mostly, underscoring what Professor Reaver had already told me—Julius Harker and his museum were in dire financial shape.

An odd bit of correspondence. Receipts. The leather-bound accounting ledger was similarly discolored, its pages sticking together. The quiet rustle of Ruan's jacket outside told me he was nearby. His discomfort with this museum and the unease between us only exacerbated my nerves. We could not stay long.

Hoping it would not be missed, I slipped the ledger into my satchel. I needed time to examine it—and we were short on the stuff. The city would wake soon. I made quick work of the drawers and bookshelves, running my hand beneath the bottom edge in search of secret compartments, but there was nothing out of the ordinary. At least, nothing I could find. At last, I gave up and moved on to Julius Harker's office.

It took me several minutes in the darkness to finally pick the lock—far longer than an interior door ought to have taken. The locking mechanism finally gave up its secrets with a satisfying click and I entered. The air in here smelled of tobacco with the strangest hint of petrol. The combination tugged at a memory of mine that did not quite want to come, a glimmer of a thread to my past. One I did not like. Not at all.

The walls of Harker's office were hung floor to ceiling with shadowboxes full of artifacts. His desk was no better, cluttered with this and that. The man hadn't found a piece of paper, pamphlet, train ticket stub, or market list he hadn't preserved for posterity. It would take years to get through the stacks of ephemera sitting before me, and even if I managed the task, it would only give me the vaguest glimpse of Harker's life. How was I to determine what was important in this sea of miscellany?

Grumbling, I sank down into Harker's stiff leather desk chair to begin digging through his mountain of refuse. I tugged on the center desk drawer.

Locked.

Of course.

I reached into my roll again and made quick work of the drawer lock before sliding it open to reveal crumpled paper, *more* ammonites, strange rocks. And a peculiar smooth roundish stone, about the size of a duck's egg. I lifted it up, turning it over in my hand. A strange hole had been bored through the center with such precision it might have been made by a machine. I placed my finger inside, running it along the roughened edge.

"What have you found?"

I dropped the stone to the desk with a startlingly loud thunk. A metallic taste flooded my mouth from where I'd bit my tongue. "Didn't anyone tell you not to sneak up on people when burgling?"

"I'll take that omission up with my tutor." Ruan glanced down, furrowing his brow, and lifted the stone from the table, turning it over in his own hand. "Where on earth did you find a milpreve?"

"In a drawer, isn't that where they come from?" I replied dryly. "What is a milpreve?"

"An adder stone—*Glain Neidr*. They're all the same thing. Different words amongst different peoples." He sighed, pressing it into my palm and resting his own hand over it lightly, careful not to touch my skin in the doing. "It's said to protect against evil magic. You should keep it on you."

"I'm not going to steal from a museum." I bristled at the mere notion, yet I wrapped my fingers around it all the same.

"It's not stealing when the man is dead. He hasn't any use for it now."

"Have I become such a bad influence on you? Weren't you recently lecturing me on my extra-legal activities?"

He gave me a half smile, glancing back to the main hall with the rows of exhibit cases back to me. His expression fell. "Milpreve or no, I don't like this place. Find what you need, and we should go."

I didn't disagree with him at all. I'd been ill at ease ever since the first time I stepped into the museum and couldn't place my finger on it. I glanced to my watch. We had only minutes left before we needed to return home lest we be discovered. "I'll be quick."

Ruan nodded, disappearing back into the museum, and I feared he was returning to that worrisome comb. I did not like the longing on his face when it came to that object. There was a determination there, a recklessness that did not suit my pellar at all.

He's not yours, Ruby—you made quite certain of that in Scotland.

Perhaps not, but the sooner we left here the better.

I gathered up a packet of letters bound with red string from the farthest corner of the drawer, along with a tattered journal. Pocketing both, I grabbed the little milpreve, without the remotest flicker of conscience. I'd already taken the ledger. I could simply review them at my leisure, and replace them all—milpreve included—once my task here was done.

I had the blessing of Mr. Mueller to find the true killer. It wasn't stealing. Not really. Simply borrowing.

Chapter Eleven

A Different Sort of Terror

HE *was gone.*

It was the only thought. Only thing in my mind.

Smoke filled my lungs.

I couldn't move.

Couldn't scream.

My senses distorted. Ear aching, the sounds around me whining like an engine as my eyes watered.

Body thick with sweat.

Darkness.

Something wet and hot dripped down the side of my face as I struggled against my unresponsive limbs.

I had to find him. Had to get to him.

And yet I could not quite recall who.

Or why.

Only the fervid need to find *growing within me. The need to possess . . .*

Unseen hands wrapped tighter around my aching wrists, pulling me backward and shoving me deeper into the dark.

I'd been caught.

I struggled against my captor, opening my mouth to scream, as something sharp pierced my side.

"Ruby..." A familiar voice reached through my dreams.

I couldn't go to it. Not yet. Not until I'd found him.

"Ruby..."

My captor let go.

And like a crack of thunder, the dream was gone. The scent of a summer storm rushed through me, pushing away the terror that had taken hold. A coldness raced through my body, easing the weight in my chest as my breath came at long last.

The sturdy round weight of my cat was nestled at the crook of my knee, and one *very* particular man sat at my side staring at me as if he could not fathom what he'd just found.

A dream.

It had only been a dream.

But good God, my nightmares never boded well, and they'd been growing increasingly worse and more prescient since I first met Ruan along that Cornish beach months before.

A fact I did not want to think much on at present.

"Oxford?" My voice came out hoarse—throat burning from the smoke of my dream. "We're in Oxford..."

"Yes... Oxford." Ruan's roughened palms framed my face, his fingers tangled in my sweaty hair as he began murmuring to me in Cornish. Words I hadn't a prayer of understanding. The reassuring pressure of his hip pressed firm against my side as he tugged me, inch by inch, from whatever horror I'd been locked in. Had *he* been what I was seeking? Or was *he* my captor? Even still as the memory of the dream fled, I could not quite recall. Could not grasp onto the ephemeral thought.

Nor did I want to.

Flecks of silver faded from his pale eyes. A remnant, I'd discovered, of him reaching for his power. He'd been listening to me—and while at one time I might have found that an intrusion—I could not feel angry about it. Not now.

My stomach heaved and I scrambled off the bed onto the cold wooden floor, gathering a nearby chamber pot, and promptly vomited up the contents of my stomach.

Silently, Ruan pressed a glass of cool water into my hand. Taking it, I rinsed out my mouth, spitting into the bowl. Uncanny how he always knew precisely what I needed, but I had grown oddly accustomed to it in our short acquaintance. Enough that I missed that same intimacy now that we were at odds with one another.

I sat down on the floor, cross-legged, and raked my gaze up from his bare feet to his misbuttoned trousers where he crouched beside me. Heat rose to my cheeks.

"You're safe," he murmured, rubbing his broad hand over my back, sending that familiar soothing rush of cold through my veins as the room once again took on the faintest scent of electricity.

My rioting pulse disagreed.

Nevertheless, I crawled back up onto the bed and slid over, making room for him to join me on the mattress. It was a silent invitation, one he'd likely reject if the uncertainty in his eyes was any measure. The temptation to flee must have been great, but instead of leaving he sat down, gathering me against his side as he had that horrible night in Scotland when I'd been so afraid. I didn't need him to vanquish my demons, I simply wanted him alongside me while I fought them myself. I closed my eyes and rested my cheek on his scarred shoulder.

"Tell me what you saw." His thumb traced gentle circles at the base of my spine. My mind eased considerably, worries chased away by whatever it was he was doing with his thumb.

"Could you not hear the dream?"

He shook his head.

"I don't know how to describe it. It wasn't like my other dreams.

I was in the dark. Trapped. There had been a fire . . . or perhaps an explosion?" I wrinkled my nose trying to recall. "But the strangest part was that my senses were all distorted. I couldn't see. Couldn't breathe. Could scarcely hear. I cannot decide what to make of it."

"Has it been like this before?"

I shook my head. "Not in years. During the war, of course, my dreams were terrible then. In the months leading up to my parents' deaths and the several years after. I . . . for a while I was quite convinced I was going mad."

Ruan let out a low, not-at-all reassuring sound in his chest.

"The dreams worry you, don't they? Do you think I'm going mad? Because *I* think I'm going mad."

"You're not mad . . . you're finally . . ." The rough stubble on his jaw caught on my hair as he thought better of what he was about to say. "No, Ruby. You're not mad."

I was too tired to argue and nuzzled closer into his neck, inhaling the green scent of him. "How can you be certain?"

He didn't answer. Ruan's fingers tenderly grazed my exposed shoulder, before he pulled the thick blankets up over me.

"Why are you being so kind? I thought you didn't like me very much."

He let out a soft laugh. "Liking you has never been the problem with us. But I intend to be clear on things this time. My feelings for you have not changed. But I refuse to live in no-man's-land with you in some hellish child's game where I do not know where I stand. I will be your friend. I will be your lover, but I cannot continue teetering between the two. I *will not* be a part of that with you. You are far too precious to me for that."

Precious. The word settled beneath my skin and I closed my eyes, allowing myself this tiny indulgence, for come morning this tenderness between us would disappear. I slowly began to fall back asleep, listening to the gentle patter of rain on the windowpane. My life had been an enduring nightmare—from the time I was a little girl in America until the moment I met Ruan on a Cornish shore when something bone-deep snapped into place. As if in finding him I'd found the answer to a question I'd been seeking my whole life. It wasn't the man himself; no, it was nothing romantic like that.

It was *me*.

I'd found some inexplicably lost shard of myself on that shore and somehow that same piece was tied to him. It made no sense at all, and yet somehow all the sense in the world.

Chapter Twelve

Nothing a Bit of Cake Won't Fix

WHEN I woke the next morning Ruan was gone. I might have thought his late night visit was a dream itself, if not for the fact that my room smelled vaguely of him. He must have stayed after I fell back asleep. The cowardly part of me was glad that he had left, for with him gone I could pour myself entirely into figuring out who killed Julius Harker.

I poured cold water from the pitcher into the cheerful yellow porcelain basin and washed my face, before taking a damp cloth to the rest of my body. Fiachna raised his furry black head from his spot on the foot of the bed and shot me a judgmental look.

"Oh, hush. I know all about what you get up to in Exeter, you little feline lothario."

Fiachna meowed pointedly.

"'He who is without sin' and all that . . ."

The great black cat purred loudly in acknowledgment that there were quite a few fluffy black kittens scattered around the city. He stretched before hopping off the bed and wriggled through the cracked-open door without even getting his morning scratch behind the ears.

It was early. The sun had not fully risen, and the street outside remained sleepy and quiet. I gathered my purloined evidence from last night's misadventures at the museum and made my way downstairs.

The rich dark scent of coffee greeted me as Mrs. Penrose pulled a loaf of bread from the oven. "The lad left an hour ago if you're wondering." Her back remained to me as she placed the steaming loaf on a nearby wooden board.

"Ruan?"

"Who else would it be sneaking out of your room in the wee hours? I don't recall you having any other suitors."

"He's not a suitor," I grumbled, glaring at my housekeeper. "Besides, nothing happened."

Her long gray hair was loosely pinned up at the nape of her neck, a few stray wisps falling from the knot. "Oh, I'm not judging, maid. You know I love the lad as my own—*something happening* might do the both of you some good."

I slid past her, grabbing a cup from the highest shelf in the cabinet, and poured my own coffee with feigned disinterest. "He's returning, I presume."

"Oh, most certainly. He had something on his mind. He ran straight past me saying he'd be back for supper, he had to go see about a book."

I let out a startled laugh. Ruan was beginning to sound like Mr. Owen. Then again, Ruan's interest in old books was precisely the reason we met in the first place. "Did he say what book he was after?" I began to lay out my day's work on the worn tabletop. Time was short, and the tea-stained ledger was as good a place to start as any.

"No, my lover. He didn't say much of anything. But who ever *does* know what he's after? He's a dear one, but Ruan Kivell's always been a bit odd. A good and righteous woman might hope that taking up with you would settle him down, but I'm afraid there's no hope in that corner."

I grinned at Mrs. Penrose. "I cannot decide if that's an insult or a compliment."

She smiled back, shoving a generous slice of yesterday's ginger cake at me. "A compliment, my lover. I never said I was a good and righteous woman. Now eat, there's no problem in this world that a slice of cake can't fix."

SEVERAL HOURS AND two pots of coffee later, I was still seated at the kitchen table poring over the letters I'd taken from the museum. I rolled the *borrowed* milpreve in my palm, something about the stone's smooth grain aided my focus. Had Julius Harker done this too? I frowned, setting one letter down on the table and picking up another.

"Any luck, maid?" Mrs. Penrose asked from the far side of the room. She'd spent most of the morning baking, her fingers sticky with butter and flour as she worked dried cherries into her scone dough.

I dropped the stone on the table. *Protect against evil indeed*, the rock was little more than a rustic paperweight.

"That was a pretty song you was humming just now."

I blinked, turning to face her. "I wasn't humming."

"Ah but you were, maid. An old melody too. I cannot think I've ever heard you hum before. Nor sing for that matter. You must be feeling better. Makes my heart soar to hear you happy."

I couldn't bear to tell her she was mistaken. If anything, I was more adrift than ever before. I picked up the milpreve again and held it to the light. "My mother used to sing when she was happy . . ." I said softly, staring at the stone. I'd not thought of it in years—perhaps it was the imposter's presence that brought it back to the forefront of my mind.

"You don't speak of her much."

No. I scarcely did, though she was never far from my thoughts, especially with this most recent imposter. "She would sing to us when we were small—my sister Opal and I. She had the most beautiful voice I'd ever heard. My father loved to listen to her. I can still recall how he'd lean in the doorway, watching her each night as we fell asleep."

Mrs. Penrose gave me a sympathetic glance. "She sounds like a lovely woman."

"She was. She loved my sister and I more than anything in this world."

Mrs. Penrose washed her hands in the sink, scrubbing at the dough beneath her nails. "Do you need some help? I am not certain what good I'll be to you, but perhaps between the two of us we might find something in all that mess you've made of my scullery table."

Blotting the memory of my mother from my mind, I handed the tea-stained ledger to Mrs. Penrose. "You've a head for numbers. See if you find anything odd in there, hmm?"

"Shall I fix us a pot of tea while we work?"

She didn't wait on my response as she set on another kettle before taking the seat across from me, and we set to work. The sun was hanging low in the sky by the time I finally gave up on the letters. Over the course of the morning, I'd learned all sorts of useless facts about Julius Harker: He was separated from his wife, who currently lived in Bath with their two grown children. He also was in possession of a vast collection of Egyptian artifacts—not a surprise as he was exhibiting said artifacts at the time of his murder—and he had an aversion to turnips. I couldn't blame him on the final point for I disliked the root vegetable myself. Beyond that, the sum of my investigation had left me with a pile of various receipts and descriptions of objects that meant nothing. The man's existence was utterly boring.

"Maid . . . look at this." Mrs. Penrose tapped an entry in the ledger with the tip of her pencil. She slid her scratch paper over to me, revealing her notes where she'd quietly been refiguring the calculations in her own exacting hand.

I scooted my chair across the cold floor, half-eaten fruit scone in hand. "What did you find?"

She removed her glasses. "I'm not entirely sure. But see here? Every few days there is a repeating transaction. See this number?"

Forty-seven pounds and six shillings. A year's wages for some.

She underlined it once, running her finger down her list. "Seven times in total. See here, where three days later precisely half of that figure goes back out. Now to whom or why, I can't tell. But mind, that's a great deal of money to be moving about with no explanation for it."

"A *great* deal of money indeed, especially for someone with so many creditors. If it was payment on a debt, he'd certainly keep record of that." I gathered up the correspondence, flipping through the pages, checking for dates to match her entries.

I pulled each letter and lay all seven on the table.

It didn't take long to spot the pattern—one utterly invisible without the aid of the ledger.

"You see something, don't you?" Mrs. Penrose's voice quivered with excitement.

I skimmed the correspondence again, annoyed at myself for missing it in the first place. Harker been conversing with a fellow at Cambridge tracking down pieces of a missing Napoleonic cache—a collection of artifacts that had been stolen during Napoleon's occupation of Egypt around the turn of the previous century. It was something I'd overlooked as Harker's ill-fated exhibition was purportedly showing off pieces from that same cache. Many of the pieces had been looted from Egypt and brought to Europe to be on display in fashionable French homes. From what the letters indicated, the original cache had been slowly broken up and sold off into various private collections over the years. However, if what I held in my hands were true, Harker had mostly reassembled it, snapping up an ungodly quantity of artifacts for his own private collection. Far more artifacts than made it into his exhibition.

I blew out an unsteady breath, not certain what to make of what I'd found. The exhibition the other evening only contained a handful of items—and the only one on the stage that was also mentioned in the letters was the very box he was found in. But if the letters were to be believed, Harker had recovered hundreds of other artifacts, including a golden racing chariot. The chariot would have been the star piece for any other collector. I flipped back through the pages again. In truth, most of the items mentioned in the letters were far more significant than what had been on display. I'd thought it a rather bare-bones exhibition at the time, but perhaps there was something more behind the omissions. Had the exhibit been intentional, or an afterthought? Now that was a question I could not answer. At least not yet.

I ran my hand through my hair, struggling to make sense of it. Where were the remaining artifacts? They certainly hadn't been on display in the cases at Harker's museum, and they hadn't been on the exhibition dais either.

I gathered the pages together, shoving them into the stolen folio before pressing a firm kiss to her forehead. "You are a genius, Mrs. Penrose. An utter genius." I grabbed my winter coat and slung my worn leather satchel over my shoulder, determined to find the one person in Oxford who might be able to shed light on the cache. I checked my watch, snapping it back shut. If I left now, I might catch Leona at the museum before she left for the day.

Chapter Thirteen

The Plot Thickens

AS much time as Leona had been spending with Julius Harker, she had to know something about his cache—some tiny detail to break open the rest of the mystery, like one of those Russian nesting dolls.

I raced down the rapidly darkening streets of Oxford toward the museum, past the schoolchildren kicking a ball around the green, and paused alongside the ancient Bodleian Library to catch my breath before taking off again. Stubborn patches of snow and ice lingered in the shadier spots, waiting for the wet spots in the sun to refreeze that evening. Harker's correspondence sat like a stone in my pocket. These unaccounted-for artifacts had to *mean* something. They simply had to.

The bells of St. Mary's rang out marking the hour when a faint motion from the periphery of my vision caught my attention. No more than a shadow or flicker of a shape, but enough to cause me to turn just as a figure disappeared into an alleyway. The person had been less than twenty feet behind me, and I'd scarcely noticed them, so caught up in my worries about Leona and the cache.

A frisson of tension worked its way up my spine.

Come now, Ruby. It's three in the afternoon and there are plenty of people about. No one is following you.

The rational voice in my head was likely correct and yet I hastened my step, nearly breaking into a run the last few cross streets to the Ashmolean. Hari's hotel was just across the way from the museum, and for a half moment I was tempted to go see him, ask if he thought it plausible that I could be followed—but he would only chastise me for getting caught up in the investigation. Especially after I'd assured him that I would not do any such thing.

No. I could not turn to Hari. Not over this.

It was my imagination. That was *all*.

It was quieter than normal inside the museum, with that hushed sort of wonder typically reserved for cathedrals and graveyards. Reason warred with the growing unease in my belly. Surely no one would be following me—after all, no one even knew that I was *actually* investigating Harker's death. The only way anyone *could* have known was if they'd somehow seen me enter his museum last night.

With a start, I recalled the scent of stale pipe smoke in Harker's office. He'd been dead for days before discovery, and by now it had been nearly a week since he'd last been in that locked room. Would the scent have lingered that long? I added that to the growing list of questions I could not answer.

I skipped steps on my way down to Leona's basement reading room and skidded to a stop in the open doorway.

"Can I help you?" Mary asked over the rim of her glasses. She was the sort of woman who wore her annoyance on her face—and she was most certainly perturbed by my appearance.

"Is Leona here today?" I craned my neck, peering around the room. It certainly didn't look like Leona was here.

Her expression shifted to concern as she removed her glasses and sat them on the large book before her. "No. The girl hasn't come in at all today and Professor Reaver has been unbearable because of it." She gestured at the pile of books behind her. "How am I to get through all this for him in six hours? Tell me that?"

I let out a sympathetic sound. "Does he often ask for your help?"

"Not usually, but Leona's absence always puts him in a temper. The only person in all of Oxford who can handle his moods is Miss Abernathy."

Something about her words pricked my conscience. "Is she gone that often?"

"Now and again. Usually, I know when she's not coming in, but this time . . ."

"Do you know where she is?"

Mary didn't answer right away, focused upon the book before her. "I haven't a clue. I went to Reaver himself this morning and he said he sent a boy around to check if she was well, but the lad returned and wouldn't answer my questions. I thought I'd stop by her flat tonight and see how she fares. Perhaps she's taken sick, there's been a terrible fever going around town this winter. It could be that."

I leaned against the doorway, crossing my ankles. How very strange. "Why wouldn't the boy answer you? It seems a rather straightforward thing. She either *is* or *is not* at home."

Mary sighed, placing her book away on the shelf, and began to file the scattered papers on her overburdened desk. "I don't know. I worry it has something to do with that Julius Harker business. She and Professor Reaver had been discussing him when they didn't think I could hear."

"What about?" I laid my hand over Harker's letters in my pocket. Not that Mary had any idea that they were in my possession.

"A collection of artifacts. At least that's what it sounded like, but anytime I would enter the room they'd hush up right away."

Then Leona *must* know more about the cache. A flicker of hope fluttered in my chest. It was a treacherous emotion, one not to be trusted, but it was all I had to go on. Hope and a smattering of letters. "Reaver doesn't seem to have liked Julius Harker much. I was told they were constantly at odds."

The woman let out a startled sound, brushing an ash-colored

strand of hair back from her eyes. "He doesn't. Can't bear the sight of him, but that one—" She tilted her head toward the empty chair at Leona's study desk. "She'd been spending too much time with him. Reaver had been lecturing her about how dangerous he was right up until Harker was found dead. I assumed Reaver meant *dangerous to her profession* . . . but now I cannot help but wonder if he meant something else altogether . . ."

As do I.

"Does Leona have many friends here?"

Mary tucked a leather-bound journal into her own carryall. "No. She keeps to herself mostly. No friends besides you and that girl she lives with. But from the way Reaver's been behaving, I worry she's gotten herself mixed up into something bad."

"Have you mentioned your fears to anyone else?"

A door farther along the hallway closed loudly, followed by low laughter. I glanced down the narrow corridor, but the others were walking away from me.

She turned to face me, gathering up her bag and slinging it over her shoulder. "Who would I tell? It's little more than supposition. Leona hasn't a mother to look after her. The rest of her family is still in Egypt. Then there's her father, who might drop in now and then, reeking of liquor and throwing his military rank about before disappearing again. The point is, the poor girl hasn't anyone at all in this town. And Professor Reaver works her to the bone. His concern with her is entirely her usefulness to him and nothing more. She's up all hours here, locked in this reading room or in some storeroom with him when no good could happen to her."

"Well . . . she has me. Whatever good that'll do her. You go on home. I'll stop by her flat, see how she is." My true friends were few, and I wasn't about to lose this one even if I had behaved abominably to her when she first came to ask for my help. I stepped out into the hallway, Mary following after.

"Are you certain it's no trouble?" Mary locked the door to the reading room.

"No. No trouble at all," I said with a faint smile before heading out of the museum and into the winter night. It had been scarcely five minutes after I left the museum when that same prickle of awareness returned. The sensation of not being alone. I turned in time to catch a glimpse of a man some thirty feet behind me, his hands shoved into his pockets. He wore a workman's cap pulled low over his brow and a dark gray coat. His hair was dark, but I could not make out his face.

Realizing I'd caught him, he quickly turned, scurrying away in the direction of St. John Street. I wasn't going mad at all. Someone *was* following me. I stood stone still, watching until he fully rounded the corner. Reassured of my sanity, I set off in the opposite direction.

Of course, now I had two problems instead of just one. First, who killed Julius Harker? And second, and more concerning at present, who exactly *was* my mysterious shadow and what did he want?

Damnation. That was three problems, not two.

I FOLLOWED THE most circuitous path to Leona's, careful to loop back once or twice, in hopes of throwing off my follower—if he even still was there. The whole ordeal took me three times as long as normal, and the evening air grew colder by the second. Flurries began to fall from the sky, making the night hazier than it had been when I set out. A snowflake stuck on my eyelashes, and I blinked it away before knocking again on Leona's door. The cracked blue paint peeled from lack of attention. Her house lay on a quieter street, not far from the castle. One of a series of two- and three-story townhomes that all looked relatively the same, with different-colored doors. Initially built for families, over the years they'd been divided up into several smaller flats for students and other less-affluent laborers. I shivered, blowing into my bare hands for warmth.

The door opened at last, and a gust of warm air greeted me. "I told you before, you need to—"

Leona's flatmate Annabelle stood before me, her words evaporating as she took me in. I'd met her a time or two since coming to Oxford—a slight creature, who'd only turned twenty last month. She kept to herself mostly, focusing on her studies, desperate to prove herself to her family who were apprehensive about sending a girl off to the University. Recognition dawned in her wide gray eyes.

"Oh. It's you, Miss Vaughn."

A car rumbled by on the street behind and I leaned closer, drinking in the warmth emanating from inside. Ordinarily, Annabelle would welcome me in, offer to pour me a couple fingers of whisky while I awaited Leona, but there was something in her face and the way she stood in the half-open doorway that told me that I would not be crossing her threshold tonight. A half dozen pairs of stockings lay drying atop the hall radiator along with Leona's worn white jumper.

"I've come to see Leona. She didn't show up at the museum today and Mary was worried for her."

The girl's eyes widened in surprise. "She didn't?"

I shook my head, perplexed by Annabelle's response. The girl wrapped her fingers tighter around the old brass door handle.

Everything inside the front hall *looked* normal. "Mary said a boy came around the house to check on her. Did you speak with him?"

"I haven't seen any boy." Her answer came too quickly. Her breath too short. "Haven't seen anyone today at all . . . been working on a paper. I thought Leona was at the museum. She left here after dawn."

Annabelle was lying. It was clear as day. But why? I tilted my head, peering into the welcoming foyer. "Can I come in? Wait until she returns home? It's damnably cold out here."

The girl shifted on her bare stockinged feet and tugged her oversized gray jumper tighter around her. "You better not, Miss Vaughn."

And that was when I heard the voices.

Annabelle heard them too, and her face visibly blanched.

One was definitely Leona's.

The second belonged to a man.

"Who is with her?" I growled, wrapping my fingers around the door just above hers.

Annabelle released the door, holding up her palms in defeat. "She's safe. She's fine. I promise you, Miss Vaughn."

I raised a brow, my voice far sharper than I'd intended. "Julius Harker is dead. I suspect he also told his own friends *he* was fine, until he wasn't."

Annabelle wet her lips, glancing back toward the room where Leona entertained her guest. "She said I wasn't to allow anyone in, to tell them she was out all day. Please, Miss Vaughn. I don't want to cause trouble with her."

"Even me?" I raised a brow.

She worried her lower lip unable to meet my gaze. "Yes, Miss Vaughn. I asked. She said even you."

She may as well have struck me across the face. I stared at her dumbfounded.

Leona had explicitly told her flatmate to not let me in. I struggled to tamp down the betrayal and rage battling within me. Annabelle was an innocent in this. But Leona . . . Leona had begged me to help her and was now keeping secrets. And secrets were the one thing I could not abide. "Tell her to meet me at the Artemis Club tomorrow morning at seven sharp. Or else I assure you I will be back here tomorrow afternoon, and I will not stand politely and wait to be turned away." I tilted my chin toward the hall. "Tell her if she wants my help, she cannot lie to me again. Those are my terms. She can accept them, or she can solve Julius Harker's murder on her own."

The worried girl nodded. "I will. I promise. I'm sorry, Miss Vaughn. I am . . ."

I turned on my heels and stormed down the street and back toward the townhome. It made no sense. Why would Leona come begging for my help and then behave in such a way? And moreover, who had been in the house that both Annabelle and Leona didn't want me to see?

Chapter Fourteen

Other, More-Academic Pursuits

GOLDEN light filtered out the windows of a nearby pub as I tugged my coat tighter around me. My temper hadn't eased one little bit in the last half hour, and I was most of the way home. All my concerns—my mysterious shadow, the prospect of yet another imposter, the fact I *might* be seeing people who aren't really there, and the tangled web with Ruan—all of those minor problems took a back seat to the fact that Leona had *lied* to me. Lied to me and explicitly had her flatmate turn me away. I blew out an irritated breath. Mary told me Leona had been arguing with Professor Reaver over Julius Harker, and now here she was having secret assignations. I'd bet my life the two things were connected.

Pausing outside the pub, I blew into my half-frozen hands. I'd forgotten my gloves when I set out this afternoon—a fact I already regretted as my fingers were quite numb and stinging from the cold. The proprietor here had trimmed the windows and doorways in cheery shades of red, gold, and green. A sprig of mistletoe hung over a nearby doorway. The main taproom was full of souls gathering around a pint—or three—and having a bite of supper before returning to their homes for the night. The door opened and a teetering rosy-cheeked old man stepped out into the cold, allowing the roar from inside to flood the street. I did not long to be inside among them—cozied up by the fire and veiled by frosted windowpanes. For some, the idea might bring a sort of wistfulness for days gone by, but I simply wanted to walk away from this world and not look back. My chest tightened.

Leona was keeping secrets from me. She might well know the answers to my questions about Harker's missing cache, but I could no longer trust her words. My heart ached at the thought. *I should go home. Wash my hands of this whole sordid affair and return to Exeter, away from murderers and antiquarians.* And yet I could no more abandon poor Mr. Mueller to his fate than I could forego the sea. It was an impossibility. Unthinkable. And if I could no longer trust Leona, then there was only one person in the world who could help now. Me.

I would simply have to return to Harker's museum and search for the missing antiquities myself. I already possessed a notion of the lay of the museum. The bulk of his collection likely lay beneath the public floors, as in any other museum. I was perfectly able to translate both hieratic and demotic on my own. While it took me longer than Leona with translation, I knew my way around an ancient text. What's more, I even knew what objects I sought. It should be a simple enough task. Let myself in, look around, leave.

Easy.

"Miss Vaughn! It's lovely to see you again this evening."

Emmanuel Laurent stepped out of the pub, the wind catching the door and slamming it hard behind him. He turned, embarrassed by the sound, before returning to my side. "My dear girl, I did not expect to see you tonight. How is Owen this evening?" He adjusted his bowler before tucking his fine red-and-navy-striped scarf into his overcoat. I met his warm smile with one of my own, unable to resist the warmth of his presence.

"Mr. Owen is well. I was headed home just now. I'm late for supper and I suspect he will be worried." It was a harmless fiction.

Mr. Owen worried in his way—but he seldom let it show. If I had to guess, he was most likely sitting in the kitchen playing gin rummy with Mrs. Penrose while she plied my greedy housecat with tinned fish.

Laurent stretched, running his hands over his belly. "I met some friends for dinner and was about to head off to a lecture tonight. You are more than welcome to join us, my dear. I do so enjoy your company. You are a breath of fresh air amongst our staid set."

I started to tell him no, that I really ought to go home, but for some strange reason I could not make the words come.

His brows drew up as he studied me. "Are you quite all right, my dear?"

I nodded, opening my mouth, then snapping it back shut. "The cold air stole my breath, that's all."

The door to the pub opened again, the merry bell jingling in the night, and I glanced up to find Ruan standing in the threshold beneath the mistletoe, none too pleased to see me. "Ruby . . ."

Laurent gave me a queer look, then turned to Ruan. "You are acquainted then?"

"We"—I suddenly felt rather ill—"are acquainted."

"That's right! All that business in Lothlel Green I'd read in the papers. I'd nearly forgotten. How silly of me."

The muscles in the edge of Ruan's jaw quirked as he watched me, struggling to control whatever fit of temper was going on inside his brain.

Are you well? I didn't know if he could hear me, but it was worth a shot.

His nostrils flared as he made a cynical sound in the back of his throat.

Apparently not.

I turned my back on my irritated pellar. "I am afraid as much as I'd love to join you this evening, I'd best get back to Mr. Owen. I did promise him I wouldn't be gone long."

Laurent checked his pocket watch and frowned. "If you are certain. I'd better be off as well. I don't want to be miss the start of the lecture. Are you ready, Kivell?"

"Go on without me, Professor. I'll be along dreckly."

Oh God.

I knew good and well what *dreckly* meant. A convenient Cornishism that Ruan employed that meant *whenever he damn well pleased*. It could be anywhere from *imminently* to *two weeks from now*. A wise woman would have felt an iota of fear at the tone of his voice—might have said or done whatever necessary to remove that strange flash of anger from Ruan's unusual green eyes—but I was not wise, certainly not when it came to him.

Oblivious to the razor's edge of tension growing between us, Laurent dipped his head and headed off down the lane, disappearing into the shadows. Ruan loomed on the sidewalk in front of me until long after Laurent was out of earshot.

The muscle in his jaw worked, as he debated what he was going to say to me. I could see from the look in his eyes he wasn't happy. But whatever it was, I wasn't having it. "Where have you been all day?" The question came out sharper than I'd intended.

He let out an aggrieved grunt, folding his arms across his chest. "It isn't as if you ever ask my permission before you decide to hare off somewhere." His tone softened. "If you must know, I've been with Laurent all day. He wanted to speak of Ernst. I lost track of time."

Ernst? Then suddenly I recalled the conversation I'd had with Professor Laurent in his library earlier this week. Of how he was waiting on his former student who had been friends with his late son, Ernst. *Ruan* must have been that student. "He was your friend . . ." I murmured. Whatever ire I'd been holding on to fled. It also certainly explained Ruan's ragged expression tonight. "I'm sorry."

"I'm not— I hadn't spoken of him in years before tonight. It felt good to be with someone who loved him. Who'd not forgotten the light he brought into this world. Ernst never treated me differently or less than—even though he knew I was a miner's son." Ruan closed his eyes, giving his head a shake. "Gods. There were times back then I thought he was only kind because he felt sorry for my lot, but I sometimes think he saw something in me. Something I've never seen in myself."

I swallowed hard, knowing that feeling intimately. "I hadn't thought—I didn't mean to bring back the past. Mrs. Penrose said you'd gone out looking for a book. I assumed you were out—"

"I had been, then I stopped by to see Laurent . . ." He let out a sad small sound. "But it is nothing. A fool's errand. My melancholy has nothing to do with you and I should not have been curt with you over it."

I sighed.

"My *temper* however, that is deserved . . ."

My relief was short-lived. I placed my hands on my hips, when I caught the edge of humor in his eyes. He was teasing. I wasn't sure what to make of that.

"Returning to Oxford brings back those last few months before I left the University. I was angry then. Ernst— he cautioned me to control my temper."

"I'm still not certain you *have* much of a temper. I've seen you cross but never truly angry."

Ruan chuckled. "Then Ernst would feel he'd done the job well . . . though I doubt he would believe it after the way I left Oxford."

"You never told me what happened. . . ."

Ruan closed his eyes, exhaling through his nose. The familiar divot of worry reappeared between his brows. I squeezed my icy fingers tight to keep from reaching up to smooth it. "It's a story for another day."

"No. . . . I didn't mean to you, I mean to him. Was it the war?"

Ruan's attention remained fixed on the empty street behind me. "He died on the first day of the Somme."

Were you there?

I didn't even realize I hadn't spoken the question aloud until he shook his head.

The pain on his face—the helplessness at the memory of his old friend dying. My fingers went to his wrist of their own accord.

He closed his eyes again and pulled away from my touch. "I heard you earlier, Ruby."

Good God, my thoughts had been a cacophony tonight. I could only imagine what he'd overheard.

"All of it." Ruan dropped his voice to little over a whisper. "But in particular, while I was finishing my supper, I heard you planning on going back to Harker's museum. I'm beginning to rethink my assessment that you aren't mad, or perhaps it is only that you are intent on driving *me* that way?"

I clenched my fingers into a fist and shoved my hands deep into my coat pockets, stinging from his rebuke. "Perhaps if *you* weren't intent upon controlling everything around you then you wouldn't be as concerned about your precious sanity."

His nostrils flared. "*Me*? Control *you*? Gods, if only one could. I am simply trying to keep you alive and am doing a poor job of it. No wonder Hecate said you'd be the death of me."

My stomach churned at his mention of the White Witch's prophesy. I almost *had* been the death of him in Scotland. My eyes dropped down to where the scar was hidden beneath his thick coat and oatmeal-colored jumper.

He'd heard that. His expression softened. "You understand, then."

My mouth felt like cotton. "I understand nothing. Least of all you—this." I gestured between us.

"Then at least we are matched in that." Bitter amusement tugged at the corner of his lips—whatever anger with me he'd harbored moments before had fled as quickly as it came, replaced by an emotion I dared not name. "Two months ago, I watched a man place a rifle against your breast, powerless to do anything to save you. Unable to look away for fear that if I did, I would lose that final second in your light. And I could not bear the thought." He reached to touch my face, but instead closed his fingers and shoved his hand into his pocket. Emotion thick in his voice. "I know that we are at odds right now."

"We're always at odds."

"But gods, I cannot bear the thought of you putting yourself needlessly at risk. I am sick at the thought of it. Whatever happens between us, I cannot bear the thought of you being in danger. Promise me, Ruby."

I leaned closer to him, close enough to catch his green scent, and inhaled deeply. In that moment I might have promised him anything his heart desired. The man was a witch indeed. My voice came out hoarse. "Promise what?"

"Promise me you will not go to Harker's museum without me. I will come back to the townhome after the lecture. Then we will go together. I will help you, but we must do it together."

I nodded, far too numb to form words. Ruan leaned closer, his breath grazing my cheek, and I thought he might bend. He might not let me touch him—might not *touch* me—but perhaps he might kiss me again as he had in Scotland and end this unpleasantness between us once and for all. But his iron will held firm. He straightened and turned, calling back over his shoulder, "Until tonight, Ruby Vaughn."

And I watched him walk away into the snowy night.

Chapter Fifteen

Old Habits Die Hard

"STUPID. Stupid girl . . ." I muttered, fiddling with my lockpicks. The street behind me was mostly empty, with only the occasional passerby to break the silence. I crouched outside the back entrance of Julius Harker's museum, hidden in the shadows. The sky overhead was clear and bright—illuminated by pinprick stars.

You're no better than Fiachna after a field mouse, Ruby Vaughn. Unable to let it rest until you come back bloodied, missing tufts of fur, your tail between your legs.

I ought to have waited on Ruan before returning to the museum. After all, I had promised him I would do that very thing. Yet when the clock chimed midnight and he still hadn't returned from that infernal lecture with Professor Laurent, I had no alternative. If I was to sort through Harker's collection to figure out what happened to him, I needed *time*—and I was quickly running out of the stuff.

Ruan would be furious when he found out—which was why he mustn't ever learn of it. I readjusted my scarf as a lonely nightingale trilled out from somewhere behind me. My eyes stung as I continued to struggle with the lock. The bitter wind caught the back of my pleated cobalt skirt, threatening to expose my practical woolen drawers to all and sundry. Then again, neither all *nor* sundry were in this frigid alley at quarter to one in the morning. I finally managed to spring the stubborn lock and stepped inside, closing the door behind me.

It was far darker than it had been the first time I'd come to the museum, or perhaps it was only my imagination. The shadows of the tall cases were longer, the silence more ominous. The wooden floorboards creaked as I took a step, and I spun on my heels, heart hammering in my chest. But there was nothing there.

Outside, the muffled sound of dogs barking gave me pause. Had I locked the door behind me? Surely I had.

Foolish girl, giving in to imagination.

Taking my flashlight in hand, I headed for the front entrance and quickly found a wooden panel concealing the narrow curving stairs to the basement. Once I closed the panel behind me and was safely hidden in the stairwell, I flicked on my flashlight and descended the curving stair. I had to be careful. If I fell, I'd be trapped here in Harker's collection until someone eventually came and discovered me.

If they ever found me.

The air in the storeroom was stale. Faint streaks of light filtered in through the small windows nearly twelve feet above my head.

Where to begin . . . where to begin . . .

I bit the edge of my thumb, scanning through the dusty, overcrowded shelves before settling upon the nearest rack. The storage apparatus was a beast of a construction, purpose-built a century or more ago. It stood a good five feet taller than me, reaching nearly to the ceiling. Its shelving extended the width of the room with a rolling ladder affixed to it, allowing access to the upper shelves. I ran my flashlight across the crates, peeking into the lid of the closest one. A collection of Roman coins. The hasty words painted on the side indicated they'd been excavated somewhere in Northumbria. Not that different from those I'd admired in Professor Laurent's own collection a few days before. I closed the rough-hewn lid and moved on to the next, which contained similarly useless shards of Etruscan pottery. Intriguing, yes—but not what I was after. The provenance and date of acquisition were painted clearly on the outside of each crate.

The storeroom was vastly different from Harker's cluttered office upstairs, and had I not known they both were owned by the same man, I would not believe it. Down here everything was neat as a pin, albeit dusty, with each artifact meticulously labelled, sorted, and stored away.

I moved from box to box, rack to rack, losing track of time in my search for . . . something . . . *anything* to explain those transactions in the ledger, and yet there was nothing to my eye out of the ordinary. Nor was there any sign of the missing artifacts. By my loose recollections there were at least a hundred items unaccounted for that Harker mentioned in his letter to his colleague, and yet the most intriguing discovery I'd made had been an unusual shade of dust mite I'd not before encountered. None of it made any sense. Perhaps he wasn't storing the objects here at all or had an accomplice? Perhaps the objects weren't objects at all, and simply code for something else?

The minutes ticked by, and I had another half dozen shelves to go through. My nose tickled, likely due to said dust mites. Rubbing it with my sleeve, I spotted a brief flash of gold on the far side of the room. I hurried over, shining my light upon what appeared to be a sort of chariot that was partially obscured by a large crate, and a half dozen canopic jars sitting loose on the shelf.

Finally.

Giddy with the thrill of discovery, I hiked my skirt up over the tops of my warm woolen stockings and climbed upon the old table. Balanced on my knees, I leaned over to better inspect the shelf behind. I wedged the flashlight between my jaw and shoulder. One by one, I pulled the jars from the higher shelf and placed them onto the rickety surface beside me until the golden object came into full view. It was most certainly a chariot. I reached down and pulled a stubby pencil from my satchel and placed my worn notebook on the shelf to take inventory of what I'd found, lips moving slightly as I counted the canopic jars alongside me on the table. *Two. Four. Six. Seven. Eight.* I craned my neck, careful to keep the flashlight steady beneath my chin. Three more on the far side, that made what? Eleven? Then the chariot—which was blocked in by a long, low crate. Unlike the others, this crate bore no paint. At least none where I could see. No provenance. No dates.

I set my flashlight down and grabbed on to both ends to better access it, but the thing was far too heavy to move on my own. I continued my hasty inventory, sorting through the smaller pieces. This had to be part of the cache. It simply *had* to be. With the jars and smaller artifacts moved out of the way, I carefully stood on the table and lifted the lid to reveal a mummified cat lying atop the straw. Fiachna would have definite *thoughts* about that one. I shifted the packing material on the other side to reveal smaller alabaster figures alongside a handful of intricately carved vessels. My nose stung from the dust I'd stirred up. Yes. Most certainly the cache.

I squeezed my eyes shut, trying to will the sneeze away, but failed.

A second threatened and I sniffled, grasping my flashlight in my left hand.

"I cannot decide whether I should bless you or accept the fact you've the devil's own mulishness . . ." Ruan grumbled from somewhere behind me in the darkness.

I turned, whacking my hip on the crate and letting out a pained yelp. A nearby canopic jar rattled in protest.

"You promised me, Ruby Vaughn," he murmured, stepping closer. I could scarcely make out more than the shape of him as he reached up, taking me roughly by the waist and setting me on the ground beside him.

It was the first time he'd touched me willingly—excepting when he woke me from my nightmare—and there was no tenderness at all in the gesture. As soon as my feet hit the floor, he removed his hands from my person, thrusting them into his pockets and turning away from me. "You promised me that you would not come without me." His voice sounded oddly strained. "Then . . . *then* I find the bloody door unlocked where anyone could have come upon you. You're lucky I'm the one who's found you and not the murderer—you know that, don't you?"

I placed my hands on my hips. "You were late. We were running out of ti—" I gestured with my flashlight toward the stairs, partially illuminating the side of his face, and my pulse stilled.

Blood.

There was blood on his face. A brownish smudge marred his forehead, along with the sleeve of his now-ripped oatmeal sweater. *What had happened?*

"What happened to me is not the point."

It was to me, but instead of arguing with him I reached up, untied the kerchief I'd used to hold back my hair, and began to wipe at the stubborn spot on his temple. It didn't *seem* to be his, or if it was, it had dried long ago.

Ruan inhaled sharply and, for half a second, I thought he would retreat, brush my hand away, and tend to his own filth—but instead he stepped closer with a weary sigh. "The blood isn't mine. Some lads got heated about the lecture. There was some pushing. Fighting. Someone rang for the police."

I raised my brows in challenge. "What on earth were they debating to cause a fistfight?"

"Does it matter? I stayed behind to help clean up the wounded." His voice was rough as I dabbed futilely at the dried blood. Needing to be useful. To fix the awkwardness between us.

He reached up, taking my hand from his temple and folding his rough palm over mine, pulling it away from his face.

I furrowed my brow, not understanding.

"You know how bad things have gotten since the war. There's no work, and what work there is doesn't pay. Even if it *does* pay a wage, the coin isn't worth what it used to be. The price of goods is abysmal. . . . A man survives the war and comes home to what? To simply starve on the streets of old *Blighty* when the children of the same men that sent them to war are given every advantage. Gods . . . it's the reason I hated this place in the first place." I'd never heard bitterness from Ruan's lips. *Blighty.* That's what the soldiers used to call Britain—home. But the way it dropped from his tongue sounded like a curse.

"So they started a fight," I said dryly. "As if knocking each other about does anything to fix the state of the country."

"It might not fix it, but when a lad's hungry enough, getting his blood up puts a fire in his belly that's hard to quelch. Maybe fire's what we need to make change in this country. The gods know that pretty speeches and promises haven't done a damn thing."

"Violence only breeds more violence—you know that as well as anyone. You saw what the war did. Change doesn't come from anger and infighting. It comes from planning. From organizing, then action."

He let out a grunt of acknowledgment in his chest. "I forgot how much I hated it here. I never belonged amongst these people, always too coarse and rough for their genteel halls. Tonight, the police thought I was one of the old soldiers that stormed the lecture theater. They looked at my clothes, heard my accent, and knew at once I didn't belong. Thought I'd come with the lot of them armed with their billy clubs and knives. It took Laurent yelling at the officers to get their attention."

My breath caught in my chest. "Were you harmed?"

His fingers were still wrapped around mine, and I detected the slightest tremor in his touch. "No." The word came out little over a whisper. "I rushed Laurent out when things went awry and flagged down a cabman to take him home."

"And then you went back . . ."

He let out a low sound of agreement in his chest. *Of course he did.* This foolish man had gone back into the fray after nearly being caught up in the conflagration himself. My heart seized up. There were no thoughts. No outside world. Nothing but the warmth of his hand holding mine. The faint scent of lemon candy on the air between us, and the agonizing regret that I'd bungled everything spectacularly.

I *could* have lost him tonight. He could have been *killed* and I'd have been down here in this stupid museum chasing after ghosts I had no business following. It was unthinkable, so I quit all thinking altogether. I stretched up on my toes and kissed him, bracing myself for the rejection that was bound to follow. He let out a pained sound, but instead of pushing me away he grabbed me by the elbows, tugging me hard against his body, and kissed me back with all the regret and longing that had been bottled up between us for too long. The evening stubble on his jaw scraped against the soft skin of my own as he hefted me up onto the rickety wooden table behind me.

The sound of pottery shattering upon brick filled the silence of the chamber, going off like a gunshot. We sprang apart. Ruan looked ruefully from me to the floor. I followed his gaze down to where a broken jar lay at his feet. Bile surged up my throat.

"Damn and blast." I hopped off the table, scooping up the flashlight that somehow had fallen from my hand, and began inspecting the thousands-of-years-old antiquity. It was little more than shards and dust, thanks to my inability to control my baser instincts. I reached down, not certain whether to grab the mummified object that had fallen out or to—

"Ruby . . ."

I couldn't breathe.

Think, Ruby, think.

"This is bad. This is catastrophic. . . . This is—"

"Give me the torch, Ruby," Ruan grumbled, taking the flashlight from my hand and dropping down on the ground beside me, examining the small powder-coated object surrounded by the shards. He nudged it with the back of his finger.

Upon closer inspection, it wasn't mummified. It wasn't even remotely desiccated yet. "That's not old . . ."

Ruan then carefully lifted the object with two fingers, tilting it into the light before growing pale. A bit of the white powder rubbed off onto Ruan's fingers, revealing a fleshy gray object in the early stages of dehydration.

"That's not mummified either," I murmured half to myself.

Ruan set the object carefully back on the ground, amidst the powder that had spilled out of the shattered jar.

"That's a . . ."

"Tongue," Ruan supplied, pressing his lips together. "It does appear to be."

It looked awfully . . .

"Fresh. Also, yes." He added dryly, "Anyone you know missing one?"

Julius Harker. My mind raced. His body in a box, his tongue in a canopic jar in his very own museum. What was his killer trying to prove? Was this some sort of a ritual or was it something else entirely?

Ruan ran the light over the floor beneath us where the powdery white substance had spilled out of the shattered jar, and a new wave of guilt washed over me. Fresh tongue be damned, I dropped down to the ground, lifting the unbroken cat-shaped head. *Bastet.* I furrowed my brow. What was Bastet doing on a canopic jar? That was highly irregular. All the ones I'd seen bore the four sons of Horus upon them. I turned the carved head over in my hand. The object was strangely lighter and smoother than it ought to be for a piece of its age. I picked up another shard, holding it to the light, when I spied a French maker's mark. "It's a forgery," I murmured in stark relief. "An empire piece perhaps? But I really don't know." I pocketed the shard and stood up, dusting my hands on my skirt, leaving white smudges on the fabric.

"The pot may be a fake, but the tongue is real enough." Ruan cocked his head toward the powder surrounding the lid bearing the visage of the cat-headed goddess. "What do you suppose that is?"

I wrinkled my nose as I toed the powder carefully. "Cocaine, perhaps? That would certainly explain the movement of money in his ledger and the secrecy about it. But I'm not about to taste it to find out."

"Probably for the best, as while I'm no chemist, I doubt cocaine would have preserved human flesh this well."

My expression fell at the sudden realization in his words. "You're right . . . the tongue doesn't smell at all . . . and it certainly ought to by now." *If it belonged to Harker*, a thought I did not want to countenance. Nor did I want to question how my country pellar was familiar with the chemical properties of cocaine.

He turned to me, his expression bleaker than I'd ever seen it. "They'd put cocaine in packages for us during the war. What better way to send a fellow to his death than to put him out of his mind in the process." He dropped his West Country accent, putting on a more genteel tone. *"Happy Christmas, Kivell, do try to take out a few Germans while you're at it. That's a lad."*

I knew the war had been hard on him. Knew Oxford had been too, but this side of Ruan—this hurt and aching one—was a new version. One with wounds I'd seen on other men, but never on him. He kept his pain all tucked deep inside the man himself, but tonight—tonight he had let me in.

I couldn't think of it—couldn't think of what it meant—so I turned away, raking my hands through my hair. Not cocaine. Then what? I began to pace, racking my brain for what could be in the jar—what might slow the decomposition process—when I realized exactly what it must be. "The ancient Egyptians used natron in the mummification ritual. It's a salt compound, that likely would delay decomposition. But I cannot fathom why Harker was experimenting with the stuff. What would a man do with natron in the twentieth century?" I gently lifted the lid of a second jar and glanced inside. It too was full of the powdery whitish substance. I placed my fingers in, rubbing them together.

"It's possible," Ruan admitted.

I frowned. There was no way to know for sure without a scientist and a laboratory. Neither of which I had. One by one I checked the contents of the jars that had surrounded the chariot. Each full to the brim of the same peculiar powder. "What was Harker *doing* with all this?"

"Enough, Ruby. If we stay any longer the sun will be up."

He was right.

Of course he was. The damned man was nearly *always* correct.

But I was perplexed. What *was* that substance, and why did Harker have so much of it here in his basement?

"*Ruby,*" Ruan growled impatiently.

Right. Time to go. I glanced once more at the collection before turning and hurrying back out into the night.

Chapter Sixteen

An Ounce of Honesty Between Friends

RUAN left me outside the townhome at half past three in the morning, muttering some half-hearted excuse about checking on Professor Laurent. In truth, he likely needed distance after what almost occurred in the basement of the museum. I'd *kissed* him, but the big stubborn bastard had kissed me right back.

But that was a problem for another day. Preferably long after I'd determined who killed Julius Harker and freed poor Mr. Mueller. I stood outside the kitchen door, a warm light glowing from inside, and reached into my pocket for the skeleton key. A twig snapped behind me, and I turned, ready to chide Ruan for lurking in the shadows, but he wasn't there. No one was. But as my vision adjusted to the darkness, I made out the shape of that same great black dog, low and still at the end of the alley, watching. Its hackles raised.

Dread lodged in my throat as I stared at it.

It's your imagination, Ruby. Just your imagination. The key trembled in the lock. I turned it and hurried inside, shutting out the beast *and* my overactive imagination.

Fiachna popped his head up from where he'd been napping on the table holding vigil for me. He meowed loudly, stretching each front paw before hopping down and trotting up the nearby stairwell, his fluffy black tail shaped like a question mark as he disappeared into the darkness, fully expecting me to follow.

After what I had found tonight, I certainly wasn't going to get any sleep. Though perhaps I could make sense of the discoveries found in the museum. I would write to my friend Howard Carter. He might still be in Egypt excavating his new discovery in the Valley of the Kings, but if anyone would have an idea about the Napoleonic cache and why Julius Harker would have natron in his basement, it would be Mr. Carter. And as he was currently thousands of miles away, I could be fairly certain that he was not involved in any of it.

I walked over to the hall table and pulled out a fresh sheet of paper, sat down, and began writing.

Dear Mr. Carter, we have a bit of a predicament here in Oxford . . .

"Morning, maid."

Neck stiff, I lifted my head, blinking in the dimly lit kitchen. Mrs. Penrose stood before me with a bemused smile, head tilted to the side to better see me.

Good God, was anything more mortifying than falling asleep at one's work and being caught by one's housekeeper? I yawned beneath my fist, smoothing the page of Mr. Mueller's account book that had served as my pillow. "What time is it?"

"Half past six, why do you ask?" she asked, setting a kettle on the hob.

"Damn and blast." I shot to my feet, glancing down at yesterday's attire still dusty from the basement of Harker's Curiosity Museum. The white handprint of powder still smeared on my skirt.

"What is it? What's the matter?"

I snatched up the letter I'd hastily written to Howard Carter and tucked it into the capacious pocket of my skirt along with my small notebook where I'd been jotting down my observations. "I'm late.

I must meet Leona at the Artemis Club at seven and . . ." I raked a hand through my hair, struggling to settle the unruly curls without aid of a mirror or a comb.

Mrs. Penrose handed me my cloche, which I stuffed onto my head.

I murmured my thanks, turning around to take my long coat from her outstretched hands.

"Well, then you'd best be off, my lover, hadn't you?"

I smiled at Mrs. Penrose, grabbing a saffron bun from the bowl beside her, and placed a kiss on her cheek. "You are a goddess, Mrs. Penrose. Never forget that."

She let out a hearty laugh and shooed me out of the kitchen.

I was going to be late. But Leona had known me long enough to know I seldom made my appointments on time, getting waylaid by my own distractibility even at the best of times, and goodness knew these were anything but those.

AFTER DROPPING MY hastily penned letter in the post, I trotted back to the Artemis Club. The city was slowly coming to life despite the early hour. The cold morning air stung my lungs, but it did not bother me—not when I had the most peculiar sense of clarity. For the first time since I foolishly agreed to help Leona, I had assembled a tidy set of clues. Julius Harker was likely dealing in fakes and was quietly reassembling this mysterious Napoleonic cache. He *also* had a great deal of natron in his basement—for what purpose, I could not yet ascertain. And somehow—some *way*—Leona was tied to it all. Her betrayal yesterday still rankled. The woman had asked me to help her and then was hiding something from me.

I pulled open the heavy carved door to the Artemis Club, the sweet winter-flower scent flooding my senses as I stepped inside. The dim glimmer of pre-dawn light dripped in through the windows of the main entrance. The young woman at the desk glanced up from her book and flashed me a bright smile.

"Miss Vaughn!" She wore the charming violet-and-black-striped uniform of the Artemis Club. Her expression faltered as she took in my disheveled appearance, but she recovered admirably. "Miss Abernathy is already in the tearoom. She said you would be coming. I put her in the usual spot. Shall I have the morning paper sent in?"

I started to shake my head but thought better of it. Considering the violence last night at the University, perhaps it would be good to see what had truly occurred. Ruan's account was tinged with an uncomfortable bitterness, and it was best to take in other sources to get a sense of things. "Yes. Please do."

"Of course, miss."

My shoes were silent on the plush carpet as I hurried down the corridor lined with floor-to-ceiling windows overlooking the gymnasium on the left and the walled garden on my right.

At least she'd decided to meet me—it was a start.

The tearoom was little more than an old solarium turned into a dining space. The walls and ceilings were made from great rectangular panes of glass with potted ferns and vining plants dripping from their great hanging pots. Blooming orchids, lush peonies, and scented climbing roses warred with the vines for sunlight. All carefully tended and cultivated. I adored it here—and breakfast in the tearoom was the other reason I came here most days since I'd been in Oxford.

Leona sat at our usual table alongside the raised fishpond full of turtles and koi, quietly stirring her cup of tea. "I do not like being threatened."

I wrapped my fingers around the back of the chair across from her. "And I don't like being lied to. We're evenly matched."

Leona took a pointed sip of her tea, her eyes downcast. "It was for your own good."

Half irritated, half relieved that she didn't deny her subterfuge,

I sank into the violet velvet cushioned chair across from her. "What is or isn't good for me is mine to decide"—I pointed to my chest—"not yours. Who was that man at your house yesterday, and why were you not at the museum?"

"I cannot say."

My pulse thrummed in my temple. "Cannot or will not?"

She sighed. "Ruby, there are things happening in Oxford right now that are dangerous for you to know about. Trust me when I say that, if this was pertinent, I would share it with you. But that person yesterday—he has no bearing on Mr. Mueller's arrest, or Julius Harker's death."

A young server came, laid out a fresh place setting before me alongside the morning paper, and poured me a cup of white tea. I held my tongue until she was out of earshot again and dropped two cubes of sugar into the cup, stirring it slowly. "How can you be certain it has no bearing?"

She wet her lips, gaze drifting to the fishpond beside me, and shook her head. "I just am. What did you come to talk to me about yesterday? Did you learn something to help clear Mr. Mueller's name?"

I stared at Leona, not at all recognizing my old friend. Oh, physically she was exactly as she'd always been. But there was a newfound wariness lurking behind her eyes—a shrewdness that I'd not noticed before. "Nothing at all. Tell me, Leona. What was Julius Harker working on before he died? I've come to understand that you were close to him."

She sniffed, as irritated with me as I with her. "It wasn't like that with him—"

I took a sip of the rapidly cooling tea, keeping my voice carefully low. "Then how was it? What am I to think when you are hiding information from *me* and all the while you are also hiding your relationship with that man from Professor Reaver? The two of them hated one another—"

"That's not true!" she snapped. "Spit it out, Ruby. I can see you are frustrated with me, and I don't blame you for it, but there are some things you cannot know. For your own safety."

Frustrated was an understatement, and yet my stubborn heart refused to abandon her in this endeavor. She had been my friend—and even if she was making it terribly difficult to trust her, I could not leave her alone to save poor Mr. Mueller. I struggled to keep my voice down. "Then tell me what you can. What was Julius Harker involved in? Mr. Mueller wondered if he might have had business dealings with his killer. He seemed to think that Harker was soon to come into a great deal of money. Enough to end their troubles forever. Mueller believed that Harker meant to sell something. Do you have any idea what it could be?"

A flurry of emotion crossed Leona's face before a sickening realization settled upon her. "Oh no . . ." Her bare fingers went to her lips in disbelief. "No . . . surely he wouldn't have done something reckless . . ."

I reached across the table and touched her forearm. "What has Harker done? What do you suspect?"

"I don't know . . . not for certain. But I do wonder . . ."

Her hand fell limp to the table. I took it in my own, giving it a reassuring squeeze.

Leona pressed her lips into a thin line, glancing around the empty breakfast room. "There are some very powerful people in Oxfordshire. Ones that Julius had crossed in the past . . ." She wet her lips again, looking back over her shoulder before turning her attention to me. "They've been involved in . . . less than legal ventures . . ."

I furrowed my brow, not quite comprehending. "Less than legal . . ."

"*Drugs*, Ruby. I'm speaking of drugs. Cocaine. Heroin. Hashish." The impatience in her voice paled in comparison to the prick of fear rising at the back of my neck. She squeezed my fingers tight.

"Julius had threatened to intercept a shipment of cocaine from one of these people. I frankly thought him mad for even considering it and told him the same. How could he do something so . . . utterly foolish, and for what end? It would risk everything he'd worked so hard to rebuild. I told him I wanted no part in that, and he assured me he would not, that it had been a foolish idea spoken of in the heat of the moment—"

"And now you think he might have done it after all . . ." My mind raced back to the urns of powder in the basement of Harker's museum.

"I do. It's the only thing that would give him that sort of money. Julius was in such terrible debt. It was only a matter of time before he lost the museum to his creditors. Can you speak with Mr. Mueller again—see if he has any idea if Julius actually *did* manage to steal the shipment?"

"Do you know *whose* shipment it was? Who it is he had in his sights?"

She shook her head. "Julius was careful not to share more than was absolutely necessary with me. He said it was dangerous enough to be associated with him. I thought . . ." Her voice cracked as her eyes grew glassy. There was no pretense here, not anymore. "I thought he meant to my professional reputation, but now I realize that he meant a great deal more than that. Oh, Julius, how could you have done something so *stupid*?"

If Julius Harker had stolen a shipment of cocaine, that would be motivation enough for murder, but I was almost certain the substance I'd found in his basement wasn't cocaine.

The clock struck eight and Leona leapt to her feet, knocking over her tea, spilling it on the tabletop. "Oh Ruby, I have to go. I am sorry. I just realized the time. I promised Reaver I'd be in early and now I'm already late."

Whatever openness she'd shared moments before had fled with each toll of the chime. We said our goodbyes and I hastily mopped up the tea with my napkin. The soggy pages of the morning paper were little more than pulp now, muddled together into a congealed mess. I paid the bill for both of us and left several pounds behind, by way of apology for the state of the table, and then took my leave of the club.

I wasn't sure what to make of Leona's sudden change in mood. It could easily be ascribed to the fact that she'd learned that Julius Harker was not only an antiquarian, but he was *also* a thief—that would certainly affect a girl's attitude. But at least we had an ounce of truth between us. It was certainly more than we'd had when I started out this morning.

Chapter Seventeen

A Great Aching Head

A cold droplet of dew fell from the eaves of the Artemis Club, hit the exposed portion of my neck, and slithered down the back of my blouse. Lovely. Just lovely.

I chose a different path home than normal, a twisting and scenic route, to clear my head and order my thoughts. Periodically, I'd pause to regain my bearings and be certain I hadn't gotten lost. I was perhaps halfway back when I stopped outside a cobbler's shop to adjust my own shoe, which had come unlaced. I'd not even *thought* consciously of where I was, but as I looked across the street, the realization sank in. For there, lying sleepily before me, was Julius Harker's Curiosity Museum. Windows darkened. Waiting in the early morning light for someone to stop by.

Hadn't I already learned my lesson?

The iron gate to the alley beside the building gaped open. I must have forgotten to shut it. Surely no harm would come from me checking to see if the back door was locked. And if it wasn't . . . then I could simply slip back down to the basement and continue examining the canopic jars. If Leona believed that Julius had been trying to intercept a shipment of drugs, could he have hidden it amongst natron in his very own museum? After all, an Egyptologist could plausibly have natron with no one batting an eye, and to the naked eye the two substances resembled one another well enough. I, for one, had certainly confused the two last night.

Ruby Vaughn, you reckless creature.

Ignoring the warning voice in my head, I darted across the street as the rain began to fall and disappeared into the space between the two buildings.

The door was open.

Open?

My heart thundered in my chest. Surely not. We'd closed it last night—of that, I was certain. But before my mind could catch up with what my eyes beheld, something hard came across my throat and I tumbled backward.

The scent of liquor and stale sweat flooded my senses. A broad-chested man hauled me against his body, burly forearm cutting off my air. He wore a balaclava covering his nose and face and I could not make him out. He was of a height with me and a great deal wider.

I clawed at the fabric of his nondescript brown jacket, the sleeve abrading the delicate skin of my throat. I slipped on the wet stones, thrashing my hip toward him, reaching for something vulnerable. An eye. A nose. An ear. Anything at all. My eyes watered from lack of air.

"You need to stop putting your nose where it doesn't belong, you little bitch." His spittle hit the side of my face. His voice was familiar, and yet in my panic I could not place it. At long last my elbow caught his rib cage, jabbing hard. He let out a pained grunt as my hip made contact with his male bits. He stumbled backward a few steps, slackening his grip on me. I started to run, but he caught me by my rain-damped skirt, ripping the fabric and pulling me toward him. He threw his arm back around my throat, squeezing tight. Dark spots appeared before my eyes like unholy stars.

This was bad.

Very bad.

"Fucking bitch," he gritted out in my ear, before slamming my head against the wall—the sound of bone on stone echoing in my ears. A splitting pain erupted at my temple and the world around me fell to black.

A SEARING ACHE shot through my temple as I opened my eyes, staring up at an unfamiliar ceiling. I turned my head, shifting on the hard wooden bench where I'd been tenderly laid out. I wasn't dead.

That was good, I supposed.

I reached up, hand latching onto a rolled-up woolen uniform coat smelling of salt and tobacco. It had been wedged beneath my neck as a makeshift pillow. An itchy woolen blanket had been laid over the top of me.

The police station.

Of course!

But how the devil did I get here? Shivering, I sat up, rubbing my arms over my still-wet shirtsleeves. I spied my jacket lying over a radiator to dry, with my soiled shoes sitting beside it.

I lifted my hand to the searing spot on my temple and drew my fingers away, sticky with dark, clotting blood.

"Morning, Miss Vaughn," Jack, the young constable, said. His expression sunny and bright as he came around the hinged counter toward me. There was a catlike air to him, graceful and quick, and I found myself liking him a great deal—especially as he'd risked his own neck allowing me to speak with Mr. Mueller earlier this week.

I blinked. "You know my name?"

He grinned, tapping the folded newspaper on the desk. "I *can* read."

Heat flushed to my cheeks. Of course he did.

If he was aggrieved by my lies, he did not let on. "Inspector Beecham found you, called to have you brought here. Said a shopkeeper phoned in with reports of a woman who'd been murdered and left outside Harker's Curiosity Museum." His gaze drifted down to my ripped skirt. "It was a lucky stroke I had phoned for a physician a few moments before you arrived. He should be here and can make certain you're all right. I hope it's not too uncomfortable on the bench, it was better than the cells at any rate." A dark flicker of worry ran across his expression as he looked at my soiled clothes.

I winced, shaking my head. "No. I'm fine. Just a little banged up is all. I hope you didn't get into too much trouble with the inspector after allowing me down to the cells. I . . . I am sorry I lied to you."

He gave me a lopsided smile. "Ah, I've had worse. Besides I'm sure Old Mueller needed some company. It gets lonely down there and he was always a nice old man." A strange expression crossed his face at mention of Mr. Mueller but he gave his head a slight shake. "I'm glad you're not too badly hurt. I was worried when you wouldn't wake."

"How long have I . . . ah . . . been here?"

He rubbed his jaw. "Not long. A half hour at most. You do know you talk in your sleep?"

I blinked at him. "I hope I didn't say anything too embarrassing." *Or incriminating, as I'd broken any number of laws lately.*

He let out a laugh. "Nah. You kept saying how sorry you were. But when you stopped—"

There were voices from behind the closed door leading to the cells. Shouting and quite the commotion. "What's that about?" I tilted my head toward the door, changing the subject from my peculiar sleeping habits and whatever it was I might have been apologizing *for* in my dreams.

"There was a bit of trouble last night at the University. We're about full to bursting, miss. Veterans, most of them. A few laborers. There's been unrest all over the country in the last few years. It was only a matter of time before it finally boiled over here in town." I noticed a faint purple blush of a bruise raising on his cheekbone. "Inspector Beecham keeps saying it wasn't a riot, but it's the closest I've ever seen to one."

Ruan had downplayed what occurred, but it must have been truly terrifying. I shifted on the bench, wrapping the blanket more tightly around me as the old radiator popped and hissed. "You said the inspector found me by the museum?"

Faint lines appeared at the edges of his mouth. "He did. He telephoned from the cobbler's shop to have you brought here and be sure you were well enough, so I did."

"Thank you, Jack."

He gave me a half-hearted smile. "It's the least I could do. I tried to clean your—" He gestured with two fingers to his temple. "I also took the liberty to be sure you weren't bleeding anywhere else. I'm sorry, miss. I'd have asked your permission if you were awake."

I smiled at him—it was difficult to be angry at such a sweet boy. "I appreciate it. Truly I do. Is Inspector Beecham still here?"

Jack cleared his throat. "Ah. No, miss. Well, he *is*, but he's been in the cells since he returned. As you can hear, there's been a bit of trouble with a couple of the rioters."

The commotion from behind the door grew louder. I raised a brow, wincing at the pull in the muscle on my temple. "Is everything all right down there?"

Jack weighed his words and opened his mouth to answer when the front door swung open and Ruan stormed into the station. As soon as he spotted me, his expression softened. Relief surged through his body as he took me in, from my bloody brow to my torn skirt.

I raised my fingers to the wound self-consciously and swallowed hard. I'd forgotten how intense it was to be the focus of his full attention.

"I'll see to it," he murmured, coming to my side and brushing my hand away with his own before tilting my head to get a better look.

"I'm fine. Perfectly fine."

"I am the judge of that." An irritated muscle jumped in his jaw as he continued to probe with his rough fingers.

I'm all right. But we should talk.

He gave me a curt nod, barely perceptible to anyone but me. He'd heard me. *Good.* I needed him to. What use was this peculiar ability if we couldn't take advantage of it at times like this?

"You must be the physician the clinic was sending over," Jack said, looking between the two of us. A sudden dawning of recognition then flashed in his eyes. "Wait, aren't you the fellow I saw at the University last night?"

Ruan stilled, his fingers gently resting beneath my chin.

The young man examined Ruan with peculiar intensity as raw panic took hold. He recognized Ruan. . . . What exactly *had* happened last night? "You are," Jack continued, sounding far more sure than before. "You're the one who helped Professor Laurent leave before you came back to tend to the wounded. I wondered why anyone in their right mind would come back into the fray . . . but it certainly makes more sense now."

Ruan exhaled softly, as anxious about the young constable's recollections as I.

Jack glanced over his shoulder to the door to the cells. "Once you've made certain that she's well, I would appreciate if you could join me downstairs. It was the reason I phoned over to the clinic. As I said to your colleague over there, some of the fellows from last night were brought in. As you can imagine, they've been giving us hell—pardon my language, miss."

Ruan opened his mouth to protest, but I was faster. "Oh, I'm perfectly fine, Doctor. You go help the authorities. I need a moment to gather myself after my recent ordeal." I held him with a meaningful gaze.

Ruan's expression went from mutinous to murderous.

"What is the problem down there anyway?" I asked before Ruan's damnable integrity could give us both away.

Jack frowned, folding his arms. "There's been an accident with one of the prisoners."

Something in the simple statement struck Ruan, I could see it in the subtle shifting of his expression and the stillness that came over him. Whether it was my desperation for him to go to the cells or if he could sense what was going on below, I couldn't tell.

"What's happened?" Ruan said softly, leaving my side and heading toward the long police desk. His dear West Country accent smoothed to the point I scarcely recognized his voice.

"One of the rioters got loose this morning and somehow got in with another prisoner. The inspector has been down there for a while now trying to keep the peace, but it might do some good to have a physician there to see if there's anything that can be done for the poor fellow who's been attacked."

That didn't sound good. Not good at all. The constable wiped a bit of sweat that had beaded at his brow. "I must warn you, the inspector . . . he can be . . . *stern*. He likely won't appreciate my calling you in—but it was only right, considering. I hope you don't take offense if he says anything unpleasant."

Now *that* was an understatement. Inspector Beecham was an utter nightmare. I sat on the bench watching as the two men disappeared through the heavy door to the stairway that led to the cells below. Leaving me and my slowly weeping wound utterly alone in the police station.

I shot to my unsteady feet, bracing myself on the arm of the wooden bench before hurrying to the police desk and lifting the counter as I'd watched Jack do earlier. I had a minute, perhaps two at most, before someone returned. Not that I even knew what I was hunting, but surely there were records somewhere pertaining to Harker's death. Perhaps a coroner's report? Something to illuminate why the police remained convinced Mr. Mueller was guilty. I made quick work of the desk, which had nothing of import other than what appeared to be a dried-out half-eaten cheese scone and the morning paper. It seemed that Harker and my own appearance in Oxford continued to dominate the news, sharing the front page with the rioters. Both articles written by the same person. V. E. Devereaux. I blew out an aggrieved breath, skimming the headlines.

MUMMY CURSE!

DEATH AND DISHONOR!

Good grief. Perhaps it was best that the tea destroyed my copy. I left the papers behind and moved to the inspector's office in hopes of finding something more enlightening. A half-empty cup of tea rested precariously atop a towering stack of papers on the desk. I took a sniff.

Not tea.

Whisky. My stomach knotted. I moved on, carefully scanning through the files on the surface. Nothing. How could they be holding Mr. Mueller in the cells below without even a hint of an investigation going on above? One would at least expect an autopsy of Harker or *something* useful lying about.

A haphazard vertical wooden filing system sat behind the desk. Some documents were kept in folders, others crammed into envelopes, and others still lying loose between things. Fiachna kept his playthings tidier than this office. I huffed out a breath in annoyance. Heart pounding in my ears, I began sorting through the papers, fingers flying over the pages.

It was foolish to think I would find something in this short amount of time—but I would never have a better opportunity. Distant voices came from behind the door, growing closer by the second as I spotted the typeset words *Harker, Julius* on a folder label. Without a thought or even checking to see what the file contained, I lifted it and tucked it into the waistband of my torn skirt, then hurried back to the bench.

I sank down on the hard wooden surface, wrapping the blanket around me seconds before Ruan stepped through the doorway. His stern expression was unreadable, but I caught the traces of silver fleeing from his pale green eyes. *Something happened down there.*

What is it?

He ran his hand over his jaw and shook his head. Jack followed him through the door, his face equally grim. Out of habit, I reached for the pocket of my skirt where I'd kept my own notes.

Empty.

I touched the other one, as casually as possible. *Also* empty.

Good God. All of my notes inventorying what I'd discovered in Harker's storeroom, the meticulous transaction details that Mrs. Penrose had found. All of it was gone.

"Terrible business." Inspector Beecham's voice boomed from deeper in the stairwell. His heavy boots echoed against the walls. "Would you mind making sure this one gets home without further incident, Doctor?"

Ruan made a sound of agreement low in his chest. "I'll see to it and be sure she doesn't find herself in any more mischief."

My nostrils flared. *Mischief?*

"Be sure she doesn't. We've enough trouble for one day."

For once, Inspector Beecham and I were in complete agreement.

Chapter Eighteen

A Sweet Distraction

ONCE the door to the police station closed behind us, Ruan's feigned professional concern for my well-being returned to his usual quiet determination. Hand on my elbow, he tugged me down the alley and back onto the bustling High Street. The sidewalks were packed with shoppers running last-minute errands to the butcher or the toy store. A workman walked down the street whistling a merry song. All the discordant sounds and scents made my headache all the worse.

I struggled to keep up with his long strides, panting. "Could you slow down for a moment and tell me what happened in the cells?"

Ruan came to a dead stop, and I almost ran into his back. He shushed me, his variegated gaze drifting over my shoulder to the street behind.

My jaw dropped. How dare he *shush* me? Of all the— But before I could finish the thought, he took me again by the elbow and pulled me into the lee of a nearby shop festooned in garland and red ribbon. "You could have been killed back there, and the very first words out of your lips are about what *I* discovered?"

"In case you didn't notice, I'm not dead and we still have a murder to solve," I replied hotly.

He muttered to himself in Cornish before looking up at the sky in what I distinctly sensed was a plea for his old gods to save him from stubborn American heiresses. "If you must know immediately, without concern for either of our safety, then Mr. Mueller is dead."

Dead? Of all the things he could have uttered, that was the last I expected. The wind whipped through the wide street.

This was bad. *Very* bad. "Natural or otherwise?"

Ruan sighed, turned, and continued to bustle me toward the corner of Cornmarket, letting out a low dark sound of amusement. "Someone cracks your head, and you ask me if the dead man in the prison cell that very same morning died of natural causes? Truly, Ruby, I am beginning to grow concerned that perhaps you are not as well as you claim."

Point taken. I folded my arms mutinously. "I was simply making certain."

"I know . . ." His expression flickered, and he wrapped his fingers painfully tight around my upper arm.

What had possessed him? Ruan didn't speak, instead he dragged me across the street and into an inviting candy shop with its brightly painted front window frames.

"Good God, Ruan, what has gotten into you? I am not a rag doll to be dragged about on your whims!" The bell rang merrily as we entered the warm storefront. I tugged my arm from him, tired of being trundled around.

"There was a woman." He leaned close to me, murmuring in my ear low enough so only I could hear. The air inside the candy shop was sweet and reminded me I'd only eaten a solitary saffron bun today—and that had been hours ago.

"Looks like I'm not the only one seeing things and jumping at shadows." I rubbed the sore spot on my arm before glancing out the window.

Ruan did not rise to the bait, keeping his focus trained on the street outside between the high-stacked jars of sweets. To all the world he appeared like a man struggling to decide between the ginger and the horehound candies. The light coming in through the multicolored jars refracting like water droplets in the sun.

"Do you see her? The woman in the gray hat." He inclined his head to a figure waiting across the street, not far from where we'd been arguing moments before. A slight woman with flaxen hair, combed and pulled back, stood waiting. Watching.

I shifted to get a better look at her, inadvertently poking my belly with the stolen file. I'd nearly forgotten I'd taken it in our haste to leave the police station. I craned my neck, peering between the lemon drops and anise. "I don't recognize her." And she certainly wasn't the one who attacked me. This woman was several inches shorter and far slighter than I, wearing an oversized dark coat, looking more like a child playing dress-up than any true threat. Had Ruan not trundled me off into the sweetshop I might not have noticed her at all. But he was right. She was waiting for someone.

A coincidence. Just a random woman waiting for a friend.

Ruan shook his head, overhearing my thoughts. "No. It's not. I saw her outside the police station when I entered. And again, now on High Street. She's following us, and she's not very good at it."

My stomach tightened at the thought. Minutes ticked on as my mind raced with ever growing panic. *I'm being followed. I've been attacked. Mr. Mueller murdered.* And yet I was no closer to finding Julius Harker's killer than I had been at the start.

At long last, Ruan cleared his throat and gestured to a glass canister. "Ginger and lemon?"

"Are you asking me to buy you candy or fixing my tea?" I grumbled, glancing up at him.

The familiar divot of worry between his dark brows had eased, and his chest trembled with amusement. I peered between the canisters and understood at once his immediate change of mood. The woman—whoever she was—had given up on us and left. "Which do you prefer?" he asked gently.

"I . . . whichever you want."

Ruan took a wax-paper bag from the counter and lifted a silver scoop. "I haven't been in here in years. . . . Ernst and I would stop in after class on our way back home. We'd take turns buying sweets, even though the gods know I couldn't afford it—but I was too bloody proud to let him buy mine."

I gave him a faint smile. "He sounds like he was a lovely person."

"He was. I hadn't thought about it in years. Not until we came into the shop. Ernst and I would always get a mixed bag. Half lemon, half ginger. I never cared for lemon myself, the flavor too sharp and biting." Ruan's voice took on a wistful tone. "Yet for years after he died, whenever I'd come across a candy shop I'd find myself buying the lemon only."

I watched him spellbound as he was lost to his own memories, my own heart breaking with his words. I knew so little about him truly. Only the glimpses he'd shared, and I wanted—*needed*—to know more.

"It seemed terribly unfair back then, that of the two of us, he would be gone and I'd remain. Somehow having the lemon . . . it kept him near. It's absurd, I know."

It wasn't absurd at all. I reached out for him, half expecting that he would shake me away as he had every other time I'd touched him, but instead he turned his palm over, closing my fingers within his, and squeezed. "What's yours?"

Confused, I gave my head a small shake as a child bumped into me from behind. "My what?"

"Favorite flavor."

"Would you believe I don't think I have one? I . . ." I couldn't think. Couldn't answer. Favorite sweets were the sort of thing people who cared for one another knew. Favorite colors, names of siblings, the way one takes their tea. That I adore my baths. That Ruan preferred ginger sweets but still purchased lemon ones to remember a long dead friend. My aching head spun. It was a devastatingly human sort of detail that I was not at all prepared for, certainly not while we were chasing a murderer.

I heard him laugh softly behind me as he let go of me and laid his left hand on the small of my back, stilling my mind as that strange coolness rushed through my veins. "It's only penny sweets, Ruby. Nothing more. Besides. I already knew you prefer ginger."

I stared at him dumbfounded. Of course I did, but the fact that he also knew that was far more dangerous than anything else I was facing in Oxford.

Chapter Nineteen

That's the Trouble with Murder

WE made it back to the townhome without spotting the woman again, and yet I could not shake the sensation that it was not the last time we would see her. Ruan pulled the sack of sweets from his pocket and placed them gently on the table next to some cut hellebore that Mrs. Penrose must have picked up on her own at the market today. Untucking my blouse, I withdrew the stolen file from my waistband and laid it on the tabletop.

"You will be the death of me, Ruby Vaughn. I swear it." His nimble fingers began unfastening the cuffs of his shirt and he rolled his sleeves up before washing his hands in the sink. He turned back to me, gesturing for me to sit.

Puzzled, I sank down onto the kitchen chair. "What are you . . ."

He took my chin in his fingers and tilted my head into the light, examining my wound. "Turn your head to the left."

I did. "Ruan, I don't understand—"

"Now right."

I sighed and complied.

"And up?"

I let out a pained groan. "Please stop coddling me."

Ruan placed his hands on his hips and raised his brows. "The blow to your head certainly isn't affecting your stubbornness."

"I'm not stubborn . . ." I grumbled. "I am *fine* as I told you. Besides, I don't have time to *not* be fine. Mr. Mueller is *dead*, and we are still no closer to finding out who the killer is. That's *two* bodies now instead of one."

He ran his thumb tenderly along my cheekbone, before turning away to fill a kettle and set it on to heat. Either he agreed with my assessment that I was perfectly well, or he had simply grown tired of arguing the point.

"How did you know I was at the police station? Was it your—" I gestured at the center of his chest, still having trouble voicing the peculiar connection between us.

"No . . . oddly enough it wasn't." A pained expression crossed his face. "But there is something I need to tell you about this morning."

I didn't like the sound of that.

Ruan folded his arms, drumming his fingers on his forearms. "I went back to Harker's museum after I left Laurent's house. I started home, but could not recall if we'd locked the door to the museum when we left. I dropped by to make certain. It was probably four or five o'clock in the morning."

I furrowed my brow. "The door was open though . . ."

He nodded grimly. "I know. It was when I arrived as well. Someone had pried it open. The wood was damaged. I decided to go inside and see if anything was taken."

"Ruan, that was incredibly—"

"Reckless?" He cocked an eyebrow. "I recognize that. Especially in light of . . ." He gestured at my brow.

The kettle began to whistle, and Ruan took it from the range.

"Was anything taken?"

He poured the water into the nearby teapot. "All of the jars.

Plus several crates near where we were standing. They also took the tongue."

"It had been lying on the floor—why cut someone's tongue out to begin with? I suppose if the jars were stolen, then this gives credence to Leona's theory of cocaine."

Ruan's brows raised as I explained what Leona had shared this morning. How Julius Harker had thoughts of intercepting a shipment of drugs from some mysterious figure and my suspicion that he was disguising it amongst a supply of natron. The alternative would be too grim to countenance—if he were planning on lacing the cocaine with natron, he would likely be signing many a death warrant. I shivered at the thought. Suddenly something else struck me. "Ruan . . . how *did* you know where to find me?"

He hesitated, taking a step back. "After I left the museum, I came here to tell you what I discovered. When I arrived, Owen told me you'd already left for the Artemis Club." He closed his eyes with a sigh. "When I got *there*, they said that you'd headed home over an hour before. As I'd already come straight from there, I returned to the museum, thinking you'd likely had the same notion as I had. It was about nine o'clock or so when I arrived, and a local shopkeeper told me a woman had been recently attacked and her body taken to the police station. She thought you were *dead*, Ruby . . ." He raked his hand through his hair. "*I* thought you were dead. I did not hear you and yet a part of me . . . a part of me knew you could not be."

"Well, you were right. I'm very alive. Sore. But here."

Something flickered in his expression. He meant to say something more, but instead checked his watch with a frown. "I don't want to leave you like this." He gestured at my head. "But I promised Laurent I'd join him for lunch in an hour. I could send word to him—"

"It's fine, Ruan." I held up my palm in pantomime of an oath. "I promise I will not risk my neck again today so you can eat at least *one* meal in peace. Besides, I have a stack of papers to go through, and I don't need you hovering."

He smiled at that, his green eyes softening. He lifted his palm to touch my cheek, but then closed his hand tight. "If you're certain . . ."

"Very. Just look at all this!" I spread the police file out across the rough wooden work surface, annoyed at having lost my notes along with Mrs. Penrose's careful accounting from Harker's museum transactions. It would take hours to replicate what was lost. Hours we did not have. And worse yet, it was very likely that the killer had it in his possession at this very moment. All my wonderings, thoughts, every name and scrap of information I'd collected like a crime-solving magpie were now in the hands of the very person I was after. "Oh God . . . what have I done? Why did I even take it with me to meet Leona?"

Ruan sat the teapot on the table between us, a soft herbal scent drifting from the spout and filling the kitchen. "Do you think your friend is in danger because of your notebook?"

"I don't know. She has her secrets—I grant you that—but she was afraid this morning. She is the one who told me of the cocaine, I hadn't brought up anything we'd found at the museum—only relayed what poor dead Mr. Mueller had told me. She assured me that her mysterious visitor was unconnected to Harker's death, but I don't know what to believe. There was a man with her, I heard *voices*. Why would she hide that from me?"

"Do you think it was the man she works for, that Reaver fellow?"

I bit my lower lip, shaking my head. "It didn't sound like him. I don't know *who* it could be. And maybe it's nothing? Perhaps she simply has a . . . friend."

Ruan leaned back against the sink, drumming his fingers on his forearms. "That's the trouble with murder. Nothing is ever simple. It's never *nothing*. There's always something more hiding beneath the surface."

"Ruan Kivell, you're starting to sound like me . . . and I cannot decide how to feel about this." My expression fell at once. "How *did* Mueller die exactly? Before you arrived, Jack said that one of the rioters broke loose."

"Jack?"

I leaned back in my chair, waving my hand airily. "The young constable who took you to the cells—he's a very sweet boy."

Ruan took a sip of the herbal tea. "As far as I can tell it was strangulation. There was bruising on his neck, and signs of a struggle. Scratches. Cuts along his hands. He'd likely been trying to fight off his attacker."

How horrible. "Do you think it was as the police said? An altercation with one of the rioters?"

"How would another prisoner get access to his cell? Besides, the rioters are more interested in fair pay and feeding their families than they are murdering a middle-aged bookkeeper."

"Do you think whoever attacked me is the same person who killed him?"

"Perhaps, though from what I can tell Mueller had been dead for hours. I don't know why the constable even bothered calling for a physician at all, unless it was to have a witness verify that Mueller was in fact dead."

Fiachna trotted into the kitchen from the sitting room and padded over to my leg, rubbing himself on it before hopping up onto the tabletop to press his feline head against my cheek with a loud purr. "And they didn't notice? I realize that I can be overly critical of the police at times but this . . . this is suspicious. Arresting Mr. Mueller without cause, then to let him die in his cell and leave his body for *hours*." My pulse throbbed in my wounded temple and I squeezed my eyes shut to blot out the sensation. "The constable behaved . . . strangely when discussing the inspector."

Ruan made a low sound in his chest. "The inspector was none too pleased to see me either. I have to say, I don't like any of this."

Nor do I.

I picked up the wax-paper bag of penny candy and took a ginger sweet, plopping it in my mouth. It clacked in my teeth. "You should go..."

Ruan cast a long glance to the papers spread out before me. "Are you certain you don't want my help? Professor Laurent is perfectly able to survive a meal without me."

I did want his help. But I also saw the pain in his eyes every time he spoke of Ernst. Spending more time with his friend's father would ease that ache a little. If I cared for him—and I did—I could give him that much.

Chapter Twenty

Other People's Secrets

I looked back at the file I'd stolen from the police station with a frustrated grunt. My tea had long grown cold, and even Mrs. Penrose was giving me wide berth. Fingers tangled in my dark curls, I continued shuffling through the papers of the stolen folio.

Honestly, Ruby. Who steals from the police?

Taking it had been a terrible mistake—worse—a *useless* mistake. I kept double-checking the dates on the documents in case I'd misread them the first hundred times I'd looked. Transposed a number. *Something*. But no. While the file *was* for Julius Harker, it was regarding an investigation that had taken place a decade ago. Long enough that the pages had yellowed. I scanned the typed reports, scarcely believing what I'd found. While it might not be useful, at least it was interesting.

"I'll be damned . . ." I muttered into the rim of my cup. If there was any doubt that Julius Harker was capable of thievery, it was put to rest now. The man had been a thief for decades.

Fiachna nudged my hand aggressively and I sat down my cup and stroked his ears. "Would you believe that the man stole a *book*?"

He purred in response, evidently unsurprised at the turn of events. Then again, neither was I, but somehow seeing it in print made it all the more real. According to the police records, roughly a decade ago Julius Harker had brazenly stolen a four-hundred-year-old manuscript from the Bodleian Library.

"Well, that certainly explains why he got thrown out on his ear, hmm, Fiachna?"

He meowed in agreement, rubbing against me. The deep rumble of his purr eased my nerves a bit. Perhaps stealing the file wasn't in vain after all. For while it didn't answer my questions about Julius Harker in the present, it certainly painted a clearer picture of the man in the past. It also told me why he'd been cast out of the University.

"You talking to me, my lover?" Mrs. Penrose asked, coming into the room with a handful of the post.

"No . . . simply trying to understand *who* Julius Harker truly was." I pulled out a sheet of paper and my pencil and began hastily dashing out notes to myself.

Mrs. Penrose gave me a look that said she had an opinion on the matter, one she did not voice. Instead, she sat a plate of biscuits down beside me and left me to my work. I began hastily copying down the names of Harker's associates who had been questioned during the previous investigation and, oddly enough, once again Mr. Owen's antiquarian friend Lord Amberley was included in that number. I underlined his name twice. Pencil tapping on the line.

This was the second time that Lord Amberley had come up in connection with Julius Harker. First, with Reaver's tale of how Harker had identified Amberley's marbles as forgeries, and now this. It was curious that he would have crossed paths twice with Harker, but collectors were curious people and the world of antiquities is a small one.

My mouth grew dry as another thought came to mind: Why would someone pull this file *now* of all times unless they believed that the root cause of Harker's death lay in the past—not the present?

"Off with you, you wee beastie." Mr. Owen gently urged Fiachna to abandon his spot of sunshine for the cold stone floor. Fiachna did not budge. The old man snatched one of my ginger biscuits and took a loud bite.

"I don't think he's keen on shooing, but you can try." I didn't bother lifting my head from my papers, too perplexed by the stolen book to pay much notice to the battle of wills between my cat and Mr. Owen.

At long last, Mr. Owen gave up, let out a harrumph, and lifted the substantial cat beneath his arm and sat him down on the bench beside me. "What's that you have? Dorothea said you had a look about you this afternoon."

I was grateful for his company. There wasn't a book published that Mr. Owen didn't know, and if his friend Amberley was somehow connected to Harker, there was no sense concealing that fact. "Have you ever heard of a book called the *Radix Maleficarum*?"

Mr. Owen's bristly white mustache twitched as he took another bite of the biscuit. "*Root of the Witches*? I've never heard of such a thing. Why do you ask?"

Strange. I glanced down at the paper before me, my lip caught between my teeth, and gave my head a slight shake. "I don't know. But apparently Harker lost his position at the University after stealing that book from the Bodleian. Why do you suppose he'd risk his career over something like that? Why would *anyone* risk that?"

Mr. Owen leaned closer, reading my hastily scratched notes. "I see you are back to your lady-detectiving again. That must be why Dorothea sent me in here."

"That's not a word." I snorted back a laugh.

He reached across the table for my papers. "Now let me see what you have there . . ." Mr. Owen adjusted his spectacles and began to read more carefully. "There isn't much about the book in here. From what it says, he was never charged at all and the book was returned to the library. How strange—it all simply—"

"Disappeared," I finished with a shake of my head. "I don't know what any of that means. Or if it means anything at all." I hesitated again before adding, "How well do you know Lord Amberley?"

He tilted his head to one side. "As well as one knows anyone, I suppose. He is mad for books, more than I am. Why do you ask, my love?"

I glanced back down to the papers. "It says he was questioned about the disappearance and denied any knowledge of the book."

Mr. Owen furrowed his brow. "Now that is strange. I would have thought if anyone knew about it, it would be Amberley." Mr. Owen pursed his lips. "I've never heard of it and if Amberley hasn't heard of it—I'd say it's quite an intriguing find. Then again, as it was returned to the library, I'd expect it's still there if you want to take a moment to see what the fuss is about."

Only Mr. Owen would treat a man losing his livelihood—and perhaps even his life—over a misplaced book as a *fuss*. "I don't have reading privileges at the Bodleian, unless you've forgotten. They don't allow just anyone in to read. Not without proper credentials."

He nudged me with his elbow and gave a conspiratorial wink. "That's never stopped you before, my love. I'm sure you'll figure out what to do." He stood, pressing a kiss to the top of my head inches above my wound, and wandered off deeper into the house.

I glanced up at the clock on the wall. Five past two. There was still plenty of daylight left. I slowly straightened the pages, placing them back in the folder. In fact, Mr. Owen's idea was a rather good one. If that book was worth Harker risking his livelihood over— *and* if the police were interested in its previous theft—then it must be important. While I might not have reading privileges at the library, Leona did. And she certainly owed me a favor after all the secrets she'd been harboring.

Chapter Twenty-one

Unto the Breach

I hired a car to bring me from the townhome to the Ashmolean. Partly due to my aching head, and partly out of fear of being followed. While I was beginning to believe that I was imagining the great black dog, I was *fairly* certain that the woman and the two separate men I had seen were flesh and bone.

"Merry Christmas," I said to the driver, pressing several pounds into his gloved hand, enough to cover several weeks' worth of wages. He looked from the banknotes back up at me, surprised by the sum I'd handed him. Despite the blow to my head, Ruan's harsh words about the sorry state of post war Britain remained stubbornly in my thoughts. Things were bad right now, truthfully they had been for quite some time. The rioters. Lack of jobs. Deflation. And yet so many of us just went on—sleepwalking through the months while our neighbors suffered. The increasing turmoil roiled beneath the surface here in Britain. Similar ripples had begun to spread all across Europe, a quiet vibration of something yet to come. I too was sleepwalking, insulated from much of the world—living with Mr. Owen, the two of us locked away in our bookshop, focused upon the past, ignoring the warning signs of what was coming—but isolation did not change the fact that the world around us was a tinderbox awaiting a spark.

Concern lined the driver's face as he looked at me. "Do you need me to wait, miss? I can pull off ahead until you've finished your business, it's no problem at all."

"No, thank you. I'll likely walk. It's a surprisingly fine day."

The driver looked at the clouds overhead and gave his head a shake before driving off. He probably believed I was mad, perhaps I was—but if he sat idling away in his car, the odds of him being noticed by whoever was following me were far too great. I would not risk this man's safety for my own comforts.

I ran up the steps and into the museum, each pound of my feet against the stone echoing in my temple. The galleries were empty, aside from the lone attendant here or there marking the minutes until the end of their shift.

The door to Leona's reading room was ajar, and a warm bright light glowed from within. I rapped twice with my knuckles on the cool wooden panels, before nudging it open with my toe.

"Come in," Leona called.

Her sleeves were rolled up and she looked very much like someone who had spent the last eight hours buried in books. An unexpected wave of relief came over me at the sight of her.

"Ruby, what are you—" Her cheery greeting faded as she noticed the creeping edge of discoloration at my temple. "What's happened to you?"

"A great deal. I want to talk about Julius Harker and his"—I wet my lips, weighing my words—"acquisitions."

Leona's eyes lit in recognition. "Did you go back to the museum?"

I nodded.

Leona's gaze flitted to the door. "Close it, would you? It's awfully drafty here."

It wasn't drafty at all. She simply wanted privacy. I shot a glance to Mary, the middle-aged researcher who shared the room with

Leona. The woman was utterly lost in the pages of a large book on the far side of the room.

"You can trust her," Leona said softly. "Mary and I have been through a great deal here, haven't we?"

The other grunted in acknowledgment as she turned a page, not even deigning to look up.

I shut the door and turned back to face her, twisting my hands before me. I wasn't ordinarily a nervous sort and yet much had occurred since I saw her this morning.

"Ruby, what's happened? You're worrying me."

I drew in a shaky breath and it all tumbled out at once, for better or worse. "Mr. Mueller is dead and the cocaine is gone."

Whatever Leona had been expecting me to say, it wasn't that. She sank down onto the wooden library chair with a sigh. The grief on her face not at all feigned as she stared past me at the closed wooden door leading into the museum.

"I don't know how long before the papers pick it up, or how the police will handle things . . . but I wanted you to know. To hear it from a friend."

"How . . . how did you find out?"

I gently lifted my hair on my temple revealing the bloody scrape and frowned. "It seems that whoever killed Harker doesn't want his secrets revealed. After you left the club, I started home. I don't know what possessed me to go back by the museum, but I did. When I arrived, I found that the door had been forced." I omitted the fact that Ruan was the one to have discovered that minor detail.

Leona worried the inside of her cheek. "And you were attacked . . ."

I laid my palms on a low, flat exhibition case used as temporary housing for several dozen old books.

"Perhaps you should leave it alone. I'd not thought you'd get harmed. I hadn't thought—hadn't dreamed . . ."

"Leona, we're talking about murder. Investigating that sort of thing often leads to this end result." I gestured at my head. "At least this time I wasn't shot."

Her expression darkened. "That's not amusing."

"No, it's not, but it's what I've been dealing with the last several months. After today, I have to believe that Julius Harker was dealing in cocaine, and that Mr. Mueller either knew what was going on and hid it from us, or someone believed he did."

"Yes, I'm afraid we must." She squeezed her eyes shut as the radiator popped and groaned in the corner. "But who had he stolen the shipment from? If we knew that then we could take it to the police. Perhaps they could help us?"

I shook my head. I didn't have the heart to tell her that I suspected the police were somehow complicit in the whole sordid affair. That was a problem for another time—namely, once I knew the identity of our killer. "There is another possibility though . . ."

Leona quirked a brow.

"I am beginning to wonder if perhaps the answer to our problem lies in the past. I made a very curious discovery today. About a decade ago, Julius Harker stole a book from the Bodleian. It has since been returned, but I think the police believe the two crimes are connected."

Leona stiffened at the mention of the book.

At long last, Mary snapped to attention. "Are you speaking of the *Radix*?"

"You know of it?" For if she did, she might be the only person besides Julius Harker and our killer to be aware of its existence.

Mary shot Leona a curious look before turning back to me. "I remember that affair quite well. It was years before you came to work at the museum, Leona."

Leona did not respond, intently studying an imperceptible stain on the floor some three feet from where she stood.

Mary tugged her glasses from her face and continued. "It was all anyone could talk about for months. I mean honestly, to go as far as to steal the book, then hand it back to the library, sacrificing his entire career—only a madman would do that."

"A madman indeed," Leona murmured.

There was something odd in her body language. The tension in her shoulders, the sudden withdrawn quality to her features—but I could not concern myself with her secrets, not when I had found someone who had knowledge of the blasted book. I was as jubilant as Mr. Owen's fictional Great-Aunt Penitence after confession. "What was special about it? Have you ever seen the thing?"

"Never laid eyes upon it. But they say it has to do with witches. It's very old, and from what I understand incredibly valuable. My best guess is Harker meant to sell it, but he'd have had a very hard time finding someone to fence it for him."

I let out a startled sound at the rather detailed knowledge Mary had of the darker aspects of dealing in antiquities.

She let out an exasperated sigh and laid her palms on the desk before her. "Miss Vaughn. I work in a museum. Artifacts have been known to go missing, only to be found years later in private collections. It is sadly the way of things in our line of work."

"Do you know anything else about the *Radix Maleficarum*?"

Leona frowned, her dark brown eyes wide. "Are you certain of the title, Ruby? *That* is the book the police are interested in?"

I nodded, careful to not tip my hand as to my source of said knowledge, lest I expose my own innumerable crimes committed in the name of lady-detecting—as Mr. Owen would say. While I did not believe Leona was involved in harming Julius Harker or Mr. Mueller, she still had secrets—and until I knew what they were, I could not trust her completely. Not with this. "Does that book mean anything to you?"

She worried her lower lip. "Only that it's the second time someone has mentioned that book to me in as many days."

My skin pricked at the newfound information. "Was it Professor Reaver?"

"Goodness no. Frederick is not at all interested in any text before it's reached a thousand years old." She laughed. An odd expression on her face. "No. No. It was someone *else*."

Else was a loaded word. Meaning all sorts of possible things, and in our current predicament it was a word I did not much care for. "*Museum*, else? Or *elsewhere* else?"

Leona darted a worried look to the door before shaking her head. "Not here. This is not the place for such conversations."

We could discuss cocaine and murder here, but not missing books? Something was not right. Not right at all. I fiddled with the smooth, cream-colored button of my jacket as Leona rushed to her desk and jotted down a note on a torn scrap of paper before thrusting it in my hand.

"Take this to Jonathan Treadway. He should still be at the natural history museum." She checked her watch. "At least for another hour."

I furrowed my brow—the name achingly familiar. *Jonathan Treadway.* I'd seen it somewhere. "Is he the one who mentioned the book to you?"

She shook her head. "Tomorrow, Ruby. No more questions now. I'll tell you everything else then, I promise. Meet me at the club at our usual time."

I took the paper from her outstretched hand. She held my gaze for several seconds. Leona was trusting me with something important—only I had no idea what that thing was. I started for the door.

"Ruby?" Leona called after me, halting me in my tracks. "Tell Jonathan it's important. He'll . . ." She hesitated, the darkness shrouding her features. "He'll know what it means."

With a looming sense of dread, I hurried out the door toward the wide stair leading to the main floor of the museum. I brushed into the fragrant holiday greenery along the balustrade on the way up the steps, taking them two at a time, when I came face-to-face with Frederick Reaver, who was on the way down. His cool affect washed over me. The man glowered at me from where he stood three steps above.

Chin defiantly high, I looked at him.

"Miss Vaughn . . ." His eyes traced over my wounded temple. "It looks like you've had a bit of trouble this morning."

My pulse thundered in my veins. "Just clumsy is all. I fell down the townhouse steps."

"Did you?" He made a curious sound in his chest. "One must be careful on the ice this time of year."

Leona's letter grew hot in my palm as I kept my fingers wrapped tight around the paper. Reaver's eyes traveled from my wound down my throat to settle unerringly on my hand. He somehow *knew* that I had a message from Leona.

I swallowed hard, trying to keep the panic from my voice. "I will keep that in mind."

"I hear you are prone to close scrapes, Miss Vaughn. They say you took a bullet in Scotland, if the rumors are true."

"I tend not to pay much mind to rumors." I said coolly. "Nasty things, Professor. I'm sure you understand. Now, if you'd excuse me." I ducked past him, not pausing until I reached the top. He remained there—stock-still—waiting midway on the stairs, watching me with a considered stare. I hurried out the door, forgetting all about my quest for the reader's card and finding the book at the Bodleian. I pushed open the heavy door to the museum and shivered—for once, it wasn't the cold.

Chapter Twenty-two

Jonathan Treadway, *the Younger*

A sense of unease settled in my chest as I left the Ashmolean and started in the direction of the natural history museum. Not that I had any *reason* to be unnerved—only a murderer on the loose, multiple people following me, hallucinations of spectral dogs, *and* I'd accidentally fallen in love with a man I'd utterly rejected. Truly, my life was going precisely to plan. I gave my head a shake and quickened my pace.

The route between the Ashmolean and the Museum of Natural History was lined on both sides by all sorts of structures. University buildings. Shopfronts. Homes. All jumbled together alongside one another as they'd grown together over the years. The street was dark and deserted. Darker than I recalled. Illuminated by the meager glow of the streetlights dotting the path. I paused beneath a gas lamp and withdrew the note from my pocket. If Leona had entrusted it to me, she surely expected me to read it. A cool breeze picked up, lifting my hair as a dog began to bay in the distance, followed by a second. The wind caught the little scrap of paper, fluttering in my palm.

IT'S HAPPENED.

How very unhelpful. Hopefully it meant more to this Jonathan

Treadway fellow than it did me. Or better yet, perhaps he would know more about the *Radix Maleficarum*. Leona had acted strangely at its mention, her entire affect shifting from ease to wariness. It had to be related to Harker's fate—it simply *had* to be. Perhaps this Treadway fellow was Leona's mysterious caller from last night. If she was sending him cryptic notes, it wasn't a stretch to believe she was meeting him in private as well.

Snow began to fall as I caught the familiar sound of footsteps on the pavers behind me. Good God, not again. Fists tight, I spun around only to find Ruan there behind me—a stubborn dozen yards away.

I sighed in relief. "It's you . . ."

He wore his brown cap pulled low over his brow, dark curls peeking out from beneath.

"How did you find me?"

The edge of his mouth curved up slightly, the tension in his shoulders ebbing. He must have feared I'd be angry with him for following me. "It shouldn't be *that* much of a surprise anymore." His gaze drifted to the scrape on my temple, and the humor fled his face. "How are you feeling?"

"Fine, Ruan. I am utterly fine." I flung an arm out to underscore the point and spun around. "See? Absolutely, miraculously fine." I narrowed my gaze at him. "But please stop asking."

He chuckled low, muttering something in Cornish. This time—hopefully—in fond amusement. He stuffed his gloved hands into his coat as he drew up beside me, tilting his head in the direction of the natural history museum. "Lead on then, Miss Vaughn."

Warmth curled in my belly, along with another less-familiar sensation. *Hope.*

"You're helping me, then?"

"It does appear that way, doesn't it?"

I tucked my hands into the pockets of my coat and matched his long strides step by step, marveling at the change in him—how quickly my country pellar had gone from urging caution to breaking into museums and walking the streets with me in search of a killer.

STEPPING INTO THE natural history museum was a gateway into another world. One of curious beasts and giants that once roamed the land. Great skeletons of long-dead creatures reached up toward the vaulting glass-and-metalwork ceiling. A veritable sanctuary of science, with columns made of various stone specimens native to Britain interspersed with marble statues of the great scientific minds throughout history. If I had my leisure, I might have spent hours here—wandering the discoveries and losing myself in them—but I hadn't any time, and I hadn't come for pleasure. It did surprise me a little that Ruan refused to set foot inside, insisting that he would wait. Alone. In the snow. He truly was peculiar at times.

It didn't take long to find Professor Treadway's office. It lay beneath a great stone archway like all the others—this one with the stenciled words PROFESSOR OF ANTHROPOLOGY recently repainted over the doorframe.

I withdrew Leona's note from my pocket and read it for a second time—as if the words would have changed in the handful of minutes since I last read it. I gathered myself and rapped upon the heavy wooden door.

"Enter," a muffled voice called from within.

I grabbed the heavy metal door hold and twisted. The old hinges groaned as the musty scent of ancient things, along with the faintest hint of tobacco, assaulted my nose. I stepped inside, the room awash in the warm glow of artificial light.

A man not much older than me looked up from a desk. An objectively attractive sort, I suppose, in the way that beautiful men can be such. He had delicately sharp features and roan, nearly black, hair that he wore cropped close and neatly combed. The combination put me in mind of the silent film actors from those American pictures that Mr. Owen dearly loved.

Jonathan Treadway's shirtsleeves were rolled up, revealing thin wrists and an almost birdlike frame. He wore an old herringbone vest that might have belonged to his predecessor in this office at one point.

"I . . . I don't believe we've met." He studied me warily before he spotted the torn scrap of paper in my hand. A sudden dawning of recognition came over his sharp features and he frowned. "Ah. Close the door please."

Close the door? With a man I scarcely knew? It was not the wisest course of action, but at the same time, Ruan was nearby. If things went pear-shaped, he'd likely sense it and come to my aid—despite whatever bizarre misgivings he had about the place itself. There was a peculiar sense of security in our connection—in knowing he was always near, even when we were apart.

I quickly did as asked, blocking out the quiet sounds of the museum staff busily at work shutting down the gallery floor for the evening, and sealed the two of us inside. He reached out a well-manicured hand for the note that I had placed on the desk.

My unsteady pulse beat in my aching temple as Jonathan Treadway read the two words that Leona had hastily scrawled out only minutes before.

He crumpled it before laying it in a silver dish on his desk and lighting a match. The scent of sulfur filled the air as the flames licked up and caught the edge of the paper. Neither Treadway nor I spoke, both watching as the orange embers slowly consumed the note, turning it to ash.

"That is unfortunate."

I stared at him unblinking. This entire week had been one *unfortunate* happening after another.

"Is she safe?" he asked softly.

"I could ask you the same question."

He stared at the pile of ashes before him. "I presume *she* sent you with it?" There was something in the cadence of his voice that caught my attention. It was *him* with her the previous evening. It had to be. *This* must be the man Leona had been meeting in private. While the voices had been muffled, the man had a distinctive rhythm to his words. One shared by Jonathan Treadway.

"Who are you?"

"Professor Jonathan Treadway. But you knew that already, as you found your way to my little corner of the earth over here."

I stared at his hands, noticing the bandage that covered his left forearm. A weeping hint of pink stained the edge. He'd been wounded. My mind raced back to Leona's frayed fingers the night Harker's body was discovered. Since when was museum work dangerous? "Do you hurt yourself often here in the collection?"

His dark brow raised as he noticed my frank inspection. He lifted his shoulder carelessly before slowly unrolling his sleeve over the bandage, fastening his cuff in a vain attempt to ward off my line of questions. "Leona sent you with that because she trusts you. I do not know you. Therefore, I do not trust you. Please don't show me false concern or try to get pleasantries from me."

This was hopeless, and yet if Leona trusted him—if Leona sent me here—then there must be some reason for it. And I'd stake my very life it pertained to that book. "You asked me if she was safe . . ."

"Is she?"

The stone walls of the room were closing in upon me. "Does your concern mean she is in danger?"

He folded his hands together, resting his chin upon his templed fingers. "Grave danger. We'd all thought, *hoped*, that Harker's death was isolated—the result of his peculiar interests, but now that appears not to be the case."

"Do you know who killed Julius Harker?"

He did not answer.

"Can *you* protect her?"

He buried his face in his hands, rocking his head slowly back and forth. A hopeless, miserable gesture. "No one can. Not now. If what Leona fears is true, then our mutual friend has made herself some very powerful enemies."

"The same enemies that Julius Harker had?"

He swallowed, picking up a cut-crystal glass of water and taking a sip. "You should leave here. Forget what you've delivered to me and go back about your life, Miss Vaughn. It would be best for all involved."

My mouth gaped open. "I did not give you my name."

"I do not need it. You've been all over the papers since the day you set foot in Oxford." He gestured with two fingers behind me. "The door."

Hands on hips, I stared at this Treadway fellow, unable to make sense of him. "You told me that Leona is in danger from the very same person who killed Julius Harker and somehow expect me to go back to my life in Exeter as if none of this had happened?" My voice came out shrill. What sort of people did Leona acquaint herself with here? A den of liars and faithless frauds, that's who.

"I did. You do not know what you are getting yourself involved in. Not all is as it seems. This glittering world"—he gestured out the door—"this bastion of learning. It is a mirage, Miss Vaughn. There are things at play that you do not understand, and I fear they are a danger to you most of all."

I furrowed my brow, catching the peculiar scent of stale tobacco smoke and petrol on the air. "Me?" My mind tripped through the years back to the war. I grabbed onto the desk for a half second, regaining my bearings. *You're not in France, Ruby. You're not in France.* My hand began to tremble upon the desk. Why should my mind go *there* of all places? And now?

"If you think I will abandon Leona because you are frightened, then you have clearly not read enough about me in your papers,"

I snapped before turning on my heels and storming out the door and out of the museum.

Ruan stood at the foot of the steps waiting for me, rubbing his hands together in the snowy night. His expression mirrored that of Jonathan Treadway's, tight and pinched. His cap was under his arm as snowflakes swirled around him, catching in his dark curls. The silver strands that laced through the black were all the more evident in the moonlight.

What's wrong?

"Everything."

I hadn't realized I'd asked the question at all, but Ruan wasn't looking at me. Instead, he remained fixated on the museum doors. "What did Treadway have to say?"

"How did you know? Never mind . . . of course you know. It is both terribly annoying and incredibly convenient how you do that."

That earned me a wry quirk of his lips.

Groaning, I ran my hands over my face as my teeth began to chatter from the cold. "You know this Treadway fellow too, don't you? From your time here. . . . I should have guessed."

"I did once." Ruan reached out, readjusting my fine cashmere scarf and tucking it into my woolen coat. "He doesn't like me. Or at least *didn't*. I haven't spoken to him in years to see if he's changed his mind on the matter."

"He doesn't like me either if it's any consolation. Shall we start home?"

Ruan hesitated, as if there were more to this distrust of the young anthropologist.

I caught a bit of movement from the street behind us out of the corner of my eye and tucked my arm into his, quickening our pace. "Was he a student when you were here?"

Ruan's head was dipped, eyes downcast as we made our way down the street. If he sensed my unease, he did not mention it.

"He's a bit older than he appears. Back then, Treadway was lecturing in Professor Laurent's department. They would occasionally butt heads over Treadway's methods. Nothing unusual. Academic jealousy, or that is what Ernst told me. Treadway believed himself destined for greatness like his father before him and always let everyone know it. Some of the lads would call him Treadway the Younger."

I glanced over my shoulder, but the street remained empty. It had only been my imagination. A trick of the wind. I nestled in closer to Ruan, using his size as a buffer against the cold. "Do you think he's a bad man?"

"I don't know," Ruan said softly. "But we'll find out soon enough, won't we?

Yes. Yes we would.

We continued on as the snow began to blanket everything around, the slate rooftops dusted with the white powder, giving them a hazy, almost dreamlike appearance. Oxford was the most beautiful town I'd ever seen, almost as if it had been cut directly from a children's fairy-story book—and yet there was a dark undercurrent flowing alongside us. Something *evil* that had come to town and that pulsed with every step as I grew closer to Julius Harker's killer.

Neither Ruan nor I spoke for most of the way home. Every few minutes, I'd cast a surreptitious glance over my shoulder to reassure myself that no one was following and would be rewarded by a cat, or a workman headed home. No peculiar dogs. No more mysterious shadows. It was four days before Christmas and the city had grown quiet. Back home, Exeter was always brimming with life in the days leading up to the holiday, but Oxford was another creature altogether.

"When were you going to tell me about the *Radix Maleficarum*?" Ruan asked softly, breaking the comfortable silence that had stretched out between us.

My gaze shot to his. "How did you know about that?"

"Owen told me earlier."

Of course he did. I pinched the bridge of my nose and gave my head a shake. "I'm not sure what to make of the book. I don't see how it fits in with the rest of the clues."

"Is that not why you went to see Treadway in the first place?" Ruan paused, turning to me with raised brows.

"I don't know, Leona had me take a note. She'd been behaving peculiarly after the book was mentioned, but the note was about something that's *happened*."

Ruan stared at me, his jaw open. "Ruby . . . there's something you should know. . . . Jonathan Treadway is the one who stole the book in the first place."

"He *what*?"

"It happened when I was a student here. Laurent was incandescent when he learned of it, threatened to turn Treadway in himself if he didn't return the book to the Bodleian at once."

"Impossible. I saw the police report. There's no mention of Jonathan Treadway there. None at all. And if he had stolen it, then why did Julius Harker end up taking the blame?"

Ruan caught his lower lip in his teeth. "I don't know. It was handled very delicately. Hardly anyone knew of the book—I only did because of the time I spent with Ernst. But Julius Harker and Jonathan Treadway were close when I was in school here—*very* close. Always having lunch together on the green. Perhaps they were friends, perhaps more. I do not know. What I *do* know is that I was at the house with Ernst when Professor Laurent confronted Treadway about the *Radix Maleficarum*. I couldn't hear all of it, but I came to understand that Treadway denied any involvement. Whatever he told the Professor must have placated him, for he let the matter die as soon as Harker confessed. Supposedly Treadway was not to teach again, and that's why he's over at the museum."

"That *is* curious. Julius Harker was thrown out on his ear and yet

Jonathan Treadway has a prime position. Do you suppose Harker actually *did* steal the book and hid it amongst Treadway's things?"

"Perhaps. Or perhaps they were in it together and Harker took the blame as he had less to lose. If there was evidence implicating Jonathan Treadway, I doubt he'd be allowed to carry on in Oxford unscathed no matter *who* his father is." Ruan hooked his thumbs into the waistband of his trousers.

"Who is his father?"

Ruan lifted a shoulder. "Only one of the most preeminent anthropologists in all of Britain."

I groaned. *Fabulous. I was enmired in a marsh of academics and murder.*

Ruan let out a low laugh. "And cocaine. Don't forget that."

"How could I *ever* forget that?"

Ruan chuckled. "It sounds to me that the book must have something to do with this."

"Or if not the book, then perhaps . . ." *Treadway.* And if that was the case, it led directly back to Leona. I was going to be sick. "I need to get my hands on that book."

The knot had begun to tighten. Leona, Harker, and Treadway were all connected. And now with Harker and Mueller dead, Leona and Treadway were left alone. And afraid. *Something had happened,* she said. Something more than simply murder, and it had to do with the book. Had Leona surmised the danger that she was in, or the danger that she'd be putting me in by enlisting me in this quest? I squeezed my eyes shut, unable—*unwilling*—to answer that question.

Ruan wet his lips. "How well do you know Leona?"

As well as I knew myself, I'd once believed. But I now questioned that too. I shook my head. "Of the two of us, she is the least likely to be entangled with criminals. But Treadway said something strange earlier. . . . He said he'd thought at first that Harker's death was *isolated.* Do you suppose that means that the killer is not who they first imagined?"

Ruan made a low sound in his chest. "I think your friend is in deeper trouble than she bargained for."

I do too. I laid my cheek against Ruan's warm coat, grateful for his company. For his easy friendship, despite the fact I did not deserve it. "Thank you . . ."

"For what?" Ruan wrapped his arm around my shoulders, not slowing his pace, nor even looking at me.

"For being here in Oxford. I don't know what I would do had you not answered my abysmal letter."

"It truly was a terrible letter, but I believe in you. I have every faith you'd have managed to crack this case one way or the other," he agreed with a laugh as we continued wordlessly into the night.

Chapter Twenty-three

A Missed Appointment

I dragged my weary body from my warm bed well before dawn and hurriedly dressed by candlelight. I couldn't sleep. Too worried about whatever information Leona wanted to share. Anxiety, I supposed, was better than nightmares—but not by much. Discovering that Leona's friend Jonathan Treadway was involved in the earlier theft of the *Radix Maleficarum* sat in my belly like a stone. Did she know of his involvement in the book's initial disappearance? Surely not. The fear on her face when she sent me to him with the note was real, and I *knew* her. At least I thought I did—and Leona was a librarian first and foremost. It was what she had trained to do before she obtained the position with Reaver at the museum. She was *not* the sort to steal a book, no matter the reason.

Fiachna lifted his ebony head, blinking slowly, eyes flashing that unnatural green in the flicker of flame. He butted into my palm, demanding attention before I left. It was still dark by the time I stepped outside the house, made more ominous by the thick blanket of fog that enveloped the city overnight, muting all sound and distorting the charming streetscape into a dreamlike world of shadows and shape. The cold air, however, was *not* the stuff of dreams—stinging my lungs with each step I took to the Artemis Club. I wrapped my scarf tighter, hurrying along the well-worn path to the club. The club's baroque facade towered arrogantly over its neighbors, alluding to its previous life a century ago as an opera house.

A muffled sound echoed in the dark, and I turned in time to see the shadowy shape of a dog disappear behind a building.

Death. A spectral dog means *death.* That's what Ruan had said.

Or—you foolish girl—it means someone was careless and forgot to lock their gate.

Not mad. I am not going mad. I repeated the words over and over, willing myself to believe them. A foggy morning, a mysterious book about witches along with a murderer afoot, and all my good sense flew out the window, replaced by superstition. While I occasionally could admit to the existence of the inexplicable—ghosts, witches, *pellars*—I wasn't about to believe in omens or signs. Now *that* was nonsense.

No. Decidedly not mad.

Still, I was not willing to test my luck. I dashed the last several yards to the grand front doors of the Artemis Club before casting a wary glance behind me.

Empty.

No dog. Nor men. Not even the strange woman Ruan had spotted following us after we left the police station.

See? Not mad.

Pulse settling to a steady beat, I stepped inside the warm, dimly lit entrance, closing my fear outside the club.

"Miss Vaughn!"

It seemed a lifetime ago that I met Leona here for breakfast, but in truth, less than twenty-four hours had passed. The stark overhead lights had been cut for the evening, leaving the room bathed in warm lamplight emanating from the desk in the center of the round room. The young receptionist leaned around a particularly large floral arrangement to smile at me.

"Has Leona arrived yet?" I unwound my scarf, unbuttoning my

field jacket with numb fingers. I'd forgotten my gloves. I stared down at my stiff hands in confusion. How had I forgotten my gloves? I could have sworn I'd grabbed them on the way out the door.

The young woman gave me a puzzled look. "No, miss. I haven't seen her since she left here in a rush yesterday morning."

A worried frown settled in my brow. Leona was always the first one to the club. She lived not far, just beyond the castle.

I blew hot air into my hands, roughly rubbing them together. "It's no matter, I'm sure she's running late."

The young clerk gestured to the lush velvet couch against the wall. "You can wait here and warm yourself. Or go on ahead into the tearoom. Breakfast won't be served for another two hours, but if you'd like to read the paper, the morning edition arrived just moments ago, I can have them put on a pot of tea for you." Her eyes were fixed upon my bare hands.

"No . . . no, I'll wait." My mind raced, searching for any possibility for Leona's absence. Either she was once again avoiding me, she was simply running behind schedule . . . or something bad had happened.

Harker. Mueller. Leona.

Two of the three were already dead.

My fingers tightened on my lapels as I hastily refastened the buttons and started toward the door. "If she arrives, will you ask her to wait on me?"

"Of course, Miss Vaughn, but I cannot make her wait if she doesn't wish to stay. You know the rules. Our members are free to come and go as they please."

I didn't hear her words. There was nothing but the riot of my pulse in my ears as I ran out the door, for I knew without a shadow of a doubt that Leona was not coming. Whether it was the fear on Jonathan Treadway's face yesterday as he warned me of the danger or the growing death toll across Oxford connected to Harker's

Curiosity Museum, that damnable truth echoed in my ears—Leona was in trouble.

St. George's Tower, the only remaining part of the old Oxford Castle, loomed high in the morning fog. It was more prison than castle, and had been for ages. The first rays of sun broke through the clouds, slowly burning away the haze. I turned from the old prison complex and ran down the street to Leona's house. Before, when I'd trod this path, I hadn't given two thoughts to who might notice my comings or goings. Nor did I worry about who might be waiting ahead. But now, with each step, my own fear pounded in my chest.

I rounded the corner onto the narrow cobbled lane leading to Leona's home and froze. Her front door was open, and light from inside flooded out onto the street. My mind miles ahead of my body, I broke into a sprint down the uneven surface and burst into the house.

"Leona!"

The hall table had been overturned, one aged leg snapped in two.

I darted up the stairs.

On an ordinary day, Leona's room was tidy with everything in its place. But today it was utterly ransacked. Drawers pulled from the dresser and cast upside down on the rug. Her undergarments and blouses scattered in heaps. Her finely painted enameled jewelry box smashed to pieces, bits of glass and broken wood littering the carpet. My own cracked reflection stared back at me in the shattered mirror.

Broken lamp.

Overturned chair.

A reddish smear on wood.

Hands shaking, I reached out for the dresser and touched the wet spot, drawing my reddened fingers back. Blood.

"Leona!" I cried out. She *had* to be here. She simply had to be, for the alternative was too much to bear. My riding boots thundered on the worn wooden floorboards as I sailed around the newel post and into the sitting room, my voice growing ever more frantic.

"Le—" I skidded to a stop. A lifeless hand lay palm up on the carpet from behind the sofa.

Annabelle.

Leona's young roommate was motionless on the floor. I dropped to my knees next to Annabelle, who lay sprawled on the far side of the sofa with an ivory-handled blade embedded in her stomach. I brushed the hair from her face with my icy hand. Her breath came faintly against my palm.

Not dead then.

Her blood pooled around the metal of the blade, seeping through the thin white lace of her nightgown and onto the woven rug. I tugged my cashmere scarf from around my neck with trembling hands.

Thick grief settled in my throat. I carefully wadded the fabric. "I have you, darling. I'm here now. I won't leave you." The rote words returned. They'd become habit after the thousands of times I'd said them to dying soldiers. Holding them in my arms at the regimental aid post as they'd asked for their mother or sweethearts. Listening to those last words meant for another's ears. The men stable enough to move went into my ambulance. The ones who couldn't . . . well . . . they were left behind. *Triage* was the word the French used for sorting through the wounded. Dying. Dead. Likely to die. Might survive.

By all appearances, Annabelle was in the first category. If I removed the blade, she'd bleed out immediately. If I left it in, I had minutes at most to save her. Not nearly long enough to seek help and return in time to save her.

"Lee—" she started, struggling against my hand.

"It's all right, darling . . ." I pressed the scarf to the wound, keeping the knife from moving, all while *hopefully* staunching the bleeding long enough for . . .

For what, Ruby Vaughn, a miracle?

My eyes stung as I rubbed my face on the rough shoulder of my coat, hoping the girl couldn't see the truth written across my face.

Annabelle whimpered.

Surely someone had to have heard the struggle. In desperation, I shouted out for help, my voice hoarse. Once. Then twice. Her hot blood soaked through the fabric. I did not feel the growing wetness on my cheeks, or the slowing of her pulse beneath my hands. Nor did I hear the quiet footsteps behind me on the rug. It wasn't until Ruan crouched beside me on the ground alongside the girl's body that I realized that we were no longer alone.

He had come.

Of course he had.

Ruan touched my shoulder softly, before setting his old British Expeditionary Force haversack down beside him.

"How did you . . ." But there was no sense finishing the question. It did not matter if he'd followed me or if he'd heard my panic with that strange ability of his.

"You've done well . . ." he murmured, rummaging around in his bag for an orangish brown concoction. He tilted it into the light, confirming the contents before removing the lid.

The familiar scent jolted me to attention. "Acriflavine?" I hadn't smelled that since the war. An antiseptic solution that had been used frequently on wounds.

"I keep some on me. Though I don't know what good it'll do her with a knife in her belly—but I can try. It's all I can do."

A strange coldness radiated from the girl's body to my own fingers as the room filled with the scent of a summer storm—the same electric sharpness that once terrified me now reassured me. The room was thick with it. My gaze shot to Ruan.

He was calling upon his abilities already—long before he'd even laid hands on her. But this time was different. This time, I could *feel* him reaching for his power. It echoed within my own body in a way it never had before. Previously, I'd only seen it in the silver flecks fleeing his eyes, smelled it in the air, felt its coldness upon me—but never like this. Never before had it run through me like a lightning rod.

"What are you doing?"

He raised a brow, confusion in his expression. "Preparing supplies. . . . We don't have time to get her to a surgeon."

He did not even know he was doing it. I stared at him in disbelief. *How could he not know?* He told me once in Cornwall that he had little understanding of how to control his abilities, that it came and went as it willed. I watched as he slowly and methodically removed items from his haversack and sat them on a nearby tea tray. "I'm going to have to be quick. *Very quick* so she doesn't bleed out. I also need to be certain none of her vital organs have been damaged."

I nodded numbly—after all, surgery on the parlor floor occurs every day, does it not?

"Are you ready?" His voice was soft and sure, lending me confidence I did not possess. "She has minutes at most. We cannot get her to a hospital in this condition, though the gods know I would prefer it. When I remove the knife, we'll have even less time. A matter of seconds."

I wasn't ready at all, but I was going to have to be.

Ruan began talking to himself in Cornish as he set about laying out his forceps and catgut sutures. He laid the cloth soaked in the antiseptic acriflavine solution on the tea tray near my left hand. "You must remove the knife quickly when I say. Straight up and out. You understand me?"

"It'll kill her."

"It's the only way. She'll die on her own if you don't—or we can give her a chance by trying to fix what's been done to her."

My hands grew slippery with her blood as I wrapped my fingers around the knife's handle. "Have you done this before?"

"Not with such a clean wound."

Did . . . did they live?

"Now, Ruby . . ."

Without a thought. Without a prayer to my mother's beloved saints, I did exactly what he said, watching as Ruan swiftly probed the wound, examining the damage. He gave me quiet instructions, swift and calm as any formally trained medical officer I'd aided before. And just as I had during the war, I complied without question. Ruan made quick work of tying off a small ligature of the large vein that had been severed before confirming the wound itself clear of any foreign materials.

Before I realized what had happened, he was finishing up the stitches on her abdomen. The whole episode took what . . . a minute or two at most? A life reduced to mere seconds on a clock, ticking silently down one by one while Ruan staved off her death until another day. Refusing the grave by the sheer force of his iron will.

I remained transfixed by his hands as he worked—scarred and strong, but with a delicate grace and speed that I'd not expected. He'd used those hands on me, fixing me. Taking care of me—but I'd never watched him work on another. There was a reason he was revered in Cornwall, why people would travel for miles to seek his help.

It was the same reason I loved him beyond all reason. Ruan was the last truly good thing in this world, and I would be damned if I'd let him walk away because of my stubbornness.

Ruan made a soft sound in his chest. "We need to get her out of here. *Now.*"

I shook my head, staring at my own bloodied hands. "Leona . . . Leona is missing."

Ruan touched my shoulder gently. "We have to go. We cannot be found here. Not like this. She needs to be in a hospital."

I opened my mouth then snapped it back shut, the words taking on some strange, unspeakable shape on my tongue. The almost-murder weapon was still in my hand. I turned the ivory-handled blade over in the light. It was a fine piece, but had no maker's mark. A well-crafted, expensive weapon. Not the sort of thing your typical burglar would have.

But who—who had done this thing? The hall clock chimed the half hour. It was nearly eight in the morning. At last, the sounds tumbled out. "Leona. They've taken Leona."

"We'll find her, I promise, but it will be after we take Annabelle to the hospital, and can be sure she survives this."

I wrapped the knife in my bloody scarf and shook my head hard. She could *not* go to the hospital. Julius Harker dead. Mr. Mueller murdered in his jail cell. Leona missing. "She has to stay with us."

He worried his lower lip. "Ruby, I might be able to do rudimentary battlefield procedures, but I am not able to—"

"There was nothing rudimentary about what you did." I rocked back onto my heels, wiping the sweat from my brow with my sleeve. "You can take care of her as well as anyone."

Ruan let out a startled sound. "In case you forget, I am only a *pellar*."

"The pellar who saved her life."

"She's not saved yet. She needs professional care, someone who can be certain she won't get infection."

How could he not see that infection was the least of all risks in this matter? There was no one in this whole city who could protect her as we could. "And allow whoever put that knife in her to finish the job? She comes home with *us*, Ruan Kivell. Someone killed Mr. Mueller under the very nose of the police—likely the police themselves, considering how strangely they've all been acting. Do you truly think that she'll be safe anywhere else? We can trust no one."

He hesitated, warring with his own sense of justice before he finally acquiesced.

"I'll go fetch my car." I glanced at the dried blood on my hands and hastily tucked the knife away into my large coat pocket. Leaning down, I tipped his chin up with the crook of my forefinger. Ruan gave me the strangest small smile and I was lost. Utterly lost. Seeing him on the floor before me, bloody and exhausted, glowing with the quiet self-satisfaction of a job well done sealed my fate. "Thank you . . ." I whispered, before brushing a brief, gentle kiss to his lips. This time, in the broad light of day, he did not pull away from my touch.

I straightened, and without a word ran out the door and home for my car to fetch Annabelle home.

Chapter Twenty-four

Now What . . . ?

RUAN and I carefully transported Annabelle back to the townhome and immediately began settling her into his room across the hall from my own. It had been a dicey couple of miles thanks to the cobbled streets between there and here, but we managed all the same.

"She's fine, Ruby," Ruan murmured from across the room where he knelt at the bedside quietly assessing the girl. Mrs. Penrose and I had removed her blood-stained clothes and cleaned her up as best we could before dressing her in one of my spare clean, white nightgowns.

She's safe here. Safer than anywhere in Oxford. It was a pure and simple fact. Yet I worried it had been a mistake. Oh, Ruan would tend to her better than any physician. There was no question about her medical care. But what if in protecting her, I had led the killer to our very door?

I brushed the thought away and immediately set myself to being useful. I began to unpack the bag of Annabelle's things I'd hastily gathered and set them into the drawers of the dresser. Her satchel, which I'd taken as we left, was now carelessly lying upon a chair where I'd dropped it. I rifled through it. Mostly books and her notes from the University . . . and then I spied something else lying loose in the bottom of the bag.

Her reading card for the Bodleian.

My skin pricked as my conscience warred with practicality. For a half second I almost disregarded it, leaving the card undisturbed. But as usual, practicality won out. I tucked it into my pocket before continuing to place her other belongings in the cedar-lined drawers. Ruan might be a good man, but I was a pragmatist. Annabelle's reading card would do her no favors in her current condition, and if it helped me find who did this to her and who had taken Leona, then it was worth overcoming any minor moral quibbles.

Ruan's expression grew grim. "I am still concerned she needs a real physician. Is there anyone you can send for who can keep their mouth shut?"

I wet my lips, shaking my head. "I could call for Dr. Heinrich in Exeter, but it'd take him well over a day to get here. But she can't wait that long, can she?"

Ruan frowned, shaking his head. "We'd need him sooner than that. If she makes it to morning, I wager she'll pull through this."

My stomach knotted. I was gambling with a girl's life no matter what I did. If we took her to the hospital, there was no guarantee we could protect her there. "No, I've seen what you can do. You've saved my life more times than I can count. Surely you can tend a girl after a scratch."

"A four-inch blade is a bit more than a scratch," Ruan corrected with a wry quirk of his lips. "But I take your point."

"If there is anyone in this world who can keep her alive, it's you."

He flushed slightly pink all the way to his ears. Ruan's fingers rested lightly on Annabelle's wrist, counting her pulse.

"Go have a bath. I'll watch her until you're done," I said absently.

His eyes followed my fingers as they rubbed over the spot where my heart pounded erratically in my chest. The worry was evident in his eyes. "I'll be quick," he murmured, brushing past me and out into the hall toward the bathing room.

I studied the young girl as she lay motionless on the narrow mattress. Had Leona been taken, or had she run away? That was the true question. Whatever Leona was going to tell me this morning had to be connected to her disappearance, and now I had nothing. No new clues. No leads and no one I could trust beyond those dwelling in this very house—and Hari, of course—but none of that would help me find her. I pulled the bloodied knife back out of my pocket, turning it over in the lamplight.

Drugs. Forgeries. Antiquities, stolen books, and petty academic rivalries. None of that ought to lead to a growing pile of dead bodies scattered across the city—and yet it did. All that was left now was for me to find out why.

Chapter Twenty-five

Back into the Arms of Chance

ANNABELLE had not awoken by the time I took my leave of her that afternoon. Ruan assured me that her pulse was steadier than he'd expected and that she should pull through the ordeal unscathed, but his cold comfort about Annabelle did nothing to ease my worries for Leona. My greatest hope now was that Annabelle would regain consciousness soon, and identify her attacker. Of course, if she *could* identify her attacker, it put all of us in even graver danger, for as soon as the killer realized that he had not succeeded, he would be back. And I was most certain that he would try to finish the job.

I quickly washed up, putting on a fresh frock and leaving my bloodied clothes in a pile on the floor in the corner before setting off—yet again—to find Professor Reaver in hopes he could shed some light on Leona's current location. The man had been an enigma. At first, he had been friendly, but lately his mood had turned and he watched me with a suspicion that made no sense. Reaver's office was tucked deep in the back of the museum, past the marbles and sculptures. Past the sarcophagi and the Roman antiquities, nestled into a spartan hallway. Inside, the room was bright and airy, with everything neatly ordered and placed away.

His desk sat in front of a large window overlooking the city's rooftops and chimneys. He had it cracked open, allowing in the cool winter air. The familiar hint of smoke was in the air, or perhaps it was only in my imagination. Reaver sat behind the desk wearing an untucked shirt and suspenders, having shed his coat sometime earlier in the day. His fair hair was tousled from where he'd been driving his hands through it as he studied whatever it was before him. Lines of worry creased his face.

I started into the room, tripping over a book lying splayed open on the threshold where it had landed after apparently being thrown. The cover was tattered and unfamiliar. A greenish gold binding. I picked it up, turning it over in my hand. *A Treatise on Ethical Excavations* by Julius A. Harker.

I looked from the book in my hand to Professor Reaver.

"Set it down, if you would. It must have fallen from my shelf."

I held the book to my chest, curious how it could have *fallen* when the nearest shelf was a good ten feet across the room. "Have you heard from Leona? Do you know where she is?"

His pale eyes raked over me, settling uncomfortably at the bruises and scab marring my temple. "In her reading room as she always is." Stark smudges of blue ink marred the fingertips of his left hand.

"She's not. I went to meet her this morning at the club. She never arrived. When I went to her home, I found it ransacked. There was blood on her dresser, and more of it on the floor of the sitting room." I omitted the fact there was *also* a body on said floor. "Do you have any idea what she's gotten herself into? Professor Reaver . . . please help me."

"Is that so?" His voice was calm. Too calm.

I struggled to make sense of his nonchalance. I'd just told him Leona was likely dead, for goodness' sake. "Is that all you have to say? I tell you that Leona is missing, she very well could be dead—and you respond as if I told you it was raining outside."

He folded his hands on the desk. His face weary, but emotionless. "What do you want me to say that would change anything about the situation?"

I clutched the book tight to my belly. "Do you know where she is? Where she might have gone?"

He raised a brow, rested his chin on his ink-stained fist, and studied me, his pale blue eyes taking in each flaw I possessed. "I could ask you the same. She had been spending more and more time with you. Behaving peculiarly. Late for work, not even coming some days, and sending the strangest excuses."

"Me? I have been trying to help her. You know as well as I do that she was involved with Julius Harker. I think . . . I think she must have discovered who his killer was."

Reaver stared at me as if I was another antiquity. Something to be decoded. "What makes you believe she figured it out?"

I opened my mouth, half-tempted to tell him about the *Radix Maleficarum*. But something stilled my tongue. Frederick Reaver *hated* Julius Harker. *Hated* that Leona was spending more and more time with him. He had a history with Harker, having been rivals for the better part of a decade. Truthfully, he was the obvious villain in this story. So obvious that I'd discounted him out of hand. "You hated him . . ." I whispered half to myself as I took a step backward out the door.

He raised a brow. "Harker? Of course I didn't hate him. I hated the way he threw away his potential, wasted that brilliant mind of his. There is a difference, I assure you—and before you go concocting wild stories in your head about me, I would point out that you yourself were on the dais when Julius Harker was discovered. *You* snuck into Mr. Mueller's cell before he was killed. *You* were the very last person to see him before his untimely death—then breaking into his very museum afterward and stealing something very valuable." He wet his lips, his gaze drifting to my brow. "See how very easy it is to play this game?"

The air left my lungs at his accusation, made even more cutting by the dispassionate expression on his face. "How did you . . . ?"

"How did I know? I know a great many things. I told you before, it's my business to *know*."

My fingers tightened into a fist as the ground moved beneath my feet. "Then do you know where Leona is?"

"That . . . I do not. Not yet. But I intend to find out." Again his expression remained blank. I might have asked him whether he preferred cake or tarts, for all the feeling he showed. "I will say it begs the question: If you are concerned for her well-being, why have you not taken this to the police before coming to me hurling baseless accusations?"

"The same police that allowed Mr. Mueller to die in their holding cells? Leona is in danger, and I need to know from whom. I thought perhaps she'd have confided in you. But it's evident she didn't trust you either."

Something flickered in his expression, the first show of *anything* other than boredom since I entered his office. "Lamentably, she did not."

I prowled closer to the table, laying a hand on his desk, clutching Harker's treatise against my chest with the other. My voice broke. "Do you not even care?"

"Julius Harker was a careless fool and got himself killed because of it. It was only a matter of time. I had told Leona this time and again. Warned her to stay clear of him and her foolish attempt to avenge him."

So Leona *had* confided in him, at least about her investigations. "And Leona? Do you not have a single care for her fate?"

Again, there was something there. The slightest twitch of a muscle at the edge of his mouth that betrayed him. I was close. Mention of Leona affected him. He must care. There must be *more* there. "She is worth dozens of him, but my hands are bound. I *cannot* help her." The words meant something. They had to. "But as I cautioned her, I shall caution you—stay clear of the Julius Harker matter. It will bring nothing but trouble upon us all." He looked up at me with his unnervingly blue eyes.

The muscles in my jaw worked. "And Leona, shall I leave her alone to her fate too?"

Again, that twitch. Not even enough of a movement to be called a twitch. Was it fear? No. Never that. Not from one like him. The man may as well be carved from granite, but even granite can crack. "I doubt even God can help her now."

It wasn't until after I left Professor Reaver's office that the peculiar words he spoke at the beginning of our conversation struck me. He accused me of *stealing* something from Harker's museum. Something of value. And while I freely admitted that I had picked up a few things—namely that silly milpreve and the records—none of it was of any true consequence. I glanced over my shoulder toward his office, of half a mind to march straight back there and make him explain his baseless accusation, when I saw Leona's colleague, Mary, standing at the far end of the hall. Her strained expression told me she'd overhead the conversation inside his office. She held my gaze for several seconds before tilting her chin in the direction of the stairs and then disappearing down them.

She wanted me to follow.

Putting Reaver aside, I hurried after her, down the stairs and straight into the musty reading room that she shared with Leona. I closed the door behind me to find her waiting, arms folded, and her spectacles hanging from her fingertips, the gold rims glinting bright against her dark blue shirt. "Did anyone follow you?"

I shook my head as she looked at the book still clutched in my arms.

"What's that?"

I'd forgotten all about the book I'd scooped off Reaver's floor.

The one that had mysteriously *flown* from the shelf all on its own, though seeing as the author of said book was none other than Julius Harker himself, I suspected the book had been tossed in a fit of pique. Heat rose to my cheeks—I suppose I'd stolen something now. "It's Reaver's . . . I . . . I hadn't meant to take it."

She leaned forward and took the book from my arms, opening the front cover. "That's curious . . ."

I leaned closer to her, reading the inscription over her shoulder.
TO MY DEAREST LEONA. J. H.

My blood ran cold in my veins.

She handed the book to me. "As you are her friend, I doubt she'd mind you keeping it safe for her."

I wet my lips, nodding. "Have you heard from Leona since yesterday?"

Mary shook her head, worry lining her face. "No, and I heard the two of you arguing. You must be careful around him. Reaver has a frightful temper. A colder, more changeable man I've never met. I never understood why Leona was taken with him, though I think it was from their time together in Egypt."

I paused, eyes wide. "What do you mean their *time* in Egypt?"

She paused, glancing at the door then back to me. "They knew each other before. It's why Reaver insisted she work with him upon his arrival here."

That was new. "Do you know from where?"

"It was kept quiet. Everything is kept quiet when it comes to that one." She tilted her head to the ceiling. She meant about Reaver. I'd noticed it too, the deference, the distance given to the man.

"Mary, Leona is missing. I worry it has something to do with Julius Harker's death."

Mary blanched, her hand rising to her chest in surprise.

"I told Reaver the same, but he was wholly unconcerned."

"Unconcerned or overly concerned. The two sides of Frederick Reaver." She swore softly before giving her head a shake. "What has that foolish girl gotten herself into?" She drummed her fingers on her waist. "She's been acting strangely, but I'd bet my life it's got something to do with the book. The one you asked her about. It has to be."

I raised a brow. "The *Radix Maleficarum*? The book that Julius Harker was interested in?"

Mary nodded. "She received a note about an hour after you left here."

Fear pricked at my neck. "What sort of a note?"

She picked up a mostly burnt scrap of paper, handing it to me. "I don't know. She left as soon as it caught fire." Her chin tilted to a small silver bowl almost identical to the one I'd noticed in Treadway's office. "I admit I pulled it away from the flames as soon as she walked out the door. She's been worrying me as well . . ."

I drew in a sharp breath as I read the words: "'wants the *Radix* . . .'"

"Who wants it?"

"I do not know. But she left like the hounds of hell were at her feet."

I took a step closer and laid a palm on Mary's slight shoulder. "Do you know who she's been meeting lately?"

Mary brushed a loose graying strand of hair from her face, tucking it behind her ear. "She never shared that with me. All I know is what I've overheard. She was close with Reaver, I know that. I wondered for a time if there was something . . . *else* . . . between them."

"Something romantic?"

Mary frowned. "Perhaps, but if there was, it's likely been over for a while now. Leona and Reaver have been quarrelling when they think no one is watching. She would arrive some mornings looking as if she hadn't slept all night, and stay well past closing. Other days, she'd be here long before the museum opens, having spent the night in the collection with him. I think she was trying to find something."

"Did their arguments begin about the time Julius Harker didn't show up for that lecture?" My mind tripped back to when I'd first heard of Julius Harker, of how he'd slighted both the museum and Frederick Reaver by not appearing at a lecture. That had been a handful of days before the discovery of his body. About the same time as Harker was murdered.

She paused, tapping her fingers again on her forearms. "About then."

"Do you have any idea what she was looking for?"

She closed her eyes. "I don't know, Miss Vaughn. All I know is that she'd been helping Reaver translate some discovery he'd made, some scrolls. . . . They were both very tight-lipped about it."

I had overheard Leona mention something of the kind to Reaver when he pulled her away from the curiosity museum the night that Julius Harker's body was discovered. "Do you mean the Saqqara scrolls? Leona and Reaver had been discussing them the night of the exhibition. Reaver had come looking for her and I heard her tell him that she was having some kind of trouble with them. Reaver seemed surprised by it—I'd not paid much attention to it at the time. Have you located them? Do you think those scrolls mean something?"

Mary frowned deeply. "Perhaps, perhaps not. But I think we have a much larger problem here. I have searched all the accession records, all the papers to locate those scrolls. The museum doesn't *have* any scrolls from Saqqara in the collection. There *are* no Saqqara scrolls. They simply don't exist."

My skin grew cold as I stared at her. "If there are no scrolls . . ."

Mary nodded with a deep frown. "Then what was Reaver doing with Leona at all hours that they didn't want the rest of us to know about?"

I swallowed hard. That was *indeed* a very good question. And just like that, I had in my possession yet another clue that amounted to absolutely nothing.

Chapter Twenty-six

An Intrepid Imposter

WITH Annabelle's stolen reading card in hand, I left the Ashmolean and made my way to the Bodleian Library. In another time, another place, I might have been excited to see inside the ancient and hallowed space—and yet a growing dread took hold of me.

You're too late, Ruby Vaughn. Leona's already dead.

Entering the square courtyard dappled with the winter afternoon shadows, I looked up at the grand fifteenth-century building housing the library with its ornate spires and great glass windows. What was I even doing here? I had no idea what I expected to find in the book, and the *Radix* certainly wouldn't tell me where Leona was. I pinched the bridge of my nose and gave my head a shake when I spied a familiar figure leaning against the yellow stone courtyard wall opposite the library.

"Hari! What are you doing here?" I cut the distance between us, oddly buoyed by my solicitor's unexpected appearance. "Never mind it, I don't care why—you are just the person I need!"

He raised his brows, studying me as I hurried across the courtyard to him. "You are impossible to track down sometimes, did you know that?"

Evidently not *too* difficult as I was currently being followed by enough people I'd lost count. I frowned. "You haven't hired anyone to keep an eye on me, have you?"

His laugh echoed off the high walls surrounding us as he cast his hazel eyes up to the gray sky overhead. "What good would it do me? You do as you please, despite my advice. It would be a great waste of your money if I did. Besides, your housekeeper told me I could find you here."

My expression faltered.

Hari spotted it right away and drew nearer, dropping his voice to a hush as he noticed the wound at my temple. "What has happened to you?"

"Nothing important." I adjusted my hair to cover more of the damage. I took a step closer, dropping my voice. "Hari, I believe I'm being watched."

He frowned. "You didn't get a scrape like that from being watched."

A half dozen little house sparrows hopped around on the cold stone before me, searching for food in the cracks of the pavers. "Yes, well. One of them did a little *more* than watch."

Hari swore, pulling his coat tighter around him as a gust of wind ripped through the walkway sending the birds up on the wing, out of the courtyard in search of food elsewhere. "One of them? Ruby, what is going on here?"

"Someone has been following me. *Several* someones. I was attacked by a man, but there was a woman too—Ruan saw her watching us not long after the attack. I thought—*hoped*—that perhaps she had something to do with the imposter." At least the imposter didn't want me dead—she likely only wanted money. That's what they all wanted in the end. Despite initial protestations to the contrary, it always came back to cash. There was an odd comfort in that.

Deep lines formed at the edges of Hari's mouth. "It is possible. It is because of her that I've been trying to find you. She is threatening to go to the papers if you don't speak with her. She's given me three days to arrange the meeting."

"Three days?" I let out a bitter laugh. "What does she think she has that is enough to tempt me to meet with her? The papers already know the worst of my secrets. What more could she expose?"

Hari shifted closer to me, wincing with the movement. The weather must have been aggravating his old wound. His voice came out scarcely over a whisper: "She is threatening to tell the world that you are not legitimate. That your parents—"

Whatever I'd expected him to say, it was certainly not *that*. "How could she possibly know that? Even *I* did not know until we found the documents after they died." I could still recall that stifling hot afternoon in my father's study. Hari had insisted on joining me in New York when I went to settle their estate. I'd been going through my father's books, boxing them up, when a slip of paper fell out. Innocuous looking, but when I unfolded it, I'd found record of my parents' marriage. A marriage that occurred a year to the day *after* my birth. I'd not thought about it in years—it hadn't mattered at all to me, but there were some in this world to whom it would matter a great deal.

Hari touched the back of my hand gently, his expression a reminder that he recalled how poorly I took that discovery, wondering what other essential truths my parents hid from me. "I do not know how she could. But this woman has told me about your strange dreams."

Hair pricked on the back of my neck as I swung my gaze to his sad, hazel eyes. Pity thick in the air.

It was impossible. Utterly impossible. The woman somehow learning of my parents' delayed marriage was one thing, but even *Hari* didn't know about my dreams, or how I sometimes saw things that later happened—how I'd witnessed their deaths on the *Lusitania* long before my family ever left America. I stepped back, shaking my head hard. I could not deal with this now and especially not with Leona in danger. "It's impossible. Make her go away, Hari. We have greater problems than an imposter."

"I do not see how that is possible." He reached out, taking my gloved hand in his, pulling me back toward him, and squeezed it gently. "You must deal with it. For your own sake. You put everyone before yourself—what would you have me do if I were in your shoes? Answer me that."

I clenched my jaw tight, then saw the surrender in Hari's eyes.

He stepped back, holding up his hands. "I ask you as a friend—speak to this woman. See what she wants."

My nostrils flared.

But Hari had not been cowed by the German artillery during the war, and he certainly wasn't threatened by my quicksilver temper now. "Sometimes I think beneath your skin you are the most frightened person I know. Every time someone gets too close to the mark you tighten your walls. Your Cornishman must be a madman or a fool to try to surmount your guard."

I closed my eyes, willing the pounding in my brain to go away. "Three days?"

"Three days," he confirmed. "What would you have me tell her?"

"Very well. We shall do it tomorrow. At eight in the morning, she has ten minutes of my time. I have no more to spare. Leona is missing. I have to find her."

The color drained from Hari's face. "Missing? Are you certain?"

A-half-dead-woman-in-my-attic certain. But I didn't voice that, at least not here. "As much as I can be. Her house was ransacked. I think it has to do with a book in the library."

"And you are investigating this, yourself." Not a question. Hari knew me far too well for that.

"I don't have a choice. I'll explain later when we have privacy."

"Do you think she is running or was taken?" he asked softly.

That was the very question I had been wondering myself. "I don't know."

"I will try to find her."

In an uncharacteristic show of affection, I threw my arms around his neck and hugged him tight. "Thank you. I mean it. And Hari . . ."

"Mmm?" he asked, stepping back and smoothing his jacket from my unseemly fit of affection.

"Be careful. I could not bear it if you came to harm because of this."

"I'll inquire discreetly. You know Leona, she has a habit of doing exactly as she pleases. Just like someone else we know. I am certain she'll come up all right."

And I could only hope that Hari was right, like he had been so many times before.

Chapter Twenty-seven

Misdirection and Misadventure

A few small fibs and a flash of my borrowed reader card gained me access inside the hallowed halls of the Bodleian. A far easier task than I'd imagined. As I waited for the librarian to return with the book, I stared out the great window of the medieval-era reading room. All around me were hundreds upon hundreds of old, rare, some one-of-a-kind, texts. A secondary gallery of books rose above where I stood, reachable only by a curving wooden stair. An impressive sight, but at present my mind remained stubbornly fixed upon Leona's fate.

The librarian ought to be back by now. I looked away from the snowy courtyard, craning my neck to better glimpse the stairwell. Empty. I checked my watch again. I'd been waiting well over a half an hour now. Long enough that a faint sheen of snow had blanketed the slates of the courtyard.

"Miss Traywick?"

I almost didn't answer to poor Annabelle's name.

The young librarian appeared right behind me and I flashed him a bright smile. "I'm sorry, I was distracted . . . the birds . . ." My hand limply gestured out the window to the snowy courtyard—conspicuously devoid of avian life.

"You are looking for the *Radix Maleficarum*?" he asked nervously.

I struggled to recall the lie that had tripped easily from my tongue downstairs. "Yes . . . I am doing a comparative study on it and the *Malleus Maleficarum*. I was hoping to be able to see the *Radix*, it's an unusual book." *Unusual* was an understatement. I'd never even heard of the *Radix* until arriving in Oxford.

He shifted his stance, growing increasingly uncomfortable by the second. "It is very rare, miss, it is. But there's a slight problem."

I raised a brow, sweat pricking my neck.

"The book is not . . . well . . . it's not here."

My heart fell as I recalled the singed note that Leona had received before her disappearance, indicating someone wanted the *Radix*. My voice was hoarse. "Pardon?"

"I'm afraid . . . it's . . . it's . . . *missing*." The librarian's expression gave the impression he couldn't quite parse the meaning of the word himself.

"How is that even possible?" The Bodleian was not a lending library where one could borrow a book and misplace it before returning it. All books had to stay in the library—to do otherwise risked repercussions, as Julius Harker keenly discovered when he lost his position over the theft of this very tome a decade ago.

The young librarian placed his palm on the window frame beside me, his eyes unfixed as he stared out the window, reeling from disbelief. "I checked the register. It hasn't been called up in at least a decade. It must have been misshelved . . . or . . ."

Stolen. The word hung in silence between us. As a librarian here, surely he knew the book's storied lore. I rocked back on my heels, casting my eyes up to the vaulted medieval ceiling of the reading room. "Can I see the ledger?"

He let out a distressed sound. "It's not . . . not customary to do so but I don't see any harm in it." The young librarian led me down to the reference desk where he pulled out a red leather-bound book and turned to a page near the middle. He laid his finger down alongside a familiar name.

RUAN KIVELL. NOVEMBER 6, 1912

"See what I mean, miss?"

My blood turned to ice in my veins. *See?* I could see nothing but the glaring fact that Ruan himself had *held* that book in his very hands, not six weeks before Julius Harker purportedly stole it, and neglected to tell me that *very* pertinent piece of information. Oh, we would have a great deal to discuss when I got back home. "Has anyone else asked about it?"

The man shook his head again, offering a distracted greeting to the pair of students passing behind me. He lowered his voice, leaning over the old desk: "Truthfully, I did not even know it existed until you came in today. Forgive me if it sounds vain, but . . . I know every medieval manuscript we have in the collection."

It wasn't vanity at all. The man likely *did* know every manuscript, especially if he'd been in his post for very long. I, for one, knew every book in the bookshop—the shape of their spines, the colors, the way they fit together on a shelf. If even one volume was out of order, I would notice at once. "Do you think it's been gone for a while then?"

"I do. Forgive me, miss, I need to take this to the head of the library. I do not know how this could have happened. This is . . . highly unusual."

Dread snaked up my spine, replacing my earlier annoyance. It was a coincidence that Ruan had taken the book out shortly before its disappearance—*it had to be*—and yet in the very marrow of my bones, I knew that could not be true. Mr. Owen taught me early in our acquaintance that there were no such things as coincidences, and that was doubly true when it came to murder.

I stepped out into the courtyard, unsteady on my feet and shielding my eyes from the winter light. The rapidly setting sun cast the golden buildings in an even more brilliant shade. The snow had blanketed the ground, making the stones slick beneath my feet. I tugged my coat tighter, uncertain which had shaken me more—the discovery that the book had been stolen, or the fact Ruan had been the last known person to hold it. The latter shouldn't be *such* a surprise, for he'd said he was familiar with the book when we spoke on it the previous evening, but he'd spoken of it in the abstract—not that he'd *held* the damnable thing in his very own hands. I tried to brush the thought away, to not feel the sting of him withholding information from me.

I paused on the street outside the library, rummaging in my sack for my silver cigarette case. I needed to clear my head. Hands shaking, I pulled one out, lit it, and inhaled sharply, struggling to order my increasingly frazzled thoughts. While the book might be a misdirection only pulling me further away from Harker's killer, the fact remained that *Leona* was afraid of whoever wanted it. Far more frightened of *them* than whoever it was she believed killed Julius Harker. The book mattered to her—and that had to mean something to the investigation.

Just as I finished my cigarette, I caught the hint of a shadow behind me. I paused before turning my head, certain I'd catch someone. And yet there was nothing there. Nothing but an empty city street. I blinked away a snowflake caught on my lashes before starting toward the shadow. Surely there had been someone there, I wasn't seeing things. I *wasn't*.

Good God, Ruby, what are you thinking, chasing after shadows?

I gave my head a good shake, wincing from the tender bruise on my temple. *That* is what chasing shadows gets you—a great aching head. I pulled my spare scarf up about my face and continued the long trek home.

Despite Ruan's painful memories of his time in Oxford and the bloody last few days, I had to admit it was a charming place—made all the more lovely by the blanket of snow covering the ground. A stark contrast to the bleakness of my present thoughts. I quickened my step, headed back to the townhome, desperate to get Mr. Owen's thoughts on the matter—and to corner Ruan about his earlier omission about the *Radix*.

A motorcar slowed beside me.

"Miss Vaughn?"

I recognized that voice. A blue Rolls-Royce Silver Ghost slowed to a stop and sat idling beside me. The back window had been lowered and Lord Amberley waved cheerily, his cheeks pink and warm.

"My Lord." I took a careful step down from the curb to where the car had pulled off to the side of the narrow street. "How are you today?"

"Capital, my dear. And you were the final person I was hoping to find. I was telling Francis here how bereft I was that you were not at home when I called upon Hawick earlier today." He gestured to his son with his free hand—the garnet signet ring on his hand catching my attention. It always took me aback when people referred to Mr. Owen by his title. He might be the Viscount of Hawick, but I sometimes forgot as I'd always known him as Mr. Owen. "I am having a holiday supper this evening, my dear, and would dearly love if you could also join us. After all, tomorrow is Christmas Eve. I suspect Hawick will want to keep you all to himself for the holidays but if you could join us, it would mean the world to me. You know how truly boring we antiquarians can be, and you brighten every room you enter."

The edge of my mouth curved up slightly. "I wish I could, but you see I . . ." I struggled to find a plausible excuse—an unusual circumstance to keep me away—but could not think of a single reason that might work. I did not have the time to spend at *another* dreadful supper with the antiquarians, no matter how much I might like Lord Amberley. But I also couldn't very well admit I was in the midst of a murder investigation with a half-dead girl at home to tend to. The exhaust pricked my nose as I struggled to come up with a plausible excuse.

Lord Amberley's son shifted in his seat, staring out the other window and giving off the impression that he had better places to be. His skin was unnaturally flushed from the warmth of the car. I opened my mouth to inquire if he was feeling quite right when Amberley interrupted. "Do say you'll come, my dear girl."

The man was overly kind. Almost *too* kind.

"I really don't think Mr. Owen is feeling up to—"

"Nonsense, Hawick already said he'd attend. It'll be a grand time. Professor Reaver has agreed to join us as well. I've only just come from the museum. It is a treat when he rouses himself from the dusty storerooms to speak with us. His tales from Egypt during the war are always a particular delight."

My expression faltered at the mention of the war. Amberley nattered for a few moments about heroism and "the making of a man." I swallowed hard. As someone who had firsthand knowledge of the war, I doubted how "delightful" anyone's experiences had been.

"Francis here went off and did his bit too. Didn't you, lad?" He elbowed his son, who let out a disgruntled bleat of agreement. "It's going to be a splendid time this evening, Miss Vaughn." Amberley grasped my hands suddenly in his own. "And young Professor Treadway is also coming. I spoke with him earlier this morning. He seemed in a bit of a muddle, truth be told. I'm not sure what's gotten into the boy, but after some convincing he came around."

My attention snapped into place. "What do you mean, a muddle? Was he unwell?"

"Scattered, skittish. Why, Francis here knocked a fossil off his desk, and you'd have thought someone shot poor Treadway, the way he leapt from his chair. I was convinced he wasn't going to come at all, but he finally changed his mind."

How very odd. "Was he was acting peculiar?"

"Very. Never seen the lad in such a state. But I suspect dinner in good company will cure whatever ails him."

I highly doubted that. Amberley's description of poor Jonathan Treadway certainly implied he'd learned of Leona's disappearance. Learned of it or was complicit. "Perhaps I should stop by the museum to check on him."

"Oh no, my dear. It would do you no good."

I raised a brow in silent question.

"Treadway left straightaway. Ran right from the room as soon as I'd told him that Reaver would attend. Said he would come and then left us alone in his office! Can you believe it?" By now, Amberley's son had fallen asleep against the window. Softly snoring.

"He left?" I could not have disguised my surprise had I tried.

Lord Amberley nodded somberly. "Come, my dear girl. Let me drive you home. You must be half frozen. He reached for the handle to open the door.

Treadway and Reaver together in the same room? Perhaps this was exactly the spark I needed to move this investigation along. "No. No . . . I don't mind the walk."

Lord Amberley settled himself deeper into the plush leather seat and patted my hand where it rested on the window of his car door. "Are you certain? It would be no trouble at all."

"I am . . . but thank you."

He lifted a gloved finger. "Do say you'll join us tonight. It's going to be the party of a century!"

Considering the last time I attended a dinner party in Oxford, Julius Harker ended up dead the next day, I feared what might follow this one—and yet the temptation was too great. I wet my lips. "That does sound intriguing. I shall try to come. May I bring a guest with me?"

"A guest, my dear?"

I absently ran my gloved finger along the chain of my locket. "A friend of Mr. Owen's from Cornwall is staying with us. I think he'd enjoy the company." A bald lie, especially as I knew Ruan would want absolutely nothing to do with any of these men. But we'd become partners in this investigation thus far—and I sensed he would insist upon joining me once he learned of my plans.

"Ah, you must mean Laurent's pet."

I bristled at that dismissive term.

"Hawick was proud of the boy when he sent him up to Oxford for school. I still recall Kivell from his time as a student here. A terribly lonely boy. Always toiling in that greenhouse with poor Ernst. The pair of them closer than brothers. It was good of Laurent to take him under his wing." A sadness clouded his expression at the mention of Laurent's dead son, and my irritation ebbed—a fraction. "We do all miss Ernst so. It is a shame what happened to him. But yes, yes, please bring your gentleman. I will have my man set another two places. I am glad that you will join us." He started to close his window, then paused again. "Are you certain that I cannot see you home? It truly is no bother."

I tugged my coat tighter about me as the wind picked up, whistling down the street. "No. I could use a walk today. Until tonight, Lord Amberley."

He touched the brim of his hat dubiously before telling his driver to go on. I watched as the car curved around the winding road, disappearing into the distance, before I started off again, overall pleased with the turn of events when my mother's voice came to mind unbidden—yet again: *Men are monsters, Ruby Vaughn. Never to be trusted. Do not forget that.*

I brushed the voice away, not pausing to wonder why my mother had always been so fearful of strangers. I didn't have time to think of my mother. Not now. The peculiar happenings here in Oxford combined with this newest imposter must have shaken me far more than I realized.

Chapter Twenty-eight

After-Dinner Entertainment

DINNER at Lord Amberley's was a far more tedious affair than I feared. And while he had promised that both professors Reaver *and* Treadway would be in attendance tonight, their continued absence grew suspicious. Would I wake in the morning to find reports of yet another dead academician? Or two? If so, I prayed Leona would not be in that number. With each second wasted here, my imaginings grew more fevered. I *had* to find her. I had to do *something* and yet I was trapped. Trapped waiting for the party to end lest anyone realize that I was investigating Harker's death.

I sat alone on a low settee in the drawing room after enduring six courses of over-sauced and painfully rich food. The walls were papered in a deep cobalt silk adorned with white birds. It was a lovely effect, accentuated by the golden accents throughout the room. Everything in here had hints of Eastern art. A Japanese screen near the fireplace; a large, intricate, blue-tinged celadon jar that reminded me of one I'd seen at the Victoria and Albert Museum last summer. Chinese in origin, if I recalled correctly. Then again, I was far better versed in books than pottery.

Lord Amberley stood by Mr. Owen's chair, his hand on the back. The two chatting and gesturing, deep in their cups. I'd ruled

Amberley out as a suspect almost immediately, but perhaps I'd been wrong to do so. He was questioned about the *Radix* the first time it went missing. He also had a known conflict with Julius Harker, which was far more motive than most. And yet he'd not given me a single reason to suspect him. But hadn't I learned my lesson before? Even the most wicked villain can wear a sheep's coat. Mingling with the flock before striking.

I wet my lips, glancing around the room. No one was paying me any mind, nor had they for the last several hours. Ruan had disappeared earlier in the evening, at the side of Professor Laurent. He did not mind the older man's attention, and I could not begrudge him that. During the war, I'd had no one who knew my family well enough to understand my pain at their loss. If I'd had, I thought it would have done me a great deal of good. As it was, I'd nearly been sent to a hospital for mental *strain*—that's what the matron diplomatically called my *episode*. Others had the right of it—whispering behind closed doors that I'd flat out cracked under pressure. Gone utterly, raving mad.

Images of the bearded man I'd seen outside the Covered Market after speaking with Mr. Mueller came back in a flash. All at once I recalled how I recognized him, and why he was so familiar.

My throat grew dry. It couldn't be.

It simply couldn't.

For the man outside the market had the same bearing, same . . . *aura*—for lack of a better word—as the man I'd seen during the war. The one I'd imagined when I cracked. I squeezed my eyes back tight. It wasn't possible. It couldn't be happening again. I was *not* imagining things.

Even Ruan had seen a woman following me. *Someone* had attacked me, and hallucinations most certainly do *not* attack.

The room was too small. Too tight to breathe.

No. Not again. I wasn't going mad. I couldn't be. Not now. Leona *needed* me. I didn't have time to have another episode. I shot to my feet, the ground oddly unsteady beneath me, and quickly slipped into the corridor. Air. I needed air. A moment of peace away from the chatter of the room and then I'd be all right.

No one would miss me.

No one at all.

I padded down the darkened corridor lit by ornate candelabras and made my way toward Lord Amberley's library. The walls on either side were lined with taxidermy of all sorts. An entire lion stood on one side with his sharp open-mouthed grin. Upon the walls were the heads of buffalo and bison. All variety of deer. Trophies mounted and hung upon the walls, row after row reaching to the ceiling. Columns of death. My stomach recoiled at such violence, such waste. Animals slaughtered, skins taken and stretched over goodness knew what.

I could not bear it. There had been far too much bloodshed in my life for me to admire this sort of sport. Whether it was a trick of the light, or my third glass of champagne, I could have sworn the glassy eyes embedded into each of Amberley's kills followed me. Watching as I moved down the hallway. Either in pity or warning.

Intruder.

Beware.

Run.

Not mad indeed. I gave my head a good shake, wrapping my fingers around the silver handle of the door to Amberley's well-appointed library. Books would make it better. They always did.

I pushed hard.

Heat suddenly rose to my cheeks as I struggled to *not* witness the amorous scene playing out before me on the great rococo-style desk in Lord Amberley's library. For there, splayed out on the top, was a very lovely woman in the throes of passion with Lord Amberley's son Francis. Sweat was beaded up on his brow as he locked eyes with me. And instead of shrinking back, pausing for decorum's sake, he continued on . . . rutting, for lack of a better word.

I took a step backward, mumbling out an apology as a faint bit of blood pooled in his nostril before creating a thin trail to his upper lip. He wiped it away with a casual flick of his wrist, the garish smear marring his face as he continued on with his paramour, heedless of my presence. Instead, the fellow appeared to enjoy the audience.

"Love, you can either stay and join our party or go back to theirs. But please shut the door—it's drafty!" The woman laughed as she stretched farther across the desk. I was not a prude—I *wasn't*—and yet the whole scene was so utterly horrifying that I could not move. I remained frozen in place. The red lacquer on her nails caught my attention as she scraped some white substance from the surface of an old mirror. I couldn't tell *exactly* what it was she was doing, but I certainly had a good idea.

One step. Then another. I backed out of the room, closing the door. I shook my head, blotting the rather absurd scene from my head.

Cocaine and carnal appetites.

Well, that put a different light on things. Perhaps the evening was not totally wasted after all. Though a man *using* drugs and a man *stealing* them are two separate things. It was something certainly worth remembering, especially in light of Lord Amberley's connection to Julius Harker. Perhaps I had been hasty to dismiss Amberley as a suspect.

Lost in thought, I made my way back down the garish, taxidermy-laden hallway. I entered the main parlor where the party had mostly reassembled. Everyone was chattering and I looked to see what had caused such excitement, as they had been rather sedate when I wandered off. Perhaps the butler had put cocaine in the pudding to liven things up a bit?

My amusement at my own little joke withered when I spotted

Frederick Reaver standing at the far end of the room boasting all his characteristic swagger and greeting a middle-aged scholar seated by the fire. Reaver was dressed impeccably, but no matter how fine the cut of his coat, there was no hiding the newfound dark circles beneath his eyes and the wariness in his step. Both of which gave me pause. For a man who showed so little emotion this morning, to be this visibly affected had to mean *something*. I settled myself back into the plush cushions of the sofa and waited.

"I cannot believe he dares show his face here."

I bit down hard on my tongue, startled by the sound of Jonathan Treadway's slurred voice. The young scholar had also arrived without my notice and had taken up a position behind me, his hand resting intimately on the back of the sofa drawing unspoken battle lines across Lord Amberley's decadent blue ballroom.

"You scared me out of my skin," I hissed, the words escaping my lips without a thought. "Leona's missing. Did you know?"

He didn't answer. But from the stains on his jacket—and the distinct smell of sweat, smoke, and alcohol radiating from him—he certainly must. Lord Amberley had not been exaggerating when he said that Treadway was out of sorts. My champagne-addled mind struggled to make sense of his current state. Had he swum across town on a river of cognac? "Do you have news of Leona?"

He made a loud harrumph, garnering the attention of the other guests.

Apparently not.

"Treadway, my boy!" Lord Amberley's voice was cheerful—though his expression grew wary as he took in Treadway's disarray.

Professor Reaver's head shot up at the sound of the other fellow's name, and he swung his sharp predatory gaze around the room before settling on Treadway, who placed his clammy hand upon my bare shoulder.

I shimmied away from his touch, skin rebelling against the unwanted contact.

"Good God, man, I can smell you from here," Reaver muttered. "Have a bit of dignity."

"Dignity?" Treadway slurred. He started toward Reaver, whacking his hip on the back of the sofa as he made the corner. His hand grabbed wildly onto the corner of the delicate piece of furniture to keep his balance. "Dignity? What dignity is there in your nonchalance? You did this to her! You are the reason she is gone. I know who you are, you cold-blooded fiend! You have poisoned her mind against the rest of us and this is the result!"

Reaver's focus drifted between me and Treadway. "I would appreciate you keeping your tongue firmly between your teeth before you further embarrass yourself."

Jonathan swore, muttering to himself about ill-bred bullies. He struggled to shed his threadbare jacket, hopping about. The scene might have been comical were the situation not dire. Frederick Reaver was built like a stevedore—muscled and strong from the rigors of fieldwork—whereas Jonathan Treadway looked as if he'd blow over in a stiff breeze. I'd thought Treadway birdlike at first, but seeing the two men together truly underscored their differences.

"I'll put something between *your* teeth." Treadway strutted across the drawing room with the bravado of a fighting cock.

I darted between the two of them, extending my arms in each direction. "Gentlemen, perhaps we could—" A foolish attempt, for Reaver could toss me to the side without even a second thought if he aimed to do so. I was scrappy, yes, but the man had a good fifty pounds of muscle over me.

"I see no *gentleman* here! Only a murdering bastard masquerading as one." Treadway pressed his bony chest into my outstretched palm. I curled my fingers into his soiled shirt, as he took me by the waist and shoved me aside. I stumbled backward, only to be steadied by a pair of unseen hands.

Ruan's green scent invaded my senses as he leaned close to my ear, humor lacing his voice. "I cannot leave you in a drawing room for five seconds without a barroom brawl breaking out, can I?"

I remained transfixed by the veritable train wreck unfolding upon Lord Amberley's Aubusson rug. "Do something," I whispered.

I could feel his movement against me as he tapped his fingers slowly on my hip—the gesture intended to get my attention and have me watch the scene ahead, but it had an entirely *different* effect upon my poor body.

I swallowed hard.

Ruan lowered his head. "There's something happening here . . ."

Treadway took a swing at Reaver, which the latter dodged.

"What do you mean, *happening*?"

I started forward, back to the fray, when Ruan's hand drifted from my waist to the back of my hand, covering it slightly, his fingers lacing through my own as he held it there, closing his fist over mine.

Do you hear something?

"Mmm." The confirmation was little more than a rumble from his chest. I caught the faintest scent of electricity in the air, as Treadway took another teetering swing. Ruan was *listening*, or whatever it was he did. Why was no one stopping them? Reaver was going to brutalize poor Treadway. Yet everyone was rapt upon the two men dancing around on the rug like a pair of prizefighters.

A footman thundered down the hall, rousing another to try to control the fracas.

Behind us, the antiquarians began wagering on Reaver coming out the victor. It was the most excitement they'd had in years.

Poor Jonathan Treadway.

Treadway could hardly keep on his feet. His eyes wide and frenzied as he grabbed a bottle of brandy from a nearby table.

"Now, now, lad. It's all right." Lord Amberley's expression sobered.

Things were quickly getting out of hand. He reached for Treadway, who shrugged the old lord away.

Reaver had not even broken a sweat. Simply sidestepping the drunken man as one would when humoring a petulant child. "Don't make a fool of yourself, Jonathan. You've more pride than that." Reaver's voice was far gentler than mine would have been in similar circumstances.

"Where is she?" Treadway took another swipe at Reaver. "I know you've done something to her. You're the reason she's gone."

Ruan tapped my hip again with his thumb. *This*. This was what he'd heard.

Professor Laurent had joined the onlookers, taking a spot to the left of me, beside Ruan. "Well, I'll say this is not what I expected when I set out this evening." An edge of humor laced the old professor's voice before his tone shifted to one of defeat. "Always a loose cannon—Jonathan was. I thought he would grow out of it with time, but it seems not. Too much of his father in him, I suspect."

Two of Lord Amberley's footmen finally managed to subdue the raving Treadway, who continued to shout obscenities at Professor Reaver. The younger's words slurred enough I could barely make them out.

"Something isn't right," I murmured over the rim of my glass.

"What do you think it means?" Ruan remained focused upon the footmen trundling poor Jonathan Treadway out the front door. Professor Reaver plucked an imperceptible piece of lint from his woolen dinner jacket. His calculating gaze met mine and his emotionless veneer dropped. A flash of unbridled hatred shone in his eyes as he stared in my direction, and I knew in that moment that he was capable of anything. Anything at all.

Ruan saw it too. His hand gripped mine and he pulled me toward the door, forgoing even my coat. He simply shoved his own dinner jacket over my bare arms and tugged me out into the night.

Reaver was a danger.

I'd never seen such venom in a man before—and I'd gone to war, confronted murderers and angry mobs. All of which paled against the rage in Frederick Reaver's eyes.

Chapter Twenty-nine
Midnight Burglary

"I don't like him," I muttered, tucking my arm into Ruan's as we walked down the darkened Oxford streets. The closeness was for warmth. *That was all.* And yet somehow my hand unerringly found his, and I slipped them both into the pocket of his coat amongst the various unusual pebbles and stones he'd collect and forget he'd pocketed away. Ruan did not pull away this time. Rather, he squeezed my fingers tighter within his own—tired of fighting whatever this was that existed between us.

Ruan for his part appeared impervious to the cold, dressed only in his shirtsleeves and waistcoat. "He certainly doesn't like *you*. What did you do to cross the fellow?"

I snorted. "Exist? Truly, I don't know. I spoke to him this morning and we didn't leave on the best of terms, but he certainly hadn't looked at me with such hatred then as he did tonight. Do you suppose he blames me for Treadway's behavior?"

Ruan made a low sound in his throat. It was a cloudless night, which made everything somehow colder—the stars shone bright overhead as the moon rose high. The scent of woodsmoke thick in the night.

"Did you hear anything useful?"

"Not about your friend. Concern. Anger. Fear. It was all swirling in both of their heads. I could not make sense of why, but the air was thick with it."

Amused, I paused, looking up at him. "You act like you can smell it. Are you also part bloodhound?"

He let out a low chuckle. "No. But emotion has a . . . perhaps *scent* isn't the right way to explain it. But emotion is a palpable thing. Perhaps *essence* is a better word. Gods, this is strange to discuss with you . . ."

"Why? Because I'm terribly ordinary?" I laughed.

Something flickered in his expression. "There is nothing ordinary about you, Ruby Vaughn."

The dim glow of the gaslights barely illuminated his dear face. Ruan leaned down, his forehead pressed against mine, and inhaled deeply, drawing the *essence* of *me* into his lungs. His willing tenderness was intoxicating. I caught the scent of ginger candy on his breath and for a moment I thought he might kiss me, but instead he pulled back, tugging me on down the lane. "We should get back and check on the girl."

His words cut through the buckets of champagne that Lord Amberley had been pouring me, crushing the moment to dust.

Right. I felt immediately rotten for having not thought of Annabelle before now, distracted as I'd been by the fracas in Amberley's drawing room.

Ruan's step grew more determined than ever before, as if he could outrun the chaos of what we were together if he merely moved fast enough. I did not even notice until long after we were back home that Ruan never released my hand. Not until we were on the way up the stairs to the room where poor Annabelle lay in her sickbed—and for the life of me, I did not know what it meant.

I waited outside in the hall as Ruan knelt on the cold wooden floor beside the girl, murmuring with Mrs. Penrose about what had happened in our absence. "No changes then?"

She shook her head. Her gray hair glinted in the warm electric lights of the room.

The muscle in his jaw tightened, and he set about checking her pulse. "I still worry we should call a physician."

I took a step farther into the room, floorboards creaking with the movement. "Is there infection?"

Ruan gave his head an imperceptible shake.

"Is she any less stable than before?"

Again, another subtle shake.

I folded my arms beneath my breasts, still wearing his jacket. "I don't see what good a hospital will do. You are far more attentive than any physician I have ever known and frankly I'd rather put myself in your hands than any number of their kind. Besides, you're a witch."

"Pellar," he corrected grumpily.

"Semantics. The point is, you've read all the same books they have. You have spent the last several years of your life learning from Dr. Quick in Lothlel Green, you may as well *be* a physician. I have seen firsthand what you can do. With or without your"—I hesitated, uncomfortable speaking of Ruan's abilities in front of Mrs. Penrose, though the woman already believed he walked on water—"your *gifts*."

Ruan let out a decidedly Mr. Owen–sounding grunt, his roughened fingers resting on the girl's pulse. Perhaps he and I had spent too much time with the old man for our own good.

Mrs. Penrose slid past me, pressing a good-night kiss to my cheek before slowly making her way down the stairs. I waited until she was fully out of earshot before I turned back to Ruan. "Do you think Reaver did something to Leona? I'd confronted him in the museum today—I cannot understand the man nor his motivations. But tonight? Tonight frightened me."

Ruan shifted, settling his hip on the bed beside the girl. "Me as well. The air was thick with his guilt and the rage— Ruby, I swear to the gods he would have killed you on that floor had I not taken you away. I'd never felt such anger."

I swallowed hard. Neither had I. "What does he think I've done?"

"It was chaotic, I couldn't hear anything beyond the emotion."

I let out an awkward huff. "Speaking of hearing, did you hear Mr. Owen tonight?"

"I did . . ." Ruan remained less amused than I was at the situation.

"The man lost ten pounds betting on Treadway. Anyone with eyes could have seen that he didn't stand a chance against Reaver. The fellow might be a beast, and wish me dead, but his arms are quite . . ."

The ghost of a smile crossed his lips. "A man wishes you to the devil for unknown reasons and you are admiring his forearms?"

My throat dried and I swallowed hard. "All that is to say, I may not like the fellow but if one admired such a thing . . ."

Ruan chuckled. "Go on to bed. Get some sleep. I'll be done soon."

I crossed the hall not at all intending to sleep. Not with Leona missing. I dropped to my knees and dug about under the bed for my own satchel. Sitting around worrying was not going to get me any closer to finding out what happened to Leona or finding Julius Harker's killer. And there was one place I had not yet checked for clues—quite possibly the most obvious place of all. *Julius Harker's home.*

The wooden floorboards creaked behind me as I pulled out my roll of lockpicks from the bag and flopped them atop the mattress.

"I take it we are headed back out this evening?"

"We haven't searched Harker's home." I continued groping around under the bed for my boots. I shucked off his coat and threw it carelessly beside the lockpicks before starting on the stubborn buttons at the back of my rose silk gown. "Close the door, would you? I'll be ready in a trice. Assuming you're up for another adventure?"

Ruan made a sound in his chest before closing the door behind him. I'd half expected him to leave me in peace to change, but instead he stepped deeper into the room, brushing my fingers away as he made quick work of the buttons on the gown. "It will take all night if I wait on you to finish. And the sooner we are gone, the sooner we are back, the sooner I can get some sleep."

I let out a breathy laugh and stepped behind the thin dressing screen before shimmying out of the gown. I flung it over the top before turning to my wardrobe and pulling out a pair of trousers and a clean blouse. In the reflection of the mirror, I caught him watching the screen with a considered expression, as if he could not quite decide how he'd ended up in this madhouse with me.

Madhouse.... I swallowed hard as the specter of my own past came back. *Not now, Ruby.* I quickly fastened the buttons of my trousers, and tucked in my blouse. I put on my riding boots and hopped out from behind the screen struggling to get my right foot fully into the thing.

Ruan handed me my roll of lockpicks. "Shall we?"

I took them from him, my fingers brushing his before I darted down the stairs. There was promise in these words. Something beyond this night and the ridiculous plan I'd hatched after far too many glasses of champagne.

We *shall*. Whatever it might be.

Chapter Thirty

An Unexpected Conspirator

ON the way to Harker's home, I filled Ruan in on all that transpired while we were apart, including my trip to the Bodleian and the unpleasant discovery of Lord Amberley's son mid-cocaine-fueled coitus. He didn't react at all to any of it—not even a flinch when I mentioned that I saw his name on the ledger as the last person to request the *Radix Maleficarum*. He simply made that irritating sound in the back of his throat that told me little.

"Why didn't you mention that part?"

"I assumed you already guessed."

"*Guessed* that you'd been reading a one-of-a-kind book about witches?" But as the words left my lips, I realized he was right, I *should* have known. The very reason I met him at all had to do with his habit of collecting ancient books on the occult, and his hunger to understand exactly *what* he was.

He gave me a wry smile.

"Do you think it signifies anything?" I looked up at him beneath the haze of the new electric streetlight.

"Which part?"

A pang of worry settled in my chest. "That it disappeared after you looked at it? Did anyone ever ask you about the book? Speak of it to you?"

Ruan scratched his jaw with the back of his hand, a faint dusting of snow settling in his dark hair. "Treadway did. He found me with it in the library. I think he was surprised I could read at all, he thought I was stupid—never missed an opportunity to let anyone know his opinion either. We . . . got into an argument that day at the Bodleian in Duke Humfrey's Library."

I raised a brow, imagining the scene.

"It got . . . *heated*. Needless to say, I left Oxford not long after that. I'd been brought up for disciplinary action over it. I'm sorry, Ruby. I assumed you knew."

I ignored his apology, and let out an involuntary growl of my own. "Jonathan Treadway deserved whatever you did to him."

The edge of his mouth quirked up. "It wasn't quite *that* dramatic. No library brawls. Those are your quarter, not mine."

I snorted, tugging my winter coat around me. The haze around the streetlamps set off a peculiar glow this time of night. I glanced behind me for the thousandth time—but the street was dead quiet. "Did anyone else know?"

"I presume Julius Harker, as he and Treadway were so close. Ernst. Professor Laurent. He tried to help me, even stood in my defense at the hearing—told them all that Treadway was out of line accosting me as he did. But it didn't matter. Even if they'd let it pass, by the time things got that far I knew I didn't belong here."

"Ruan . . . you do belong—"

Ruan took my gloved hand in his and pulled me to a stop beside a row of darkened houses. "Laurent helped me understand what I *am*. Helped me accept that part of myself. He and Ernst knew I was different and treated me as you do. As if I was just an ordinary boy. They gave me peace to grow and learn and I will be forever grateful for that."

The fleeting sadness in his eyes was almost too much to bear. "I'm sorry."

"Don't give me your pity, Ruby. It was long ago. I don't begrudge Jonathan Treadway for being an arse. Based on the things he said to Reaver tonight, not much has changed between then and now."

I huffed out a little laugh. It seemed my pellar was becoming as good at avoiding uncomfortable truths as I. I glanced up at the street sign affixed to the wall of the corner shop. We were close. Tucking my hands into my pockets, I continued down the darkened lane. "What do you make of it, the two of them? Do you think Jonathan Treadway stole the book again? But if so, then what does Reaver have to do with the *Radix*? He's behaving suspiciously, but even Leona discounted his interest in the book. Our clues point in two directions. There's the book that is tied to Julius Harker, Leona, and Jonathan Treadway. Then there are the antiquities and the old animosity between Reaver and Harker. I do not see how they all tie together, not unless Reaver also was after the book for reasons we don't know."

"And the cocaine," Ruan added grimly.

"Yes. *That*." Images of Lord Amberley's son with that faint trickle of blood returned to my mind. I squeezed my eyes shut to blot it out. "Which also pulls Lord Amberley back into the equation."

"You told me earlier that Harker had publicly humiliated Lord Amberley."

My shoes made an eerie echo as Ruan and I struggled to keep our voices down in the quiet of the night. "Amberley does also love his books . . . but he doesn't strike me as a killer."

"Ruby . . ."

Right. I'd been wrong in the past, and could easily be wrong now. I raked my hand through my hair. "The book, then. Amberley is the only one who had a quarrel with Harker, ties to cocaine and antiquities, and is mad for books. What else do you recall about the *Radix*? This—*in case you are wondering*—is important to our investigations."

Another man might have taken offense at that, but instead Ruan simply smiled at me, leaning closer. "I gathered that much. But we can discuss this when we return home. Don't you have a house to burgle?" He tilted his chin toward the looming shadow of Julius Harker's darkened home, rising in the distance like something from a bad dream as the snow began to fall in earnest.

Twenty minutes later, having let ourselves in, I quickly set about pulling the curtains so we could use our flashlights. I did not expect to find the *Radix Maleficarum* here. Hoped, perhaps, but Leona was too clever to have hidden something important amongst Harker's things. If she and Treadway had secreted the book away, it wasn't about to be here. No, that would be too obvious. My main aim in coming to the house was to see if I could find out who Harker had been doing business with. Something that would definitively shove me in one direction or the other.

The house itself was a spare and plain building, three stories tall and wedged between two larger homes. The rooms were exceptionally narrow, the furnishings new and modern in style. A surprising choice for a scholar of antiquity. In truth, his home—like his storeroom—was immaculate. Orderly, with a sheen of dust from disuse. It gave the impression of an abandoned dollhouse, discarded. Forgotten. The air here was stale and damp. I didn't like it. Not one bit.

Ruan set off at once for the bedrooms on the first floor while I stayed below on the ground to see what I could make of things. Quickly, I examined all the obvious hiding spots—and found nothing amiss. With every tick of the clock my hope that we'd find something useful waned. A wooden tray full of unopened post sat by his desk. Carefully I went through the stack piece by piece.

Nothing but a sea of creditors' notes and overdue bills. Julius Harker was pockets to let and had been for a very long time. This was not news at all, though the sum of his debt was staggering. If his correspondence was to be believed, the man had tens of thousands of pounds of unpaid obligations—and that was just what was waiting in the post. I ran a rough hand over my face, staring at the crisp pages before me.

"Ruby..." Ruan called, breaking my train of thought. He slowly descended the narrow wooden stair, a lockbox from the last century cradled in his arms.

Now that was an intriguing find, certainly more interesting than a pile of past-due bills.

He set it down on the floor beside me with a thud. The strongbox was around eighteen inches high, and about twice as long. Made of some sort of metal—tin perhaps—over wood, and painted a middling green. Metal bands curved over the lid, reinforcing it. It was the sort of chest a shopkeeper might have had to keep important documents. Paper money, contracts. Valuables. "What's in it?"

"That was why I brought it to you." He hooked his thumbs into the waistband of his trousers, dropping his gaze to the satchel where I'd tucked my roll of lockpicks.

I pulled out the smallest of the picks and began to fiddle with the stubborn built-in locking mechanism. My hand grew damp, causing the pick to slip. "Damn and blast!"

It gave on the second try with a satisfying click. I lifted the lid, half expecting to find something truly grotesque inside, but instead was met with more paper.

Ruan shone his light into the box. Correspondence mostly. Bound in ribbons and separated into stacks. A great leather-bound diary for his schedule lay atop a thick layer of newsprint. I shifted the paper aside and hissed.

For there, at the bottom of the chest, hidden beneath his correspondence, lay a substantial number of twenty-pound banknotes.

Bound and counted in thick little parcels just as his letters had been. There were at least ten of them sitting mingled amongst stray receipts and handwritten promises to pay. I quickly counted until my head began to spin. "Ruan . . . there are thousands of pounds in here . . ."

"Is that unusual?"

I let out a strangled sound. "For a man who is in monumental debt, yes. Yes, I daresay it is. Will you count it all for me, add it to these other promises to pay, and let me know how much money he had all together, mmm?" I set the money aside and picked up the parcel of letters. "With all he owed, he must have kept his money here for safekeeping. Hidden."

Ruan settled himself cross-legged and pulled out all the money. The two of us sprawled out like a pair of highwaymen taking stock of our quarry. I wedged the flashlight under my jaw, scanning over the letters. These were from a different correspondent than the letters I'd taken from the museum. Not the fellow from Cambridge. This was a Mr. Aldate, whoever that might be, the pair of them discussing a transfer of artifacts.

The previous letters had been stale, sterile almost. These letters, however, were all dated within the last three months and possessed an entirely different tone than the ones I'd stolen from his office, ranging from intensely intimate to violently heated. Passionate letters, written by someone who cared deeply about Julius Harker and his work. Any fool could see it. The intimacy was in the casual turns of phrase. The little jokes, and references to past events that only two friends would share.

The only two people I knew of who gave a damn about the man were poor Mr. Mueller and Leona. One of whom was dead, and the other—a knot lodged itself in my throat at the thought. No. She was not dead. I would not allow it. *Could* not allow it.

I swallowed hard and continued reading, eyes burning from exhaustion until I came to one particular phrase. My heart sank. "Good God . . ."

"What did you find?" Ruan leaned closer to get a better look at the letter.

I handed him the paper. "I don't know. It's mostly about movement of artifacts into Harker's collection. Purchases and loans, quite boring reading material—but . . ."

He arched an eyebrow.

"It sounds mad—I cannot even believe I'm thinking it—but I don't believe Professor Reaver is who he says he is."

"Why would that be mad?"

I glanced down at the letter in my hand. "What if this Aldate fellow is Reaver? Or Reaver is Aldate?"

Ruan gave me a skeptical look.

"See here?" I pointed at the words typed on the paper:

You keep increasingly unpleasant bedfellows, old friend. I beg you, cease in this endeavor. If you do not, then not even I can keep you from your sorry fate. You will deserve it for your recklessness. If you will not cease for my affection for you—think of her safety. Or that of your associate. You are not the only life on the line here.

Ruan glanced from the paper to me, his brow furrowed and that endearing divot appearing between his brows.

"Reaver said the same thing to me the day after Harker was found dead. That he kept unpleasant bedfellows and deserved whatever fate befell him. Reaver was concerned for Leona, he was concerned for Mueller. The pieces *fit*."

Ruan let out a sound of amusement. "It is a common sentiment. I would wager that most of Oxford agrees with him. Frederick Reaver loathed Harker."

I licked my teeth, still trying to make sense of the letters. "But what if he didn't? What if it was a ruse to protect Reaver's reputation? A connection to Julius Harker would have ruined him. It's why Leona kept their acquaintance a secret."

"Ruby, we are discussing a man who very likely was storing cocaine in his museum's basement." Ruan gestured to the growing pile of paper money spread across the floor. "This is not complicated. He was dealing with unsavory people and he was killed for it. It is as straightforward as it can get. The only question to me is what has happened to your friend and the extent of her dealings with Harker. Did she know of the drugs, and if so, when?"

"But what if it isn't drugs at all? Neither you nor I have actually *seen* the cocaine. We've seen natron, a natural salt." Suddenly I realized I'd been jabbing my finger into Ruan's chest while talking. Flushing, I closed my fist, pulling it back and folding my arms.

The edge of his mouth curved up. He was humoring me in my wild suppositions—tolerating my conjecture—but the truth was that it was nearly two in the morning and I was no closer now to Harker's killer than when we started. With a defeated groan, I tucked Harker's diary and the package of letters into my pocket.

No one would miss them here. The entire place was coated with a fine sheen of dust. It didn't look like anyone had been here in months. And yet if that was the case, then how did these letters get into the box to begin with?

Peculiar, when you come to think of it.

"Where do you suppose he's been living?" Ruan asked, evidently overhearing my train of thought.

"Would you stop that?" I grumbled, shaking my head before letting out a weary sigh. "I suppose we'll have to figure that part out too, won't we?"

"Ruby . . ." Ruan asked softly. "You asked if Aldate was Reaver, but what if this Aldate person is actually Leona?"

I opened my mouth to say no, then paused. I laid a hand over my pocket. They were typewritten. Unsigned. The cadence, the sentences. He was right. It *could* easily be Leona—and if it was, then I'd learned no more than I already knew. I raked a hand through my hair, tugging at the roots. Both Reaver and Leona worked at the

Ashmolean, both were experts in ancient Egypt. However, of the two, Leona *cared* for Julius Harker. Cared for Mr. Mueller. Suddenly her guilt for Mueller's fate became clear, and why she did not want him to suffer for what she'd done.

My mind raced. Scrambling to piece together all the tiny clues I'd amassed over the last few days. The conversations. The things I'd seen. The things I'd found. Reaver and Leona had been arguing. Mary had said it was growing worse by the day until Harker died. Leona was not supposed to be at the exhibition that night—she had hidden her presence from Reaver, had likely been hiding a great deal more than that. I squeezed my eyes shut. The rage in Frederick Reaver's expression tonight took on a far more sinister light.

"My thoughts exactly," Ruan finished.

My jaw worked unpleasantly as I realized I'd not spoken in quite some time.

"Sorry." He gave me a rueful look.

"You think Reaver went to her house, they argued . . . Annabelle got in the way . . ." I searched his eyes, wishing that the grim possibility was not the likeliest answer.

"Now we just have to wait for Annabelle to wake, so we can prove our hypothesis."

I turned away, snapped the trunk shut, the sound echoing in the tomb-like sitting room. "Then we'd better get back, hadn't we?"

Chapter Thirty-One

The Best Defense . . .

SNOW fell in torrents as we raced through the streets of Oxford back to the townhome. Everyone with a lick of sense had long been asleep, leaving us alone in the night. A lone dog howled in the distance as we crunched along in the newly fallen snow. My teeth chattered. Neither of us said a word, both struggling to make sense of what we found in Julius Harker's home. No matter how badly I wanted to paint Frederick Reaver as the villain, something deep down told me he was not. A dreadful man, yes. A cad of the highest order? Also yes.

But he wouldn't harm Leona. That was the piece that did not fit. He cared for her, he would not have done anything to risk her. He'd more or less told me the same in his office.

The clues had been there all along. The tenderness in the way he touched Leona the night of the exhibition. The way that her name subtly affected him, even when he wore his chilly mask. "We have to find out who his buyer was . . ."

"His *what*?" Ruan asked incredulously.

"Regardless of whether it's drugs or antiquities he's dealing in, someone was buying from Harker." My sigh was visible in the night air. "We've been going about it all wrong. I've been trying to figure out the why of the crime, thinking it would lead me to the killer's identity. But all that's done is take us in circles. We need to change tack and figure out *who* might have done it, then we can worry about why."

Ruan made a strangled sound in his throat before muttering something in Cornish that sounded an awful lot like a prayer to his old gods.

The townhome was the next street over. I dipped into a narrow alley to cut the distance. It was dark between the tall buildings, and just wide enough I could touch both sides if I extended my arms. A fat rat scurried ahead, disturbed by our presence, and climbed up the wall, disappearing into the darkness. There was a time when rats frightened me, but during the war I saw enough of the things that they'd become rather commonplace now.

"How do you think you're going to find out *who* killed Harker, if we don't know why?"

I paused, turning back to him, resting my hands on my hips ready to ask if he had any better ideas, when I noticed an unusual glow coming from the townhome. Something large brushed my ankles. I glanced down half expecting to see the damn rat had returned, but instead it was Fiachna. He butted his head against me and let out a throaty meow.

"What are you doing . . . ?" I scooped him up into my arms. As I stood, I realized how he'd gotten out. The door to the townhouse was wide open, all the ground-floor lights burning bright. Panic climbed up my throat as I held onto my oversized housecat, running my fingers through his coat and struggling to make sense of the scene.

Mr. Owen and Mrs. Penrose were asleep when we left, and Annabelle was in no condition to be turning on or off lamps.

The house had been dark.

I broke into a run, cat in my arms, until I reached the doorway and came to a skidding halt. Fiachna wriggled his way out of my grasp with an aggrieved meow and hopped onto the cold floor.

Mr. Owen stood in the middle of the kitchen, clad in his long white nightshirt, his sturdy legs bare from the thigh down. My—well, *his*—revolver pointed at the chest of a man bound up with kitchen twine.

Mrs. Penrose, for her part, stood over the intruder with a heavy copper pan gripped in her hand. Gauging by the knot already growing on their captive's temple, she had already employed said pan at least once. Fiachna purred loudly before hopping up on the table, his fluffy tail proudly flicking in the air.

"May I ask what happened here?" I stepped around Mr. Owen to get a better look at their prisoner and my heart sank.

Good God, this was bad.

I stared unblinking at the unconscious form of Inspector Beecham. The same dreadful man from the police station who'd discovered me in Mr. Mueller's cell and threatened the kind, young constable, Jack. The same one who couldn't be bothered to bring me back from outside the museum after my attack, and instead phoned for the constable to carry my insensate form back to the station. I dropped my voice to a whisper. "Are you out of your minds? That man is a police *inspector*!"

"I don't care if he's the Almighty himself!" Mrs. Penrose exclaimed. "He was after the poor maid upstairs. What else were we to do, let him finish the job he started?" Mrs. Penrose gestured with her large copper pan to the upstairs floor where young Annabelle was recovering.

"Is Annabelle all right?" Ruan asked, closing the door behind him lest any passersby discover we had a man held at gunpoint in the kitchen.

Mr. Owen gestured with the revolver. "She is. I went up to check on her in the night—you know how I have trouble sleeping—and found him in her room trying to smother the poor lamb. We got into a bit of a tussle."

"This certainly explains how Mr. Mueller was killed under the nose of the police." I watched Beecham's unconscious form, running a rough hand over my face. It also explained who accosted me in that alley. While I couldn't fault Mr. Owen for his actions, a wave of nausea struck. *How the devil would we get out of this?*

"I think we have to assume that this Beecham fellow killed Mueller." Ruan crossed the room, pouring water into a kettle before putting it on to heat. "Perhaps you can ask him when he wakes up?" he added dryly.

"Very amusing. I suppose we found our killer, haven't we?" I folded my arms.

The muscles in Ruan's jaw worked slowly as he watched me across the chilly kitchen.

"Ruan, go see to Annabelle. Be sure she's not harmed. I doubt much will be happening down here until Beecham wakes up."

"This is bad, Ruby. *Very* bad."

Oh, I knew that all too well. "Mr. Owen has this all in hand, we'll muddle through."

Ruan made a gruff sound of disagreement before running up the stairs after the poor wounded girl.

"Lass . . . there is something else."

I turned slowly to face Mr. Owen. "What else happened tonight?"

He inclined his head encouragingly to Mrs. Penrose. The older woman reached into the pocket of her thick woolen housecoat and withdrew a very familiar scrimshaw comb from her pocket. She hesitated, offering it to me on an outstretched palm.

This day got stranger and stranger. Mrs. Penrose was holding the comb from Harker's Curiosity Museum. The same one that captivated Ruan when we broke in the first time. I reached out with a cautious hand, taking it from her.

It was cool to the touch, unnaturally so. Perhaps it was the material it was made from, but the object seemed to absorb the air around it. Up close it was even lovelier than it had been under glass. I closed my eyes, wrapping my fingers around it, and the scent of salt and a bone-deep longing for home grew in my belly. "Where did you find this?" My voice cracked.

"In his pocket. It's an odd piece, isn't it?" Mr. Owen asked, his dark brown eyes lingering on my face. "Yet you seem to know what it is."

"It was in Harker's museum. Ruan was fascinated by it."

Mrs. Penrose's breath hitched softly as she darted her gaze to Mr. Owen, who looked a shade paler than he had a moment before.

"Does it mean something?"

Mr. Owen rubbed his bristly white beard and gave his head a shake. "Of course not, my lamb."

"Pay it no mind, my lover," Mrs. Penrose quickly added.

"He must have stolen it from the museum." I turned the comb over in my hand. Ruan had been transfixed by it. Such a small object, to hold his attention. Ruan's response to the little comb had unnerved me at Harker's museum, but even more now that I knew of his ties to the *Radix Maleficarum* as well. Inspector Beecham was most certainly in league with whoever killed Julius Harker—if he wasn't the killer himself. First the book, now the comb. There were a growing number of questions that led back to Ruan and I didn't like that one bit. But any questions about why Beecham had taken the comb would have to wait until the inspector had awoken—for he certainly wasn't answering anything in his current condition.

RUAN SAT BESIDE Annabelle on the narrow mattress, talking to himself in Cornish as he changed the bandages on her belly. I sometimes wondered if he even realized he did it.

"You were right." He finished removing the soiled dressings from her abdomen, exposing the damaged flesh beneath.

"About what?"

"That her attacker meant to finish the job. We cannot leave her unguarded again. It was a mistake to do it tonight. We are lucky that the inspector didn't come when we were at Lord Amberley's with only Dorothea here. At least she had Owen with her." Ruan applied a strong-smelling liquid to a small piece of cloth and began gently cleaning around the stitches. An herbal scent flooded the room. "If you'd listened to me and put her in the hospital, she'd be as dead as Mueller."

"You must have more faith in Mrs. Penrose and her skill with copper pots. Dorothea Penrose is a woman not to be trifled with."

Ruan shot me an unamused look and I sobered immediately. "Mr. Owen would never let any harm happen to her. Do not blame yourself for this evening."

"He's an old man. Dorothea isn't much younger."

I raised my brows. "And the pair of them together saved her life. But I agree with you. She must be the key to understanding what happened, otherwise Beecham would not have risked coming here to kill her."

He nodded, casting his eyes to the whitewashed wooden ceiling. "We need her healthy enough to tell us what she saw."

"I think the inspector is the one who attacked me. I must have stumbled across him when he went back to steal something else from the museum."

"The comb." Ruan's voice was soft. Defeated almost.

"How did you know?"

He let out a dry laugh. "You forget what I am."

"You hear it . . ."

"I do." He scratched his nose with the shoulder of his coat and continued cleaning Annabelle's wound. "It and you."

"Are you afraid of it? Mr. Owen and Mrs. Penrose were acting very strangely just now. Mrs. Penrose gave me the impression that she knew what it was and didn't want to talk about it."

His expression grew pained. "No. It's nothing. It simply reminds me of home, that's all. It has nothing to do with Dorothea at all . . ."

But it does with you. He didn't say it, but the unspoken words hung heavily in the air between us. He continued tending to Annabelle's injuries. Wordless seconds ticked by. Liquid sloshing in the bottle. The rustle of fabric. The wet pop of a cork as he opened a jar. So excruciatingly familiar and domestic. It was on the tip of my tongue to probe him, to ask more about the comb, and yet there were things about us and our peculiar connection that he feared. Things I was not certain I ever wanted to know, for knowing them would not change the way I felt about him. What lived between us was sure and strong as the tide—and I would not risk the safety of those shores for mere curiosity.

"I have to meet Hari in a few hours." My voice cracked as I changed the subject.

Ruan turned, his hand resting on the girl's freshly bandaged abdomen. "Your solicitor? Do you think he can help us?"

Holding up a finger to pause him, I quietly shut the door behind me. Not that I kept many secrets from Mr. Owen, but this business with the imposter was one I wasn't ready for him to hear. "The timing could not be worse."

Annabelle's chest rose and fell steadily. My eyes remained fixed upon that slow and reassuring movement, as I told him the other thing that had occurred at the Bodleian earlier today—about Hari and the imposter's demands.

"You do not have to confront her."

"I think I must. It will only take ten minutes at most. I've also asked him to see what he can find out about Leona. He has friends in Whitehall. People who *know* things."

"Government men, you mean?"

I nodded. "I'm not sure what Hari got up to after he was injured in the war, but he certainly has friends in very useful places."

Ruan made a low sound of agreement. "And you think that these friends might be able to help?"

I lifted a shoulder. "It certainly can't hurt to inquire."

"Are you certain you want to do this? See this woman?" Ruan's voice grew strained.

"I appreciate your concern for me, but I've come around on this. Hari is right. I have nothing to lose by speaking with her. My mother is dead. She has been for years. There is no way she could have survived out on the sea."

"Ruby . . . I . . ." He rubbed his jaw with his left hand as he stifled a yawn. "I am tired. I should check on the fellow downstairs. We'll be in even more trouble if Dorothea accidentally killed him with her pot. Besides, Owen will need help . . ."

"It would be far simpler if he *were* dead. Then we could hide his body somewhere remote and hope for the best."

Ruan made a strangled sound in his chest. "You frighten me sometimes."

"I frighten myself. Besides, I'm not going to kill the man. I'm not *that* wicked." I gathered up the soiled bandages to burn them downstairs. "You should get some rest. Mr. Owen will be fine. I don't think Inspector Beecham is waking up anytime soon, and you know as well as I do that the old man craves a little excitement now and then."

Ruan muttered to himself in Cornish and paused, brushing the girl's hair back from her brow, running his thumb over her temple. The air grew sharp again, the scent of a summer storm in the air.

Annabelle would be fine.

Ruan had her, and if anyone could save her, it was him.

He stood at last, hand falling to his side as the air grew still around us.

I held my hand out to him, palm up. "Come on to bed, pellar.

You've done well. I'll come along after I speak with Mrs. Penrose and Mr. Owen. I need to tell them the rest of what we've learned tonight."

He furrowed his brow, not understanding my words. For the last few nights, Ruan had been sprawled out on the small sofa in the drawing room, his long limbs slung over the arm. It was a wonder he was on his feet at all—and yet rather than go stay with Professor Laurent where he could have several rooms to himself, Ruan had stubbornly remained in this cramped townhome with an eccentric octogenarian bookseller, our Cornish housekeeper . . . and me.

"You want me to come to bed?" he repeated slowly.

"Yes."

"With you?"

Again, yes.

He drew in an uncertain breath.

"It's not the first time we've shared a bed—and this one is at least twice as big as the one in Scotland. I promise not to ravish you, if that's your concern. Or I could send you down to share Mr. Owen's, he has one large enough for a king, but I must warn you he snores like an old hound."

He let out a hoarse laugh, raking his hand through his tangled hair. "I'm too bloody tired to be ravished, but I appreciate the sentiment. It's only that I . . ." He caught himself again.

Something about his uncertainty struck a chord. Ruan was afraid of us too. I sighed and took a step closer to him. "I'm more than certain how I feel about you, Ruan. I'm sorry for what I said in Scotland. For what I did. If it makes you feel better, I'll take the sofa. At least *I* fit on it. We still have to find Leona and you're no good to me with an aching neck and bad temper. You need a decent night's sleep."

He didn't speak for several seconds, didn't move at all. His clever mind likely reminding him what a bad bet I was all around. Then the edge of his mouth turned up into a weary smile. "No . . . it's all right. I accept your olive branch, Miss Vaughn, such that it is." He stifled another yawn behind his fist before placing his palm in mine. He was trying to make light of it, but it *was* an olive branch. A truce and a promise for better days ahead for the both of us.

Chapter Thirty-two

Crime Before Breakfast

AN unfamiliar weight lay across my body. My eyes shot open, panic rising in my chest until I recalled the circumstances of said weight. Ruan was fast asleep on the edge of the narrow bed. His left arm thrown over his eyes, his right leg tangled with my own. I'd scarcely hit the mattress before falling fast asleep—still fully dressed from the previous evening's misadventures. Too tired for ravishment indeed. There ought to be a word for that level of pure exhaustion.

Fiachna had positioned himself at his usual spot at the back of my knee. Ordinarily, it was not a problem, as I hadn't shared a bed with anyone in a scandalously long time. I leaned over Ruan and grabbed my pin watch. It was still dark out—but I had an appointment with Hari and the imposter.

Six o'clock.

I snapped it back shut.

I'd have to hurry. I wriggled out of the bed gently. As soon as I was up, Ruan rolled over onto the warm spot I'd left. I quickly changed into a fresh set of clothes and started out the door.

Fiachna meowed at me, stretching in the bed.

"Take care of things will you, old man?"

The cat meowed again and nestled himself against Ruan's chest, purring loudly.

My cat and I were in accord when it came to Ruan Kivell.

OUR CAPTIVE REMAINED bound in the kitchen, but this time he was awake. A pang of conscience struck me. In my utter exhaustion, I'd left a probable murderer with my octogenarian employer. What sort of a reckless fool did that? Mr. Owen, for his part, was enjoying himself immensely, sitting guard with his Webley revolver in his left hand, a teacup in his right. His dark brown eyes met mine. "How's the lass?"

"Same as last night. She's awakened but isn't speaking sense. At least, not yet."

He lifted a piece of buttered toast from a plate, casting Inspector Beecham a dark glance. Beecham's nostrils flared and he struggled against his makeshift restraints. Mr. Owen must have changed his bindings, as now his wrists were held fast by a leather belt. An old dust cloth was jammed into his mouth.

I quirked a brow. "And him? I take it he's been talking a great deal."

"Aye, I didn't care to listen to his blathering," the old Scot grumbled, gesturing with the revolver. The inspector let out a squeak through the gag.

"Anything enlightening come up during said blathering?"

Mr. Owen rubbed his thick white beard with the back of his hand. "No, but I managed to find this in his other pocket when I replaced the twine with the belt." He handed me a familiar notebook.

I took it and flipped open the journal to a middle page. My own reassuring script looked back at me. From page to page,

I scoured the book for clues I might have forgotten. My hand stilled.

"What's wrong, lass?" Mr. Owen took another bite of his toast.

I wet my lips. "A page . . . a page is missing." I ran my finger over the rough edge where it had been cut out of the journal with a blade. I flipped back a page, then returned to the missing one before going forward a few more. Cold dread inched up my spine.

Hari's address.

The page they took had Hari's address, along with Leona's.

I was going to be sick.

Certain words had been underlined by an unfamiliar hand.

L. A. *Leona.*

ARTIFACTS

HARKER

MUSEUM

THE RANDOLPH

Tiny words, meaningless on their own, but together it told the killer that I was on his trail.

It also told them where to find Hari.

Had that stolen page inadvertently led him to Leona as well? Guilty tears pricked my eyes. "Mr. Owen, tell Ruan I'm meeting *my friend* early this morning like we discussed. I'll be back soon."

He wiped a few crumbs from his lap. "Of course, lamb. Is something wrong?"

Everything. But there was no time. There never was enough time. "I'll likely be back within the hour. Two at most."

Mr. Owen's eyes glittered merrily as he took another sip of his tea. Inspector Beecham's brow grew damp despite the damnably cold temperature in the kitchen. Good. The bastard deserved to be uncomfortable.

"Aye, my love. Go on and see your friend. I'll be fine." The mirth in his voice did not match the dangerous gleam in his eye. He was enjoying this far more than a man ought.

I brushed a kiss to his temple. "See if Ruan can make heads or tails of him, will you?"

Mr. Owen cheerfully shooed me out the door, as if we weren't breaking dozens of laws before breakfast.

Chapter Thirty-Three

Imposters, All

I was getting closer—I *had* to be, especially with Inspector Beecham coming around to try to kill the only remaining witness. While I was quite certain he killed Mr. Mueller and would have killed Annabelle—I did not believe he was acting alone. He was simply the blade, someone else was giving the orders. I blew out an uneasy breath. While the clues were finally beginning to align, they still brought me no closer to who actually *killed* Julius Harker, nor did it answer where Leona had gone? Had she been taken, or had she run? There were too many unknowns still lingering at the edges of the investigation.

I racked my brain trying to recall what other thoughts or facts I may have scribbled on the missing page but came up blank. My usually infallible ability to remember meaningless minutiae had failed me at last. The snowy streets of Oxford passed by in muted silence from the inside of the cab. I scarcely spoke to the driver, remaining nestled in the back seat watching the buildings rush by outside the fogged-up window. I rested my forehead against the cold glass and closed my eyes until the driver stopped outside the hotel.

The Randolph sat directly across from the Ashmolean like two warring giants set in limestone. It was a grand hotel, all decorated for the holidays. And even at this early hour the lobby was bustling with guests. Mostly businessmen or travelers on their way to some far-flung location for Christmas. The electric lights burned bright as I trotted up the main stair and off to the second-floor corridor in search of Hari's suite. I was early for our appointment, but we needed to speak in private before the imposter arrived. I checked my pin watch, eyes fixed on the smooth white enamel face. The second hand ticked away with a stuttering motion underscoring our urgency.

I rapped twice on the fine dark wood door.

Hari swung it open at once, dressed for the day aside from the fact he wore no shoes. "You are early."

"It's been an eventful eighteen hours. Can I come in?"

He swung the door wider, gesturing with his arm. "It is just as well. I have news too."

"About Leona? Already?" I dared not hope.

He nodded, shutting the door behind me before slowly walking over to a glass pitcher on a nearby table, pouring a glass of water, and handing it to me. Hari gestured to a chair, urging me to sit. "The woman will be here soon I suspect. She was eager to speak with you."

I glanced down at the water glass, running my finger over the cut crystal. "Tell me what you learned."

Hari sank down onto the edge of the brocade high-backed chair, rubbing at the spot where his prosthetic affixed to his thigh. He seldom complained about anything, but I recalled that mornings had always been a challenge. He splayed his fingers across the bright blue of his trousers. "You had said she worked for this Frederick Reaver fellow."

I wet my lips uncertainly. "She did. I don't trust him, Hari. Not at all—but I don't get a sense that he's our killer."

"Your mistrust is good." His hazel eyes remained unfocused in the dim morning light of his hotel room. "I do not know this for certain . . ."

"But you suspect something."

Hari leaned forward. "I looked into the fellow. Everyone I have met here in Oxford during my inquiries spoke highly of his war record. I thought it prudent to phone an acquaintance of mine in the War Department, see what he was up to back then."

"And?"

"He doesn't have one."

I blinked. "What do you mean? Doesn't have *what*?"

"Doesn't have a war record. Not under the name Frederick Reaver, that's for certain."

"The man is a professor, and the Keeper of the Egyptology collection at the Ashmolean. You cannot expect me to believe that one in such a prominent position has"—my hands flew of their own accord—"simply manufactured a war record for himself. Surely someone would have known, questioned it . . ."

Hari frowned. "One would think . . . and yet when I inquired, I was told in no uncertain terms to let the matter be. A quick denial, then told to stop asking. Typically, one either does or does not have a war record. It's a straightforward question."

Treadway and Leona both intimated that there was something *else* at play here in Oxford. Some undercurrent that was none of my affair. "Are you telling me that you believe that whatever he did during the war . . . he didn't do as Frederick Reaver at all . . ."

Hari unfolded his arms. "That is exactly what I think. Either he did it under another name, or his own record is sealed. I have never been denied this type of information in such a way. But there's more." He hesitated, moving to the window and pulling the curtains before peering out onto the bustling street below. "I also mentioned *you* on the call . . ."

"You mentioned me . . . *to the War Department*."

"They know your name. In truth, they know a great deal about you, my old friend. More than I expected."

A door slammed somewhere down the hall, followed by the laughter of a couple heading out for the day. "Who doesn't? That dreadful reporter is adamant on exaggerating my every movement lately."

"I'm afraid it is more than your public persona they are interested in . . ." He stared at the entrance to the Ashmolean. "Do you remember during the war when you asked me if a person would know if they'd gone mad?"

His words brought back a flurry of memories. None of them good. It wasn't long after we'd first met. I'd liked Hari from the very start—a great deal more than any of the other wounded men I'd brought back. Enough that the two of us would sneak out some nights when I was off duty. I'd take him in his chair into the woods behind the hospital. We'd sit by the pond there, watching the planes overhead. Under the cover of darkness, we'd talk of our fears. Of losing our families. His worry that he might never walk again, and once—late at night—after far too much gin and far too little supper, I asked him if he thought I was mad. He told me no, but even *he* knew why I went away for a week. When I returned, I no longer asked questions. I did my bit, and kept my mouth shut.

A light had gone out of me. One that took a very long time to turn back on.

I'd been scarcely twenty-four years old back then. Sent to an abandoned field hospital near Armentières to bring back a wounded American officer who'd escaped German captivity. The matron gave me no papers—a thing that should have struck me as odd at the time—but I was young. Young and naïve. As soon as I reached that bombed-out aid station, I knew it was all a lie. The American was missing the better part of his face, clinging to life in the arms of a wounded British aviator, rocking him like a newborn babe. They'd not escaped German lines at all. They'd been retrieved from them. Retrieved and waiting for me to bring them to hospital.

> *"Will he survive?" I had asked the British airman after we arrived back at the hospital in Amiens, while watching two strangers gently load the groaning American into another vehicle. The Brit had a wicked wound below his right eye, going down toward his ear, from where someone had recently taken a blade to him. His coat smelled of petrol and castor oil from the engine of his plane. Some of it still smeared across his face. The wound hadn't been stitched, just badly scabbed over. He leaned close and murmured, "Don't fear for him, love, he's already dead."*

He's already dead . . .
The words haunted me for weeks.
The American was badly wounded, but no more dead than I.

I never saw either man again. According to the matron, no one else saw them either. There were no men. I'd not even been sent to that bombed-out hospital—my orders, the paper ones she pulled from my jacket pocket, said I had gone to Rouen. A city in the entirely opposite direction.

At first, I thought the fellow another of my dreams—like those I had of my mother—but never before had I confused my dreams with reality.

"Ruby . . ." Hari's gentle voice snapped me back to the present. "What I'm trying to say to you, is I did not think you mad then, and I do not think you mad now. I saw you that day when you returned from that assignment. Matron said you would be gone for two days to fetch supplies, and I had believed her. That was until I saw the man being taken from the back of your ambulance. I was so bloody pleased to see you. I started over to tell you the same— but that's when I *saw* a soldier speaking to you. An aviator with a bloody gash beneath his eye."

My eyes widened in disbelief. For all these years, I thought I was the only one to have seen that man. My heart hammered in my chest. "What do you mean you *saw* him?"

"I also saw that poor sod they loaded up onto the other lorry. The mess the Germans had made of his face. How he was alive but wounded so grievously. . . . It made me sick, the death—the senselessness of it." He tapped his prosthetic leg hidden beneath his fashionably cut trousers. "Looking at what remained of that poor man's face, then the heartbroken expression on your own—I could not bear it. Not then. I turned my chair around and went back inside. I was a coward, Ruby. I am sorry."

I wanted to deny it—to tell him he wasn't, but I was too lost to my own emotions. My head swam.

Hari had seen the men.

The men were *real*.

Flesh and bone and blood.

But my relief was short-lived as another thought came. "Why had matron lied to me?"

Hari gave me a sad smile. "Do you need to ask?"

I rubbed my eyes as the sorry truth settled into my chest.

They used you, Ruby Vaughn. Used you and disposed of you once you'd served your purpose.

"It gets worse." Hari dropped the curtain, moving slowly over to my side and sitting on the chair across from me. "The reason I bring this up now, is that I saw that very man—the one with the gash below his eye. He is *here* in Oxford. I'd almost forgotten that dreadful day. Consigned it to some hellish place not to think upon. But he passed me on the street yesterday and it was as if I'd seen a ghost."

His words were a blur. I could not quite keep up—quite make sense of them. "What . . . what did you do?"

Hari shook his head. "Nothing. He did not recognize me, I do not know why he would. I was another wounded soldier in a hospital full of them. The man nodded politely, and crossed the street before entering the Ashmolean."

The men had been real. *Real.* I wasn't mad at all. And yet there was no victory in the knowledge, only despair. "You are certain it was him—the aviator?"

Hari plucked a grape from a nearby bowl and popped it into his mouth, chewing slowly. "Yes. He must be a member of British Intelligence. It is the only thing that makes sense. I came across others doing similar work later in the war once I was relegated to desk duty. The less anyone knew of them the better. Unsavory business, but necessary. I would stake my life that you had been sent on a mission and then threatened with a madhouse to ensure your silence."

I dug my nails into the wooden arm of the chair. Rage thrumming through my body. Outside the window, the city was coming to life. I snatched a grape of my own and chewed it angrily, the juice running down my throat. "And you think that whatever is going on in Oxford . . . that British Intelligence is *also* involved. Hari . . . I have to admit it's hard to believe. These are antiquities. Not state secrets."

Hari took my hand and squeezed it. "Julius Harker is dead, as is his business associate. Your friend, who was also affiliated with Harker, is missing. We are drowning in secrets and conspiracies."

"And every single clue has led to a dead end."

"I waited outside for over an hour watching the gates to the museum. The scarred man did not leave, or if he did, it wasn't through the main entrance. Afterward, was when I called my friend in the Home Office for a favor. Once they said to let the matter drop, I knew that this was more than simple murder."

The pieces clicked together at long last, and I exhaled on a rush. "Reaver. . . . He must be in league with Frederick Reaver."

"It is the only thing that makes any sense."

I took another grape and chewed slowly. "Do you think Leona is involved in the government business as well?"

"Perhaps. Perhaps not. My contact denied knowledge of her, but that means little now."

I fell heavily back into the chair. The sunlight from the window caught on the glass light fixture overhead, sending a rainbow of refracted color across the plaster ceiling. My mind flitted back to the bearded man I saw outside the Covered Market after I first spoke with Mr. Mueller. The familiar cut of his shoulders. The knowing way he watched me before tipping his hat and walking away.

"Hari . . . did the man you saw yesterday have a beard?"

He gestured to his cheek with his forefinger. "Yes, but the scar was unmistakable."

The ground beneath my feet grew unsteady, slipping away like wet sand. "I think . . . Hari, I think you might be right. We must—" My words were cut off by a sharp rap on the door. "The imposter!" I'd forgotten all about her.

"Shall we see what she wants?" Hari asked with a half-hearted smile. "I am sorry for it. The timing could not be worse."

I reached up, took his hand in my own, and gave it a squeeze. "I am not afraid of ghosts. Be it that soldier, or some false shade of my mother."

Hari patted my hand before answering the door. A uniformed bellman stood on the other side bearing a silver tray with an envelope on top. Hari took it, dropping several coins into the young man's palm, and closed the door before unfolding the correspondence. His expression dropped with each tick of the ornate carriage clock on the table. I shot to my feet, coming to his side and looking down at the page in his hand.

I AM SORRY, MR. ANAND. I CANNOT.

"How very strange. . . . To go to such lengths to find you and then not appear at all."

My mouth grew dry at the thought. Could the imposter be another trick by our killer—something to keep me occupied? Absently, I toyed with the chain of my locket, brushing the thought away at once—it was impossible. The imposter knew things she oughtn't, ones that even Hari's friends at the Home Office could not know.

"Go," Hari said softly. "I'll call upon you as soon as I have more information."

I brushed a kiss to Hari's cheek and nodded, running out the door and straight into the lion's maw.

Chapter Thirty-four

Missing Men

AS I stepped out onto the street outside the Randolph Hotel, my stomach knotted. Not only had I been used in France, I had been *expendable*. Risked—without warning—lied to, and sent on a recovery mission. Whether or not *I* survived was immaterial. My sole use was to bring back that dying man. I struggled to link the then and the now—we were no longer at war, but there was unrest in Oxford. Unrest in Britain itself, a great roiling undercurrent of social and political tension beneath the storybook surface.

My gaze traveled up the facade of the Ashmolean, glittering in the morning sun. If Frederick Reaver was connected to that shadowy arm of the government, the peculiarities about the man, his habits, and the secretive nature of his past all suddenly made a great deal more sense. I doubted the British government was interested in the trafficking of antiquities, nor that they would kill a man like Julius Harker in such a grotesque way—but what if Harker hadn't been the target of these men at all? What if it was someone else—someone a great deal more powerful?

My stomach sank.

More clues, and *still* I was no closer to finding the killer, though I could be reasonably assured that it was not Frederick Reaver. For while I did not think kindly upon the scarred man and his associates, my mistreatment during the war had been a strategic decision, a means to an end rather than capricious cruelty.

And what is more capricious than taking out a man's tongue and locking him into a box? That was a crime of passion, of rage.

There were two different things at play here in Oxford, and I was not afraid of Frederick Reaver. Not anymore.

I entered the Ashmolean again, determined to get answers about the scarred man from Reaver. If what Hari said was true—that the scarred man was somehow tied to British Intelligence—interfering in such a way was the height of recklessness. But I was out of options if I was to find Leona.

"What do you *mean*?" I furrowed my brow, studying the young guide standing at the main desk. He couldn't be twenty, if that. Fresh faced and round, still more boyish than a man in full.

"I'm sorry, miss. But, as I said before, Professor Reaver left yesterday afternoon in a hurry."

"About when, would you say?"

He rubbed his jaw with the back of his hand thoughtfully, before glancing up at the high carved ceilings of the main entrance. "One. Perhaps two? A pair of well-dressed gentlemen came in asking to speak to him. He left right away."

One or two? After I had spoken to him—certainly—but curiously enough, *before* the mysterious scarred fellow arrived. *Two* men . . . Lord Amberley and his son. It *had* to be. That was roughly when they would have come to invite him to last night's ill-fated party. "Was it a father and son, the older man was balding?"

The guide gave me a nod. "I think so, miss. I didn't get a good look at him, but I got that impression yes. The younger one was bored, as if he had better places to be, the older did most of the talking."

"And the Professor has not been back since?" My mind raced. Amberley certainly had a motive to kill Julius Harker and the position to attract the attention of the government. Not to mention his son's newly discovered penchant for cocaine.

Could it be that simple?

The young man shook his head again. His voice was low, as the galleries were all but empty today. "Not as I've seen, though he often does use the side entrance if he's working late. I'm sorry if you've come all this way for naught. Shall I tell him you were looking for him, if I see him?"

"No . . . no, I'll just try again later," I said with a smile I did not feel, before disappearing out the door and back across town in the dying golden hues of the afternoon.

"LORD HAVE YOU, maid!" Mrs. Penrose turned to face me as I burst into the warmth of the kitchen. The air was filled with the faintest scent of ginger and cloves coming from the plate of biscuits sitting alongside the range. I cautiously glanced around the empty room.

It was quiet.

Too quiet, considering there was supposed to be a prisoner in this house.

"Where is the inspector? What have the pair of you done with him?"

Mrs. Penrose cocked her head toward the drawing room and removed her apron, hanging it on a hook by the back door. "Oh, Owen trundled him off into the sitting room earlier today. Thought to give me a bit of space to fix our tea in peace without all the grunting and sweating."

I ignored this newfound familiarity between Mrs. Penrose and the old man. "And Ruan, is he with them? Did he learn anything from the inspector this morning?"

Mrs. Penrose placed her hands on her hips. "No, my lover. I haven't seen him since he took off after you this morning. But I'm sure he'll be home dreckly."

Took off after me? A peculiar numbness took over my fingers as I flexed them against my thigh. "How long ago did he leave?"

Mrs. Penrose brushed a stray wisp of long graying hair from her temple. "Why, almost ten minutes after you did. He told Owen that he was going to the Randolph. Didn't want you dealing with that imposter nonsense alone."

The heat rose into my cheeks. "He told you about the imposter?"

"He didn't have to say a word. It was written all over his face. There's not a thing the lad wouldn't do for you. Surely you know that."

Mrs. Penrose gave me an affectionate smile, fully misreading the surprise on my face. It wasn't that Ruan had followed me that concerned me—it was that Ruan hadn't *made it* to the hotel that did. I'd been with Hari for well over an hour. Ruan should have arrived long before we received the note from the imposter.

My hand went to my chest, rubbing at the scar as I struggled to come up with any other possible explanation. Perhaps he'd gone to see Emmanuel Laurent. . . . Perhaps he'd gone to the museum on his own and we'd simply missed one another. Perhaps . . . perhaps . . . perhaps . . .

The radiator popped and cracked, the room growing stiflingly warm. My clumsy fingers struggled with the wool of my scarf as I tugged it from my neck, setting it on the table alongside Fiachna. "And he hasn't returned? Sent a note around? *Anything?*" My voice grew shrill with the last word.

She took me by the arms. "Are you worried for him? He's a good strong lad, I'm sure he'll be all right. Why don't I fix you a cup of tea while you wait on him to come back? Perhaps he went to pick up a Christmas gift?"

I raised a brow. There was no world in which Ruan would be doing last-minute Christmas shopping when we were in the middle of a murder investigation.

He's likely with Emmanuel Laurent, Ruby. The rational voice in my head did little to soothe my fears. I could not raise my eyes from the stone flags of the kitchen floor. "No. No tea, thank you. . . . I'm sure you're right." I swallowed hard, willing it to be so. Yet disappearing was unlike him, especially as adamant as he was about not leaving Annabelle alone.

My pulse rioted in my very veins as I pushed open the door to the snug where Mr. Owen was sitting. A serial novel in his lap and his old Webley revolver on the side table. Ordinarily the sight would give me a little comfort, but now it only underscored the peculiarity of Ruan's absence.

He slid his wire-rimmed glasses down his nose. "Successful outing, my lamb?"

"You could say that." I drew closer to the sweat-soaked inspector. His already porcine face had grown dark pink above the gag shoved into his mouth. "You think he's all right? Should you . . . maybe loosen his restraints? I mean to ask him some questions and would like him conscious enough to *answer* them when I do."

Mr. Owen shrugged, turning a page in his book. "I do not care *how* he fares. The villain tried to hurt that poor lass upstairs. If you ask me, he deserves a great deal *more* than what he's received thus far, and I've half a mind to give it to him myself."

While I didn't disagree that the inspector deserved retribution for what he did to poor Annabelle, vengeance was not ours to deliver.

Mr. Owen took a sip from a chipped gold-rimmed teacup and set it down on the table beside him.

"Has he said anything useful?"

Mr. Owen's white mustache twitched as he stood with a groan and grabbed another log, throwing it onto the fire. "If you count swearing and threatening me with dismemberment as *useful*."

No. No, I daresay I didn't. "Perhaps it's for the best he's gagged."

Mr. Owen let out a dark laugh, his fingers wrapped around an old iron poker, and jabbed at the orange embers at the bottom of the grate, sending up sparks. "I think you'll find more information from the lass than this one."

I brightened immediately. "She's talking?"

"Aye, asked Dorothea for a bit of broth this morning."

I threw my arms around his neck, giving him an uncharacteristic hug. "Oh, Mr. Owen, you have no idea how happy that makes me."

I darted up the stairs to the makeshift sickroom and pushed open the door. Ruan had not slept in here in days and yet it still smelled of him. His herbs, his salves, his silly ginger candies. My eye caught on his worn British Expeditionary Force haversack sitting in the corner. A fresh box of medicines sat atop the dresser. That bone-deep wariness returned in force. Everything was precisely as it should be, but Ruan himself had vanished.

The girl slept easily in the narrow bed. Her breathing steadier and stronger than it had been when we first brought her here. I pulled the sheet up over her legs, and gently lifted the nightshirt we'd dressed her in to inspect the bandages at her belly.

The dressing was hours old. Likely from when Ruan saw to it this morning before leaving for the hotel. Fluid had seeped through the linen, staining the fabric.

I hurried to his haversack, reaching for the clean bandages he'd rerolled last night. With clumsy movements, I pulled that and a bottle of antiseptic, along with one of his salves. I uncorked the jar, taking in a heady sniff of the liniment to be sure it was the one I needed. Mint and honey. Calendula too, I thought.

I knew this one well. It was the same one he'd put on my wounds in Cornwall when I'd been stoned by the angry mob. My fingers tightened around the jar. First Leona. Now Ruan. Their disappearances had to be connected. He would not leave this place willingly.

He would not leave *me*.

And he most certainly wouldn't leave *Annabelle* in this condition.

The *Radix*. If the killer was after the *Radix*, then it was only logical he'd want the last person known to have held it. Stupid. Stupid girl. I bit the inside of my cheek.

I'd been incautious, had not even dreamt that he would be in any real danger or else I'd have never let him out of my sight. Better yet, I'd have sent him back to Cornwall, where I knew he'd be safe.

Safe.

Four letters that meant everything in this moment.

I squeezed my eyes shut, blotting out the unhelpful sentiment. Ruan would never forgive me if I allowed Annabelle's wound to go putrid. I peeled away the bandage tenderly. The girl mumbled something as I removed the soiled cloth from her soft warm skin.

"It's all right, darling. It'll only sting for a moment." I laid a clean piece of linen soaked in the antiseptic mixture on her skin, mindful of the stitches, and dabbed away at the clear fluid that had oozed from the sutures.

"I dreamt of the man," she whimpered as I finished cleaning the incision and began to apply the sweet-smelling ointment to her damaged flesh.

"What sort of a man?" I asked absently, wiping the excess liniment on my skirt and placing a clean bandage over the stitches.

"I saw him again . . ." She groaned, pushing herself up by her elbows to ease my passing the bandage back around her.

My ears pricked. "*Who* did you see, Annabelle? Was it the man that attacked you?"

"Ye—" She sucked in a pained breath as I helped her back onto the pillows. "I saw him again in my dreams. With eyes. Eyes cold and black like ice."

"Was that the man who took Leona?" I grabbed the pitcher on the nearby table and poured water into a tin cup before handing it to her. She drank greedily, a dribble running down her chin to settle in the shallow hollow of her throat. "Yes. There were two . . . two of them."

I took the cup from her trembling fingers and set it on the

nightstand, grabbing a clean cloth to dab at the dampness at her throat. Her hand shot up, latching onto my wrist with unnatural strength. "He took Leona. He was here. I saw him."

"*Who* took her, Annabelle? Was Leona still alive?" I needed every drop of information she had. The wind rattled the glass in the windows, sending a draft into the airy damp attic room.

"I don't know." She winced with a subtle bob of her head. "He stabbed her with a syringe. I tried to stop him and he . . ."

I pulled a soft, quilted blanket from the nearby table and spread it over her as a bulwark against the winter winds battering the windows.

How very strange. Annabelle had been *stabbed*—with a knife—but Leona had been stuck with a syringe and then *taken*. "A syringe? Like a doctor would use? Had you ever seen this man before? Was there anything unusual about him?"

But the girl had already fallen back asleep. Probably for the best, as the pain must have been unbearable. I would simply have to wait until she was stronger to probe more. I stroked her brow gently, wishing I possessed an ounce of the healing power Ruan did, before tucking the blankets around her slight form.

If the attacker had drugged Leona, it gave me hope that she might still be alive.

Cold black eyes.

My nostrils flared. I closed the door quietly behind me and started down the back stair to the ground floor when I heard a knock at the kitchen door. Quickening my step, I arrived as Mrs. Penrose opened it. A cold wind blew in, lifting the cloth on the table. Hari stood on the other side, fist raised ready to rap upon it a second time—his expression as bleak as I'd ever seen it.

"What is it? What's happened?"

He stepped over the threshold with a frown and reached into his pocket, pulling out a familiar silver half hunter. *Ruan's watch.* I closed the distance between us, taking the dented pocket watch into my hand—turning it over, running my thumb over the simple engraved letters, R. KIVELL.

My eyes pricked.

It was the same watch Mr. Owen had given him when he sent him to Oxford as a young man.

"Where did you . . ."

"On the street outside the hotel. A boy found it and had brought it to the front desk as I was leaving. I asked to see it and recognized the name. I've been searching for you all over town. They said you had gone to the museum. I followed after."

I stared at him, fingers closing around the cold metal. "What do you mean he found it? Where's Ruan?"

Hari's worried eyes met mine. "Sit, Ruby. Please."

"I do not need to sit," I bit out. "And do not treat me like I'm some wilting flower in need of tending. If you have something to tell me, tell me."

"Very well. A man matching your Cornishman's description was seen by a porter conversing with a gentleman outside the hotel this morning. I am to understand that your Cornishman checked his watch and within seconds stumbled, overcome by some fit, unable to stand on his own two feet."

"That's not possible. Ruan doesn't get sick . . . he doesn't . . . stumble . . ." And though I said the words, my mind had already connected the pieces my heart refused to countenance.

"That's what they saw. He was suddenly overcome by weakness and was aided into a nearby vehicle."

The person who took Leona had injected her with something before kidnapping her. She'd been drugged. Likely the same thing had happened to Ruan.

"Ruby. Say something."

I shook my head, chewing on my lower lip. But *who* could have done it? The inspector was currently tied up on the other side of the hall, under the watchful eye of Mr. Owen. I seriously doubted that Lord Amberley or his son had the mettle to do it, even if they were behind it all. Not to mention the method was too clinical, too precise. Harker's killer might be the same person to take Leona and Ruan, but what if he was not? The specter of the scarred man that Hari spied outside the museum returned to my mind in full force.

Hari wet his lips hesitantly. "The porter said that your man could hardly keep his head up when he was put into the vehicle."

"My poor lad!" Mrs. Penrose exclaimed, her hands at her own throat in shock. I'd nearly forgotten she was even in the room.

My voice came out oddly calm. Resolved, despite the bone-deep ache forming in my chest. "Did anyone recognize the person who took him? Was there . . . any *scar* or distinctive marking?" I gestured to my cheekbone.

Hari shook his head, understanding at once my meaning. "I asked the same. The doorman didn't get a good look at the other fellow, but he was finely dressed."

"The car?" I whispered, reaching for anything at all to help me find both Ruan and Leona.

"A Morris Cowley."

That was no help at all. There were dozens of those on the road. Ruan could have been put into any number of vehicles. I slowly looked up, meeting Hari's worried hazel eyes.

He reached out and wrapped me in his arms, hugging me tight. "We shall find him, Ruby. We shall find them both."

I swallowed hard, rested my cheek on Hari's shoulder, and closed my eyes, inhaling the faint vetiver on his clothes. It was all wrong. "Whoever took Leona has him too. It's all my fault . . ." My mind darted back to the page in my notebook. The killer had stolen the page with Hari's address from my journal because they knew I would be seeing him again.

I stepped back, raking my hands through my hair, and gave my head a good shake before beginning to pace the kitchen. Feeling sorry for myself wouldn't bring either of them home. I'd simply have to go get them.

"You have a look, Ruby . . ." Hari murmured.

The edge of my mouth curved up into a dark smile. "Am I that easy to read?" I glanced from Mrs. Penrose back to Hari. "Can you forget, for a time, that you are a man of the law?"

He flashed me a quicksilver grin, the same one I'd seen many times during the war. "How much trouble are you truly in, Ruby? As your friend this time."

Mrs. Penrose disappeared through the door into the snug as I began to tell Hari all the things I'd kept from him these last few days. Mr. Owen wasn't the only one good at keeping secrets.

Chapter Thirty-Five

The Die Is Cast

HARI quickly came around to my way of thinking. But it took far longer than I would have liked to convince Mr. Owen of the rightness of my plan to let the inspector go and to see where he led me. If the man wanted Annabelle dead, it meant he was working for our killer. The same killer who likely held both Leona and Ruan. There was no time to waste and no alternative.

It was a perfectly simple plan, though Mr. Owen bristled at the mere thought of it. He furrowed his brow in that way of his, hands on hips and coffee-colored eyes wary. Mrs. Penrose, on the other hand—with her beloved pellar in peril—was eager to join the scheme. And once she agreed, Mr. Owen slowly came around as well to our way of thinking, especially after my attempt at questioning our prisoner failed. Inspector Beecham was incapable of doing anything but to smugly sit there and refuse to answer any of my questions. He believed he had the upper hand—and a part of me feared he did.

Later that evening, before bed, Mr. Owen readjusted the inspector's bindings, leaving the rope a fraction of an inch too loose. All the while I prepared myself to track a murderer across the darkening streets of Oxford.

Mr. Owen closed the door between the snug and the kitchen and gave me a skeptical frown. "Are you certain you want to do this, my lamb?"

I was. There were no other alternatives. It was the only outcome.

Mr. Owen let out a sad sigh before handing me Hari's small bulldog pistol. I tucked it into the pocket of my skirt as he helped me into my coat.

He pressed a bristly kiss to my cheek, brushing my dark curls out of my face. "Be careful."

"Take care of them." I tugged a dark blue kerchief from my coat pocket and tied my hair back before hurrying out the door and into the street beyond.

Doubt clung to me like woodsmoke, pricking at my throat. I could only hope the man would take this window to try to escape. If he didn't . . . I didn't know what I would do or how I would find them.

I pulled the dark coat tight, obscuring all of my cream-colored dress. I ducked into the alleyway behind the house to see if my gamble would pay off. I settled myself into the shadows, swallowed up by the ivy, and waited to hear the groan of the window sash.

It wasn't long before I was rewarded with the wooden creak followed by the soft thump of boots hitting the pavers below. Inspector Beecham's footsteps grew softer as he darted out and around the far side of the house as expected. I eased myself out of the shrubbery, brushing the chaff from my jacket, and followed a killer into the night.

The moon was bright overhead in the cold December night—the wind cutting through the layers of my clothing. My coat did little to keep me warm. A thick haze veiled the world around me, giving it a dreamlike appearance. Icy air pricked my lungs as I hurried along after him, keeping to the shadows as best I could. From somewhere in the distance, low church bells announced the hour. Nine o'clock on Christmas Eve. No wonder the streets were so empty. The inspector carried on down High Street at a breakneck pace before starting to turn toward the river.

During the summertime the Thames would be full of geese and swans and rowers and canal boats moving up and down the river. It was a busy hub of people. Even in winter, bicyclists would take the path alongside the river to hasten their journey. It might be lovely, but now the stillness of the dark water gave an ominous tinge to the evening.

I remained about a hundred yards behind the inspector, watching as he turned off onto the riverside path. We passed a small field with fluffy sheep huddled together against the cold. Homes grew farther and fewer between, replaced by the occasional barn or cottage set off the path. Each step I took transformed the urban sounds of the city to a wilder hue. Night in winter was always still, with all the creatures asleep. Only the occasional nocturnal beast calling out its eerie warnings. A twig broke behind me, and I caught the shadowy shape of a dog darting off into the nearby wood.

Voices from somewhere ahead drew my attention back to the river. A glow of lights came from a canal boat docked some thirty or more yards ahead. There was a lorry idling beside it, the lights cut on illuminating the space between the two vehicles. A pair of men carried boxes and loaded them onto the boat. The inspector slowed as he approached them. I fell farther into the shadows. So *this* was where he was going. Beecham called to another man who was silhouetted in the lights from the small craft. I couldn't be certain, but I'd wager that those were the stolen crates from Julius Harker's museum.

Ruan had mentioned that several boxes had disappeared along with the canopic jars filled with God only knew what. Cocaine or natron, it made no difference now. The only thing that mattered was finding him and Leona and bringing them safely home.

I couldn't make out their conversation, only the furious intonation of the inspector's voice. An occasional word here or there.

"... Shipment...."

"... Already late..."

I edged closer, dipping beneath the leafless canopy of a willow tree, counting the men and straining my ears in hopes I'd hear mention of any captives.

Two. No, there were three men now. One on the boat, and another on land speaking to the inspector. The pair of them were pointing back toward town. I swallowed hard, fingers curling around the pistol in my dress pocket. Another man had left the lorry and headed for the boat. Could this be where Leona and Ruan were being kept? A faint bubble of hope welled up in me. I was close—I could feel it.

An owl called out, piercing the silence of the night, and I froze, watching the men slowly disappear into the canal boat, one by one. Once they were all inside, I finally exhaled and took a step from the shelter of the tree and darted for the truck.

I approached from the far side, steps silent in the snow as I climbed up into the lorry and began rummaging about seeking something—anything at all. My fingers found a familiar sheet of paper lying on the seat. Holding it up in the moonlight I made out my own writing—it was the missing page. I scanned over it before hastily shoving it into my pocket.

Four crates remained in the back bearing similar painted markings to those I'd seen in the museum's basement. Heart thundering in my ears, I quickly pulled off a lid, shoving the straw from the top and revealing large, wrapped bricks. Bricks? Head spinning, I picked one up and had started to unwrap it when I felt the cold pressure of steel against the wound on my temple.

Chapter Thirty-six

Boom

"YOU truly are the most impossible woman . . ." Frederick Reaver growled, dragging me backward away from the boat and the truck full of what I could only guess was *actually* cocaine. I stumbled, falling into his sturdy form. Reaver was more fortress than man—a fortress who presently had a gun pressed into my freshly scabbed wound. The cold metal disturbed the healing flesh, sending a warm trickle of blood down my cheek. "And do not even *think* of warning your friends or I will shoot you now."

Friends? Good grief, Reaver must think I'm somehow working with the dreadful inspector.

"Let me go. You misunderstand." I wriggled against him, but he simply tightened his grasp upon my upper arm, pulling me along beside him until we were back under the shelter of the large willow tree that I'd paused beneath earlier.

"I think not. I finally understand *all* too well." He let out a dark and angry sound.

My mind raced over the past few days, over every single clue. Every crumb I'd collected that led us to this point, and I came up empty. I'd not once done anything to give the impression that I was in league with the inspector. "Where is Leona? What have you done to her?" I growled, wriggling again—but he jerked me tighter against him.

"That is what I'm hoping you will be able to tell me." He pressed the gun tighter to my temple.

My breath hitched in my chest. Reaver was also looking for Leona. "I don't know. But I am looking—"

He shushed me angrily. "Be quiet, I'm trying to concentrate."

Concentrate on what? I followed his gaze, struggling to make sense of him. Of *this*. A shadowed figure appeared in the distance, pausing alongside the lorry. There was a shout, then a second and third fellow arrived to assist with bringing in the final boxes from the truck. I could scarcely believe my eyes. Julius Harker must have managed to intercept the shipment of cocaine, as Leona feared. It was the only thing that made sense, especially in light of the crates I found inside the truck. And *these* men, whoever they might be, had stolen it right back. But I still did not understand how Frederick Reaver and Leona figured in. Were they truly in league with Harker? As the former currently had his pistol digging into my flesh, it certainly was a plausible theory. I also doubted he'd enlighten me anytime soon.

I ought to be afraid. And yet I could not summon the sentiment. Not with both Leona and Ruan still out there. They needed me, and I had to keep focused on escaping. On saving them.

Within seconds, all the inspector's men, along with the remaining boxes from Harker's museum, had disappeared into the belly of the canal boat. Reaver exhaled loudly against my skin, warming the side of my neck as another trickle of blood oozed out from my raw scab. My eyes pricked from the cold wind.

"Now," he murmured.

But before I could comprehend the word he uttered, Reaver jerked me to the side, thrust me hard upon the ground, and covered me with his own body. We landed with a grunt, his weight crushing the air from my lungs.

The ground beneath us shook as a blinding flash lit the night sky bright as day. A rush of heat chased after with the ferocious roar of a munition going off. The intensity of the blast whirred loud enough that my eyes watered. Something hot and sticky oozed from my right ear, slowly making its way down to the collar of my cream dress, soaking through to my skin. For a moment—only that—I thought I'd been blown back to France and was lying there on the muddy ground. That the last few years had been a fever dream from which I'd finally awoken. Dazed, I stared into Frederick Reaver's face. His own eyes were closed. He lay like a stone atop me. While he'd anticipated the blast, he'd evidently not expected the intensity of it.

With a grunt he rolled off me, lying flat on his back in the wet snow, gulping in the acrid air. Reaver was as disoriented as I. The ringing in my ear blotted out everything else. I couldn't think. Could scarcely hear over the sound inside my own head. The pain burned itself into my brain. Small pieces of debris from the sky fell like singed snowflakes making their way to the earth.

The small vessel had been reduced to little more than flames and flotsam floating atop the water. My chest seized up as I pulled myself to standing and stumbled a few steps toward the water. My legs unsteady beneath me. Had Leona and Ruan been on that boat?

Reaver snagged me again by the arm, jamming the metal of his gun back into my side, and pulled me into the woods. "Don't think your tears move me, Miss Vaughn. I may have been fooled before, but I know precisely what you are."

Thickness grew in my throat as I stared at the dark waters, scarcely registering his words. "What have you done?"

"Solved two problems at once," he grumbled. "Come now, Miss Vaughn. I was told you were terribly clever. Solve this puzzle, mmm? I find you in the bloody lorry up to your elbows in cocaine and you ask me what *I* have done? I thought your concern for Leona true at first, but then I saw you with him. Cozied up with that murderous swine. Now . . ." He leaned closer, his hot breath at my neck smelling sweetly of peppermint. "Now I know better."

Leona. I'd nearly forgotten his words from before. Reaver was also looking for Leona. That stray bubble of hope returned. Faint, but there all the same. If Reaver wanted to protect Leona, then she couldn't have been on the boat he destroyed. She just *couldn't* have been. "Do you know where she is? I can help you, please. Please tell me that she's safe."

"You had better hope she is safe and whole, for your own sake," Reaver muttered, jerking a coarse burlap sack over my head as my vision went dark. He tightened it around my throat, shutting off all light as he pulled me along beside him. With the loss of my sight, panic finally set in. I was well and truly caught. I stumbled, tripping on roots and debris, as Reaver led me at a breakneck pace away from the boat's debris. My senses blunted. Disoriented. Despite being at a severe disadvantage—bound and unable to see, bleeding from goodness only knew where—I could not help but grasp onto the slightest glimmer of light in this dreadful situation. For Frederick Reaver was *not* the villain. Oh, he was certainly a rotten scoundrel, but he hadn't killed me yet. And more than that—he was *also* looking for Leona, which meant that, as improbable as it seemed, Frederick Reaver and I were on the same side in all this. If only I could make him realize it.

Suddenly his words took on new meaning, striking a chord in my memory. Reaver said I'd "cozied up" with the killer. It must have been Amberley's dinner party. My throat grew thick. Lord Amberley. *Of course.* How could I have been such a fool? Amberley had been there from the start. At the antiquarian meeting. Butting heads with Harker. At the museum the night Harker's body was discovered. At the Ashmolean.

The final pieces clicked into place. That must have been why Reaver agreed to go to Amberley's dinner party. Why he left the museum so quickly after Amberley and his son arrived. Reaver had been after Lord Amberley all along.

The strong calloused hands that had painfully gripped my wrists were replaced by a rough rope. Twisting once, then again as he fastened my hands together. My palms grew slippery with my own blood. If only I could get him to understand, to listen to *reason*. Then perhaps we might stand a chance of saving her.

"I am on your side in this!" I tried again.

He responded, but I couldn't make out his words between the whirring in my ear and the sack muting the sound. "I want to help Leona too. I'm not what you think I am!"

But no matter my protests, it was no use. Reaver wouldn't listen. He continued to drag me along beside him to God only knew where. Occasionally a flicker of light would come through the loose weave of my sack. We must be going back to town. It was the only explanation for the brightness. Was he taking me to Amberley thinking he could make a trade for Leona's life? Good God, it would get us all killed.

"You mean to bargain me, don't you?" Panic began to rise within me. "I am on your side, Reaver. We want the same things!"

To that he let out a muffled curse and gave me another stout jerk. "Your lies do you no favors, Miss Vaughn." I stumbled again, jamming my toe on a curbstone.

Yes. We were definitely back in Oxford.

My hands were nearly frozen from the cold air congealing my sticky blood. I flexed my fingers, unable to feel them. At least the hot moisture had stopped oozing from my ear—that, or I'd simply grown numb enough I couldn't feel it. Suddenly, through my sack and over the ringing in my ear, I heard the muffled crack of a gunshot.

Reaver tensed before throwing me down on a step. I struck the stone hard, swearing loudly at the impact.

A great crash followed. Splintering wood from what must have been a door rained over my body. I flinched, waiting for a blow that did not come. Instead of striking me as I'd expected, Reaver hoisted me back up onto my feet and dragged me inside to meet my sorry fate.

Chapter Thirty-seven

The Devil Meets His Match

IT was a home. At least I thought that's where Frederick Reaver had brought me. My senses were still muted from the blast—I could scarcely hear, let alone think straight. Had he brought me to Amberley's home intent on trading me for Leona? If so, he was in for a sore disappointment once Lord Amberley arrived. My stomach lurched. Why would Reaver simply not *listen* to me?

The scent of leather and candle wax drifted through the loose weave as Reaver pulled me along the warm corridor. The sore muscles in my legs began to give way, and for the second time in as many minutes I was thrust onto my knees. Thick, soft carpet met the skin of my shins through the holes in my bloodied stockings. Reaver ripped the rough-hewn sack from my head. Tears streamed down my face from the sudden onslaught of light. The world inside was too bright, too loud. Reaver placed his meaty palm between my shoulder blades and shoved hard, sending me face-first onto the floor. My own hands were still bound behind my back and I twisted at the last moment, catching myself with my shoulder. A hot sharp pain shot through me.

"Blast and hell, you are going to get everyone killed—" I started before the words died away.

This wasn't Lord Amberley's drawing room.

I blinked slowly, taking in the room around me.

This wasn't Lord Amberley's home.

I was going to be sick. The dawning recognition of exactly where he'd brought me finally sank in. I had been here before. Sat on the fine antique sofa in the center of this room. Sought refuge here from the antiquarians' dinner party just a handful of days before. Oh God . . . how could I have been so wrong?

My eyes slowly adjusted to the light as I beheld the walls lined with row after row of curio cabinets housing a lifetime of collecting antiquities.

The life's work of Emmanuel Laurent.

Ruan's mentor. Famed Antiquarian. Soon to be Member of Parliament. Emmanuel Laurent.

Why would Reaver bring me to Emmanuel Laurent?

I swallowed hard, not wanting to believe Laurent capable of such a thing. It made no sense. How . . . why would he? Laurent had been kind. Attentive even. My mind tripped on ahead of me as I turned my head to the side, finding young Jack—the kindly young constable from the police station—sprawled out on the floor alongside me, suffering from a gunshot wound. What was *he* doing here? Earlier tonight a part of me wondered if he might not have been one of the men who perished on the canal boat, though Jack had always been at odds with the inspector.

Jack's bloodied palm covered his belly, his eyes wide as he looked up at Reaver, his skin pale from the loss of blood. Reaver cast the young man a pitying look. His own expression softening for a fraction of a second. Was Jack in league with Reaver or was there yet someone else involved in this macabre pantomime?

"I have a trade for you, Laurent! I've brought your pet," Reaver shouted, interrupting my thoughts. "Now give me Leona."

I had to get free. Had to get myself out of this before Reaver got all of us killed. I tugged against the ropes binding my hands.

The slipperiness of my own blood allowed my one thumb to come free right away. I folded my fingers as tight as I could, and my right hand slid a bit farther up the rope. That was something.

Pain shot through my shoulder as I drew myself up on my knees with my hands awkwardly behind me.

"Why would I want *her*?" Emmanuel Laurent stood in the doorway, his voice impossibly even as I stared into his dark gray eyes. The color of slate.

The devil's eyes.

The air left my lungs on a rush. It was *Emmanuel Laurent* that Annabelle had seen, not the inspector at all. My gaze dropped to the gun held casually in his hand as the unlikely truth settled into my gut. My mind raced to catch up with what I already knew without a doubt.

Emmanuel Laurent was the killer.

I should have known. Should have guessed. Frantic, I looked to Jack, whose pained gaze remained fixed upon Reaver—as if somehow the prickly, hardheaded scholar had the power to save us all. The man was more likely to get us all killed than to get us out of this alive.

Foolish, foolish girl.

The answer had been before me all along, I just hadn't paused to think on it. Laurent been connected to Harker long before the latter's disgrace and expulsion from Oxford. I'd never even stopped to suspect him of the crime, despite the fact that Laurent had been connected to this whole affair from the very first act.

He knew of the theft of the *Radix Maleficarum*.

He knew the truth about Ruan.

He'd killed Harker. Killed him and then taken Leona to hide his crimes.

Of course Ruan would have stopped to talk to him. To check the time, not seeing the drug-filled syringe before it was too late.

He'd shot Jack, the young constable. The litany of Laurent's crimes echoed in my head. It all made perfect sense and I could not understand how I missed it.

I could scarcely breathe, mind running through the last few days, gathering all the things I knew of Laurent—none of which brought me any closer to *why* a man who had so much to lose would risk it all.

"I would appreciate if you wouldn't leave her to ruin the rug." Laurent stepped deeper into the room, his eyes raking over my bloody form. "You see, Frederick, this is precisely why I do not own a cat. They always drag in the most woebegone things, disemboweling them on the floor as if their violence could impress me. I assure you it does not. It took me years to acquire that carpet and now *how* am I to get those stains out? Hmm?"

I glanced down to the bloody splotches I'd left and rubbed my palm on it, adding another rust-colored smudge to the pattern.

"Perhaps you should have thought about that before you shot Jack," Reaver growled, gesturing to the poor constable bleeding out across from me. Who *was* this man, and was there more to Reaver than met the eye? Yes, he was a scholar—one couldn't hide that fact—but the way Jack kept looking to him. The almost protective growl in his voice. Reaver cared for the younger man. Almost as one would a protégé. Or someone one was training.

A protégé.

Suddenly the last clue slipped into place. On the night of Lord Amberley's party, Laurent had occupied Ruan for most of the evening. But at the end—when Reaver and Jonathan Treadway were in conflict—it was Emmanuel Laurent who had been at my elbow. *That* was the reason for Reaver's venom that evening. He thought I was in league with Laurent. No wonder the fool man believed I had a hand in Leona's disappearance and wouldn't listen to reason. I was often in Laurent's company, Ruan himself going back and forth between the two homes. Had the roles been reversed, I would have been just as intractable as Reaver.

"Ruan, Leona . . . where are they?" My voice sounded far stronger than I felt at present.

Reaver's expression faltered as he looked at me, evidently coming to the same realization as I about our allegiances.

"Perfectly safe. They both are. I take excellent care of my collection."

"You cannot collect people," I growled, settling on my haunches, my bound hands numb behind my back.

"Oh, but that is where you are wrong, Miss Vaughn. People are the most valuable and difficult pieces to acquire. You never know what one can do, the *power* one can hold over another."

"You cannot think you can control a person's life—"

"I do not think. I *know*." He chuckled. "People, my dear foolish girl, are the path to power. And power is all anyone can ask for. There's safety in it. Comfort. One might not be able to achieve the divine, but with enough power a man can make himself invincible. Untouchable. A veritable god amongst sheep."

"You drugged them both," I murmured in disgust. "A god wouldn't need to drug people into compliance."

"It certainly helps make people more accommodating to reasonable requests, and in time they always come around, with gentle encouragement," Laurent said with a huff. His gaze slithered from his rug back to my face. "Less mess that way."

"Less mess?" I let out a startled sound, as I managed to free my left hand from the ropes and flex my fingers, willing what was left of my blood to begin flowing through my veins again. "You killed Julius Harker and took out his *tongue*, for goodness' sake! It didn't seem you minded mess then."

He waved his hand airily with the gun. "It had to be done. The idiot stole my shipment. Stole it and rubbed my nose in it. He had to be dealt with and it was an expedient means to an end."

"Leona had nothing to do with that sordid trade," Reaver spat out, stepping closer to Professor Laurent. "Harker was a fool, everyone knew that—but Leona had nothing to do with your shipment. Let her go, she has nothing to give you."

"Nothing to give?" Laurent clicked his tongue with a shake of his head. "You never did realize what you had on your hands. Frederick. That was always your great failing. Missing what was right before your eyes."

Reaver bristled.

"Did you know she can read nine languages and speak at least that many? The value of a woman like that is substantial," Laurent said with a tender tone. "Oh, what am I thinking. Of course you know her worth. After all, everyone knows about your . . . *tendresse* toward the little Egyptian chit. I daresay, jealous rages suit you, Frederick. In fact . . ." His mouth curved up into a sinister smile. "Come to think of it, I have just come up with a tidy little solution to our problem here. For we both know that the three of you cannot leave this house alive."

"You cannot possibly think you can kill *us all* and no one will notice."

"Oh, come now, Freddie dear." Laurent's tone grew mocking. "Everyone in Oxford knew that Harker had been tweaking your nose over your professional failures ever since you returned from the east. It's almost as if"—Laurent toyed with the edge of his sleeve—"almost as if Harker knew who you really were . . . *what* you really are . . . and enjoyed reminding you of it. Who is to say you did not put him in that box all on your own to hide your own secrets from the world?"

I drove my thumb under the ropes, pulling them off my other wrist, flexing my fingers. The feeling was slowly beginning to return. Slippery with blood, my skin burned with the motion, but I was fully free at last. The young constable, Jack, had slipped from consciousness, his pulse slowing. He was going to die if we didn't get Laurent to stop talking soon.

Think, Ruby, think!

"What I don't understand is why you killed Harker. You could have gone on and taken your seat as MP. The police looked the other way when it came to your drug trade. They had been overlooking it for years. Why *him* and why *now*, when you have everything to lose?" Reaver stepped forward, shielding me from Laurent's attention as he asked the very question that had been on the tip of my tongue.

Hari's pistol dug into the flesh of my thigh. I'd nearly forgotten I'd tucked it into my dress pocket. Reaver had searched my jacket pockets when he captured me, but he hadn't thought to touch my dress.

"Julius Harker could not leave well enough alone. Much like you, Frederick. If you'd stayed in your museum with your scrolls and your mummies, I wouldn't have need to kill you. *Either* of you." He pointed his pistol cavalierly at me. "You will be a lovely corpse, Miss Vaughn. A pity to waste you. You're nearly as bright of a star as Leona. I am certain the boy will grieve you, but there's naught to be done. He in time forgot all about Ernst, and I am quite certain he will forget about you."

My nostrils flared as I pulled myself up onto my knees, once again shifting and giving me access to the large pocket of my dress in hopes I could pull out the gun without him noticing. My pellar was *not* going to be grieving anything, if I had a say in the matter.

Reaver must have realized what I was about, as his gaze dropped to my unbound hand, which had found its way to my pocket—perhaps he recalled that he'd forgotten to check it. Reaver pressed his lips tight, holding me with his icy gaze, and I could have sworn he gave me a slight nod.

"Why take Leona? Why not simply ask for her assistance?" he immediately asked, drawing Laurent's attention back to himself and allowing me to withdraw the gun from my pocket unnoticed.

Laurent moved closer to Reaver, his movements sinuous and smooth as I wrapped my fingers around the grip of the pistol. His liar's mouth curved up into a sickening smile as he drew nearer to Reaver, dropping his voice low. "She did not like me much. And the little bitch still has not given me the book. I've offered a fortune for its recovery and yet it *conveniently* has disappeared again."

The *Radix*.

"You don't have it?" The words escaped my lips of their own volition. I could not have hidden my surprise if I tried.

"Of course you would know about the *Radix*. Kivell is always quite chatty when he believes someone actually cares about what he has to say. His melancholy grows tiresome. I don't know how Ernst put up with it all those years."

My fingers tightened around the butt of the gun. "Why do you want the *Radix*? It's just a book."

He lifted a shoulder. "Look around this room, Miss Vaughn. Everything in here is rare. Unusual. One of a kind. Just like Ruan and the lovely Miss Abernathy. Use that clever mind of yours one last time, then ask me why I want it again." But Laurent was no longer paying attention to me, he was walking toward Reaver, a syringe in his left hand hanging casually by his side. Inconspicuous enough one might not even notice the small silver needle running alongside his forefinger. Reaver didn't see it, his attention fixed upon the gun in Laurent's other hand—the obvious threat. He didn't see the more subtle danger coming. Without a thought, I lifted Hari's pistol and fired, hitting Laurent in the shoulder. The syringe hit the ground with a clank alongside young Jack.

Reaver lost no time, scooping up the bloodied rope that I'd wriggled free of and wrapping it around Laurent's arms, tying them behind his back much as he had mine.

Laurent screamed.

"Quick. See to Jack before he bleeds out any more," Reaver called over his shoulder as he worked to restrain the older gentleman.

But I was already on my feet and at the boy's side.

The young constable's eyes fluttered open. "Sorry, miss."

"You've got nothing to be sorry for. Let me see to you, mmm?" I shifted his weight onto my lap, unfastening his uniform jacket and assessing the gunshot wound. It was only the one—on the side of his belly. Dark blood oozed out over his stained fingers. I reached down, placing the hem of my dress in between my teeth, and ripped hard until I had a large wad of fabric in my hands. I laid it over the wound and applied pressure. "There we go. We'll hold this here until we can get you help."

He opened his eyes and blinked at me uncertainly. "I didn't think you were working with Laurent, miss. Not really. I didn't care what they said."

I gave him a faint smile. "At least someone had faith in me, Jack."

He laid his bloodied hand over mine and squeezed, breaking my heart. He was young. Scarcely older than Ruan had been when he left Oxford. Far too young to die. "Reaver . . . he told me to not come. Said he had tonight's assignment handled with the captain."

The captain?

"All clear upstairs." An eerily familiar voice rang out, and before I knew what was happening, a large black Labrador bounded over and gave me a single lick on the cheek. It whimpered, lowering its head to Jack's hand, and nuzzled it. Jack smiled at the big dog.

"'Allo, Shadow. That's a good lad . . ." His bloodied other hand rested atop the dog's ebony head. Shadow let out a high-pitched whimper, laying his large body alongside his human, and lifted his head to watch me, big brown eyes pleading.

Not an omen of death after all. At least I hoped not.

My hands were soaked with Jack's blood as I watched the man coming down the stairs. The same man I'd seen outside the Covered Market. Hari had been right. *As usual.* The Royal Flying Corps officer was older now—*weren't we all*—his golden hair longer, neatly styled back beneath his fashionable homburg. The years between now and then disappeared and it was as if I was staring at a ghost. An echo of the man who had held that dying soldier in his lap on the long road back to Amiens. The same man that matron told me did not exist. The man I could have sworn I had seen all over Oxford, trailing me. Watching me. He was no ghost. He was real. Flesh and bone and walking toward me. His thick woolen military-style coat reached his knees, and he wore the exhaustion of a decade on his face. The aviator was just as handsome now as he'd been back then when we first met. The gash beneath his eye that he'd ignored for all those miles as he held the dying man in his arms had healed now to a jagged raised pink scar, partially hidden by his short-cropped beard. It was no wonder Hari recognized him right away—I would have known him in a heartbeat as well.

This man must be the "captain" that Jack had mentioned. The aviator's keen eyes caught mine and he flashed me a weary smile. "Hello again, Miss Vaughn. I'm terribly glad you're not dead."

"Sorry, Captain . . ." Jack said, looking up at the man.

Jack's blood soaked through my bandage onto my palm. "Help him."

"They're on their way," he said softly. "I've seen to the two upstairs. I assume the big one is yours."

Ruan. One less thing to worry about, I supposed. I nodded.

"And Leona?" Reaver asked as he finished binding Professor Laurent and walked over to join us. He crouched down on the carpet to lay a tender hand on Jack's shoulder and gave him a squeeze, before ruffling the dog's fur.

The edge of the scarred man's mouth quirked up. "Yes, yours is up there too, Freddie."

Jack looked up at me with a frown. "I tried to help you, miss. The inspector . . . he killed Mr. Mueller. I told the captain what happened . . ."

"You did do well, Jack. I suspect a promotion will be in your future if you can keep yourself from dying." The scarred man crouched down on the floor across from me. He stroked Jack's hair with a frightening solemnity. The faint scent of petrol and pipe smoke permeated his jacket. For the second time in my life this man had crossed my path, and for the second time I found myself lost. Confused and questioning my own sanity. He had been constantly two steps ahead of me. He must have been the reason my mind flicked back to the war every time I got close. The faint scent of him, achingly familiar from those hours we'd spent in the lorry on the way back to Amiens. Familiar enough to recall, but not quite enough to remember.

"You're the one they call captain?" I asked softly. "Jack was working for you . . ."

He nodded with a sad expression. "My office had been watching Laurent for months now, waiting for him to make his move. Jack has been particularly useful monitoring the inspector. I met the lad during the war. He's been my very shadow ever since. As has this great brute." The captain looked fondly at the large black Labrador lying on the floor beside us.

Jack let out a pained sound, but I could not help but see the pride in his young eyes. I swallowed hard, struggling to keep up with the revelations, and yet it all made perfect sense. I wasn't going mad at all—I only possessed half the facts.

The scarred man—the *captain*—rubbed his jaw with the back of his sleeve, an almost apologetic look on his face. "There was some question on whether Laurent had become a threat to the crown with some of his other activities. With the frequency at which you'd been to his house—and then your Cornishman spending so much time here . . . I am sorry, Miss Vaughn, but we believed you were in league with him as well. Especially once Leona disappeared. Jack believed you innocent, but . . . I suppose the lad was right after all."

"I don't care about any of that, Jack needs a doctor!" I insisted. His pulse was slowing under my hand. My voice grew panicked.

"Let me take care of my man," the captain said tenderly, lifting Jack's hand from mine and reaching for the cloth I was pressing against the bullet wound. "A few of my lads are on the way. Things just happened here a bit faster than I was anticipating. They'll be in soon to get him to the hospital. I promise you, Miss Vaughn, I've not lost a man yet—and I don't aim to start tonight."

"And the American? The one I helped bring back to the hospital for you during the war?" I asked, alluding to that fateful day along the Western Front, with that poor soldier who'd been missing half his face.

He gave a wistful smile. "Living in Iowa now, married to his sweetheart, with two children. As I said, I do not let my men down, Miss Vaughn. No matter the odds. I assure you of that. Jack's a good lad, we'll see him through this. Won't we, Jack?"

My shoulders relaxed slightly as I allowed the scarred man to place his hand over mine on the bloody cloth. "You were in the woods tonight with us too. You're the one that blew up the canal boat." It wasn't quite an accusation, but it wasn't *not* one either.

He lowered his golden lashes and sniffed. "I did what had to be done tonight. As did you." He gestured dismissively to the bound form of Laurent lying on the floor. "You've done the crown a service. It is a debt that will need to be repaid." He gave me a meaningful look. "Go see Freddie in the morning at the museum. Tell no one what's happened here tonight. It will be well, I promise you that, Miss Vaughn."

I stared at him unblinking. "Tomorrow is Christmas Day . . . the museum will be closed."

He gave me a wink. "You and I know locks have never stopped you. Let me see to my man, you go see to yours."

Ruan. I wet my lips and gently brushed Jack's hair from his brow with my left hand. "Promise me you will do everything you can to help him."

"Upon my honor. Such that it is."

I pulled my own palm from beneath his, shifting the boy onto the captain's lap.

"I hear my men already. Go on, Miss Vaughn. No harm will come to young Jack tonight."

And for the first time in a long time, I believed.

Chapter Thirty-eight

Love Like the Tide

RUAN was upstairs, exactly as promised. My ear throbbed, but it didn't matter. Not when I'd found him. He was alive. Granted, he wasn't *conscious*, but he was safe and whole and I had never been more relieved in my life. Reaver had bundled Leona out of the house and to the hospital along with Jack, leaving Ruan and me alone on the upper floor. The scarred man—"the captain," as Jack kept calling him—had a half dozen men downstairs searching through Laurent's collection, presumably for any other stolen goods.

Laurent had placed Ruan upon an old iron bed, bound at his wrists and ankles to the rails with nineteenth-century neckcloths. I hurried to his side, heedless of the blood that splattered my cream-colored dress, and stroked his cheek with the back of my hand.

I'd actually done it.

I'd saved them both, found Julius Harker's killer, and—aside from an aching head and likely a burst eardrum—I had seen it through.

Ruan wore clean pajamas two sizes too small. Bathed and washed with an unfamiliar lemony soap. When I last saw him, he'd still been fast asleep, bearing the dark shadow of night on his cheek, but now he was clean-shaven, his hair washed and combed.

Laurent had tended him and placed him in another man's pajamas like a human doll. A piece of his collection dressed in moth-eaten clothes.

I ran my palm against the smooth skin of his jaw, eyes pricking with tears.

He knew what I was.

That's what Ruan said. Laurent confirmed the same downstairs. Good God, I would shoot him again if I could—and this time I'd aim for something other than a shoulder. He deserved more than that for what he'd done to Ruan. The betrayal. The irreparable harm.

I pressed a chaste kiss to Ruan's lips and rested my cheek against his shoulder, waiting impatiently for him to wake. Surely whatever Laurent had injected him with would wear off as it had with Leona. The bells of Christ Church Cathedral began to ring out in the snowy night, breaking the silence and announcing Christmas Day. Others around town began to join them. One by one, as if prompted.

You're all right, my little love . . . you're all right . . . My mother's voice echoed from somewhere in the back of my mind—over the throbbing in my ear, even over the thunder of my own pulse. The last thread of my strength failed, and I collapsed, boneless and sobbing softly.

Ruan shifted, grumbling as he opened his eyes, and looked at me. Confusion clouded his expression as he studied my filthy face. His gaze lingered on the trail of blood-tinged fluid that came from my ear, staining the shoulder of my dress.

He shifted, tugging against the neckcloths tying him to the bed. "Ruby . . ."

I wiped my damp nose on my sleeve and sniffled, scrambling to sit upright. "I am sorry. I'm sorry for all of it."

He ran his tongue over his teeth, weighing his words carefully. "I am grateful for your apology. But why are you *weeping* and why . . . why exactly am I tied to this bed?"

I'd not even thought to free him earlier, so inordinately grateful he was alive. I began to ramble, words bursting out of me as I explained what had happened between the time I crept out of the house at dawn and my finding him here. How Laurent had kidnapped both Leona and him. How Reaver mistakenly believed I was in league with Laurent. How Jack, the young constable, was evidently working for the government alongside Reaver.

"That is all that happened?" he asked slowly, his gaze fixed upon the bit of ash that fell from my hair to the clean sheets of the bed. Perhaps I forgot to mention the exploding canal boat.

"*All?* I rather think I've done quite a lot in the last dozen hours."

His expression grew sober. "So, it's over then."

"It is. I am sorry. I am so utterly sorry."

He furrowed his brow. "Sorry for what?"

All of it? "Laurent was your mentor. Your friend's father. And he . . . he turned out to be—"

"A monster," Ruan finished, voice grave. "I may grieve for the pain he caused us, but never apologize to me, Ruby Vaughn, for something you did not do."

I wiped the remaining moisture from my face with my sleeve, annoyed that I had turned into a watering pot.

If a girl cannot cry after rescuing the one she loves from a murderer, then when can she weep?

Ruan startled as if he'd been stung by a bee. Eyes wide. "You *love* me?"

I couldn't bring myself to look at him, after he'd so clearly heard my riotous thoughts. I slid to the foot of the bed and began struggling with the neckcloth holding his left ankle, making use of my hands. The sooner we could leave this house, the sooner I could reassure myself he was safe. "Of course I do, you daft man. Though it is rather inconvenient that you heard that. I was hoping to manage some grand romantic gesture, perhaps some groveling involved after that abysmal letter I wrote you."

He let out a low throaty laugh, pulling against the remaining cloth bindings.

"Stop moving, you're making the knot tighter. But yes, if you must know. I'm afraid I do love you." I pulled at the stubborn fabric at his ankle that he'd only managed to make harder for me to unravel. "It scares me to death, and I still am not convinced that you will not wake up tomorrow and realize this was an utter mistake, but—"

"*You* love *me*."

I nodded solemnly as I finished freeing one of his legs, before moving to the next. My fingers trembled as I brushed the exposed skin of his foot, making quick work of the second restraint, fixating on my own hands rather than looking up into his dear face. "I am utterly terrified. I love you and I do not trust it. The very thought that one day you might change your mind—or worse, me watching you die . . . I could not bear it."

"Oh, Ruby . . ." Ruan's voice broke as he muttered something to himself in Cornish. I slid up the bed, leaning over him as I worked at the ties on his remaining wrist. He leaned up, brushing an awkward kiss against the stained cotton lace covering my collarbone, the only part of me he could reach in our current predicament. "Gods, do I love you, woman." He let out a dark laugh, his free hand reaching up to cup my cheek. "My life is nothing but chaos and danger and yet I would not trade a second of it for a peaceful life. You *are* a tempest, as I told you that afternoon in Cornwall after we solved our first murder together. Violent and angry and beautiful, and I would not have you any other way."

Only Ruan Kivell would speak of *murder* in the same breath as *love*, and I would not change him either. My throat constricted as I leaned down, taking his lips in a kiss that quickly grew out of control, and I was not certain in that moment if the salt I tasted was from *his* tears or my own. Nor did it matter. At long last, he broke the kiss with a groan. "Ruby?"

Dazed, I sat up, half concerned I'd hurt him. "What is it?"

He wet his lips, eyes dark. "Would you mind untying me the rest of the way so we can go home, take a bath, and finish this thing in a proper bed like civilized folk?"

I wiped at my cheeks with both hands, swallowing down a laugh. "I think I'd like that very much."

Chapter Thirty-nine

The Final Play

RUAN insisted on walking home from Laurent's, despite the fact he was unsteady on his feet. I think part of him needed to reassure himself he was well after being sedated for most of a day. Hand in hand, we made our way through the night. Mrs. Penrose and Mr. Owen fussed over me the moment we entered the house, but in time they allowed us to go upstairs. Ruan refused to leave my side, insisting on bathing me himself, removing the blood and soot and filth from me with his own hands. Checking my ear and my scrapes and cuts to make certain that no true harm had befallen me.

Then at long last, once satisfied I wasn't about to die from my assortment of injuries—and heedless of his own more interior wounds—he took me to bed. Twice. The first time was fast, desperate, and needy. The second unhurried, patient. And each broken kiss and foolish word uttered between us in the predawn hours underscored those absurd words we said to one another at Laurent's home. This was not lust, not in the least.

It was love.

And I'd be damned if I knew what to do with it, but I would try.

I did not deserve this man. I knew that much, but there was

something between us that would always bring us back together. Be it fate or love or his old gods' schemes. I knew in my very bones that I would always come home to Ruan Kivell and he to me. Like the tide to the shore . . . returning each day without fail.

WHEN I LET myself into the darkened halls of the Ashmolean the next morning, I remained uncertain what to expect from Frederick Reaver. I'd read the morning paper while still in bed with Ruan, the headline staring back at me:

CELEBRATED ANTHROPOLOGIST DEAD OF HEART ATTACK AGED 72

A much younger photograph of Emmanuel Laurent sat below the newsprint, showing the man alongside his son before the latter went off to war. Ruan had a peculiar expression on his face when he saw Ernst's face smiling back from the newsprint. He'd been so impossibly young when he died. I hastily folded the paper and put it away. I did not like the pain that flickered to life whenever Laurent was mentioned in Ruan's presence. And I was quite certain the two of us would have a great deal to talk about when it came to Ernst and his devious father. But for now, I was grateful that Ruan was safe in body—even if his spirit had taken a beating. He did not offer to join me at the Ashmolean, nor did I ask him to. It was painfully clear that the less he learned about Laurent's perfidy, the better. With a kiss on his forehead, I'd left him there in the warmth of our upstairs room with Fiachna devotedly purring at his side.

I knocked twice on Reaver's office door, slipping my lockpicks back into my satchel.

"Come in. Come in." His voice was muffled through the wooden paneling.

I nudged the door open with my toe, half expecting to find the bristly, growling man I had thought my enemy these last several days but instead found an altogether different one sitting behind the desk.

Leona sat in a practical armchair across from him. She cast me a rueful look as she drank her tea. Her legs drawn up beneath her.

"Am I interrupting?"

Reaver shook his head, his singular dimple flashing as Leona studied the depths of her cup. "No. I wanted Leona here as well for this. She arrived a few moments ago."

My fingers curved around the door suspiciously.

"Close it, if you would?"

I did as he asked, stepping into the bright office, and took the seat beside Leona. Every muscle in my body rebelled from the night before. A great deal had happened over the last week, and I wasn't certain how I felt about having been lied to, suspected of treachery, and nearly killed *again*. This was becoming a bad habit. "How is Jack?"

Reaver exhaled at the question, grateful for a starting point to a conversation that was long overdue. "Better than expected. He's at the hospital. Surgeons say that he should recover within a few weeks. He's a good lad with a bright future ahead of him serving his majesty, should he choose to continue on."

Good. At least one less drop of blood stained my hands. "And your other friend.... What about him?"

He folded his hands upon his desk. "I do not know who you mean."

"The *captain*. That fellow who arrived at the house last night at the perfect moment. The same one who *blew up* the canal boat."

He stared at me unblinking.

"Charming scar beneath his eye. Took Jack to the hospital," I added dryly, as if there could be any confusion of whom I spoke.

Reaver drummed his fingertips on the tabletop, visibly debating whether to admit the captain's existence in the light of day. Finally, he nodded again, half to himself. "He is well, thank you for your concern."

I exhaled loudly through my nose and shot to my feet, pacing the room. It was good to move, to do something. "*Who* is he? I've met him before, during the war about the time he received that scar of his. Every time I cross his path, my recollection of the event does not concur with the official record of the same and last time that occurred, things did not go so well for me." I laid the morning's paper down on the table between us, tapping the fictitious headline lamenting Laurent's death of *natural* causes. "Hopefully no one will try to lock me in an asylum this time."

Reaver chuckled half to himself. "Why am I not surprised? That was how I first met him too. The captain has had many names over the years, he is brilliant at his work—that was until he was nearly captured. After that he was sent back to the home front to hunt domestic spies rather than foreign ones."

I blinked, not quite believing my ears. "He believed Professor Laurent to be a *spy*?"

"I do not know what *he* believed, but the crown certainly did. That's why he was sent to Oxford. There were concerns that Laurent had been keeping the wrong sort of company. The *seditious* kind."

I opened my mouth, then snapped it back shut again.

"Come now, Miss Vaughn. You cannot think that the threats against our country ended with the armistice?"

Of course not. "So you would allow the world to believe a lie—that Laurent died peacefully in his sleep—rather than to know the truth about him? If what you say about him is true, and Britain is not fully safe, even now . . ."

"Safety is an illusion even at the best of times," he said with a deep frown. "And the lie is better than the truth in any event. Emmanuel Laurent has been dealt with and paid for his crimes. Does it matter what the truth is?"

"But no one knows he committed any crime at all. There will likely be some absurd plaque installed, lauding his achievements when he ought to be pilloried."

Reaver furrowed his brow. "Would you prefer that the entire country knew that the man poised to be a MP was a kidnapper and a murderer, funding his political aspirations and peculiar personal habits through the sale of intoxicants to the very people who elected him? Let us not even go into the whispers about dealings he had with the Germans. A traitor willing to sell his soul to the highest bidder being that close to the levers of power? It is unthinkable, Ruby. Unthinkable that the crown would let that stand when a simpler explanation ties things up neatly and with fewer questions. A plaque is a small price to pay."

"Yes. Yes I would. At least if people knew, they would not be so easily deceived the next time it occurs. Because you know as well as I do that a fellow like him will come along again."

Reaver frowned. "Then we are in disagreement."

My nostrils flared. "Is it that simple then? A lie rather than an uncomfortable truth? Then you and that man . . . you both work for the crown?"

He shrugged. "I work for the museum."

"You're not as good at the vague answers as your captain friend from last night."

The edge of his mouth curved up. "No one is as good as he. He was born to perform it, I was simply dragooned into his service, as were you. Be careful, Ruby Vaughn. He has taken a liking to you, and you may end up ensnared in his web again."

My gaze shot to Leona. "Do you also work for the crown? For this . . ." My hands fluttered before me as I could not quite form the words. "For that man?"

Reaver's expression darkened. "No. Leona's involvement was an entirely unanticipated occurrence."

I hugged myself tight to keep my hands from shaking.

"Harker and Leona had a deal unbeknownst to me." Reaver's voice was grim as he poured a glass of Scotch from a bottle and took a sip.

"What sort of a deal?"

"We were acquiring goods," Leona interrupted. She looked well this morning, with no hints of the trauma from the days before. Her eyes bright, and hair loose and unbraided.

"What sort of goods?"

"Artifacts. Antiquities. Objects that had been stolen from their homeland. Julius and I were . . ." she hesitated, wetting her lips "Collecting . . . with the intention of repatriating them. Sending them home where they belonged."

Repatriation? I'd not heard of such a thing. "And that's how Julius Harker crossed Laurent initially?"

Reaver took another sip of the amber liquid. "Mmm. I believe that is what started their animosity, yes. Laurent would likely have continued on as he had been, quietly amassing power, surrounding himself with those who would do his bidding without question, dealing in cocaine, and buying up antiquities had Harker not tweaked his nose. At the time, I did not know that Leona had become involved in Harker's scheme. It was an honorable pursuit, truly. He would quietly acquire small pieces, then larger ones, building a cache for safekeeping until it could be returned to its country of origin. From time to time, he would ask my opinion, and I would quietly help him determine provenance of an object."

"You are Mr. Aldate then," I asked, referencing the letters I found in Harker's home. The person who clearly cared a great deal for Harker.

Reaver gave me a sad, small smile. "Yes. I could not correspond with him openly. But we used to work together at the University. We used to frequent a pub along St. Aldate's and it seemed an appropriate enough name. I'd always been fond of him. Julius was a passionate man, a good one—if incautious—but recently he'd started behaving erratically. We went along this way for years, corresponding with one another about this artifact or that. If something was dubiously acquired, then Julius would go about and acquire the object and return the items to where they belong. That was how he met Leona the first time, back when we were all in Egypt. It was where I met her as well." His gaze settled warmly on Leona as she flushed beneath his attention.

I stared at the two of them, unable to form words. It was unconventional. It was radical . . . it was . . . *extraordinary*. I could not help but be impressed, and a little part of me wished I'd thought of it myself. It certainly would be a better use of my funds than supporting Mr. Owen's expensive book habit.

Leona tugged her jumper tighter around her.

"But the drugs? Were either of you involved in that?"

Leona shook her head. "Harker needed money to keep up the acquisitions. It was as I told you before—I'd not believed he was serious about it. There isn't much money in archaeology, you see. At least if one has a moral compass. I tried not to ask too many questions, but Julius grew bolder and bolder with each item he recovered. He hated Laurent for his avarice. The way the man would buy up entire collections and lock them away in his home."

"But wasn't Harker doing the same thing with his museum?"

"The museum was an illusion. It created a veneer of respectability and a place to hide the true objects amongst fakes. The museum allowed Harker to acquire things, create forgeries, then secrete the authentic ones back to where they belonged with no one suspecting."

"It's a rather clever scheme."

Reaver nodded in agreement. "It was. I admired him for it, even if I couldn't say as much publicly. But Leona—for a time, she served as a go-between for Harker and me. As I mentioned before, the Home Office had been watching Laurent for years, waiting for the moment to strike. Then when Julius Harker was found dead . . ."

"It brought it all to a head," I finished.

Reaver confirmed it with a sigh. He rubbed at his temple. "I did not realize anyone knew of Harker's connection to Leona, but Laurent must have found out about their collaboration somehow."

"I am sorry that I ever thought you the villain."

"As am I. We were both mistaken." He gave me a rueful smile. "Though I grant you most people do dislike me. The only reason I am telling you this now is you have seen too much, and honesty at this point is better than continuing as we were."

I opened my mouth, then snapped it back shut, glancing between the two of them. Seconds ticked on in silence before I finally managed to voice the question lingering at the edges of my mind. "Where is the remainder of Harker's collection? The items that he was intending to repatriate?"

"It is all safe," Leona said softly. "That's all you need know."

"Does the government know about what he was doing?"

Leona glanced across the table at Reaver. "No. No one knows but the three of us now."

"And the *Radix*? Jonathan Treadway? How do they fit in?"

Leona shook her head, moving to the far side of Reaver's office and pulling out a large book from the shelf, which she laid on my lap. "Julius was brilliant at forgeries." She gave me a faint smile. "He was convinced that someone would steal the *Radix*. Julius asked his old friend Jonathan Treadway to retrieve it again and to hide the original somewhere that not even he could find it. Then, not long before he died, he'd arranged for a forgery to be made, a duplicate of the book. We'd hidden the forgery in Harker's own collection. Eventually, we were going to move the fake back into the Bodleian, keeping the original safe. But the forgery had been stolen from Harker's museum before we could complete Harker's plan to switch the true *Radix* with the false one."

"Who has the forgery now?"

Reaver winced. "I think it was on the canal boat."

I let out a startled sound. Well, we certainly wouldn't get it back then. I lifted the hide-bound cover, revealing the brilliantly colored title page with the words *Radix Maleficarum* in a strong and artful hand. There was a bit of foxing on the pages there. My fingers hovered over the paper longingly. It must have been more recent than first assumed. I was told it was written in conversation with the *Malleus Maleficarum*, but it was unusual to see foxing in fifteenth-century books. "So this is it. . . . The original?"

Leona nodded. "It is. It's been here all along, in Freddie's office. Hidden in plain sight."

I wet my lips, closed the book, then pressed it into Leona's hands. "It belongs to the Bodleian."

Leona took it and quickly replaced it on the shelf. "Freddie will figure out a way to get it back without any questions asked. I think with Laurent dead it should be safe. At least for a time."

"As always." Reaver rubbed his temples with a small laugh. "Frederick Reaver, fixer of problems."

It was admirable, really, what she and Julius Harker had been doing—a far sight riskier than anything I'd ever done on my own. "I'm glad."

She gave me a strange look. "Glad of what?"

"Of what you've been doing. It was brave. Dangerous—yes—but brave."

"I thought you might tell me it was reckless. I certainly thought it was at the time."

I laughed, raking a hand through my hair. "It is. Exceedingly reckless. But sometimes doing what is right means being a little reckless."

Leona laughed, the newfound tension between us dissolved at once. "You truly haven't changed that much. I am sorry for saying otherwise when you were reluctant to help me at first. You aren't a coward."

"Don't be sorry. I certainly deserved the accusations, and a little more."

"You are hard on yourself. You were only speaking from experience." Leona chewed on her lower lip before looking up at me. Almost sheepish. "How long are you still here?"

"The second of January, why?"

"Then you still owe me one more round—best out of three at the Artemis Club. I don't feel like being cooped up in the basement today and I don't suspect that Freddie is going to complain about my absence now that I'm back to translate for him at all hours. My body is craving a little bit of exercise."

He gave her a slow smile. The sort that I should have seen from the beginning. The man was utterly besotted with Leona Abernathy, and she him.

"*Fencing.*" I mouthed the word to myself for good measure. "You are thinking of *fencing* after nearly getting killed?"

"Life is for living, Ruby Vaughn. It's a wonder that you always forget that part."

Epilogue

FOUR weeks later, I stood outside a familiar storefront in Exeter. The worn gilt lettering of Owen & Sons painted some twenty years ago full of hope and promise had begun to fleck off in spots. We'd likely have to get it re-lettered in the new year, but that was a problem for another day. Hope, I was learning, was a transient thing, ever changing with the seasons. A motorcar rumbled past me on the street and for the first time, as I stood on the threshold between the world outside and the bookshop, I was not afraid. I did not fear my future, nor what had come to pass.

It was a novel thing, being brave.

I suppose I'd have to get used to it.

It was almost February now, and I'd spent the last three weeks rusticating—as Mr. Owen called it—in Lothlel Green with Ruan. He hadn't been himself after what happened in Oxford. To all the world, my pellar was an impenetrable mountain of a man, but I could see how fragile he'd become—broken and chipped away by Laurent's betrayal. I'd have liked to say that I stayed with him that long because we were happy in Cornwall. And we were happy, in a fashion. But there was a newfound darkness haunting Ruan's eyes and a wound far deeper than either of us cared to admit. I spent most of my days reading by the fire, while he worked in his garden preparing for spring. We'd walk, sometimes for hours at a time, and not say much to one another. The long, silent cliffside walks gave him the most pleasure. We'd traversed hundreds of miles over those weeks. It was a strange, peaceful sort of existence there. Sometimes he'd take me with him when he called on the villagers, other times he'd leave me behind at the cottage, but I did not belong in his world. Not for long. I missed Exeter and my life here. No matter how much I loved the man, a part of me would always be trapped between these two worlds. His and my own, until we figured out the balance of things.

And so, I was back—most of me at least. My heart, however, remained stubbornly in Cornwall.

The glass-paneled door gave with a creak, its cheery bell announcing my arrival. The familiar thump of my cat landing on the floor welcomed me home. Fiachna trotted across the bookshop and nuzzled my leg, followed by two mewling black-and-white kittens who looked as if they were dressed for supper. Fiachna purred loudly and began to roughly groom one of them. Now this was new. I scooped up the two kittens and wandered deeper into the bookshop.

"You're back, my love?" Mr. Owen's voice rumbled from somewhere deep in the bookshop. I inhaled slowly, reveling in the scent of old books. I craned my neck, peering past stack after stack of books lining the walls. Some were piled two to three tomes thick. I often fussed at him for his cavalier nature in maintaining such things, but it was his shop, not mine, and I'd been gone a scandalously long time.

"I thought it was time I came home." I edged around a particularly precarious stack. "Where *are* you anyway, or did your pile of books fall on your head?"

"Not amusing, Ruby. I'm in the back. I got a new shipment in today. Care to join me?"

I squeezed between two overburdened shelves and lifted the curtain before joining him in the cramped storeroom. The tiny room was little more than a glorified cupboard and was crammed with even more oddities than the main room of the bookshop. Mr. Owen was seated on a large pillow, pulling books from a crate and setting them beside him on the floor.

"When were you going to tell me Fiachna had kittens?" I asked, setting the two little fluff balls onto a nearby pillow.

Mr. Owen harrumphed. "Well, *he* didn't have them, mind you, but I get your point. I'm not sure *whose* kittens they are, but he has taken a shine to them. They showed up at the doorstep the other night and the old rogue insists on grooming them and carrying them about. Perhaps he's decided to settle down at long last."

I couldn't disguise my smile at the thought of Fiachna as a doting feline father. Mr. Owen grunted as he lifted another book from the crate.

"You know you could hire someone to help you with this. You don't have to do everything on your own." I took the book from his hands and placed it on a nearby pile.

He stared up at me over the top of his wire-rimmed glasses. "Why would I hire someone when I have you? That is, unless you've decided to quit—leave me high and dry here while you go off and gallivant with your witch. First the bloody cat settling down, now you." He reached yet again into the crate.

"I'm not gallivanting anywhere, but you know this is far more than we can do between the two of us. Now go sit in your chair—I'll handle this." I took Halley's *Astronomical Tables* from his hands, admiring the fine condition. "Good God, who did you kill for this?"

He let out a low laugh. "I have my ways, lass, you know that. Now tell me, how is young Kivell these days?" Mr. Owen came to his knees, using a heavy chair to pull himself up to standing. He stretched, rubbing at the base of his spine before sitting down. One of the kittens took the opportunity to climb up his trouser leg onto his lap before continuing up to his shoulder.

"Ruan is . . ." I wasn't sure *what* he was, but he certainly wasn't himself. He was quieter, more withdrawn. He wasn't sullen or angry—it wasn't like that at all. But something had shifted inside him and I was not sure if I could reach him anymore—at least, not in the way I had before.

He frowned, seeing my answer all over my face. "I suspected as much with what happened in Oxford. The lad's been surrounded by people but he's been alone his entire life. No one ever understood him, no matter how much they might care for him. Then for him to lose Ernst like that—his first true friend—and for Laurent to do such a horrible thing. It would only make sense the lad would be melancholy."

Melancholy was one way to put it. I exhaled, hugging the large book to my chest, drawing strength from the tome.

"Why didn't you stay with him? If you need more time, I can take on another girl to help me around here. I am partial to *you* of course, but I can make do with another if I must. Maybe I could convince my progeny to come home at last to help a doddering old man and his growing herd of cats."

My chest trembled at the thought. I was still growing accustomed to the fact Mr. Owen *had* a living descendent—until a few months ago, neither of us were aware he had a daughter—though I hadn't seen her since we parted ways in Scotland back in October. "Have you heard from her?"

Mr. Owen waved me off. "The lass wrote me for the holidays. Was thinking of coming to visit in the new year. Enough about me. Tell me, why aren't you still in Cornwall with your pellar?"

I wet my lips, hesitating. "He . . . Nellie Smythe's babies came early. Do you recall her from Lothlel Green? She's living at Penryth Hall now. She had twins, you see, and Ruan is staying up at the house until Nellie is well enough and he's certain the twins are safe. I thought I'd come home for a few days." That, and I could not bear being alone with my own thoughts on the windswept Cornish cliffs. Nor did I particularly want to spend more time than necessary at Penryth Hall. Ruan offered to let me join him there, but the old manor house carried far more ghosts than I cared to revisit. Even Mrs. Penrose fled that place at the first opportunity.

Mr. Owen furrowed his brow. "The lad needs you—you know that, don't you?"

I did. I needed him too, but I sensed that our path was not meant to be simple or easy. And we'd traverse it as we would, and it would do neither of us good to be caught up in the other and give up our own lives. Not when he was utterly vital to his people. But how would I ever explain that to Mr. Owen? To Mr. Owen there were no insurmountable burdens, no impediments to love except for death—and even that was negotiable.

The bell at the door rang, interrupting my thoughts.

"We're in the back," I called, pulling the curtain aside, still clutching the ancient text to my belly. Fiachna followed me out along with one of his two kittens.

A young messenger stood there by the front desk, eyes wide as he looked up at the books towering above him. I understood the sentiment. This place was magical. The first time I set foot inside the seventeenth-century walls of the bookshop I fell in love, and that hadn't changed much over the last several years—no matter the trouble Mr. Owen had gotten me into.

"Can I help you?"

"Are you Ruby Vaughn?" the boy asked.

I laid the book on the countertop, and huffed my hair from my eyes. "I am."

He thrust a telegram in my hand. I rummaged in my pocket for some coins and dropped them into his gloved fist. "Thank you."

He mumbled out a polite acknowledgment as he hurried out and back on his way.

"Who was that, my love?" Mr. Owen stepped out of the dusty storeroom, the second pint-sized kitten still perched upon his shoulder.

"Just a boy . . ." I said absently and opened the telegram, heart sinking as I read the words.

I'VE NEWS OF THE IMPOSTER AND YOUR MOTHER. AT LEAST I THINK I HAVE. COME TO LONDON AT ONCE. HARI.

I drew in a shaky breath and looked up at Mr. Owen. "It seems I'm going on another adventure."

"Shall I get my coat?"

I let out a laugh and threw my arms around him, kitten and all. Whatever it was I'd find, wherever it was I'd go, like the tide to the shores, I knew I would always return home.

ACKNOWLEDGMENTS

Writing the acknowledgments for the third Ruby Vaughn mystery is no easier than it was the first time. It almost feels harder to do because there are so many folks who have had a hand in bringing these books to life, whether it's through the production of the book itself, the editorial process, being a sounding board, or simply being a friend. I want you to know that I am grateful to each and every one of you for believing in me and these rompy gothic murder mysteries.

These stories wouldn't be here at all if it weren't for Team Ruby and the folks at Minotaur Books. You have been amazing every step of the way, and your belief in these stories means the world to me. From copyediting to the gorgeous covers to publicity and marketing—publishing is truly a team effort. I am grateful for how hard you work to help bring the books into the world. The world of Ruby Vaughn exists because you believe in her. To my editor, Madeline Houpt—you have this incredible ability to see right to the heart of my books. Ever since we first spoke about the books, you've understood the story I'm trying to tell. These books are so much better for your insight. Thank you. Also, my fabulous agent, Jill Marr, who has been a champion for my stories and by my side every step of the way—I cannot imagine a better partner in all this. Thanks for being my partner in crime fiction!

Ashley. Elizabeth. Paulette. Reine. Rose. Your friendship through this whole writing journey has been far more precious to me than you can ever understand. Thank you for being there whenever I need an ear, a sounding board, a walk, or a cup of coffee. Writing can be a lonely endeavor at times, but you make it so much better.

For Mom—who has hand-sold my books to her dentist, doctors, random people on planes, walking groups, and her multiple book clubs. You were my first and strongest advocate, and I am so grateful for you. You are literally the best mom a girl could ask for.

For J and the boys—who have lived the deadline-life right along with me these last three years. Willingly letting me disappear for hours on end, handing me cheese (when I inevitably forget to eat), keeping me hydrated (when I *also* forget to drink something other than coffee), and supporting me as I chase my dreams—all the while knowing that I'll be back again just as soon as I hit send on the manuscript. I am constantly amazed by the faith you have in me and my stories. I love you three so much. You are my inspiration, my joy, and my peace in a world trying its damnedest to take that peace away. Writing would be impossible without you.

And last—but certainly not least—for you, my readers, who love these characters as much as I do. Thank you from the bottom of my heart for being along for the ride.

ABOUT THE AUTHOR

Jess Armstrong is the *USA Today* bestselling author of the Ruby Vaughn Mysteries. Her debut novel, *The Curse of Penryth Hall,* won the Minotaur Books/Mystery Writers of America First Crime Novel Award. She has a master's degree in American history but prefers writing about imaginary people to the real thing. Jess lives in New Orleans with her historian husband, two sons, and a growing number of pets and plants. And when she's not working on her next project, she's probably thinking about cheese, baking, on social media, or some combination of the above.